Maggie Without a Clue

BOOKS BY KASEY MICHAELS

Can't Take My Eyes off of You

Too Good to Be True

Love to Love You Baby

Be My Baby Tonight

This Must Be Love

This Can't Be Love

Maggie Needs an Alibi

Maggie by the Book

Maggie Without a Clue

Published by Kensington Publishing Corp.

Kasey Michaels

Maggie Without a Clue

KENSINGTON BOOKS
www.kensingtonbooks.com

KENSINGTON BOOKS are published by

Kensington Publishing Corp.
850 Third Avenue
New York, NY 10022

All Kensington titles, imprints, and distributed lines are available at special quantity discounts for bulk purchases for sales promotions, premiums, fund-raising, educational, or institutional use.

Special book excerpts or customized printings can also be created to fit specific needs. For details, write or phone the office of the Kensington special sales manager: Kensington Publishing Corp., 850 Third Avenue, New York, NY 10022, attn: Special Sales Department; phone 1-800-221-2647.

Library of Congress Card Catalogue Number: 2003116204
ISBN 1-57566-883-1

First printing: August 2004
10 9 8 7 6 5 4 3 2 1

Printed in the United States of America

To Stan Gorzelany, with thanks.

The past lies like a nightmare upon the present.
—Karl Marx

Don't look back. Something may be gaining on you.
—Satchel Paige

Maggie Without a Clue

PROLOGUE

I've decided to keep a journal. Maggie says a lot of writers do, except she doesn't because she can't see the point of writing anything if she can't sell it. But, as I am not a writer by vocation, I suppose this isn't a complete frittering away of time for me, so here I am, penning my first entry.

The weather remains warm here in Manhattan as we move through September. The park is delightfully sparse of school age children and I can sit here, my scooter resting against the bench as I write. I should describe the scene in more detail, I suppose, as Maggie told me people tend to wax poetical in their journals, but it's a park. Trees, flowers, paths. What else is there to be said about a park?

My name is Sterling Balder, by the way, in chance hundreds of years from now someone discovers this journal tucked away inside an ice floe or some such thing, and wonders who I might have been. Until a few months ago I lived inside the pages of Maggie's mystery novels, along with my dearest friend, Alexandre Blake, the Viscount Saint Just. He solves crimes in Maggie's books, and I, as I once overheard her refer to me, am the Comic Relief. Oh. Maggie's books are set in England, Regency England to be specific about the thing. I probably should have already said that.

For several years Saint Just was fairly content to exist inside Maggie's head, as it were, until he decided he was sufficiently versed in how to properly comport himself in Manhattan. At that time we . . . we . . . well, we *poofed* out of Maggie's head and into her apartment. That probably sounds more difficult (and possibly painful) than it was. Really. Learning to zip things? Now *that's* difficult.

Saint Just is Alex Blakely to everyone here except me, and Maggie introduces us as her distant English cousin Alex and his friend Sterling, on whom she patterned her mystery series, using both our names and our physical . . . attributes, I believe she terms them.

Things have been wonderfully interesting ever since. We've met a multitude of people. I suppose I should say who they are, and then the journal won't be a hodgepodge and all of that. Very well.

Maggie is Maggie Kelly, although she used to be Alicia Tate Evans when she wrote historical romances and now she's Cleo Dooley as she writes her marvelously successful Saint Just mysteries. That's clear, isn't it?

Bernice Toland-James is Maggie's editor at Toland Books, and her very best friend, although Tabitha Leighton, Maggie's literary agent, is also a boon companion.

After Maggie's publisher was murdered we became acquainted with Lieutenant Steve Wendell. The good lieutenant continues to wander in and out of Maggie's life, which depresses Saint Just more than he will admit, although the two gentlemen seem to have formed a bond lately, much to Maggie's surprise and, I believe, dismay.

There's Snake and Killer, of course, and Mary Louise. They're all cousins, and little more than children, really. Once denizens of the street, they have become the nucleus of Saint Just's ever-expanding group of Street Corner Orators and Players, one of my friend's endeavors to become financially solvent without dirtying his hands with trade or anything even vaguely smelling of the shop.

Oh, dear, that sounds cruel. Saint Just is a marvelous man,

truly. A trifle high in the instep at times, granted, but a good one for all of that. If only he wouldn't persist in believing himself a wealthy viscount from 1811 who is also a master at mystery detecting. He dove right into the fray when Maggie's publisher was murdered, and just again a few weeks ago he deliberately insinuated himself into a rather muddled affair of pranking and murder at a writers convention we all attended.

Once again, Saint Just had been looking for a way to pad his pocketbook, and he found that at this same convention by entering a cover-model contest which he did not win. He did, however, manage to be noticed by Mr. Pierre, who has taken up both Saint Just and Mary Louise to tout his perfumes.

Mary Louise is still much the urchin, but she cleans up extraordinarily well.

This new endeavor of simply being himself as he poses for photographs is important, because now Saint Just and I have enough blunt to vacate Maggie's condominium and relocate ourselves across the hall to Mrs. Goldblum's apartment while she visits with her sister in Boca Raton, where we are about to install a most wonderful large screen television machine.

I am to be in charge of the apartment, by my own wishes, and because Saint Just may be a champion detective, but he wouldn't have the first idea on how to go on with anything as complicated as a motorized can opener. He'd much rather continue to excel at what he does best. That, dear journal, would be in being Saint Just.

Is that it? No, there's one more, isn't there? Felicity Boothe Simmons. May I say—shudder! Miss Simmons used to be Faith Simmons, and one of Maggie's best friends, but then she became *NYT*—whatever that is—and dropped Maggie like the proverbial hot potato. Maggie is also *NYT* now, and Miss Simmons cannot forgive her for her even greater success (this is Saint Just's explanation at any rate). Although, now that Maggie has very recently saved Miss Simmons from a Dire Fate, it would appear the woman is attempting to worm her way back into Maggie's life.

Maggie is not best pleased by this turn of events. Saint Just says Maggie tends to be prickly in an effort to keep from having herself hurt. Did I mention that he fair dotes on her? Not that he wishes that sort of thing bandied about, of course.

Now I'm done, I'm sure of it. I hadn't realized journaling could be quite so difficult. I seem to have been scribbling for hours, and I would dearly like to toddle over and purchase a flavored ice. It's Saturday, so I am allowed a blue one. Saint Just limits me to two blue ices a week, as he seems to be inordinately put off by blue lips and tongue. As I said, he can be a bit of a stickler, although his heart is pure.

You see, I have deduced—Saint Just is not the only one who can deduce—that as Maggie invented Saint Just, Saint Just is partly Maggie, and the other way round. They are different, and yet they are alike. Sometimes enough alike to disconcert each other mightily.

I'm still wondering if the same can be said for me.

Have I forgotten anyone? Should I mention Doctor Bob? I've yet to have the pleasure, but Doctor Bob is Maggie's confidante and advisor, much to Saint Just's disgust. Maggie refers to the gentleman as her *shrink,* but as I've already said, I've yet to meet the fellow, so I myself won't comment on his size.

I've also yet to be introduced to Maggie's parents, most especially her mother. Maggie mostly talks to Doctor Bob about her mother, and about Dame Nicotine, the most persistent bane of the dear girl's existence.

And Socks! How could I forget Socks? He's really Argyle Jackson, doorman of our building, but we know him as Socks, aspiring actor. He's also my friend.

So that's it, finally. We're here, and we're enjoying ourselves immensely. I've purchased a few tomes on something called feng shui, and hope to devote myself to arranging Mrs. Goldblum's apartment in tune with nature and the environment and serenity and good health and wealth, and all of that.

Now if only Maggie would stop stumbling over murders, I

should think everything will be just as I'd hoped it would be when Saint Just first proposed coming here. A Most Edifying Adventure.

Respectfully,

Sterling Balder

P.S. Did I mention Henry? I don't think I mentioned Henry. Where is my head? Henry is my mouse. His nose twitches and he enjoys running on a wheel inside the cage Maggie purchased for him. It's so good to have someone else to care for, don't you think?

CHAPTER 1

Maggie sat hunched at her computer desk in the living room, staring at the screen. She'd been staring at the screen for five minutes, wishing the words displayed on it to change, reassemble themselves in a more pleasing manner, but it wasn't working. They were still there, damning her.

"Amazon.com? *Again?* Really, Maggie, self-flagellation is so unbecoming," Saint Just said, leaning over her shoulder to press a Post-it note on the edge of the computer. "There. Does this help?"

Maggie took off her computer glasses, threw them to the desktop, and grabbed the note. " 'The trade of critic, in literature, music, and the drama, is the most degraded of all trades.' Mark Twain."

"You seem to enjoy him," Saint Just said when she turned her chair to glare up at him. "I've become a bit of a devotee myself. A pity he wrote after the Regency. I would dearly love to quote the fellow in our books."

Maggie crumpled the note and threw it into the garbage can. "Mark Twain didn't have to put up with these damn reader reviews."

"Maggie. Dear Maggie. There are, at last count, seventy–three reviews posted there on our most recent opus. A starred review from *Publishers Weekly,* a quite flattering review from *Booklist,* and *Kirkus* was its usual damning-with-faint-praise self. Add to that sixty-seven unremittingly marvelous remarks from readers."

"And three one-star rips," Maggie said, reaching for her nicotine inhaler. "They drive me nuts. I can't answer them, I can't do a thing about them. Why in *hell* would a Web site that wants to sell books show reviews that say a book is the worst piece of drivel they've ever read? And this one," she said, turning her chair to the screen once more. "See this one? It gives away the murderer, for crying out loud."

"That would be the reader from Iowa? The reference was oblique at best. I wouldn't say she spilled all the gravy. Mostly, she complained that if you knew anything at all, you'd know that English gentlemen of the Regency era did not swear or take the Lord's name in vain."

"Yeah, right. We invented all that in the last fifty years or so. I can hear Wellington now." She dropped into a British accent. "*'Please, my dear fellows, if the spirit so moves you and I'm not interrupting your tea break, might you redirect that lovely cannon over there, as I do believe the Frenchies are advancing up the hill at us in a rather sprightly manner.'* "

"God's teeth, woman, if I might further depress the hopes of our Iowa reader with some mild swearing, would you please *stop* obsessing? And your accent is atrocious."

Maggie wasn't listening. "And this one. This guy said he figured out the murderer halfway through the book. That's not good, Alex. That's really not good."

Saint Just leaned closer. "And does it also say that he most likely peeked at the ending before he began to read?"

"You can't know he did that."

"You can't know he did not do that. You can't know if he's just another frustrated—what are we not supposed to call such people? Oh, yes, another frustrated wannabe. That's it. Can't do, so he attempts to rip apart those that can. Anyone with a computer and a modem—and an axe to grind—can submit a review on these things. Now, are we quite done with this morning's descent into the pits of self-pity?"

"No, we're not. This last one's the worst. She says you and

Leticia weren't together enough. You know what that means, don't you, Alex? It means there wasn't enough *sex* for her. The 'together' enough bit is a tip-off. So's 'I wish there had been more emotion.' And 'It was a little light on the romance.' There's a dozen ways they say it, but they all mean the same thing. Didn't feel the romantic tension, the characters didn't connect enough, on and on. They're all buzz words. What they mean is there wasn't enough nooky for them. Not enough hot, sweaty, jungle sex. Why don't they just say it? Why don't they just say, Hey, lady, put them in bed on page three and keep them there? Better yet, have them do it in public. On horseback."

"Well, my dear, speaking as the hero in question, may I say it's not—minus the horse—an entirely unpalatable idea."

"If I wrote soft porn, no. I'm writing mysteries, damn it. I'm writing about people, not positions. I'm writing characters, not fifty ways to screw your lover. Can't they just get subscriptions to *Playgirl* and stop pretending they're looking for anything more than a cheap thrill?"

Maggie sank against the back of the chair, inhaled deeply, and blew the air out on a sigh, her bravado gone, to be replaced by her usual insecurity. "Maybe they're right, Alex. Maybe the books need more sex."

"Do I get a vote?" Saint Just asked, waggling his eyebrows.

"No, you don't. And maybe you shouldn't say 'Christ on a crutch' anymore."

"I shouldn't?"

"No, maybe you shouldn't. Or 'God's teeth.' "

"Perhaps, just perhaps, I should be all things to all people. Has anyone ever succeeded in that sort of lofty endeavor?"

"Only until after they win on election day. Whoops, can't talk like that, either. Democrats and Republicans. Saint Just's Whigs and Tories. You name it. You saw the e-mails I got. There are people out there who'd like me lined up against a wall and shot for treason and heresy, just because I uttered one little opinion on free speech at the WAR conference and that reporter ran with it."

"Ah," Saint Just murmured. "We Are Romance. The mind still boggles over that unfortunate name."

"Yeah, yeah. Back to me, okay? I'm in pain here." Maggie clicked the mouse over the SIGN OFF menu. "I'm nuts, aren't I? Bernie says I'm nuts. Hell, Bernie said if I ever talk to another reporter *she's* having me shot."

"Never be afraid to speak your mind, Maggie. You simply tend to worry overmuch about everyone else's opinion," Saint Just said, holding out a hand to her as she rose from her chair. "It's a failing you mercifully did not pass along to me. Simply stop obsessing."

Maggie pushed a hand through her recently clipped and streaked hair. "I am not obsessing. I do not obsess. Really. I'm not obsessing." She flung herself inelegantly on one couch as Saint Just gracefully lowered himself onto the facing couch. "Okay, okay, stop grinning at me. I'm obsessing. Just a little. Why do I even *read* these reviews?"

"Again, dear love, you're insecure. You are, in fact, the greatest mass of insecurities I have ever encountered, and I have resided with Sterling. Oh, wait, you know that. You created him."

Maggie looked at her nicotine inhaler, then at the pack of cigarettes on the coffee table. Would she really sell her soul to the Devil for a cigarette? Good thing that so far all her imagination had managed to dredge up was Alex and Sterling. If she could summon a guy with horns and hooves and a tail, she'd be in some serious trouble. "Poor Sterling. I think I gave him all my more vulnerable traits."

"Yes, and gifted me with everything you wish yourself to be, and could be if you'd only believe in your own considerable worth. Now, having said that, you might notice that I am holding a key in my hand."

Maggie felt her stomach do a small flip. Was this it? Was this really the big day? Was she ready for the big day? "Mrs. Goldblum's key?"

"Until recently, yes. But, as of this morning, all mine. Mrs. Goldblum wasn't to leave for another few weeks, but her sister took a tumble on the shuffleboard court or some such place and fractured her hip, as she informed me last evening. Mrs. Goldblum rushed off at first light, leaving us full access. In quite a dither to be gone, poor woman. We'll be transferring the remainder of our belongings as soon as Socks arrives. What will you do without us, Maggie?"

She tipped up her chin (the better not to see the pack of cigarettes on the coffee table). So this was it. Mrs. Goldblum had (verbally—she put nothing in writing) subleased her apartment to Alex and Sterling while she left for a lengthy, open-ended stay with her sister in Boca Raton. "You're moving across the hall. I think I can manage."

Saint Just crossed one long leg over the other. He was the picture of sophisticated elegance, even in modern-day clothing, although in her mind's eye, he was the perfect hero when dressed, by her, in Regency costume.

She'd made him perfect, at least her idea of perfect. The man every woman drools for, to be honest. Handsome, with Val Kilmer's sensuous lips. Physically long and lean and muscular, like Clint Eastwood in those old spaghetti westerns women still sighed over on cable. Eyes blue, Paul Newman in *Hud* blue. Tanned skin, smile lines, a tumble of ebony hair. The voice of a young Sean Connery as James Bond—that Scottish burr mixed with an English accent that had been melting feminine knees for decades. Peter O'Toole's aristocratic nose. To die for; that was the Viscount Saint Just.

She'd made him self-confident, which she was not. She'd made him witty, which she could only be on paper, and so seldom in public—having lived her life as one of those people who wake at two in the morning to say, "*That's* what I should have said when she made that crack about my hips!"

She'd made him brave, to cover her own fears, made him independent of his parents because she was still fighting to saw through a cast iron umbilical. She'd made him daring, witty, cuttingly sarcastic, deliciously sophisticated.

The perfect hero—perfect Regency hero, that is.

And then she'd given him a few flaws, because a totally perfect person would be nothing more than a stereotype; plastic, unbelievable. The sort of flaws that would make him more real, and yet weren't really flaws in Regency England, where the gentlemen ruled and the ladies poured tea. She'd made him arrogant. A tad selfish. A bit domineering.

A know-it-all.

Which had been all well and good, as long as he stayed between the pages of her books, solving crimes and bedding the ladies. Having the perfect hero live in her apartment? That had proved problematic.

Maggie knew she could leap into this man's arms and yell, "Take me, you gorgeous man, you!" If she were that sort of girl, which she wasn't. If she didn't worry that he might one day poof out of her life as unexpectedly as he'd poofed into it. If she was the chase 'em down and tackle 'em type, which she most definitely wasn't.

Although, right now, at this very moment, he was looking pretty damn good . . .

"Maggie? Maggie, please be so kind as to at least pretend you're paying attention."

"What? Oh, sorry, Alex. What were you saying?"

"I was saying, I think Sterling and I should celebrate our first evening in our new home by escorting you to dinner. I've already taken the liberty of making reservations at Bellini's, as a matter of fact. For eight o'clock. Unless you'd rather remain here all day and night, punishing yourself with other people's opinions?"

"I'm not going to read any more reviews, all right? Ever. Because you're right. They don't help me, do they?"

"Not unless you can be convinced to allow me another romantic tryst per book, no, I would say they aid none of us."

"Okay, okay, give it a rest, you made your point. I really have to write today. What time is it now?"

Saint Just looked at the small clock on the table beside the couch. "It's already gone ten. Sterling was up and about early, for his daily constitutional in the park. He should return soon, with shining eyes and dreadfully blue lips. Why?"

"Because I want to call Bernie. Or hadn't you thought about inviting her?"

"The reservation is for four people, yes, allowing you a guest of your own choosing. Bernice would also have been my choice."

"Ten, huh? I'll wake her up if I call now. You know how she is on Friday nights."

"Drunk and Disorderly, I believe was the charge last month. There's a lot to admire about our dearest Bernice. And one recent development in her life to lament. That would be her ever-increasing affection for the grape."

Maggie leaned over the arm of the couch and snagged the portable phone. She hit the speed dial button and punched 1, for Bernie. "She doesn't have it easy, Alex. Kirk left behind a mess when he was killed, and she's still reorganizing. Damn, I got her machine. She never checks her machine. I'll call again later. In the meantime, what can I help you carry across the hall?"

Saint Just blinked. "I beg your pardon?"

"Carry. Across the hall. Your things?"

"Me?" He pressed both hands to his chest in mock dismay.

"Oh, cut it out. Of course, you. What? You were going to hire movers for some clothes and a few boxes?"

There was a knock at the door, and Saint Just rose to answer it. "Ah, Snake, Killer. And you, the most estimable Socks. Just in time, in the nick of time, actually. The boxes are stacked in the bedroom on the left, directly down that hall. Yes, there you go. Have a care with the clothing in the closet, if you please."

Maggie watched as Snake (unfortunately christened Vernon), Killer (handsome in a downtrodden, Byronic sort of way), and

Socks headed for the hallway. "You hired all three of them, didn't you? No, wait, scratch that. They *volunteered.*"

"Absolutely. Vernon and George no longer labor on Saturdays now that they've been elevated to management in our small enterprise."

"Your street corner orators. I still can't believe you turn a profit."

"Minimal, I agree, but an opportunity is an opportunity, and it pleases me to have found a legitimate device for George and Vernon to pad their pockets. I should think you'd be proud of me. Now, if you'll excuse me, I do believe I will adjourn to my new apartment, to direct the placement of my belongings."

"Yeah, yeah, you do that," Maggie said, waving him away as the phone rang. "Hello?"

"Maggie? *Maggie!*"

"Bernie? I just called you to—"

"Maggie! Ohmigod, Maggie! I was sleeping! The phone rang! I had to pee, so I—he's dead, Maggie. Sweet Jesus, Buddy's dead!"

Maggie closed her eyes, hugging the phone close to her. Oh, yeah. Her friend had tied on a big one last night. "Bernie, calm down. Buddy's dead. Yes, he is. He's been dead for a long time, honey. What were you doing last night?"

"What? He's *dead,* Maggie! It's terrible!"

Maggie was already on her feet, heading across the hall to motion to Saint Just. "Bernie, I want you to calm down," she said, raising her eyebrows to Saint Just, who followed her back into her apartment and took the second portable phone she handed him.

"Keep her talking," Saint Just said, then lifted the phone to his ear.

Maggie did her best, even as her hands shook, because this one was bad, very bad. "Do you want to talk about Buddy, Bernie?"

Had Bernie gotten some bad drugs? She only snorted a little

cocaine a couple of times a year, for dietary purposes, Bernie promised, but the woman also drank like a fish. In these past weeks? Like a whale. Maggie felt tears stinging her eyes; why couldn't she do something to help Bernie?

Saint Just was moving his hand in a circular motion, urging her to keep talking.

"Bernie, honey, Buddy went out on his boat seven years ago and he never came back. He's dead. We know that. *You* know that. A couple more weeks and it's officially official. He's dead. What happened, honey? Did you have a bad night? Bernie? Stop crying, honey. Talk to me."

"I . . . I don't know. I don't know. I don't *remember.* I—damn it, Maggie, he's *dead*! I woke up, and there was this *blood.* All over. Blood. And . . . and there he was. God, look at all this blood! I'm blood all over! Help me, Maggie. What do I do?"

"Bernice," Saint Just said and Maggie looked to him in relief. He sounded so calm. "Bernice, darling, this is Alex. Now, you're at home?"

"Alex, thank God! He's in my bed. Alex! Buddy's dead in my bed!"

"Call nine-one-one," Maggie suggested, earning herself a frown from Saint Just. "No. Stupid idea. Scratch that, Bernie. Don't call nine-one-one. Alex?"

"Bernice," Saint Just said soothingly, even as he took the phone from Maggie and hit the Off button. "Maggie and I will be with you in ten minutes. In the meantime, exactly where are you?"

"In . . . in the living room. The blood, Alex. It . . . please come! Maggie, I need Maggie."

"We're already on our way. I want you to sit down, take several deep, cleansing breaths, and await our arrival. Do nothing. Touch nothing. We'll be right there, and you will let us in, and then we will see all this blood. All right?"

"Blood? What blood? Who's seeing blood?"

"Not now, Socks," Maggie said as the doorman stood in the

living room, half of Saint Just's wardrobe over his arm. She grabbed her purse, checked to make sure her cell phone was in it. Tossed in her cigarette pack; there was a time to abstain and a time to suck in that nicotine for all she was worth, damn it. "Just drop that junk and run down to hail us a cab, okay?"

"Correction. Place my clothing back where you found it, and then go downstairs and secure a hack for us. Oh, and I'll take the blue jacket, if you don't mind," Saint Just said, crossing the room to pick up his cane (the one with the sword in it—when Maggie wrote fiction, she wrote fiction she liked, and fiction she liked had her hero a whiz with weapons).

"Alex, we don't have time to—"

"Maggie, dearest, there is always time to be properly attired. That, in case you may be wondering, is offered in the form of a polite hint. Ah, thank you, Socks," he said, taking the jacket. "Now, please hold the elevator for us. We're right behind you. Maggie?" he asked, extending his arm.

"What do you think, Alex? Is she drunk? High on something? She sounded so *scared*. And Buddy? God, she hated him. Why would she dream about Buddy? Let's go. Damn it, let's just *go*."

Saint Just motioned for Maggie to enter the elevator ahead of him. "There is such a thing as a nightmare, Maggie. Now, I'm afraid I'm woefully uninformed about this Buddy person. Please correct that lapse."

"Okay, okay," Maggie said, dashing out of the elevator, only to have Socks pass her as he jogged to the front doors and the street. "Buddy is—was—Buddy James. Bernie's second husband, after Kirk. Bernice Toland-James, remember? I never met him."

"Interesting," Saint Just said, waving to Sterling, who was scootering toward them, his lips distressingly blue to anyone who didn't know his proclivities in confections, a large red-covered book tucked under his arm. "Come along, Sterling," he said. "Give the scooter to Socks and join us. It would appear Bernice is having a bit of a come-apart."

Maggie stood back so that Sterling could enter the taxi first, then crawled in after him, only then noticing that she was wearing her pajama top with her shorts. Had she combed her hair? No, she couldn't remember combing her hair. But she had brushed her teeth after drinking her morning orange juice. That had to count for something.

She looked at Saint Just as he issued calm commands to the driver, at his neatly creased slacks, his expensive sport coat, his pristine white shirt. "I could hate you."

"A gentleman is always prepared for any circumstance," he said, smoothing down his slacks. "Now, Buddy?"

"I don't know his real name. After Kirk dumped Bernie for ten or twelve younger versions, she went for the first guy who was as far from Kirk as she could find. Buddy James. They married, bought a house somewhere in Connecticut. Near the water. He wasn't in the business. Sold insurance, I think."

"Fascinating man, I'm sure, but perhaps we can move on? The marriage was a happy one?"

"Sure, until Bernie got sick of the commute, and being domestic. Bernie was born for high-rises and doormen and limousine service. Sailing made her hair frizz. Just being near the water in Connecticut made her hair frizz. After a while, just looking at her gardens and her snazzy kitchen and weathered clapboard and anything that looked remotely like an Early American antique made her hair frizz. She was planning to divorce Buddy when he took his boat out one day. A storm came up, and they never found him. Not even the boat. Just some wreckage of some sort."

"A boating tragedy. I see."

Maggie nodded, then leaned forward and knocked on the glass. "Hey, you up there. Cut through the park, all right?"

Sterling was still attempting to fasten his seat belt, as well as trying to catch up. "I don't understand. Bernie married a buddy? A friend?"

"In good time, Sterling, in good time. Now, Maggie. How long ago was this boating mishap?"

"Seven years ago. Well, almost seven years ago. Buddy left behind a pile of debt, but Bernie had no proof he was dead, so she couldn't even get his life insurance money, and he had a bunch of that, because he was an agent, remember. She's been paying off his bills for years. I think she's planning to have a party next month, when he's officially dead. A Bury Buddy party, she calls it, or something like that."

"And yet, according to Bernice, he's dead now. In her apartment. In her bed."

"What?" Sterling abandoned his search for the end of the seat belt and grabbed at the hand strap.

"Obviously Bernice had a difficult evening last night, Sterling," Saint Just said, patting Maggie's hand.

"Don't pat my hand," Maggie said, drawing away, holding her spread fingers out in front of her. "I'm hanging on by a thread here. I never heard her sound like that before. You think she's hallucinating? God, Alex, what are we going to do? Should I call Doctor Bob?"

"For you? Never. For Bernice? It is a tantalizing prospect, as she'd eat him alive. But no, Maggie, we'll handle this. Hopefully. Ah, here we are, and I'm afraid I am not quite as prepared as I believed. Maggie? Pay the gentleman, please?"

Maggie glared at him, then searched in her purse, coming up with a ten dollar bill. The fare was four dollars and eighty-five cents. And she knew she could wait for change until hell froze over.

"Perfect," Saint Just said, snatching the bill from her as the taxi pulled to the curb on Park Avenue.

"Yeah, yeah, I know. The last of the big tippers. Just get a receipt."

"Of course, as you are the last of the cheeseparers." Saint Just helped her out of the taxi and, with Sterling following behind, still looking bemused, they gave their names to the concierge. As they were all named on Bernie's list of allowed visitors, they then were imperiously directed to proceed to the elevator that would take them to the penthouse condominium.

CHAPTER 2

"Wait," Maggie said, stopping in front of the elevator. She began digging in her purse for her cell phone.

She looked so frazzled, and yet so incredibly beautiful. A tall, slim woman wearing wrinkled shorts and a robin's-egg-blue pajama top with little grinning white sheep on it. A woman with uncombed hair and no make-up. A woman who wore her insecurities on her sleeve, almost as a badge of courage, as she did her best to convince the world she had worth; she really did have worth.

Saint Just felt his heart squeeze, and immediately struck a nonchalant pose. Maggie wasn't the only one who felt it safest to hide embarrassing vulnerabilities.

"My dear girl, whatever is wrong now? You've suddenly remembered that you're still *sheep-clad*?"

"Very funny. Just be happy I'm wearing shoes, okay? But maybe we shouldn't be doing this. Maybe I should call Steve, have him go up with us? I mean, cripes, Alex, what if Bernie isn't hallucinating?"

Saint Just refused to react, although he'd been harboring much the same thought. Bernice was a dear of a woman, but she could be a tad . . . unpredictable.

"Maggie, you have to make up your mind. Either Bernice is hallucinating as a result of ingesting some substance, legal or otherwise, or she has a dead Buddy in her bed and blood on her hands. Either scenario, do you really think we need the New York police at this moment?"

She pressed her hands against her head, her fingers curling into her hair. "I don't know. I'm panicking." She gave her hair a pull as she added, "I *hate* panicking."

"Come here," he said, pulling her against his chest as, neatly, efficiently, he employed the tip of his cane to depress the CALL button. "It's all right, Maggie. Everything will be fine. I'm here."

Maggie wrapped her arms around him and clung. Just for a moment. Then she pushed herself free, saying, "Oh, brother. That was a terrible line. And a terrible lie. If Bernie's in trouble, it doesn't matter who's here."

"I'm here, too, Maggie," Sterling said, gently patting her shoulder.

Saint Just winced. Sympathy from Sterling? He reached into his pocket and extracted a clean square of folded linen, handing it to Maggie as she let out a subdued yet unnerving wail.

"Never sympathy, Sterling. Not from anyone save me, because she knows that, at heart, I'm only offering comfort in order to make her angry enough not to dissolve in a moment of crisis."

"I'll never understand you, Saint Just," Sterling said, stepping into the elevator and holding the door open for Maggie, who was wiping her moist eyes. "I'll never understand either of you. Like you well enough and all of that, but understand you? Never."

Saint Just glared imperiously at the concierge, who was looking at them questioningly as the doors slid closed, then began examining the elevator as it rose to the top floor. "Is this the only elevator? The only access?"

Maggie blew her nose in his handkerchief and dared to try to hand it back to him. "I suppose so. I've only been here a couple of times since Bernie moved in. No, wait. There's probably some sort of service elevator, too. And a stairwell, in case of fire. Why?"

"Nothing. I was just thinking. If Bernice entered her penthouse with a gentleman in tow last night, someone would have seen her, probably someone much like that suspicious gentleman we encountered just now in the foyer. And, that person would have to sign in as we did, even if he arrived with Bernice, I would suppose. I should have requested a peek at the register. Sterling, we'll have to see to that."

"Absolutely, Saint Just."

Maggie held up one finger. "*If* she came in with Buddy. That's what you're saying. But she couldn't have come in with Buddy, because Buddy was fish bait seven years ago."

"I really wish you'd stop saying things like that, Maggie," Sterling said, wincing. "I can't swim, you know. Never could."

"Hush, Sterling. Yes, Buddy is supposedly dead, as you say, Maggie. That is problematic, I agree, but not an insurmountable obstacle to sweet reason, if applied correctly."

"Uh-oh, there he goes," Sterling said, looking at Maggie. "He's detecting."

Saint Just ignored his friend, choosing instead to examine the control panel in the elevator. Passengers went all the way up, or all the way down, with no buttons listing the other floors. "Kirk lived well," he said, arching an eyebrow at Maggie, knowing that this had been Kirk Toland's penthouse until his untimely and rather spectacular demise not that long ago.

"I know," Maggie said. "Bernie had to give up most everything else, but she's keeping the penthouse. Forgetting to change his will after the divorce was the only decent thing that man ever did. Guess he thought he'd live forever."

The car stopped, the doors whispered open, and Saint Just stepped directly into a black and white marble foyer complete with twelve foot ceilings and thick white marble pillars. A towering arrangement of fresh flowers sat on a round table. Obviously the very tasteless Kirk had hired a decorator. "Sterling, if you'll keep Maggie here for the nonce?"

"No way! I'm coming with you. Bernie! Bernie, it's Maggie! Where are you, honey?"

Maggie's words echoed in the large foyer, but there was no answer.

"Oh, God, she's not answering. That can't be good," Maggie said, trying to break free of Sterling's grasp, but Sterling had been given a commission by Saint Just, and he held on tight.

Saint Just proceeded slowly, grasping his sword cane midway down in his left hand, leaving his right hand free. Ordinarily, he would be pretending not to be impressed by the opulence unfolding before him as he passed through the foyer and into an immense cavern of a room, the furnishings of which could have graced Buckingham Palace, even Versailles. But he was impressed.

"Bernice?" he called softly, searching the dimness, for heavy drapes hung in front of floor-to-ceiling windows, banishing the sunlight. "Bernice, darling, it's Alex."

And then he saw her. She was crouching in a corner, her knees drawn up to her chest, her head buried against those knees. Her glorious long mane of Titian curls tangled like a bird's nest. Her lime green satin pajamas had an odd design. . . .

"Bernice?"

Bernie looked up at him, her eyes wide. She moaned low in her throat.

"Bernice, darling. Maggie's here, too. And Sterling. You wouldn't want them to see you like this, would you?"

Bernice Toland-James was a beautiful woman. She worked at remaining a beautiful woman as she ventured more deeply into her forties (at least that's the decade she claimed), via cosmetic surgery, liposuction, Botox injections, starvation diets, a couture wardrobe, and a hair colorist who had to be a genius.

She was brilliant, both in her coloring and in her mind. She was kind, generous, amusing, a loyal friend; Maggie's loyal friend, as well as her editor. She was now sole owner and publisher of Toland Books.

She had become, in these past weeks, something else: a dedicated—and seemingly happy about it—drunk.

"Alex?"

Bernie's voice was little more than a whisper.

"Yes, Bernice. That's right. Alex. Here, allow me to assist you to a chair." He held out his hand and, slowly, definitely reluctantly, she took it. As she stood up, the design on her pajamas became clear. There was no design at all. There was blood. Quite a bit of blood. Still wet, definitely sticky. More blood was on her hands, on her face. Even matted into her hair.

"Alex? Buddy . . ."

"Yes, my dear," he said soothingly, wishing Maggie at the other end of the earth, but as she was here, he knew he had to call her, gain her assistance. "Here you go. Just sit down on this lovely couch, and I'll fetch Maggie. All right?"

"Maggie," Bernie said, swallowing hard. "Yes . . . yes . . . Maggie. I called Maggie. I remember."

Saint Just looked down at his hand, saw the blood on it, and wished back his handkerchief. Instead, he tucked his right hand into his pocket so that Maggie wouldn't immediately see the blood on him, mentally putting paid to his favorite jacket, and returned to the foyer.

"Is she all right?" Maggie asked, standing quietly, without Sterling's having to restrain her. "I heard you talking to her. She's still hallucinating?"

"Unfortunately, no," Saint Just said, looking to Sterling. "Maggie, I need you to be very brave. There could be a problem. There's blood on Bernice's pajamas, a rather copious amount. Mine was only a cursory examination, but I think I am safe in saying it is *not* her blood. Now, I want you to go to her, don't ask about the blood, and just sit with her. Possibly fetch her something restorative to drink. Sterling, come with me, if you please. Touching nothing, as *Left*-tenant Wendell will have to be summoned at some point, I'm sure."

Maggie had already brushed past him, so that when he and Sterling reentered the living room, it was to see the two women on one of the immense couches, hugging each other, Bernie sobbing soundlessly.

"There are stairs, Sterling," Saint Just said, pointing toward another hallway and the landing he'd already seen. "We'll assume the bedchambers are up there. Come along. Again, touch nothing."

"Do you think there's a body, Saint Just?"

"Conjecture seems rather pointless, as we're soon to find out definitively, but yes, Sterling, I'm very much afraid we will shortly discover a body."

He stopped at the head of the broad, winding staircase, confronted with a long hallway lined with several doors. Then he looked down at the Oriental carpet and saw the blood. There also were three bloody hand prints on the wall, as if Bernie had repeatedly staggered against that wall as she escaped the bedroom. Poor terrified woman.

"Sterling, if you would be so kind?" Saint Just stripped off his jacket and handed it to his friend—perhaps it could be saved—then unbuttoned his shirt and removed it.

How he enjoyed these moments, this clarity of sight he felt when put to the test. He had been born for this. Well, *made* for this, at the least.

Using one shirt sleeve as a glove, ineffective as that was, he stepped carefully, avoiding the blood, and then pushed open the already slightly ajar door that was second on the left.

"Oh, gracious," Sterling said from behind him as they both proceeded into the dimly lit bed chamber.

"Indeed," Saint Just said, raising the bulk of his shirt to his nose, the better to cover the sour-sweet smell of blood, of bodily fluids. "I don't know who that is, Sterling, but the gentleman in question is most definitely quite dead."

"All that blood, Saint Just. On the bed, on the ceiling, on the walls. Everywhere. Just like *The Case of the Lingering Lightskirt.* Only that was a woman, of course, and this is most definitely a man. He's so white, Saint Just. The parts that aren't bloody, that is."

"Exsanguination, Sterling. Our victim bled to death." Saint

Just moved closer, mentally cataloguing all that he saw, as he feared that once Wendell was on the scene, he would be banished from the room. The man's neck had been cut, ear to ear, transecting both carotids. "See the wound?"

"Uh . . . no, that's all right. As I said, we saw something very like this is *Lightskirt,* and I distinctly remember Maggie's description of the wound," Sterling said, already backing from the room.

"Very well, you may wait downstairs with the ladies. The less we disturb the scene the better, I suppose. No need to summon Maggie, as she never had the acquaintance of Mr. James. We'll have to believe Bernice, unless she was too muddled to be certain of her identification. Poor thing, to awaken to this. I'll only be another few moments."

He thought about Sterling's observation. The scene was rather reminiscent of *Lightskirt,* Maggie's third Saint Just mystery. The victim had been female, of course, and the first of four dispatched in such a way until he, Saint Just, had solved the murders and apprehended the titled and powerful miscreant. *Lightskirt* had ridden the *New York Times* best-seller list for three months.

But this? This was not fiction. This was fact.

And he, Saint Just, was once more on the case.

He could move no closer, not without stepping in blood. But he was close enough to see where Bernie had been lying on the far side of the wide mattress, her body crudely outlined by blood spatter. Close enough to see the naked man's exposed and slit windpipe; a stronger hand with the knife, and the man's neck would have been completely severed. Close enough to see the very large knife lying tangled in the sheets.

Retracing his steps, Saint Just pulled the door shut and headed down the hallway, in search of a bathroom. After washing his hands, he retrieved his jacket from the stair post, where Sterling had left it, and extracted his cell phone, punching in memorized numbers.

"Alex?"

He turned quickly, blocking Maggie's sight of the bloody wallpaper. He slipped his arms into his shirt, buttoning it. "There's a body, yes. I'm phoning *Left*-tenant Wendell now. Please rejoin Sterling and Bernice in the living room."

"Oh, God! Sterling just nodded when he came back downstairs and I thought . . . but I didn't want to ask in front of Bernie. It's Buddy?"

"That I don't know. Please, Maggie. Bad news doesn't improve with keeping, and I want Wendell here rather than anyone else." He turned away from her and spoke into the phone. "Yes, Wendell, so happy you're answering your phone at last. Blakely here. I was wondering, would it be possible for you to come by Park Avenue? The Bernice Toland-James residence, to be precise. Excuse me—Maggie? The exact address? Ah, thank you."

He repeated the address to the lieutenant. "Yes, very near the museum as a matter of fact. Lovely neighborhood, quite a step up in the world for you, so you might wish to brush the doughnut crumbs from your shirt before joining us. What's that? No, no. No problem. I'm always delighted to provide sartorial advice to those in need."

He flipped the cell phone shut.

"Why didn't you tell him?"

"I didn't tell him, Maggie, because I'd rather he didn't enter leading a parade of his compatriots. He expects me to be snarky, to descend to your vernacular for a moment, and I was not about to disappoint him. He's a copper and, friend or nay, he thinks like a copper."

"Okay, I guess, although he's going to be angry."

"How relieved I am to have your approval. Wendell's displeasure is merely an added gift, isn't it? You do know you're now fairly well covered in blood? I fear we'll be waving a fond, final farewell to the sheep upon our return to our domicile. But enough of joy, how is Bernice? And how are you?"

"Bernie's sipping scotch and spazzing out about her bloody

pajamas. I know you said restorative, and you probably meant a cup of Earl Grey tea or something, but, well, it's Bernie. And I washed her hands. I know I shouldn't have, but she was really starting to freak out about them, so I washed them for her. And her face. Me? I . . . I'm fine."

"Really?"

"No, not really. Not even close, or I would have been able to think up something snappy to say to you about my pajamas, that I *like,* damn it. God, Alex, what's going on?"

"There is a very dead man in Bernice's bed, there is blood virtually everywhere, there is a knife most conveniently lying on that bed, and Bernice is even more conveniently covered in blood. Her fingerprints, I'm convinced, will be on that knife. Other than that? I missed breakfast this morning because Sterling was in a rush to get to the park, but I do believe I can now forgo lunch without any great personal sacrifice."

"Oh, God." Maggie sat down on the top step. Collapsed onto the top step. "I asked her what happened last night, and she says she doesn't remember. All she remembers is waking up with Buddy next to her—like you said. Bloody and dead. Everyone's going to think she did it."

"Most assuredly."

"Well, she didn't! You know she didn't. I know she didn't. Bernie wouldn't hurt a fly."

"On the contrary. If I were to go into battle, I would very much appreciate having the valiant Bernice guarding my back. She's an exceedingly strong-willed woman who has, if you'll recall, on more than one occasion declared herself capable of killing without a blink, if she felt herself threatened. And, much as it pains me to remind you, Bernice was a prime suspect in the murder of her first husband not that long ago."

"But we know who killed Kirk, and it wasn't Bernie. And Buddy disappeared seven years ago. You know what? It can't be Buddy. Bernie's just so strung out, she thinks it's him. I saw a photograph of him once. How about I take a look?"

"Not if you clutched the hem of my garments and begged," Saint Just said as Maggie got to her feet. "And, now that Wendell is on his way, we cannot in good conscience disturb the scene. We might even destroy evidence that would exonerate Bernice."

"Really bloody, huh?" Maggie wrinkled her nose. "That's what you're saying."

"The deceased is also nude. It would not be proper for you to view a nude male body."

Maggie rolled her eyes, as he knew she would. "Oh, bite me, Alex. Like I haven't seen a nude man before."

"Not in my presence, you haven't. Come along downstairs. Wendell was already in his vehicle. He'll be here in approximately a half hour, traffic permitting. Have you seen the kitchen?"

Maggie rubbed at her forehead. "No. I used the powder room to get a towel and washcloth for Bernie. Why?"

"I would like to see Bernice's knife collection, if that is what it's called," he said, retrieving his sport coat. "Such as the block of wood filled with knives you have on the counter in your kitchen?"

Maggie followed behind him as he returned to the first floor, stopped a moment, then headed to his right, around the staircase, through a magnificent dining room, and pushed through a swinging door. "There you go," she said. "One kitchen. One big-assed kitchen, too. But I thought we weren't supposed to disturb anything. Oh, and if it isn't too much trouble, would you mind telling me why you took off your shirt?"

"Because I didn't think to bring rubber gloves with me?" Saint Just offered, walking around a large center island topped in butcher block, stopping when he noticed that one side of the island sported a slotted piece of wood holding a dozen knives.

And one empty slot.

"Ah, our murder weapon. I recognize the handles. Convenient."

Maggie pushed him aside and took a look. "I know you hate when anyone states the obvious, but there's a knife missing. You think it really is the murder weapon? That's at least something, Alex. I mean, that makes it seem a crime of opportunity. Just the sort of thing Bernie might do if she was suddenly confronted with Buddy, who she thought was dead. Wished was dead. But at least there's a chance of second degree, not a first degree charge. Maybe even involuntary manslaughter? You can get bail with those, I think."

Saint Just arched a brow. "You've convicted her already? Your best friend?"

"No, of course not. But it looks bad, Alex, and if she's charged, I want her able to get out on bail. I told you she doesn't remember anything, right? She was drunk. Hell, she's even been having some blackouts lately, which is why I've been begging her to see Doctor Bob, get some help. Go away somewhere. Do the Betty Ford thing. Something. But she says she can't, because of everything going on at Toland Books."

"Just as you say you'll stop smoking once you've made your next deadline. Or was that when you've lost five pounds? Or perhaps it was after you've gotten your apartment back and Sterling and I are on our own? I know you well enough to be fairly positive you've made a list of excuses and refer to it from time to time. Which is it this week, Maggie?"

"Go to hell."

"That's my girl. Now, no more thoughts of Bernice being dragged away in chains. I know you like to think out loud, but this is neither the time nor the place. Who is her solicitor?"

"Her lawyer? Oh, right." Maggie took a deep breath. "Sorry. But I'm pretty creeped out here. I've never been in the same place as a corpse, unless you count my Uncle John's wake, and he was wearing a suit and the mortician had put a smile on his face, so he sort of looked happy about being dead. My mind's been racing. Bernie's lawyer, you said? I don't know. He's corporate anyway, I'm sure. Bernie needs a criminal lawyer. But Steve won't like it if we call a lawyer before he's had a chance to talk to her."

"My condolences to the *left*-tenant, of course, but Bernice will not speak to anyone unless there is a lawyer present. Not a single syllable. To the good cop, or to the bad cop."

"Watching all those *Law and Order* reruns again, aren't you?" Maggie said, then nodded. "Okay, you're right. Definitely right. She'll look guilty as sin, though."

"My dear girl, she looks guilty as sin now. How much blacker can prudent silence paint her? Now, where do you suppose her telephone directory is located?"

"I think she keeps everything on her Palm Pilot. Shall I go get it?"

Saint Just nodded, even as he opened drawers, on the hunt for the Manhattan phone book. He wished to keep Maggie busy, but didn't want the name of Bernie's corporate lawyer. He wanted a shark. A big one. He wanted a lawyer who had no life, who worked on weekends, who would devote himself to one Bernice Toland-James. If he couldn't get all of that, he'd settle for anyone he could get for the moment, and find his shark later.

Locating the phone book, he hefted its weight onto the counter and paged through it until he found the listings for attorneys. Those listings were a small book on their own.

He ran his finger down page after page, curiously inspecting the large individual advertisements, until he saw the one for J.P. Boxer, Criminal Law. There was an ink drawing of a teeth-bared boxer dog in one corner of the small ad, and a telephone number. That was it, other than a Park Avenue address, one not three blocks away. It seemed providential.

Saint Just called the number. The phone was answered on the first ring.

"Boxer here. Talk to me, because if you're calling on Saturday, you've got as little life as I do on weekends, you're in deep shit, and you need me bad," said a gruff voice made even worse thanks to the poor connection on his cell phone.

"I also need you now," Saint Just said smoothly, already halfway to being satisfied with J.P. Boxer. He recited the address, promising to meet the lawyer in the vestibule. "Ten minutes, or I call someone else. Oh, and the name is Blakely. Alex Blakely."

"Yeah, yeah, good for you. And I don't take cases unless I like them."

"Good. I don't hire barristers unless I like them. Nine minutes, my good fellow. The constabulary is already on its way."

"You called them first? I don't work with idiots. What is it? Your wife ran up her charge at Tiffany's and you beaned her with your squash racket?"

"Eight minutes," Saint Just said, and flipped his cell phone closed, already heading for the living room as he slipped his arms into his sport coat. "Maggie? You needn't look further. I'm going downstairs to await the arrivial of the lawyer. Kindly call the concierge and pretend you're Bernice, tell him that J.P. Boxer is allowed up."

"I'll do it myself," Bernie said, getting rather unsteadily to her feet, Sterling quickly moving to take her elbow. "Really. I can do that."

"Of course you can," Maggie said soothingly as Saint Just hit the button for the elevator, the gold-veined mirrored doors opening at once.

He stood in the vestibule, smiling as the phone rang and the concierge spoke into it, shooting him curious looks as he listened.

Five minutes later, Wendell still not on the scene, the doorman held open the door for an Amazon.

Saint Just's eyelids widened almost imperceptibly as J.P. Boxer employed a baritone growl to announce herself to the concierge.

The woman was dressed in bright green sweats with blue stripes running up the outside of each pant leg. She was at least two inches over six feet tall. Her hair, what there was of it, was cut to within a half inch of her well-shaped but quite large skull. Her ankle-high sneakers were orange, the laces untied. She was a garish rainbow, and seemed to be quite proud of that fact.

"Blakely? You look like you sound, Englishman," the woman said in her gravelly voice, slipping off her mirrored sunglasses.

"Boxer?" Saint Just responded, still rather nonplussed.

"Yeah, that's me," she said, grabbing a pen from the desk and signing her name on the guest register. "I'm big, I'm black, I'm ugly. I'm fifty-six and hormonal, and I'm your best friend or your worst nightmare, depending on whether or not I came running up here for nothing and left my onion bagel to get stale. Let's get to it."

"By all means," Saint Just said, motioning for her to precede him into the penthouse elevator. "Your client is—"

"Not yet, gorgeous. Wait until the doors close."

"Of course." Saint Just kept a smile on his face as, inwardly, he was reconsidering his choice. "There, alone at last. Now, as I was saying, your client is Bernice Toland-James."

"Know her, know her, this is good," J.P. said, nodding her head. "Classy redhead. Don't let your eyes bug out, Englishman. We travel in the same circles, we just don't look like it. I've seen her around. Who's the stiff?"

"I beg your pardon?"

"The stiff, the body, the victim. This is murder, right? Saturday calls have to be murder. Who is it?"

"We're not certain," Saint Just told her, and Boxer reached out, slamming her palm against the STOP button.

"You're not *certain.* What are you *certain* of, bucko? Are you sure there's a body? My bagel, remember?"

Saint Just believed it was time he took charge. And, if he had the faintest idea how to do that, he would. As it was, he knew himself to be outgunned and even outbullied. By a woman. It was disconcerting.

He did his best to fill her in, including the fact that Wendell was on his way.

"Wendell. Know him, too. Tough. But decent. Dresses like a bum, but that's all an act. Likes to play Good Cop. Who else is up there? You look like the sort that wants an audience. I don't like surprises."

"Really? I would think you rather enjoyed them. Handing them out, that is."

"Funny man." She glared at him. "I hate funny men. Who else?"

Saint Just told her.

"Don't know them. A writer, huh? I hate writers, too, especially crime writers. They never get their facts right. But you're all friends of my client? How much has she said to any of you? You'll be subpoenaed, you know."

"Bernice hasn't said much of anything, claiming to know nothing, except to say that she awoke this morning to discover the deceased in bed with her. She believes the body to be that of her husband, Buddy James, who supposedly was lost at sea seven years ago. And yes, there he was."

"You shitting me?" Boxer grinned. It was an unholy grin. She hit the STOP button again, and the elevator began to rise once more. "Oh, Blakely, you beautiful, beautiful man, this is going to be *fun.*"

"How edifying for you, I'm sure," Saint Just said, at last discovering some empathy for Maggie and her tendency to retreat in the face of large, blustering, supremely assured people. A woman? God's teeth!

CHAPTER 3

Maggie heard the soft swish of the elevator doors, handed Bernie a fresh tumbler of Scotch, and headed for the foyer. "Alex?" she said, looking at J.P. Boxer.

"This the crime writer?" J.P. asked, hooking a thumb at Maggie. "Stay out of my way, sweetcakes."

"Excuse me?" Maggie said, stepping back a pace. "I'm Bernie's best friend."

"Good for you. I'm her lawyer. Quick, who does she need right now? Oh, wait, I know. *Me.* Where is she?"

"In . . . in there," Maggie said, stepping back even more. It was either that or be mown down by this huge woman in orange sneakers. "Alex?"

"It's all right, Maggie. Miss Boxer—"

"*Ms.* Boxer, Englishman," J.P. called over her shoulder. "Better yet, *Attorney* Boxer. My mama scrubbed a lot of floors just so I could say that. You can start writing it that way on my retainer check. That would be a two and a five, gorgeous, with three zeroes on the end."

"Who . . . who *is* that woman?" Maggie asked Alex. "She's *horrible.*"

"Exceedingly and, I have no doubt, purposefully so, yes," Saint Just agreed, taking Maggie's arm. "However, she's here, and as Wendell will also be on the premises very shortly, we'll simply have to muddle along. You did bring your checkbook, didn't you, my dear?"

"Traveling with you? I'd have to, wouldn't I?" Maggie said irritably. "Come on, we can't leave Bernie alone in there with that woman."

"She's not alone. Sterling is with—ah, yes, I see your point."

Maggie was still shaking, both inwardly and outwardly. Wishing herself stronger for Bernie's sake, doing her best to keep herself in check, to not start screaming or crying. She reentered the living room and approached one of the chairs.

"Don't sit!"

"I beg your pardon?"

"I said, don't sit," J.P. commanded. "Don't sit, don't touch, don't breathe deep. This whole place is evidence. Go over there and stand with your chubby friend in front of the fireplace, like good little soldiers."

"Maggie?" Bernie held out her hand. "I want you here, with me."

J.P. grabbed the tumbler of scotch out of Bernie's hand. "Say bye-bye to Johnny Walker, Ms. Toland-James. From this moment on, you're officially on the wagon."

"But . . . but . . ." Bernie's panic was palpable.

"Oh, screw this," Maggie said in exasperation that overcame her insecurities, quickly heading for Bernie and sitting down beside her. "It's okay, sweetie. It's okay."

"I said—"

"Good day, Attorney Boxer," Saint Just said, stepping up behind her. "So sorry for your inconvenience, but we won't be needing you after all."

J.P. turned to face him. Looked him up and down. Slowly. "You don't like me, do you, Englishman? That's good, because I work at being unlikable. But you know what else? I'm good at what I do. I am fucking excellent. So excellent I can see the blood all over my client here. You called me, but from here on out, I call the shots. Now, if you can't live with that, if you want some namby–pamby to hold her hand, hold all your hands, and try to get her to cop a plea in exchange for ten to twenty upstate, that's no never mind to me. Otherwise—like it or not, I'm Big Mama here, even if that means playing rough with your cute little writer girlfriend. So, what is it? I stay, or I go?"

Maggie bit her bottom lip as she watched Saint Just. His blue eyes gave nothing away, but she could see the slight tic working in his left cheek, just beneath his eye. The Viscount Saint Just did not take orders.

"You stay," Saint Just said, and Maggie could hear Sterling's sigh of relief. "You stay, Maggie is allowed to render moral support, *and* Bernie gets her drink. Other than that, we're yours to command. You see, I am not above sensible compromise."

J.P. stuck out her hand. "I guess I'm not, either. But we detox her before the trial. Like I said, I've seen her around."

"Trial?" Bernie moaned low in her throat and grabbed Maggie's hand once more. "I have to have a trial?"

"Maybe," J.P. said, all her attention on Bernie once more. "We'll get there when we get there, okay? For now, tell me what you know."

Bernie gripped Maggie's hand even harder. "I don't know *anything*. I went out last night. It was Friday, right?" she asked Maggie, who nodded, blinking back tears. "I woke up this morning, and Buddy was . . . Buddy was . . ."

J.P. had pulled a pad and pen from her jacket pocket. "Went out. When? Where?"

"Um . . . there was a party. Yes, a party. At Binky Halstead's brownstone. You know Binky, Maggie. She used to be married to Walter Yeager, the financier? He's . . . *upstate* now, for insider trading. Oh, God, and we were *laughing* about it, and now I—"

"Charming circle of friends," J.P. said, scribbling. "I'll need her number and address later. Where else? Did you go anywhere else?"

Maggie used her free hand to rub Bernie's back. "Think, Bernie, honey. Anywhere else?"

"I . . . I came back here. Yes, I came back here. In the limo. But then I didn't want to come upstairs yet, so I walked a little and . . . I think I went to Brenda's. You know? Two down, around the corner, three over?"

J.P. scribbled on the pad. "Brenda's. I know the place. High-toned watering hole. They'd remember seeing you. Anywhere else?"

Bernie shrugged. "I don't know. Maybe. I'm not sure. Binky was handing out tequila shooters."

"Ah, Bernie, you should have come to me," Maggie said. "If you were lonely or something."

"Were you lonely, Bernie?" J.P. asked, dropping all formality. "Were you alone?"

Bernie turned her head toward the stairs. "I couldn't have been, could I? I mean, I don't remember. God, Maggie, *I don't remember*!"

The elevator doors opened and Maggie stiffened, knowing Steve Wendell had arrived. "Bernie, let go. Steve's here."

"I'll handle this," J.P. said.

"Actually, no, you won't, not just yet," Saint Just said silkily. "Maggie, go fetch the good *left*-tenant before he becomes hopelessly lost, saying little, if you please."

"Thanks, Alex," Maggie said, and hurried out to the foyer, to see Steve standing there in his usual rumpled khakis and knit shirt and ill-fitting jacket, his sandy hair blown by the wind, glad to see her, his smile warm—and quickly disappearing.

"Maggie? Is that blood?" he asked, pointing to her pajama top. "Are you all right? Are you hurt?"

"Oh, Steve, I'm so glad to see you. She didn't do it. I know she didn't do it."

He took her hand, bent to kiss her cheek. Good old Steve. So reliable, so without his own agenda. So unlike Alex, who maddened her, intrigued her, *bothered* her so very much. Steve was comfortable, safe . . . as long as she didn't think about the dangers of his job . . . as long as she fought down her attraction to an imaginary character who could disappear from her life just as she'd be telling him she loved him.

"Who? You're talking about Bernie? She didn't do what?"

"Kill Buddy," Maggie said. "Her husband. He's dead, if it's him. Somebody's dead upstairs. She called us and told us. But she didn't do it. You know Bernie. You know she didn't do it."

Steve held up one hand. "You're telling me there's a body in here? Jesus, Maggie, why didn't Blakely—"

"He thought . . . I thought . . . we thought it would be better if you came first, took a look around. That would make you primary, right? You'd be in charge of the case?"

"Technically. But probably not. I know Bernie personally, remember? I might be pulled off. Where's Blakely? More important, where's the body? Where's Bernie?"

"We're in there," Maggie said, pointing to the living room. "Except the body. That's upstairs, in Bernie's bed."

"In her bed? I'd say heart attack during sex then, if it weren't for the blood on you, Maggie. Why is there blood on your clothes?"

"I hugged Bernie. She's covered in it. Alex went upstairs to see if there really was a body, and he said the bedroom was covered in blood too, and—"

"He went upstairs? He disturbed the scene? Damn it, Maggie. Next he'll be giving me his cockamamie ideas on who did it."

"Well, he has been giving that some thought," Maggie said quietly.

"Keep him away from me, Maggie, I mean it. If Bernie didn't do this, I'm her best friend."

"Wrong, Wendell, that would be me," J.P. said, entering the foyer. "If you two are quite done, maybe you want to call the crime scene guys and get the stiff out of my client's house? You know how it is, they start to stink after a while."

"J.P.," Steve said, rolling his eyes. "Gee, my day just keeps getting better and better. Still chasing ambulances for your supper?"

"Only if you're in 'em, sweet knees," J.P. said, winking. "Now, before you call in the dogs, what do you say we all go upstairs and take a look around."

Steve laughed, but he was clearly not amused. "Oh, yeah, sure, let's do that. Hey, call out for pizza and we can make a party of it."

"Forever droll," Saint Just said, already heading for the stairs. "But, being reasonable, Wendell, something you may have just a fleeting acquaintance with, you really should be sure in your own mind that there is a body upstairs before you call in reinforcements."

"I hate when he has a point," Steve said. "You stay here, Maggie. You too, Sterling, Bernie."

"Are you nuts?" Bernie said, and took a deep drink from her tumbler. "I'm not going back up there. I didn't like looking at him when he was alive."

"Nice, real nice. Anyone want to hear my vote as to whether or not Red over there takes the stand in her own defense? I didn't think so. Lead on, Wendell," J.P. said. "Have you got any extra gloves?"

"Not in giant size, no," Wendell said, and Maggie bit her bottom lip. She waited until they were all upstairs, then followed after them, to stand just beside the doorway, the better to hear anything anyone said. After all, if Alex could be there, so could she.

"Yup, that's a body, all right," Steve said. "Blakely, keep back."

"In these shoes? I should most certainly say so. Do you see the knife? Wonderfully convenient, don't you think?"

"She was probably drunk."

"Never assume, Wendell," J.P. said. "Little weenie, ain't it? Pitiful. All shriveled up and all."

What followed was silence, and Maggie had to cover her mouth, so as not to laugh out loud as she pictured Steve blushing and Alex—well, God knew what Alex was doing. Probably keeping himself busy sticking his quizzing glass to his eye.

"We'll have a tough time separating bodily fluids in this mess."

"Sperm, Wendell. You can say it around me. Sperm. Little swimmers. Very little swimmers, I'd say. Guess it is true, what they say about you white guys. You want a rape kit? What will you give me to get it?"

"We're not playing *Let's Make a Deal* here, J.P. This is a crime scene."

"And Ms. Toland-James is my client. Now, what will you give me? I know what I want. I want the sexual assault team here. No hospital. You get her clothes, you get access. But she stays here. And I want it now, so she can get a shower. The woman's covered in blood, for cripes sake."

"I get to talk to her?"

"Oh, Englishman, do you hear the man? He dreams. Wendell, she talks to you when I say she talks to you. Pretend I've got the police commissioner's ear, Wendell, which means I've got your ass in my hands. Figuratively."

"I liked you better when you were a cop, J.P."

"If we might return our attention to the clues, leaving this descent into personalities and sentimental waxing over times gone by to some other more appropriate moment?"

"Jesus, Blakely, you're talking clues? And stop saying clues. It's evidence. *Evidence.* We have a body, we have a wound, we have a knife. We've got a suspect downstairs. I think that's enough to start with. What else do you want?"

"I want, *Left*-tenant, to know how this gentlemen came to be dead in Bernice's bed. I want to know how he arrived here, with whom, when. I want to know if it was self-defense. I want to understand why there is an imprint of Bernie's body on the far side of the mattress, outlined in blood."

"She slashes him, then passes out right after, while he plays Fountain Man," Steve suggested.

"I don't know, Wendell," J.P. said. "That's one hell of a slice. I could make it, I'm a big strapping kind of gal, but I don't think Twinkletoes downstairs could have done it. Especially drunk."

"Who says she was drunk?"

"I thought you said Wendell knows her," J.P. said, obviously talking to Alex.

"Okay, okay, I get your point. But this guy was invited in. There's no sign of a struggle here."

"No, Wendell, there's not," Saint Just said. "You know what else there isn't? There are no items of male clothing here. Now why, do you suppose, is that?"

"They're somewhere," Steve said, and Maggie heard his voice trailing off as he moved farther from the doorway. "I see three doors. Closet, bathroom, something else."

"Sauna," Maggie said, then clapped her hands over her mouth, her eyes opened wide. "Oops."

"Margaret," Saint Just pronounced in taut, even tones. "Shame on you."

Maggie stepped into the doorway, trying to peek past J.P.'s large frame, to the bed. "I'm her friend, too. And who do you think really solves all those murders, anyway? You? I mean—um, never mind."

Man, she'd almost blown it, almost said that Alex Blakely was really Alexandre Blake, Viscount Saint Just, the perfect hero of her imagination come to life here in Manhattan, and not just in her imagination anymore. Oh yeah. Sure. That would have gone over big.

"Some small hysterics," Saint Just was saying. "My American cousin writes fiction, you understand, but we have, together, stumbled over two bodies in the past little space, at which time I stepped in and solved both cases. With nominal help from her, I agree, as I am a magnanimous man."

"And I'm supposed to care? Be impressed? Don't hold your breath, handsome," J.P. said. "Wendell? I want a full report as soon as you get it. Hair, fibers, fingerprints, blood type, fluids. Rape kit. The whole magilla. I know you love to share. Are we done here?"

Maggie watched as Steve pulled out his cell phone and

flipped it open. "We're done here, yes. I'll meet you all downstairs. Don't touch anything."

"Gee, and here I was, about to go to the kitchen and make myself a sandwich. Come on, Englishman. Let the man call his little friends. We've seen enough."

Maggie got one good look at the bed, which was more than enough for her, and quickly preceded J.P. and Alex down the stairs, back into the living room.

Bernie, Maggie noted, was looking better, even wearing those blood-soaked pajamas. The booze had helped, having her friends here had helped, but Bernie had also helped herself. She was a strong woman, something you had to be if you wanted to swim with the sharks in the publishing world, and win. "Maggie? Is it Buddy? I'm sure it's Buddy."

"Ah-ah, you talk to me, Bernie, not little Mary Sunshine here. You sure this is your dead husband?"

Bernie looked to Maggie. Maggie looked to Alex. Saint Just said, "Approximately six feet tall, muscular build going to fat. Thinning blond hair, eyes brown, teeth capped, at least in the front. Rather large brownish mole approximately three inches below the left shoulder blade. Healed incision on the left knee. Flat feet."

"You saw all that?" Maggie was impressed. "In all that blood, you saw all that?"

"Simple observation by a trained eye, my dear. May I suggest your next corpse have his eyes open and fixed, his jaw slack? It's quite a dramatic image."

"Dead a while, long enough for the eyes to start to cloud a little," J.P. added. "I'm impressed, Englishman."

"Alex. Please, call me Alex. And of course you are. I am nothing if not impressive."

"All right. Alex. God, you're weird. Almost as weird as me. But you missed the good stuff."

"Really? By the good stuff, I imagine you're referring to the bruising around the body's wrists and ankles, and possibly also the faint hint of what could be adhesive residue on his right cheek?"

"Damn. Okay, Alex, weird or not, you can join the team. Everybody else? Out."

"I need Maggie," Bernie said, grabbing Maggie's hand and unceremoniously pulling her down onto the couch. "I'm hanging on by a thread here. Don't leave me, Maggie."

"I won't," Maggie promised, glaring up at J.P. Boxer, then sparing a little of that glare for Alex, who was preening now. Definitely preening, the bum.

"And I'll just be leaving," Sterling said, before anyone could throw him out. "Pausing downstairs to slip a few Andrew Jacksons to the concierge for a peek at the guest register, isn't that right, Saint Just?"

"They watch a lot of television," Maggie offered weakly to J.P. "My purse is over there, Sterling."

"Okay, one gone," J.P. said once Sterling had entered the elevator. "Now, who's Saint Just?"

"That would be me. Maggie borrowed our names for characters in her book, and gifted me with the title Viscount Saint Just. Sterling finds it amusing to address me as Saint Just. He's a simple man. A good man."

"You're all nuts, that's what I think. Okay, Bernie, we'll do this again, from the stiff on. Does anything we've said sound like Buddy?"

Bernie nodded furiously. "He had knee surgery about six months before he disappeared. Had me waiting on him hand and foot, the louse."

"There she goes again. Word of advice, babe. Newly deceased spouses, especially those found murdered in your bed, are not referred to as louses by the suspect. Drowned, right? I got to tell you, Bernie, that corpse upstairs looks in pretty good shape to have been in the water for seven years. Tell me about the boating accident."

Bernie shrugged. "What's to tell? He took his boat out. We

lived in Connecticut, right near the water. Buddy was always taking that damn boat out. This time there was a storm, and he never came back. They found stuff, the Coast Guard. A few life preservers, some other debris. It will be seven years in two months, six days, and a couple of hours. Maggie? What date did I reserve the Rainbow Roof for, do you remember?"

Maggie grinned weakly. "Bernie hired the Rainbow Roof at the Waldorf for her Buddy's Officially Dead celebration. That isn't going to sound good if the newspapers get ahold of it, is it?"

"I'm not doing handsprings," J.P. said, rolling her eyes. "You fell into a lot of bucks when your first husband was murdered, didn't you, Bernie? Toland Books? Lots of press, as I remember, especially when you were a suspect. Lot-a-lot-a press."

"And a lot of debt. The papers never mentioned that. Oh. Wait a minute. I think I see where this is going," Maggie said. "You're thinking Buddy wasn't really dead, that he faked his death, and he heard about Bernie inheriting everything from Kirk and then came around looking for his share? Because it isn't seven years yet and they're still officially married?"

"And Bernie didn't want to share. Yes, that's one theory, if the stiff really turns out to be James," Steve said from the hallway. "Bernie? Was Buddy in financial trouble when he took the boat out that day?"

Bernie snorted. "He was—"

"Zipper it, Bernie. Wendell, I told you. She doesn't talk to you. If you overheard anything, you overheard privileged conversation between lawyer and client and I'll have your scrotum and its contents bronzed and on my mantle if you try to use any of it."

Saint Just, who was standing behind the couch, leaned forward slightly to whisper to Maggie, "I grow to appreciate this fairly obnoxious woman more with each breath she takes. Crude, but definitely effective."

The elevator opened again and suddenly the living room was crowded with uniformed cops, technicians dressed in blue jumpsuits and lugging large metal suitcases and cameras as Steve jerked a thumb toward the stairs, a female uniform escorting a middle-aged man carrying a medical bag.

Steve had stuck his flip-badge into his belt, and looked every inch the cop. "I want the bedroom, any adjoining rooms. This room, the elevator, the kitchen. Hallway and stairs. Any access in or out. Anything I didn't think of. Get it all. Don't touch the body. M.E. should be here any minute. He goes first. By the book, people."

"Wow, some digs," one of the techs said, turning in a full circle before following after the rest of his team.

"There's another bedroom, Bernie?" J.P. asked as Steve followed after the techs, redirecting two of them to the kitchen. "You'll have to be examined."

Maggie couldn't be sure, but she believed her metatarsals were "kissing," Bernie's grip on her hand suddenly became so fierce. "It's okay, Bernie. They . . . they want to check you over, make sure you're all right. Since you can't remember. I'll stay with you, I promise."

"Just a minute, Bernie," Steve said, turning over a page in his notebook as he reentered the living room. "You say the deceased is Buddy. Buddy James? Buddy's his first name?"

"That one you can answer," J.P. told her.

"Willard. Willard James. But he liked Buddy."

"There's no accounting for tastes," Saint Just murmured, picking up his cane. "If I'm no longer needed?"

"Oh, you're needed, Blakely. You've all been all over this place. I need all your prints, to rule them out. Where's Sterling?"

"I'm sorry, Steve. Sterling left. But he didn't touch anything. Alex told him not to touch anything. He just stood next to the fireplace, with his hands in his pockets. I mean, he's very . . . obedient. I'll bet he kept his hands in his pockets when he went upstairs. Didn't he, Alex?"

"He went upstairs? Is there anyone here who *didn't* go upstairs?"

Saint Just looked at Maggie. "No, I think we all wandered up there at one time or another, Wendell," he said. "My apologies."

"Yeah, like you mean it. All right. I'll be a few hours, but then I'll come over and get Sterling's prints. Sorry, Maggie, but it could be late. I'm going to be pretty busy here."

"I understand. As long as you promise to keep an open mind, Steve, because even if it looks bad, we all know Bernie didn't do this."

"Maggie?"

Maggie hastened to follow after Bernie, who was being led away by the female uniform cop. "Here I come, Bernie."

They went through the dining room and into another hallway that led to several rooms, including a large study Maggie remembered from her last visit to the penthouse.

The room was forest green, with immense white moldings and miles of bookshelves. The couches were burgundy leather, the fireplace was brick, and Kirk's temperature-controlled cigar humidor table still took up one corner of the room. Bernie enjoyed the occasional cigar, when she was feeling macho.

Bernie looked at the couches, but Maggie turned when she heard voices, to see a litter being wheeled into the room, the sort used by ambulance crews.

"That . . . that's for me?"

"Star treatment, dearie," the female cop said rather sarcastically. "We need fibers, hair, blood, fingernail scrapings, mouth swabs, any trace. Those pajamas. And the sexual assault kit. Lieutenant Wendell says your friend can stay with you. We'll try to make this as painless as possible."

Bernie's eyes went wide and she began to tremble. "This is real, isn't it, Maggie? Oh, God, this is *real.*"

CHAPTER 4

Socks hastened to open the cab door and helped Maggie onto the sidewalk. "Something's up, Maggie, Alex. You'd better go upstairs."

Saint Just handed the taxi receipt to Maggie and looked at Socks. Was it possible the young man was pale? Yes, it was. His lips seemed rather bloodless, his eyes wide and anxious. Just the image he wished Socks to project at his audition next week, for the Mel Gibson movie set to film in Queens in November.

Not that he'd have much time to closely manage Socks's acting career, not with Bernice's troubles being necessarily moved to the front burner of his increasingly active life. Assisting Socks with his career, including that book-cover-model contest he won at the WAR conference, managing the Streetcorner Orators and Players, signing a contract next week for Mary Louise and himself with Fragrances by Pierre. And now Bernice.

For a gentleman of leisure, Saint Just was an inordinately busy man. If Sterling harbored any love for him, he'd not choose this moment to tumble himself into a briar patch.

"What is it, Socks?" Saint Just asked, as Maggie seemed fully occupied in sucking on her nicotine inhaler. He decided to be hopeful, and believe Sterling was not involved. "You're experiencing a difficulty of some sort and wish to speak to me upstairs?"

"Not me," Socks said, pressing his hands to his chest. "And I didn't see anything, because my shift was over and I was upstairs, moving the rest of your stuff, and Snake and Killer took off, so it was just me." He blinked. "I haven't seen you wear that yellow shirt. You know, the *Dior,* the one with the tapered sides? It would be bitchin' with my—"

"Yours. Done and done. Now, what happened that you didn't witness? And please don't tell me Sterling decided to take apart the plasma television machine to see how it works."

"No, no, nothing like that. And it didn't fall down, either. It's good and bolted to the wall; I watched them install it while you were gone. But Sterling . . . Sterling had some company."

Maggie, who had been slipping a new nicotine cartridge into the holder and making rude comments under her breath about how sucking air and pretending it was a real cigarette was like standing outside a bakery and hoping the smells would fill her belly, said, "Sterling had company? Who?"

Socks looked to the curb, where another cab was pulling up. "Duty calls, sorry. Go ask Sterling. He'll tell you all about it."

"Maggie?" Saint Just said, offering her his arm. "Unless you'd rather we take advantage of that now unoccupied hack and proceed to the airport. I've yet to fly, you may recall, and purchasing a ticket to Anywhere But Here seems a viable option at the moment, don't you think?"

Maggie used her key card to open the interior security door to the building. "Oh, cut it out. I couldn't leave Bernie. And neither could you. You want to solve the murder. Admit it."

"True. Although I could leave Ms. J.P. Boxer with few regrets, we cannot desert Bernice. Or Sterling, whatever problem he seems to have stumbled into in our short absence. And you wonder why I fret, watching him scootering off alone to the park."

But Maggie still wasn't giving him her full attention. "I'm so glad J.P. said no to Steve when he asked if Bernie would go with him, to make a formal statement. How long do you think she can keep her away from the cop shop?"

"I beg your pardon?"

"The cop shop. I think that's what they called it in some movie I saw. The precinct. The station. The guard house? Does that help? Anyway, how long do you think J.P. can keep Bernie away from the cops?"

"That depends on the evidence, I would imagine, and how well Ms. Boxer's blustering protestations concerning *Miranda* rights and chains of evidence and compromised crime scenes carry her. Right now," he said as they entered the elevator, "I suggest we take comfort in this one small victory. Bernice has yet to be hauled off to the cop shop in bracelets."

"Bracelets? Now who's using cop show words? And you don't mind if J.P. brings her over here later? I mean, she isn't being allowed to stay at . . . at the crime scene, and she's too messed up to check into a hotel alone. Socks seems to think he's done moving you and Sterling out of the guest room. I mean, it should work, right?"

"It depends. Do you know a liquor establishment that delivers? By the gallon?"

The elevator doors opened just as Maggie was glaring at him. "Bernie's been a pretty heavy social drinker as long as I know her, but I won't say I haven't noticed how bad it's been getting lately. I'm going to help her quit."

"The lady says as she rummages in her purse for her lighter," Saint Just said, because Maggie already had a cigarette between her lips. He extracted a lighter from his sport coat pocket. "Here, allow me. Shall we go inspect my new, definitely not destined to be smoke-free quarters?"

Maggie drew almost desperately on the cigarette. Her eyes closed as she then exhaled a thin blue stream of smoke. "The real thing. God, that's good. And only my second today. Or my third?"

"I tip my figurative hat to you, my dear," Saint Just said, slipping his key into the lock of his new door, which led to his new home. The sense of independence this gave him was immeasurable, and he'd have enjoyed the feeling to the top of his bent had it not been for his worry about Bernice. As it was, any celebration he and Sterling decided upon would necessarily be muted.

"Sterling? Where are you hiding?" he said as Maggie entered the apartment ahead of him.

"Oh, wow. I've never been in here. Look at all the antiques." Maggie frowned. "And she has a separate dining room? Damn. How many rooms are there?"

"Six," Saint Just said. "This room, the aforementioned separate dining room, kitchen, two bedrooms, and a small secluded room behind the kitchen I shall employ as my private study. Oh, would you care to see our view? We have one, you know."

"So do I," Maggie muttered. "Of a brick wall and somebody's windows. You know, Alex, I can sometimes hate you. You just seem to fall into good luck, you know?"

"What can I say? I am the man you made me," Saint Just said, smiling at the plasma television screen that now held pride of place above the working fireplace, Mrs. Goldblum's rather uninspired oil landscape presumably having been banished to the depths of a closet. "Although I prefer to think of myself as capable of seizing opportunities, rather than being merely lucky. Sterling? Front and center, if you please."

Maggie slid her fingertips over the shiny black top of the baby grand piano, on her way to the Louis XV credenza propped against the wall. "Hiya, Henry, nice piece of lettuce," she said, bending down to peer in the cage at Sterling's pet mouse, a small white creature with a constantly twitching pink nose and a rapidly expanding waistline, thanks to Sterling's doting attendance. "Where's your owner?"

"Oh, no, Maggie, I don't *own* Henry. We're friends," Sterling said, entering the living room.

"Sterling, whatever are you wearing?" Saint Just asked, looking at *his* friend.

Sterling pushed his spectacles back up his nose and grinned sheepishly as he looked down at the bright blue bib-apron on which was sewn, in day-glo pink, KISS THE COOK. "You like it? It's my housewarming present from Socks. Along with a cookbook. An English cookbook at that. I'm preparing a pudding even as we speak, and must get back to it. Yours is a box of very thin cigars. It's over there, on the coffee table. How's Bernie?"

"Coming along, coming along," Saint Just said, sparing a moment to cast his gaze over the cigar box on the table. "Socks, however, seems to think you might have experienced some sort of problem?"

"Me? No, I don't think so. I was a little worried, I admit that, but I'm sure it's all right now. Just a mistake."

"On whose part was this mistake?"

"Why, on the part of the gentlemen who came here, of course. And possibly Mrs. Goldblum, if that doesn't sound ungracious. I had nothing to do with it."

"Let me," Maggie said, walking over to Sterling. "From the top, Sterling honey, okay?"

"The top of what?" Sterling asked, clearly perplexed. "The top of the two gentlemen? Well, if you really want to know, they wore hats. Black hats. But I don't see—"

"You made him this literal, my dear," Saint Just reminded Maggie as she dropped into a chair, grabbing a crystal candy dish and dumping out a few decades-old hard candies, to use the dish as an ash tray. "You thought it amusing."

"I thought I made you the perfect hero, too," Maggie said. "Am I excused if I admit I was wrong?"

"If I could get back to my pudding? I'm nearly at a critical stage, I believe."

"Not yet, Sterling, if you don't mind. You said you had visitors. Shall we begin with opening the door to the men in hats, and you can take it from there?"

"Very well. You just had to say so."

Saint Just ignored Maggie's snort of amusement.

"Thank you, Sterling. I'm most appreciative."

"I heard the knock on the door—"

"Hold it, Sterling. You heard the knock on the door? Nobody buzzed you, to ask you to buzz them in?"

Sterling frowned. "Uh . . . no, Maggie, there was no buzzing, by anybody. I suppose they just slipped in, when someone else opened the door? Is that all right? I do it sometimes, when the door is already open for somebody else. Especially when I have my scooter with me."

Saint Just was no longer amused. "Go on, Sterling."

"As I said, I heard the knock on the door, and I opened it to see two gentlemen standing just outside, in the hallway. They were very large gentlemen, even if they removed their hats, although they didn't, not even when they came in."

"You invited two very large strange men into our domicile?"

"Well, actually, Saint Just, I did not, so there's no need to cut up stiff about it and all of that. They rather walked in without invitation, asking to see the old lady. That's what the bigger one said. The old lady. I assumed they meant Mrs. Goldblum, they said yes, and I told them she was away, on an extended vacation. They weren't best pleased about that, I'm afraid. Unhappy."

Maggie lit another cigarette. "Define unhappy, Sterling."

"Well, they . . . um . . . one of them, that is, rather grabbed at me." Sterling put a hand to his throat. "Here. At which point he asked where it was. When I told him I had no idea what *it* was, the second gentleman took umbrage and became rather volatile. I hope it wasn't a valuable vase, or one with sentimental value."

Saint Just cast his gaze around the room, stopping at the Sheraton writing desk. He remembered a rather inferior blue and white vase he had already decided to banish to the closet along with the landscape. But it was already gone. "What happened to the vase, Sterling?" he asked with deceptive calm.

"It's beyond repair, I'm afraid. As I said, volatile. But now it's all explained, and they've gone, and there's nothing to worry about."

"I need some aspirin. About six of them," Maggie said, and disappeared in the direction of her condo. "Get the rest of this, will you, Alex, and feed it to me in one go when I get back."

Saint Just watched her leave, then followed Sterling into the kitchen. "What exploded?" he asked, looking at the mess that seemed to cover every counter.

"Oh, this? It's just me, cooking. Did you know that you should turn off the blender before you add more ingredients? And I think I should probably have taken out the little stopper and poured through there, rather than remove the entire lid. Ah, well, we learn as we go on, don't we, Saint Just? I'll get the ceiling later."

Saint Just looked up, wished he hadn't. "I'll leave you to it, then, once I understand everything that happened with your visitors."

"Mrs. Goldblum's visitors," Sterling corrected, carrying bowls to the sink. "It's just as I said, Saint Just. They were under the impression that they had an appointment with Mrs. Goldblum this afternoon, to pick up *it*. I still don't know what *it* is, but when they realized that Mrs. Goldblum was gone, they finally left."

"I see," Saint Just said, still not seeing, not at all. "Then they won't return?"

"I shouldn't think why. Mrs. Goldblum isn't here. We're here. Really, Saint Just, I would have thought you'd realize that. You're usually so sharp."

"Thank you, Sterling. Carry on," Saint Just said, gratefully departing the kitchen.

Maggie was in the living room when he returned. She looked tired, worried, perilously close to frazzled. "So?"

"I don't know," Saint Just said honestly. "Mrs. Goldblum had an appointment with those two men who frightened Sterling and broke a vase. You know, Mrs. Goldblum departed in quite the hurry when she received the news about her sister's accident. Perhaps she forgot the appointment?"

"And perhaps not? Right? Because you're wearing your skeptical face."

"Am I that obvious? Perhaps I'm seeing mare's nests, and

there's a simple explanation for everythng. The questions remain, however. Who were these men, and why, if we are not wrong to be suspicious of her hasty departure, did she take such pains to avoid them?"

Maggie shrugged. "You could call her, I suppose. She's got to be there by now, it's after four o'clock."

"She did leave a number when I suggested it, in the event of some emergency," Saint Just said, walking over to the desk to pick up the scrap of notepaper Mrs. Goldblum had placed there.

He thought back to his meeting in the hallway yesterday with Mrs. Goldblum. She'd told him she would leave in the morning, she'd all but shoved the key to the apartment into his hand, and he'd had to inquire twice before she agreed to leave a number where she could be reached. It had all seemed the nervous anxiety of an old woman worried about her sibling. Now, however, it seemed more like panic, and a crushing need to be gone in a hurry.

"Alex? You're just standing and staring. How about you let me make the call? You know, woman to woman? Mrs. Goldblum's an old lady, and you wouldn't want to frighten her."

"As you say," Saint Just said, handing Maggie both the paper and his cell phone. "I would very much like to know the identity of our visitors. Duns, do you suppose?"

"Bill collectors, you mean. Nobody calls them duns anymore. They dun, yes, but they aren't . . . aren't dunners. Okay? And could be. Maybe they'll be back Monday with an eviction notice. No, that's my luck, not yours. Besides, look at this place. I didn't realize it, but Mrs. Goldblum is *rolling* in it. Now hush, this is a lot of numbers to push."

Saint Just took up his seat on the facing couch and waited, listened.

"Yes, hello. Would you repeat that, please?" Maggie asked, looking at Saint Just. "I'm sorry, and your number is . . . ?" The frown deepened. "Yes, yes, I must have the wrong number. Thank you."

She shut the cell phone and tossed it back to Saint Just.

He slipped the cell phone into his jacket pocket. "You didn't dial incorrectly?"

"Nope," Maggie said, reaching for a cigarette, then sitting back again, leaving the cigarette in the pack. "I dialed correctly, if I wanted to talk to somebody at Hartman's Drug Store in Boca." She crumpled the note in her hand. "She gave you a bogus number, Alex. I don't like this. I don't like this at all. And how are you supposed to pay her? She just gave you a telephone number, no address."

"You . . . that is, I recompensed her for six months rental before she departed for Boca Raton. Now, now, don't climb up into the boughs, my dear. I sign that contract with Mr. Pierre on Monday, at which time all debts will be paid in full."

"I don't care about that," Maggie said, waving him off. "Oh, all right, I do care, but we've got more important things to think about right now. This could be bad, Alex."

"Already weaving a scenario in that agile, yet fiction-oriented mind of yours, Maggie?" Saint Just asked, shaking his head. "Surely not. I mean, this is Mrs. Goldblum we're talking about, correct? Nice old tabby?"

"That nice old tabby was supposedly married to a lawyer for the mob, Alex. Remember me telling you that?"

"The mob." Saint Just considered this. "What, precisely, is the *mob?*"

Maggie spread her hands. "The *mob.* It's the *mob.* It's . . . okay. I'd say it's a bunch of Italian guys running around doing illegal things, except that now there are a lot of mobs, and they aren't all Italian. Sicilian. Whatever. Anyway, they do illegal things, like loan sharking and protection rackets and prostitution, money laundering, and drugs—lots of them are into selling drugs these days, I think. And one mob hates the other mob and sometimes there are wars, and they go to the mattresses and then pop out to go around shooting each other."

"I'm sure you think this is helping," Saint Just said, taking out his quizzing glass and dangling it from its black grosgrain ribbon.

"I'm not really making this clear, am I? I mean, except for watching *The Sopranos* and that old *Untouchables* movie, I really don't know what they do. They're just the mob. Organized crime."

"Yes, it does all sound rather organized. And, unforunately, as clear as mud. Suffice it to say, these are violent men?"

"Oh, yeah. Cement shoes, swimming with the fishes, bullets to the head while eating a plate of pasta, you name it. Not nice guys. Not the sort who say, Okay, she's not here, sorry, we'll go now, please excuse the intrusion."

"And you think the two men who visited Sterling are representatives of this mob?"

"I don't know," Maggie said, pushing her fingers through her hair. "I mean, I only *heard* that Mrs. Goldblum's late husband was a lawyer for them. I don't know it for certain. But remember how she didn't want to sign any sort of sublease with you guys? How she said her husband—what was his name? Oh, yeah, Harry—told her never to put anything in writing? Lawyers kill forests every day, for all the paper they use. So, what kind of a lawyer was Harry?"

"I can see your highly inventive brain is percolating. Pray, continue," Saint Just said, steepling his fingers in front of his chin.

"Okay. Let's say, for the sake of discussion, that Harry Goldblum *was* a lawyer for the mob. How did he die? When did he die? And, did he have something that could put some big cheeses in the mob behind bars for the next seventy years if the Fibbies got hold of it?"

"We'll soon need the services of a translator, I'm afraid. And these Fibbies are—?"

"Federal agents. FBI. Writers always seem to call them Fibbies. I think they're the ones who go after the mob. And the IRS—that's the tax collector. The IRS got Al Capone for filing false tax returns or something. Couldn't get him for anything else, the murders and that kind of thing, but they got him for tax evasion. But accountants keep financial records, not lawyers."

"And you're certain the late Mr. Goldblum was a lawyer?"

Maggie frowned. "Yeah. No." She sighed. "I really don't pay a lot of attention to my neighbors."

"Now there's a revelation. You don't pay much attention to anything but your work, Maggie, ergo that muddled definition of gangs."

"Hey, I write historicals. Ask me about the Bow Street Runners and I can give you chapter and verse. And it's 'mobs.' Gangs are different."

"I stand corrected, and humbly beg you decide not to further enlighten me. That said, if not for Sterling and myself, you'd soon be a recluse, walking around all day in your pajamas and talking to your cats."

"Ha. Ha. I've got a life."

"So does Henry over there. But, the sad state of your existence to one side, only recently made better by my decision to come into your life and give it—shall we say, *life?*—how do we go about learning more about Mr. Harry Goldblum? And Mrs. Irene Goldblum, for that matter?"

"We could start with Socks? He was already here when I moved in two years ago."

Considering this a splendid idea, as well as their only idea, Saint Just used the intercom to call down to Socks and request his presence.

Two minutes later, looking nervous, Socks entered the apartment, peering around curiously. "They didn't come back?"

"No, we're quite alone," Saint Just said, motioning the doorman to a chair. "We'd appreciate some information, Socks, about Mrs. Goldblum. What can you tell us?"

"About Mrs. Goldblum?" Socks asked, looking at Maggie. "I don't know. She's a nice old lady. Good tipper at Christmas. Oh, you want more than that, right? Okay. I don't know when she moved in, but I do know that until it got changed, the name plate over her mailbox had her name on it and her husband's, but his was crossed off. So I guess they both lived here, until he died."

"Interesting," Saint Just said, slipping his quizzing glass back into his pocket. "Continue."

"Yeah, sure. This place is rent controlled, if you can believe that. Last unit in the building that is, since it started going condo. Me, I don't really believe it, but Mrs. Goldblum told me it is. Do you think she's lying about the rent control, that she really bought the place, you know, like Maggie bought hers? I don't think she has that much money, you know? But why would she lie about that? Is that what you want to know? Because I don't know anything else."

"Oh, but on the contrary, Socks, you do, you do. For instance, did Mrs. Goldblum have many visitors?"

"Visitors?"

"Socks, please concentrate on what I say, and then on answering the question, not repeating it, all right? Yes, visitors."

"You know, I don't think so. She goes away, sometimes for months at a time. Probably to see that sister in Boca, right, the one she's visiting now? I take in her mail then, save it for her. I take it in a lot, actually. Okay, all the time."

"Ah-ha, we progress. Socks, do you remember what sort of mail Mrs. Goldblum receives?"

Socks shrugged. "What kind of—oh, sorry. Bills, mostly. Doctor bills, lots of those. She gives me fifty dollars every couple of months, to bring her mail to her, even when she's here, and it was mostly bills, and her Social Security check once a month. Sometimes a postcard. You know, one of those 'wish you were here' picture postcards."

Maggie came to attention. "Oh, that's good, Socks, that's very good. You read the postcards, right? People always read postcards."

"I don't . . . oh, okay, Maggie, yeah, I read them. But they all said the same thing. Like I said, 'wish you were here.' I remember one in particular. It showed a castle, one of those big old stone ones? And it had an arrow drawn to one window, and it said 'my room.' It wasn't, though, because it was just a printed postcard. Funny card."

"Anything else?" Saint Just prodded. "Any other pretty pictures?"

"Hey, I didn't really look. You're not supposed to look, you know. I mean, maybe while I was in the elevator I might have looked a little, but . . . Paris. There was one from Paris. And Greece, I think. One of those islands over there. Everything was over there, now that I think about it. Europe, you know? I have to get back to work."

"Yes, thank you, Socks, you've been most helpful. If you recall anything else you feel might be pertinent, please let Maggie or me know at once."

The door had barely closed when Maggie was on her feet, pacing. "He isn't dead, he's just hiding, and she sticks around, going to him when she can, like she's going on vacation. But the mob gets wind of it, comes knocking on her door, wanting secret books or records of some kind, and she hands the keys to you and splits, leaving you and Sterling holding the bag. And what are you going to do about it? Nothing, that's what. You have no lease, no papers, no receipt, no proof. You're just squatting here. After a while, she calls you, sees if the coast is clear, and then she comes back. It works. It really works."

Saint Just applauded softly. "A great mind at work. Perceive me as wonderfully impressed."

"Oh, shut up. What's wrong with it?"

"You mean other than the fact that, as Buddy James has just come back from the dead to die again, your brain is automatically resurrecting Harry Goldblum as well? I forgive you that, as it is a logical conclusion, considering what has already occurred today. But, what's *wrong* with your scenario, my dear woman, is Mrs. Goldblum's continued occupation of this apartment. Why not simply leave the country, travel with her husband as he avoids this mob of yours?"

"It's not *my* mob. And I don't know. Maybe Steve will know more about Harry Goldblum?"

"Don't you believe the good *left*-tenant has more than enough on his plate at the moment, with Bernice's woes? Chasing down one of your flights of fiction seems rather unimportant."

"You're not worried? Those guys broke a vase, Alex. One of them picked up Sterling by the *throat*."

Saint Just was well aware of that. He was aware that hidden deep inside him was an anger that, if released, could be A Most Terrible Thing. Especially since, at least for the moment, he had no target. So he beat down his anger, and looked at Maggie levelly, intent only on keeping her calm.

"And then they left. Obviously Sterling, a very credible man and a terrible liar, convinced them that Mrs. Goldblum is no longer in residence. Whatever they wanted, mob or dun or whomever, whatever, they now know it is not here. She is not here. And Sterling, dear man, seems none the worse for wear. Alas, if only I could say the same for our kitchen."

CHAPTER 5

Maggie closed the door behind her and looked around the living room. Her empty living room.

Well, not empty. Napoleon and Wellington were in the room, Wellington draped over the back of one of the couches, shedding black hair everywhere, and Napper contentedly curled up on her desk chair, obviously after having typed a million lines of *zzzzzzzziidooooeeffffssssuuuuu22222ktt34-dxnkkkkkkhhh* onto Maggie's computer screen. That was one way of adding pages to her manuscript.

The ridiculously large, and really pretty ugly vase of flowers Faith had sent over two days ago was still there, on the coffee table, some of the lily petals dropping off and making what was going to be a big mess in another two days.

She liked Faith better as a former friend. She didn't like her as what she was attempting to become, which was a born-again friend, or whatever.

Faith Simmons, now known as Felicity Boothe Simmons, had once been Maggie's friend. But then Faith had hit the big time and forgotten she knew Maggie, until Maggie hit the big time too, which was when Faith decided that she hated Maggie. Saint Just had told her that Faith couldn't forgive her for being a success; Maggie just thought Faith was a jerk with a bad boob job.

But now, ever since the We Are Romance convention two weeks ago, and ever since Maggie had stupidly pushed Faith out of harm's way and, okay, maybe saved the woman's life, Faith had been calling and stopping by and sending presents.

Like these fugly flowers.

Maggie picked up the vase and carried it into the guest room. Maybe Bernie would appreciate them. Bernie liked exotic. Maggie would have preferred daisies, something simple. And Faith knew that.

"And I know she knows it," Maggie said, giving the single bird-of-paradise topping the arrangement a last disapproving look.

Then she stripped the queen-size bed and fitted it with clean sheets from the linen closet, checked the dresser drawers and closet to be sure they were empty, and pulled the drapes, darkening the room, pretty sure Bernie wouldn't be in the mood for sunlight.

"Dinner," she said, heading for the kitchen. There'd be no celebration at Bellini's tonight, she thought, mentally waving goodbye to delicious garlic, rosemary, and sage chicken, and lemon ice for dessert.

She opened the refrigerator and frowned at the contents. A half dozen eggs. An open pack of bacon. Orange juice; six half gallons, because orange juice had been on sale. Well, at least she was ready for Sunday breakfast.

"Soup," she said, closing the refrigerator and opening the cabinet next to it, standing on tiptoe to look inside. "Chicken noodle, chicken rice, chicken with stars, chicken vegetable, chicken broth. Damn, I eat a lot of chicken soup."

"You also talk to yourself quite often, another very valid reason for my more substantial entry into your life."

"Alex!" Maggie whirled around, nearly losing her balance. "Don't *do* that. And stop just barging in like you're freaking Cosmo Kramer and I'm Jerry Seinfeld. You don't live here anymore. I am alone again. A-lone. Remember?"

"You'll be wanting your key returned?"

"No-o-o, I won't be wanting my key returned," she sniped

angrily, opening the refrigerator and yanking out a bottle of spring water. "I'm sorry, Alex. I'm just . . . just on edge. Bernie, and now Sterling? Have some pity here, okay?"

Her eyes widened as Saint Just stepped forward and pulled her into his arms, pressing her head against his strong chest. She hadn't been in his arms, *really* in his arms, since that night at the WAR convention. She'd been trying to forget that momentary weakness . . . even as she replayed the memory about five times a day.

"This . . . this isn't quite what I had in mind," she said, her words sort of slurred, because her mouth was pressed against his shirt.

"I should let go?"

"Shut up," Maggie said, sliding her arms around his waist. "Just shut up and hold me."

"My pleasure," Saint Just said, lightly stroking her back. "Everything will right itself in time, Maggie, I promise. Bernice will be exonerated, the true culprit will be apprehended, and Sterling will be safe in his kitchen, unless he persists in wearing that most atrocious apron, upon which time I shall myself threaten him with bodily harm."

Maggie laughed against his chest, then lifted her head to look up into his face. "I think he looks cute. Just a cuddly teddy bear."

"Precisely as you made him, my dear, and I thank you for that. Now, don't you think it time you showered and got out of this dreadful creation?"

"It's not that much blood. Do you think it can be saved? I mean, I like this pajama top." Then she closed her eyes. "No, don't answer that. I could never wear it again, not without thinking of Bernie today. Alex, you should have seen her when they explained what a rape kit was and what they wanted to do to her. She . . . she made a joke, a really terrible joke, but I was holding her hand, and it was shaking. *She* was shaking, all over. I just—"

His mouth closed over hers, cutting off what she might say

next, even if she knew she'd run out of words and was rapidly being taken over by her emotions.

He kissed her once, twice, then trailed a string of kisses across her cheek, into her hair. "You were very brave today, Maggie," he whispered into her ear. "I was extraordinarily proud of you. I am always proud of you."

Maggie sagged against him, her arms still tight around his waist. "I was so scared."

"You were a Trojan, a brick. And you will continue to be so, for Bernice's sake. Now," he said, his hands on her shoulders as he held her slightly away from him, "why don't you go shower and change, before Bernice and Ms. Boxer arrive. I'll phone Bellini's and add the amazon to our table. The reservation is at eight, remember?"

"You . . . you don't really think Bernie will want to go out for dinner, do you?"

"I have no idea what Bernice desires. I do know what she will do, and that will be to do what she normally does, with no change in her routine. She is, after all, innocent. She should behave as such."

"With her criminal lawyer in tow?" Maggie asked, wondering if there was some way she could wrangle another kiss . . . and then wondering why she'd want to, since she told herself every day that she had to keep her distance from this man who was, after all, a figment of her imagination . . . with a very solid-feeling chest.

"Ms. Boxer lends cachet, my dear. Now, I've got telephone calls to make, and you've got to attend to your toilette." He dragged her close and kissed her once more, a definitely hard, definitely tongue-probing kiss, then let her go. "Oh, and I'll be borrowing a few towels, as we seem to have forgotten to purchase any as yet and Mrs. Goldblum's are all, well, they're Mrs. Goldblum's towels. I'm sure you won't mind."

"Uh-huh. Sure. Anything you need," she said, lifting a hand to wave weakly at his back as he headed for the door. "God, I'm *so* easy, and he knows it, damn it," she said, talking to herself again, and went off to take a long, cold shower.

She was dumping ice into the bucket in the living room, having checked the level on her scotch bottle and unearthed a fresh one from underneath the drinks table, when her houseguest arrived, lawyer in tow.

"I've got a message for you from Wendell," J.P. said, kicking the door shut behind her, as her arms were full of luggage. "He'll be busy tonight, attempting to lynch my client, but will come by tomorrow to roll Sterling's prints."

"Oh, okay. Thanks, I think. Bernie, how are you?" Maggie asked, hugging her friend even as she dragged her over to the couch.

"How am I? You mean after being poked and prodded and fingerprinted and generally violated? Oh, and after being bled on by Buddy. Let's not forget that part. I don't know. How should I be?"

Maggie nearly said *devastated,* but bit the word back in time. "In need of a stiff one?"

"True, true," Bernie said, winking at her. "But I'll take a drink instead."

"And that, Bernie," J.P. said, settling her large frame in the facing couch, "is exactly the way you are *not* going to talk from here on out. I thought we settled this."

Bernie flipped back her curly mane of bright red hair. "It's only Maggie."

"Who can be subpoenaed," J.P. said, folding her arms beneath what could only be called her generous bosom. No, magnanimous.

"I'd never repeat anything like that," Maggie said, handing Bernie a tumbler one-third full of scotch and ice.

"That's my girl. Loyal. I love you, Mags."

"Oh, cut me a break. What are you two looking for, adjoining cells?"

Maggie picked up the pair of large suitcases J.P. had carried into the room and took them down the hall to the guest room, where she stopped, took three long, deep breaths, then returned to the living room. "I thought you were getting Bernie off?"

"Oh, good. An optimist. Little Mary Sunshine is an optimist. Get her off? I'd love to. But this one isn't going to be easy. Wendell wants her, wants her bad."

"Steve wants me," Bernie said, raising her empty glass. "How about that, Maggie? Your guy's after me."

"Actually," J.P. said, "he's after the truth. Wendell's a good guy, as cops go. Let's just hope he can find it without us."

Maggie sat down next to Bernie. "We're not going to help him?"

"No, Little Mary, we're not. We're going to help our precious booze hound here. And we're going to start by taking away her hootch. That's it, Bernie. No more."

"Oh, God," Bernie said, sinking low on the cushions as Maggie took the glass from her hand.

"Um . . . J.P.? Do you think we could start tomorrow? Alex wants us all to go to Bellini's for dinner tonight."

"The Englishman? Is he out of his—wait a minute. That could be good." J.P. got up and began to pace, nearly stepping on Wellington, who hurriedly hid underneath the computer desk. "Make her public, make her visible. Keep her visible. She's innocent, right? Innocent people don't hide. I think I like it."

Maggie considered this for a moment. It only took a moment. "And you want her doing this cold turkey?"

"I'm doomed. Doomed," Bernie said, falling over onto her side, her hands clutched to her chest.

J.P. looked down at her client. "She's never sober?"

"I . . . I really don't know," Maggie said honestly. "She's just Bernie. I think she has a . . . a capacity."

"She's a drunk. Rich, so she's a poor distressed soul with a problem, but she's still a drunk. A functioning drunk."

"Well, she was," Maggie said, wincing.

"Meaning?"

"I'm doomed, doomed. . . ."

"Shh, Bernie, it's all right," Maggie said, rubbing Bernie's hip. "Lately . . . lately she's not been so good. Since Kirk was murdered, I'd say. He left her everything, the company, the penthouse, all his toys. But that's not as great as it sounds. He had a lot of debt. And then there was the money Toland Books lost thanks to—"

"Yes, I remember that. So she's had problems."

Maggie nodded. "She's been reorganizing the company, selling off Kirk's toys. The place in the Hamptons, his plane, stuff like that. But when Buddy's life insurance comes to her she'll be—oh, God."

"Doomed . . ."

"Hello? Am I missing anything? Has the ladies' sewing circle convened without me?"

"Alex!" Maggie got to her feet and motioned for him to close the door behind him. "I just realized something."

"Doomed . . ."

"Yes, and now she's going to share, isn't she?" J.P. said, seating herself in Maggie's desk chair (a sin punishable by death, but Maggie was too upset to think about that).

"Buddy's insurance, Alex—J.P." Maggie pushed her hands through her hair. "He sold insurance, remember? That meant he wrote a lot of it for himself while he was at it. Cheap. The premiums, not the policies. I think he was insured for about three million. Bernie? Is it three million?"

"Doomed . . ."

"Stop saying that!" Maggie looked at J.P., who wasn't looking ready to do cartwheels at the news. "When Buddy disappeared Bernie said insurance investigators were haunting her, for months and months, sure Buddy had either faked his death in some plan with her, or that Bernie had poked a hole in his boat—or something. Isn't that right, Bernie?"

"Mmmmm," Bernie said, having passed beyond doom, into complete inarticulation.

"I should have asked for a larger retainer," J.P. said, spinning the computer chair in a circle, then bracing her feet on the floor and glaring at Maggie. "Let me get this straight. Seven years ago—almost seven years ago, let's not forget the Hip Hip Hooray, Buddy's Dead party—insurance investigators thought Bernie might have killed husband number two. Husband number *one* dies a little bit back, and she's suspected of killing him, too. Now husband number two is dead. Really dead this time. And our gal over there stands to rake in three million in insurance payoffs? Beautiful. Maybe I should be the one downing the hootch."

"It does look bad, doesn't it?" Maggie asked Saint Just.

"It could be problematic, yes. If her inheritance would banish the last of any financial embarrassment, and Willard were to resurface just as the funds were about to come due, one could suppose Bernice's . . . displeasure. Her reluctance to share."

Silence descended on the room, not broken until Sterling burst in, all excited, as only someone without a firm grasp on the severity of events could be. "I say, everyone, turn on the television machine. They're going to talk about Bernie after the commercial."

Maggie grabbed the remote. "What station, Sterling?"

"I'm not sure. But it's that nice Fox lady."

"Miss Holly Spivak, Maggie, Fox News," Saint Just told her.

"Got it," Maggie said, and turned up the volume as everyone, even Bernie, focused on the screen, watching some demented woman dance with a floor mop.

And then there was the anchor's smiling face and a quick segue to Holly Spivak, just another in Alex's strange coterie of acquaintances, and a pretty decent investigative reporter:

"Thank you, Jim. As you can see, I'm standing outside the Park Avenue building containing the Toland penthouse, home of the late Kirk Toland, the socialite and businessman who was murdered not quite two months ago, and the residence of his ex-wife, Bernice Toland-James."

"She's making it sound like Bernie lived with Kirk," Maggie

said, only to be shushed by everyone else in the room. "Well, she is."

"In a Fox News exclusive, this reporter has learned that police were called to the Toland-James penthouse before noon today and discovered the body of one Willard James, a.k.a. Buddy James, Toland-James's second husband. And here's the kicker, Jim. James supposedly died at sea seven years ago."

Spivak nodded, an obvious signal, and suddenly they were looking at a tape recorded earlier, with Spivak talking over the tape.

"The litter containing Willard Buddy James is being wheeled out behind me, his body, according to my source inside the police department, discovered nude and mutilated in the bed of Bernice Toland-James, his wife, now his widow. James, who had been reported lost at sea nearly seven years ago after taking his boat out in a storm off Connecticut, had been presumed dead until this afternoon, when he was positively identified through photographs taken from the Toland-James residence."

"You kept pictures of the guy?" This question, directed at Bernie, came from J.P.

"Wedding pictures," Bernie said, clutching a cushion to her breast. "I looked good in them. Wore a Vera Wang."

The camera panned up the building, all the way to the fifty-fourth floor, the penthouse, then trailed down again, zeroing in on the black bag being loaded into the coroner's SUV.

"Ms. Toland-James," Holly Spivak's voice droned on, as tape of Bernie and J.P. leaving the building was shown, "refuses all comment at this time and police are investigating."

"Damn, they're good. I didn't even see a camera," J.P. said. "They got the sneakers, too. Looking good. This goes to trial, maybe I can get an endorsement fee, if I wear them to court."

Maggie tossed her a dirty look.

The tape ended and Holly Spivak's smiling face was back on the screen. "One thing more, Jim, taken from the Fox News archives. A statement made by Ms. Toland-James during the investigation into her *first* husband's murder."

Tape rolled again, this time a clear close-up of Bernie speaking into a phalanx of microphones and tape recorders outside Toland Books.

She looked beautiful, her smile vibrant, her glorious hair tangling around her shoulders, a lock blowing across her face. She was wearing that damned black and white striped pantsuit she'd worn as a joke, saying she wanted to get into the mood for prison uniforms. Sure. Designer prison stripes.

But it was when she spoke that even Sterling said, "Oh, dear. Oh, dear me," for what she said was: "No, I didn't kill him. But I could have. Him and my second husband, both. Man, can I pick the losers."

"Off the cuff? An amusing anecdote? Or a foreshadowing of this morning's violence? Needless to say, Jim, we'll be following this story closely." Holly Spivak was grinning—flat-out grinning—into the camera as she ended, "Back to you, Jim." Maggie switched off the power.

"My big mouth . . ." Bernie said, falling onto her side again, this time to cover her head with the pillow.

J.P. stood up, began to pace. J.P. pacing was rather like a tiger looking for a way out of its cage, and with a pretty good chance of finding one. "Somebody get her a drink," she said, hooking a thumb at Bernie. "Get me one, too. A double."

"I'll do it," Sterling, always helpful, said, hastening to the portable bar.

Maggie lit a cigarette with trembling hands.

Saint Just took out his quizzing glass, draped it over his head, and began swinging the glass from its riband.

Everyone was very busy being very busy.

"At least they don't know where she is," Saint Just said at last. "Unless . . . ?"

"I don't think anyone followed us," J.P. said, taking the glass from Sterling.

"You didn't see Ms. Spivak's cameraperson," Saint Just pointed out, heading for the windows that overlooked the front of the building. "Nobody's down there. Not yet, at least. That's in our favor."

"But it won't last," J.P. said, and Bernie, still under the pillow, groaned.

"What we can't avoid, we embrace," Saint Just said, looking at Maggie. "Isn't that right, my dear?"

Maggie mulled this for a moment. "Oh. *The Case of the Pilfered Pearls.*"

"Exactly."

"Do you really think it could work?"

"Possibly. I might even be able to solicit assistance from Miss Spivak, if we were to grant her—what is the term? Oh, yes. An *exclusive* interview?"

"Okay, you two, a moment here," J.P. said, stepping between them, her hands held up in the age-old time-out signal. "What am I missing? What do pearls have to do with anything?"

"Oh, not just pearls, Miss Boxer," Sterling said, beaming at Saint Just. "Pilfered pearls. One of Maggie's books about Saint Just. *The Case of the Pilfered Pearls.* Very good book. And a brilliant bit of detecting by our Saint Just. But that's all I know. I don't understand what they're talking about now," he ended, stepping back, out of the way again.

"It's relatively simple, J.P.," Saint Just said. "In my . . . in Maggie's book, a jewel thief cum murderer was skulking about London, and it was Saint Just's mission to ferret him out."

"So, since he seemed to always be after the best jewels, I had Saint Just arrange for a demi-rep ball—"

"The cream of the demimonde. Ladies of negotiable affections to you, my dear," Saint Just interrupted.

"Pros," J.P. said. "Go ahead."

Maggie began again. "I had Saint Just give this ball. You could do that in Regency times, you know. Gentlemen would host pretty outrageous balls that were for their friends and their mistresses. Anyway, all the females were to wear pieces of the famed Saint Just collection. The murderer took the bait, couldn't stay away."

She turned to Saint Just. "Is that what you meant?"

"Something like that. What I actually meant was that if we are as public as possible Bernie will not be chased, hounded by the press. What is easily accessible is never as tantalizing as what is hidden."

"You've never seen a full-fledged feeding frenzy from the press, have you, Englishman?"

"Actually, I have had the pleasure," Saint Just said, winking at Maggie, who remembered how they'd met Holly Spivak in the first place. "And I still put forward that hiding Bernice away here in Maggie's apartment will only fuel the press to further outlandish behavior such as the airing of that rather unfortunate statement we just saw."

"Yeah. She can make *more* unfortunate statements for them to air. No. She stays locked up here. No press, no exclusives. It's a bad idea. Stupid book, too."

"Oh, yeah? It went to number two on the *NYT*, lady, and stayed there for a long, long time. And the paperback—"

"Calm yourself, Maggie, my dear," Saint Just said, patting her arm. "Consider the source. Amazon.com, remember? You know your own worth, and you're no longer reacting to criticism."

"Thank you, Doctor Bob," Maggie said, reaching for another cigarette. "And now make me believe it."

"If you two are done?"

"Pardon us, J.P.," Saint Just said, bowing slightly. "Artistic temperament, you understand. Now, where were we?"

"I was putting the kibosh on your harebrained idea of parading Bernie around the city like some pet pony, that's where we were. Tonight's one thing, but not a steady diet of it, okay? However, I'm beginning to like the idea of an exclusive interview with this Spivak dame. The cops will go nuts when Bernie talks to her instead of to them—you know, the JonBenet Ramsey case? Her parents talked to everybody but the cops. It could sway public opinion in Bernie's favor."

She turned to look down at Bernie, what was visible of her

now that she'd pulled two more large cushions on top of her body. "So, now that you've given it some thought, how is she better, on or off the booze?"

Maggie looked at Saint Just. "I'll lay in more scotch?"

"Splendid idea," Saint Just said, swinging his quizzing glass. "I'll phone Miss Spivak and arrange a meeting here at Maggie's. Is Monday morning too soon?"

J.P. sighed. "Just do it."

"Excuse me, now that this is all settled," Sterling said, "but I'm afraid I have some bad news. The pudding, Saint Just? It . . . it wasn't quite a success. I'm so sorry. Shall I toddle down to Mario's for some meat and salads?"

"No, Sterling. We'll all be going to Bellini's later. Isn't that what you said, J.P.?"

"Yes. I must be out of my mind, but yes. I'm that desperate, considering how bad things look now. What was it? 'What we can't avoid, we embrace'? What a bunch of crap that is. This had better work."

"I'll see that you get a copy of the book, J.P. Autographed, of course," Saint Just said, and Maggie wanted to hug him.

CHAPTER 6

Saint Just awoke early, happy to be in his own room and no longer sharing a bed with a softly snoring Sterling. He quickly showered in his private bathroom, the one holding his toiletries and a lingering scent of lilacs, Mrs. Goldblum's fragrance of choice.

He dressed in black slacks and a soft black knit pullover, slid on his favorite Hessians—brought with him when he stepped out of Maggie's imagination and into her life—and used the pair of silver-backed brushes on his ebony hair.

He penned a quick note to Sterling and taped it to the man's favorite appliance, the toaster oven, then picked up his sword cane, slipped Raybans over his startling blue eyes, and departed the apartment.

Mario's opened early on Sunday mornings, serving the bagel and coffee and Sunday papers crowd, and Holly Spivak was already seated at one of the impossibly small tables Mario's wife had ordered set up at the rear of the store, in hopes of attracting more customers.

Saint Just accepted a cup of coffee, black, from a grinning, bowing Mario, and headed for the tables.

Holly Spivak was Fox–News–blonde, wore too much red lipstick, and either lived on air and water or exercised for hours each day, because her five-foot frame couldn't be carrying more than six stone.

"Miss Spivak, so good to see you again."

"Holly, Alex, remember? Call me Holly. And it's so good to see you again, too. God, you're gorgeous in those sunglasses," she said, lifting a hand for him to bow over. Saint Just had learned that, far from being a customary greeting, bowing over a woman's hand had the power to melt a generous majority of them into jelly. And what he knew, he invariably used to his advantage.

"Holly, my dear, you are too kind, and ravishing, as usual," he said as he sat down, leaning his cane against the back wall. "And how very good of you to meet with me."

"Yes, and how very naughty of you to throw out hints like that. I barely slept last night, wondering what I'm going to receive in return for this," she said, leaning down and removing a file from a lizard-skin briefcase.

Saint Just eyed the folder. "Am I going to be happy, Holly?"

"I don't know how you're going to be, because you're not going to see any of it until you tell me what you've got to trade. You said it was big."

J.P. Boxer would hate him for this. Maggie, being more dramatic and yet, bless her, pragmatic as well, would have his liver and lights for not letting her in on what he was about to do.

But he was Saint Just. And he did what he did.

"I have Bernice Toland-James, my dear, and am now dangling her, tantalizing you with her in point of fact. Do you want her? Exclusively?"

Holly, to be crude about the thing, instantly began to drool with excitement. "You've got Toland-James? You've really got her? Don't play with me, Alex. That wouldn't be nice."

"I am not always nice, I fear, but I am rarely untruthful. Yes, I've got her, as you put the thing. Safely tucked away and ready to talk. To you. As already mentioned, exclusively. On camera. If you're a good girl."

"Oh, I'm a *very* good girl, Alex, and I can do a whole lot more for you than this bunch of old news," she said, leaning her elbows on the folder. "Why don't we go back to my place?"

Saint Just took her hands in his, pressed a kiss against her knuckles. "How you tempt me, my dear."

"But no, right?" Holly said, pulling her hands free.

"For my sins, yes, you're right."

Holly slapped her forehead. "You're gay, right? I told myself. I mean, I knew it. All the good ones are gay."

By now Saint Just had become accustomed to this entirely unreasonable reaction to what to him, a gentleman of the English Regency, were only common good manners, a precise way of speaking, and an attention to his toilette that was only, well, only gentlemanly. "Think what you wish, my dear, as I would not so demean myself as to launch a protest if your deduction pleases you, but I very much need the information you've collected for me."

Holly recovered quickly, instantly on the attack again. "Why? It's like I said, old news. Unless you know something I don't?"

"Always the reporter," Saint Just said, smiling. "Much as I'd like nothing more than to prostrate myself at your feet, telling you all, it is, alas, not my secret to divulge. I do promise you—what is it called? Oh, yes, first dibs, if anything should come of it."

"You'd damn well better," Holly said, pulling a notepad from her briefcase. "Now, back to the Merry Widow."

"I beg your pardon?"

"You didn't see it? That's what the papers are calling her this morning. The Merry Widow. I think it's pretty lame, but they'll come up with something else by tomorrow. They always do. Of course, that something else will be my tag line. I'm calling it the Twice Dead case. Like it?"

"Not particularly, no," Saint Just said. "I won't condone a circus, Holly."

She sat back in her chair. "Well, excuse me, Mr. Perfect. What do you want?"

"Decorum would be a start, and quite refreshing, actually. A man is dead, Holly. A terrified and totally innocent woman is fast becoming the target of a media intent only on selling newspapers and raising television ratings. For shame, trading on tragedy."

"Yeah, right. Wait here, I've got to run back to my place and get into my sackcloth and ashes, repent for all the media who are *only doing their jobs,* Alex. It's the public's right to know."

"Yes, I believe I've already heard that ludicrous excuse. Tell me, if the public wanted to know about *your* private life, would they have a right?"

"If I killed my husband, yeah."

"Ah, but therein lies the rub, as well as the gaping hole in your logic, if I may be so blunt. *Did* Bernice murder her husband? You can't know that, and yet you, meaning the media in its entirety, not just you, dear lady, are already citing the public's right to know as your excuse to exploit poor Bernice. I find that contradictory."

"They found him stiff in her bed. Considering her as the prime suspect isn't much of a stretch, you know. What do *you* think?"

"That is immaterial. But what I most fervently hope, Holly, is that your American law, your marvelous Constitution, although admittedly under assault, remains quite firm on the concept of innocent until proved guilty. Why is it, do you wonder, that the media is always so happy to seek out guilt, but never innocence?"

"You don't understand market shares, Alex, that's for sure, never mind the First Amendment. Do you know how long we'd last if we played this down while every other station in town is in a feeding frenzy? If we refused to let the talking heads loose on Toland-James's carcass every night of the week and twice on Sunday, now, and all the way through the trial? If we said, hey, she's innocent until proven guilty, there have been no new developments and won't be for months, and now we'll hear from Gerry about the forecast for a sunny weekend? Give me a break. Toland-James is a gift, Alex. A *gift.*"

"I see," Saint Just said, retrieving his cane. "In that case, I'm very much afraid that this discussion is closed. Forgive me for calling you out so early on what is proving to be a fruitless errand."

"Whoa! Wait a minute, Alex. Sit down, sit down. Nothing's written in stone."

"Including your Constitution, I would say, at least since nine-eleven. Bernice's right to privacy to one side, did you ever wonder how much *you* might lose when you begin giving up someone else's rights and freedoms? Good day, Miss Spivak."

"Holly. Call me Holly, remember? Look, no sermons. I don't make the laws. And I may be part of the media, but I don't control it. What's going to happen to Toland-James is going to happen with or without me, so don't go all ACLU on me for trying to do my job. Cripes, you British make our media look like a Sunday school class. Sit down, Alex. Please. I know we can deal. Tell me what you want."

Saint Just replaced the cane. This was going well. First a well-baited hook, and then the demands. "Having spent most of the night researching high profile murder cases on the Internet, commentaries on the garish and often biased reporting of such cases, I have come up with a few, shall we say, guidelines."

"You mean ground rules."

"Another term, yes, if you wish. First, you will bring a single cameraperson with you."

"Agreed."

"Second, you will allow Bernice to answer any question in full, and not edit her words in any way in order to—again, I'm struggling with these new terms—in order to *spin* them in any one direction."

"Next you'll want me to show you the tape before it airs. Is that what you're saying? I don't do that, Alex. I'm a reporter. Hard news. I don't do puff pieces."

Saint Just smiled. "Never assume, my dear. No, I shan't demand to view what you've done. I trust you to remain true to any promise you make here, now. I trust you not to set out deliberately to show Bernice in a bad light, or any light at all other than that of impeccably fair and impartial reporting. I trust you to ask intelligent questions, and allow ample time for her answers."

"What if I ask her if she killed him?"

"I most sincerely hope you will."

Holly shrugged. "All right. What about her lawyer? Will she be there?"

"In the room? I would imagine so. As a part of the interview? Definitely not. Oh, and one more very small thing."

"Here we go," Holly said, flipping her notebook shut. "Go ahead, shoot. You already know you've got me."

"That's high praise indeed, thank you. Very well. You will not advertise the airing of the interview every five minutes by showing highly volatile excerpts and telling the viewing audience in what the dear Maggie would term a *snarky* tone that Bernice is denying killing her husband."

"Damn, you must have been reading my mind. Okay, what the hell am I supposed to say?"

"I'm not a scribe or a reporter, Holly. However, since you are so kind as to have asked? I would most sincerely wish that you simply tell the viewers that there will be an in-depth, exclusive interview with Bernice Toland–James on your network, and then announce the time."

"That's boring," Holly said, then grabbed Saint Just's forearm as he reached for his cane. "Okay, okay, I'll do it. But she did it, right?"

Saint Just inhaled deeply, sighed. "Holly, dear Holly, you are a journalist. You don't have opinions, correct?"

"You're a real pain, you know that, Alex? Do you want this file or not?"

"Oh, I want it, most assuredly. Is there anything not in it that you can tell me?"

"Not much. Just that no one was ever charged, but that's not unusual. Are you going to tell me why you want this stuff?"

"As I said, Holly, all in good time. Until tomorrow morning? Let's say at nine, as Bernice cannot neglect her responsibilities at Toland Books."

"She's still going to go to work?"

"Innocent, dearest Holly. Innocent people continue with their lives as the wheels of justice grind slowly but inexorably toward the truth. And exoneration."

"With your help, right? I remember that horseback rescue, you know. And that WAR business. A thing of beauty—both of them were. What are you up to this time, hero man?"

"Why, simply being heroic, of course," Saint Just said, getting to his feet and saluting Holly Spivak with the cane before departing Mario's, picking up copies of each of the Sunday newspapers as he went. Mario would put the cost on Maggie's bill, as always.

"Good morning, Socks," he said as he approached his building. "When did you begin working on the weekends? I thought you were studying for your audition."

"I'm filling in. Paul's got a toothache. I see you saw the newspapers. It's bad, isn't it?"

"It's typical of your sensationalistic culture, Socks," Saint Just said, readjusting the thick papers under his arm. The move secured the newspapers, but the file folder slipped to the ground, opening, and papers were quickly set scattering by the morning breeze.

"I'll get those, Alex," Socks said, bending to pick up the pages, then piling them back into the folder. He held onto one of them, his eyes wide. "Oh, damn. Would you look at that? I think my breakfast is knocking at the back of my throat."

Saint Just took the paper, realizing that it was a photocopy of a photograph. He saw a body lying in what looked to be a garbage-strewn alleyway. A body, but without its head and hands. Holding the paper closer, he could make out a stamp on the bottom of the photograph stating that it was an official police photo.

"Hmmm, it would appear Miss Spivak has very good sources. Socks, you are to forget you saw this."

"Sure, Alex, like that's going to happen in the next twenty years. I think it's burned into my retinas. What *is* that?"

"That is, or should I say *was,* one Mr. Harry Goldblum, or at least I presume so," Saint Just said, replacing the photocopy inside the folder.

"Mrs. Goldblum's husband? Oh, now that's just gross." Socks wiped his hands on his uniform. "And I touched it."

Saint Just flipped through the reassembled pages. "There are more, Socks. Would you like it if I stood out here with you and shared them?"

"No thanks, no way, not hardly," Socks said, backing away.

"Very well. I think I know of someone who will want to see this."

He rode the elevator up, still trying to balance the newspapers, his cane, and the open folder as he attempted to scan all of its contents, and didn't have to feign surprise when the doors opened and Maggie was standing there, her arms folded as she tapped her foot.

She was wearing blue knit shorts, a pullover top of bright green sporting the message IN YOUR DREAMS, and a pair of bright pink fuzzy slippers. Her hair spiked all over her head, and her expression could only be called dangerous.

That was his Maggie. Definitely a morning person.

"My felicitations on your ensemble, Maggie, my dear. Aren't you up bright and early."

"Stuff it, Alex. Yes, I'm up early. I'm up early because I couldn't sleep because I'm worried about Bernie. Who snores, by the way. *Loudly.* Tonight I close both our bedroom doors. So you know what I did? Huh? I'll tell you what I did. I got up, and I wandered into the living room, and I looked out the window. I don't know why, I just did. And what did I see out there? Huh? I'll tell you what I—"

"Maggie, my dearest girl, please stop, you might strain something vital. I know what you saw. You saw a white automobile with the words 'Fox News' on the door parked at the curb. You saw me. You put two and two together and got—"

"Holly Spivak. How could you do that, Alex? I wanted to talk to her. She's got to understand that she can't come in here and—"

"Done and done, my dear," Saint Just said, motioning with his cane for her to precede him down the hall, to his apartment. "I've something to show you."

"Oh, yeah? Maybe I don't want to see it. I would have liked to see a bag holding some bagels and coffee, but I'm not seeing those, Alex."

"Ah, we're going to be mulish, I see. Such feigned reluctance is not becoming, my dear."

"I don't care." She opened the unlocked door, then turned to look at him. "Yes, I do. What do you have? I see the newspapers. What else?"

"We'll leave the newspapers for later, as I'm sure they'll be depressing," Saint Just said, closing the door and placing the newspapers on a table. "What I have that is definitely more interesting is all of Holly Spivak's information on one Harry Goldblum."

"You have—that folder is about—oh, God, Alex, you're sneaky. You traded Bernie for Harry, didn't you? That's cold." She grabbed the folder. "And *brilliant.*"

"It was rather inspired, I agree, and the interview, in case you don't think to ask, is set for nine tomorrow morning in your apartment, which, I might add, could probably do with a dust and brush up, especially your desk area," Saint Just said, waiting for Maggie to sit down on one of the couches, then sitting down beside her. "Perhaps we could look at this together? There are a few rather . . . disturbing photographs."

"Like what?" Maggie asked, paging through the half-inch stack of papers. "Oh, *eeeuuuwww.* Like this one?"

"Precisely. Perhaps I'd better take the papers, and keep the rest of the disturbing photographs hidden?"

"Ordinarily I'd say I could see anything you could see, but I think I'll make an exception in this case. There was no head, was there?"

"And no hands."

"Oh. Missed that." Maggie pulled her nicotine inhaler out of her shorts pocket. "Glad I missed that."

Within a half hour, they had pieced together the entire story. First, because both were the sort who could readily sift and distill facts, pertinent information; and second, because there wasn't all that much of it.

Harold Goldblum had been an attorney with a flourishing practice made up of thieves, thugs, and various other undesirables, including some rather high-profile members of one of the local mob families.

Nine years ago Harold disappeared, although his wife did not report him missing. She said nothing, actually, even denying his absence when the police came to her with the possibility that the headless, handless corpse recovered from a vacant lot in Hell's Kitchen could be that husband.

She said nothing until a package containing Harold's head and hands was delivered to her, and then she spoke up only to ask for the rest of the corpse in order to bury Harold all in the same box.

There had been a fluttering of media attention, some rousting of the usual suspects, but in the end, no one had been charged. Harry's name had been scratched off Irene's mailbox and life went on, or, for Harry, didn't.

"So why now?" Maggie asked as Saint Just closed the folder. "Nine years, Alex. If the mob was going to go after Irene, they would have done it by now, right?"

"True," he said. "Unless something new has occurred to once more pique their interest in the woman."

"Like what?"

"I have no idea, my dear," Saint Just said, sliding the folder beneath the couch, out of sight, as Sterling's sensibilities would not be best pleased to see those photographs. "But, clearly, something has changed."

"It," Maggie said, sucking on her inhaler. "Sterling said they were demanding he hand *it* over." She pressed her hands on the couch cushion and pushed herself up, her head and shoulders swiveling to look all around the living room, rather like a hunting dog going on point. "God, Alex, there's something in this apartment, isn't there?"

"I doubt that," Saint Just said, having already considered and discarded that possibility.

"Oh, well, then I'll just have to forget the whole idea, won't I? Silly me. *Duh."*

Saint Just patted her hand. "Don't fly into the treetops, my dear. But do you really think, if this *it* exists, and Irene Goldblum was aware that some very bad people knew *it* exists, and that they had contacted her and planned a visit to collect *it,* that *it* would still be here?"

Maggie made a face. "Okay. So she took it with her?"

"My thought, yes."

"So we've both agreed that there is an it. A journal, do you think? Something detailing Harry's exploits with the mob? Or maybe just a collection of incriminating evidence?"

"Sterling's visitors said *it,* which makes me believe that we're speaking of one thing."

"Unless the one thing is a file, like the one you got from Holly Spivak. A file can have a lot of *its* in it."

"I believe we're traveling in circles, Maggie, not to mention drowning in *its.* What's clear is that we have no idea what those men wanted."

"True. But they'll be back. Count on it. You two have to get out of here."

"I don't think so," Saint Just said, reaching into his pocket for his quizzing glass, then rubbing it as he would a talisman or a worry stone.

"Oh, right. Saint Just doesn't run. Saint Just is the big bad hero type. But what about Sterling?"

"I should imagine he'll make his own decision, given what we know, once we share it with him."

"I could hate you. You know damn full well Sterling will go where you go, even if you planned a swan dive straight into the mouth of hell."

Saint Just sat silent for long moments, moments in which he didn't quite care for himself very much (a novel experience on its own). It was all so much easier in his books, where he was assured, because, after all, he was a continuing series, that no matter how dire his position, he and Sterling would survive to adventure again another day . . . in another book.

It was Sterling who had discovered that no matter how he exercised since his arrival in New York, he did not lose weight. And, no matter what he ate, he did not gain weight. Saint Just had a scar from a pistol ball on his shoulder, but Maggie had put that there, describing it in one of her books. They were what Maggie had made them, how she had created them, and would not age, sicken, or die, unless she wrote about it.

Hence her occasional jokes about writing him a wart on the end of his nose.

Still, he was safe. Unless coming to life had changed things. Not the little things, but possibly the big things? Like their possibility of mortality? And could he take that chance? He could, for himself. He was, after all, a hero, and could not imagine himself in any other role, no matter how, in small ways, he had felt his attitudes *evolving* in his new surroundings.

But not for Sterling. He could not take that chance for Sterling.

"Well? Aren't you going to say anything?"

Saint Just shook himself back to attention. "I will not, I cannot, in good conscience remove myself from this building, desert my post, leave you ladies to fend for yourselves. I'm no white feather man, and you won't turn me into a sniveling coward, or Sterling, who has more backbone than you seem to imagine."

"You're such a—"

He held up a hand, cutting her off. "That said, we will, however, return to the hospitality you have shown us on the morrow, or as soon as Bernice is allowed to return to her own domicile."

"Boy, that really torked you, didn't it, saying all of that? And don't think I didn't notice that you got a few swipes in there as you were giving in. But good for you, Alex. You're doing the right thing. Now, how about you let me search this place? You know, humor me? I've always loved treasure hunts."

"If you must. I'm sure Sterling will be happy to assist you. Do you think Bernice has awakened for the day? I should begin preparing her for her interview."

"J.P.'s coming over at eleven to do that. Although I'm betting she doesn't realize you could actually set it up for tomorrow. And I guess I have to tell you, I was pretty impressed at how you handled J.P. last night at Bellini's. Do you think it was the wine, or is she really letting you be in charge of Bernie's publicity?"

"You doubt my powers of persuasion?"

"No, not me. You've persuaded the world you're real, you know. But we had a free ride last night. Nobody knew anything yet, or not enough to start stalking Bernie. Today, and from now on, it's going to be a different story. The barracudas are going to be circling."

"Knock knock. Yoo-hoo, are you in there? Olly-olly-umstead-free."

"Oh, shit," Maggie said, sliding down on the couch. "Speaking of barracudas . . ."

Saint Just stood up and smiled at Felicity Boothe Simmons. "Good morning, Miss Simmons. I hadn't realized I left the door unlatched. How remiss of me."

"Bernie told me you probably were over here. I know it's still early, but I rushed right over, as soon as I saw the morning papers, to lend my support," Felicity said, advancing into the room, bringing her strong floral scent with her. "Wow, very nice. Maggie, you could learn something from the way Alex decorates."

"Bite me," Maggie said, but only loud enough for Saint Just to hear her, then added, "How did you know Bernie was here?"

"You haven't seen the papers? There's a photograph of you, Alex, leaving Bernie's building yesterday. You were *unidentified man.* I think you're there, too, Maggie, but luckily all that's visible are your legs. I recognized those skinny ankles."

"Hold me back, Alex, or I'm going to kill her."

"Shhh," Saint Just soothed, sitting down beside her once more.

"Anyway," Felicity said, crossing her long legs and reaching into her purse for a tissue she then used to dab at the corners of her mouth, "I put two and two together and figured out that if Bernie wasn't under arrest and she couldn't stay at the crime scene, she had to be here, with you. Is that a Steinway?" she asked, pointing at the grand piano. "I play, you know."

"How wonderful for you," Saint Just said, the better to cover Maggie's low growl. "So you raced right over? Tell me, are there many members of the press camped outside?"

"Only two or three," Felicity said, frowning. Then she brightened. "But I told them. I told them all."

Maggie sat up, would have stood up if Saint Just hadn't grabbed her arm. "What did you say, Faith? Damn it, can't you ever walk past a camera or a microphone without sticking out that pair of silicone marvels and opening your big mouth?"

Felicity smiled, a soft, sympathetic, *you poor flatchested thing* smile. "Maggie. Maggie, Maggie, Maggie. I know how you loathe public speaking, what with that way you have of speaking too quickly, or mumbling, but some us of know the value of self-promotion."

"You were promoting yourself?" Saint Just asked, wondering if it would soon be time for Maggie to hold *him* back.

"No," Felicity said, waving her manicured hands to wipe away that impression. "Of course not. I was just speaking generally. But to use poor Bernie's tragedy to promote myself? My dear editor? My very good *friend*? How could you think such a thing?"

"Easy. I know you, remember," Maggie said, sucking on her nicotine inhaler.

(There was much to compare and contrast between Maggie and Felicity, Saint Just thought. One of those things would be how Maggie had heard from Bernice and raced hotfoot to her aid still clad in those unfortunate sheep, while Felicity would doubtless have taken a good hour with her toilette, and shown up prepared to face the cameras.)

"Always making jokes, aren't you, Maggie? But that's just because you're so loyal. Loyal to Bernie, and definitely loyal to me, saving my life that way. I'll never forget it, Maggie. I really won't."

"Try. Please," Maggie said, and Saint Just busied himself with his quizzing glass, carefully keeping his features blank.

"Don't be silly. Oh, I forgot. I brought you something. Just a little something I saw in Tiffany's the other day."

"Faith, you've got to stop this. Really. I don't want any more presents."

"They weigh heavily on her, you understand, Miss Simmons. Presents, any expression of kindness or even praise. She is much more comfortable when ignored," Saint Just explained as Felicity pulled a Tiffany blue box from her large purse and tossed it to Maggie, who missed it, because she was glaring at Saint Just.

Saint Just retrieved the box from the floor and handed it to her.

Maggie slid off the ribbon and opened the box, lifted out a soft Tiffany blue cloth holder and slipped out the small silver pen within. "Pretty."

"Say thank you," Saint Just prodded.

"Thank you, Faith."

"I knew you'd like it. I saw you using a Bic at the WAR convention. It's really time you displayed some cachet (she pronounced it *catch-it*), Maggie, now that you've been lucky enough to make the list. I had it engraved. Look."

Saint Just took the pen and squinted at the necessarily small letters. "'Maggie Kelly, heroine.' How . . . how very thoughtful."

"I know. I wanted *heroine extraordiniare*"—Saint Just visibly winced at that pronunciation—"only it was too long, and we weren't sure how to spell it. You like it, Maggie? You really like it? You can use it at autographings. Oh, wait, you don't do those."

"Yes, I do. Sometimes I do," Maggie said, looking at Saint Just, obviously in the hope he'd rescue her heroine self.

"Ah, yes, that's done now, isn't it? Now, please tell us what you said to the reporters downstairs?"

Felicity openly preened. "I was brilliant. I told them that nobody who knows Bernie, *really* knows her, would ever believe she'd kill anyone, even if she certainly had a good reason. Oh, and that I was convinced that nowhere in the length and breadth of this great country will she receive such a fair trial as right here, in my beloved Manhattan."

Maggie pressed a hand to her forehead. "Jesus. She's already got her arrested and going to trial."

"Maggie's right, Miss Simmons. Bernice is yet to be charged, you know."

"Oh, well, that's only a matter of time. But I'm sure it was self-defense."

"Out," Maggie said, getting to her feet before Saint Just could stop her. "I mean it, Faith. *Out.* And don't call, don't try to see Bernie again, and for God's sake don't let her see you once *she* hears what you said."

"I . . . I don't understand," Felicity said, grabbing her purse and holding it in front of her as she rose and backed toward the door, Maggie stalking after her. "What did I say wrong? Did I really say something wrong?"

"Your choice of words could be termed . . . unfortunate,"

Saint Just said, stepping in front of Maggie and escorting Felicity to the door.

"I didn't mean them to be. I thought they were good words."

"Yeah, you think that about your stupid books, too," Maggie said, and Saint Just quickly shoved Felicity out and closed the door, just as the pen hit it. "Damn, Alex, with friends like Faith, Bernie doesn't need any enemies."

"No, she doesn't. Although, if we're correct and Bernice is innocent, she certainly has one."

CHAPTER 7

Maggie was torn. Part of her wanted to rip into Mrs. Goldblum's apartment, looking for journals taped on the underside of drawers or hidden behind paintings. But another part of her knew she had to be, as Saint Just would have said, a "supporting prop to Bernice in her hour of need."

It was that part of her that stopped only long enough to peek behind the very uninspired oil painting of a dark cavern on a dark day in hopes of finding a wall safe, before crossing the hallway to reenter her own apartment . . . to see Bernie sitting on the couch, dressed in a turquoise silk blouse and black slacks, her make-up in place, one foot propped against the coffee table.

The foot was bare. There was cotton between the toes. And the apartment reeked of nail polish.

"What are you doing?" Maggie asked, not sure if she was disappointed not to see Bernie lying on the couch in a fetal position, overcome with dread, or just unhappy with the smell of nail polish. Who said smokers didn't have sensitive noses?

Bernie dipped the brush in the bottle, coming out with fire engine red, and concentrated on painting the nail on her big toe. "Well, Maggie, it's like this. Either I curl up and die, or I fight back. Or didn't you figure out that someone did this to me?"

"Well, actually, Alex and I did come to that conclusion. But I thought you said you couldn't remember anything."

"I didn't. I don't. But I didn't kill Buddy. Turn him over to the cops for faking his death, sure. Turn him in to the IRS because the forgetful little bugger hadn't filed in five years before he took his hike—we filed separately, I insisted on that, and the pre-nup. But kill him? I'd rather see him in jail. I could go visit him once a month, and bring him prunes. He hated prunes."

"Right," Maggie said, sitting down on the opposing couch. "That sounds like you. A long, slow torture, right?"

"Absolutely. Besides, why would I kill him in my own house? It doesn't make sense."

"It does if you wanted to use the defense that it doesn't make sense," Maggie said, watching as Bernie, hands as steady as the proverbial rock, put a first coat on the second toe of her right foot. "But you're right. You wouldn't have—wait a minute. You had Buddy sign a pre-nup?"

Bernie used her free hand to push back her tangled curls. "Um-hmm, everyone was doing that back then. It had cachet."

"Or *catch-it,* depending on who's saying the word," Maggie said, pulling out her nicotine inhaler and taking a deep drag of unsatisfying chemicals. "So, Buddy would have gotten nothing if you divorced? If you died?"

"Right. He sold insurance, Maggie, and not very successfully. He even had to take a second job, once the bloom was off the rose and I took away his allowance. Kirk was a worm, but he was pretty fair in our divorce. I mean, I was able to buy that house in Connecticut. It's in my name."

"Still is?"

"Uh-huh. Damn! Get me a tissue, will you, Maggie. I'm all smudged."

Maggie grabbed a box of tissues from the end table and held it out to Bernie. "I'm shocked. I thought I knew everything about you. You still own a house in Connecticut? Why?"

Bernie shrugged, smudging another nail. "Because everyone in town thought I'd killed Buddy and buried him in the backyard, that's why. So I kept my backyard, just to drive them nuts."

She looked up at Maggie. "You do know me, Maggie. I'm a nasty woman, right?"

"One of the reasons I love you. Is it leased?"

Bernie looked at her right foot, sighed, and reached for the bottle of polish remover. "Can we change the subject? I was doing great until we started talking about this stuff."

"In a minute. Is it leased, Bernie?"

Bernie sat back, sighed. "Yes, it's leased." Then she sort of rolled her eyes. "I think it's leased. It used to be leased by the week, you know, in the summer. You know, Maggie, I don't know. I really haven't been paying attention. I go through an agent, you understand."

"Call him," Maggie said, grabbing the portable phone and holding it out to Bernie. "Call him now."

"Why?"

"I don't know. But if Buddy wasn't dead, and he wasn't, maybe when he came back he went first to Connecticut, thinking you still lived there. The realtor can ask the people leasing the house if anyone came sniffing around, looking for you. If the house was leased, that is. Oh, just call."

"And this would be in aid of . . . ?"

"Buddy tracking you down. He heard about Kirk, wherever he was hiding, heard about your inheriting and taking over. He was getting a little tired of Mexico, or Brazil, or wherever the heck he'd stashed himself, and decided to come back, hop on the gravy train. It would be logical for him to go first to your house in Connecticut, right?"

Bernie finished wiping off the newly applied polish. "I hope you're happy now, Maggie. I have to face the world with bare toenails. You don't wear Ferragamos with bare toenails. It's sacrilege."

"Bernie, honey, concentrate. If Buddy showed up at the Connecticut house, that proves he was after you, not the other way around."

"Nobody has opined that Bernice was hunting Buddy," Saint

Just said from the doorway. "Only that they so obviously found each other."

"I gotta remember to lock that door," Maggie said, sucking on the inhaler. "Either that, or we buy out the other two condos on this floor and just use the whole place."

"An interesting idea, but four kitchens would be a tad superfluous, don't you think? Actually, two are superfluous, unless you're planning on cultivating a heretofore hidden talent, my dear."

"Bite me," Maggie said absently. "And you're right, Alex, nobody has said that Bernie was hunting Buddy. Crime of opportunity, crime of passion, that's what they'll be saying."

"They, that nebulous they, are already saying just that," Saint Just said, holding up the front page of one of the newspapers.

"The Merry Widow?" Bernie slammed down her bare feet and headed for the portable bar. "Cut me a freaking break. That's so cliched."

"Miss Spivak plans to go with Twice Dead, I believe."

"Better," Bernie said, gesturing toward him, empty tumbler in hand. "If it was a book, it could be *Bumping Off Buddy.*" She lifted the top of the ice bucket. "Maggie?"

"Bernie, nobody has scotch for breakfast."

"I already ate a health bar I had in my purse. Now I want a drink. J.P. said I could, at least for a while. Don't harp on me Maggie, please. I only look like I'm holding on." She held the bucket higher.

"Going," Maggie said, giving Saint Just a look before taking the ice bucket and heading for the kitchen.

Once there, she stood in front of the open freezer door, rethinking her reasons for learning about the Connecticut house. They didn't change, not if she put herself in Buddy's shoes. Even if he'd had access to the Internet, all he'd get from that would be that Bernie had an apartment in the city, and a house in Connecticut. He'd think she lived in town during the week, went to Connecticut on the weekend.

Or at least he *could* think that way.

He could have been there, lying in wait like a snake in the grass. But, when she didn't show up? Next move—Manhattan. It made sense. She thought it made sense. Maybe it made sense. . . .

Maggie filled the ice bucket and returned to the living room, to see Saint Just sitting on the couch she'd vacated, leaving room for her. He stood at once, because he was a Regency gentleman, then motioned to the couch as if beckoning her to join him, because he was arrogant and bossy and just assumed she'd want to sit next to him. *Here, girl. Sit.*

Man, she was feeling snarky. But, then, she'd been awake for only about ninety minutes, and it wasn't looking like it was going to be a great day to be happy.

She put down the ice bucket and headed for her computer chair, then glared at Saint Just.

He smiled back at her, just as if he knew that she wanted to be sitting next to him, which was why she wasn't sitting next to him. How could he read her so well? No, scratch that. She knew why he could read her so well. Because she'd given him parts of her, just as she'd given Sterling parts of her, never thinking that one day she'd look at the two of them and see herself.

The self she was; the self she wished she was; the self she hoped she could be; stronger, smarter, more daring, more "I want it, so I'm going after it."

More Saint Just, less Sterling.

"Maggie? Bernice and I were discussing Connecticut, and I believe you have a very valid idea."

"You do?" she asked hopefully, then cleared her throat and said, "Well, duh, of course you do. It's a good idea. A brilliant idea."

"Oh, my dear, I wouldn't go quite that far," Saint Just said, and she recognized the twinkle in his eyes. He was deliberately trying to make her angry.

It was working.

"Bernie? What's the name of your realty company? I'll look it up on Google, get a telephone number. Realtors always work on Sundays. My mom was a realtor, for all the vacation condos in Ocean City. Sundays were good days."

Five minutes later, Bernie was speaking to one Lureen O'Boyle, saying yes, of course she remembered her (even as she made a face and shook her head at Maggie), saying yes, she wished she had time to summer in Connecticut (while rolling her eyes), and finally snapping her fingers for Maggie to hand her pen and paper so she could scribble as she said, "Uh-huh, okay, thanks, Lureen. And say hello to Gordie for me. Oh, he did? Isn't that just like a man? Bye now."

She clicked off the phone and took a sip of her drink.

"Well?" Maggie asked impatiently.

"Well, what? Oh, Gordie's gone."

"Who? Oh, your realtor's husband? He left her?"

"He died."

Saint Just looked at Maggie, who was mouthing, " 'Isn't that just like a man. . . .' "

"J.P. does have a point, doesn't she, about putting a muzzle on our dearest Bernice?"

"Oh, yeah," Maggie said, glaring at her friend. "Bernie, you have to stop saying stuff like that. I think you're funny, Alex here thinks you're funny, but the rest of the world could think you're being . . . flippant."

"Good, because I was being flippant. Gordie got me backed into a corner at the annual let's all pretend we're hicks celebration, or whatever it was. I had to knee him, which I enjoyed." She waved the note. "Do you want to know what Lureen said?"

"I don't know," Maggie said, dropping her head in her hands. "I'm beginning to wonder what it was I wanted to know."

"Have a cigarette, Maggie. Trust me, the vice of your choice will go a long way toward keeping you sane."

"Right up until the moment it kills you, I'd imagine," Saint Just purred, earning himself another dirty look from Maggie.

"Anyway, Lureen says my last tenant left the end of July.

She'd been trying to rent it, but she swears the economy is keeping everyone at home this year. So, Maggie, my house is empty. I forget. Is this supposed to help me or hurt me?"

Maggie looked at Saint Just. He inclined his head slightly, allowing her the floor. Not that she wasn't capable of taking it on her own, although it might be better if she knew what she wanted to say.

She'd have to wing it. "Okay," she said, "the house is empty. Has been empty since the end of July. So, since we can't find out if Buddy came there at any time, looking for you, that idea's shot. However, that doesn't mean he wasn't there."

"And . . . so what?" Bernie asked, sipping her scotch.

"So," Maggie said, and then hesitated. "I don't know. Alex, do we need to know if Buddy was there? I mean, would that help Bernie or hurt her? Like, if the cops thought she knew he was there and visited him there, maybe? That he could have been trying to hit her up for money or something? Part of the insurance money, at the least, even if he didn't know about her inheritance from Kirk?"

Saint Just steepled his fingers in front of his chin. "Go on."

"Okay. The timing makes sense on the insurance money, I'd say. Like, he'd promise to stay dead if she split the insurance with him? But that would mean that maybe Bernie knew that no blackmailer bites once and then goes away, so that then maybe she lured him here, and murdered him? Wow, why do I keep making cases *against* Bernie?"

"I hate scenarios," Bernie said, pulling cotton from between her toes.

"Or," Saint Just said, "Buddy returned, hid at the Connecticut house in order to prepare himself for coming to the city to confront Bernice, demand money from her? He may have felt safe there, although I would think the first place he'd be noticed and remarked upon would be in the area in which the two of them resided. You know, Maggie, I think we've come to a dead end. Unless, purely for purposes of discussion, and in an attempt to track Buddy's movements before his death, we at some point decide it necessary to explore that avenue."

"At some point? You've got another street to travel?" Maggie asked, still trying to figure out why she'd thought this was such a good idea. But that was like looking for a motive for Buddy to want to get himself murdered, and she was pretty sure that idea wasn't going to get off the ground for anyone but the prosecution.

"In point of fact?" Saint Just said. "No, I don't have any other streets to travel. Not yet. Not until J.P. extracts as much information as possible from the good *left*-tenant. And, speaking of J.P., remember that she'll be arriving shortly, to prepare Bernice for her television debut, which will make us fairly superfluous for most of the day. Bernice, would you happen to have a key to the Connecticut house with you?"

"No," Bernie said. "I haven't been there, oh, for at least four years. But Lureen has to have one. Why?"

"Oh, nothing," Saint Just said, speaking to Bernie, but looking at Maggie. "I just thought, as there's little else for us to do today, Maggie, Sterling and I could drive to this Connecticut and inspect the house."

"For clues," Maggie said, shaking her head. "I mean it, Alex, for clues, right? Not just to humor me?"

"Or to keep you out of the way while J.P. preps me," Bernie said, then winced. "Sorry, Mags. I am using your place, aren't I?"

"No, no, that's okay, Bernie," Maggie said, already heading down the hall. "Alex?" she called over her shoulder. "Let me shower and get dressed. You can go collect Sterling, he likes taking rides. Oh, and call Socks, see if we can borrow his car. I'll be ready in twenty minutes."

Twenty minutes stretched to thirty, and when Maggie exited the foyer of the building it was to see Saint Just and Socks standing together, talking. "Where's Sterling?"

Saint Just held open the car door on the driver's side. "Sterling is upstairs, aligning his bedroom in harmony with the elements. To that end, he and Socks will be shopping this afternoon, as Sterling has put forth a desire to visit Chinatown, where he plans to purchase some brass amphibians he calls three-legged money frogs, of all things, plus a quantity of Chinese coins tied with red ribbon that he intends to employ in a way I was not interested enough to linger and listen to, I'm afraid. Oh, and brass elephants with their trunks raised."

"Very important, Maggie, that the trunks are pointing up," Socks said, holding the door as Saint Just walked around to the passenger side. "Sterling's really into this feng shui stuff, Maggie. We're going to stop by my apartment first and pick up my bagua. That helps you figure out which part of your place is the wealth area, which is the health area, which is the—"

"Thanks, Socks," Maggie said, starting the car, trying to ignore the fact that the key chain was in the shape of a naked man, waist down, and anatomically correct—perhaps more optimistic than correct. "Tell Sterling to make sure he locks up before you two go shopping, okay? And thanks for the loan of the car. I'll make sure to fill it up before I bring it back."

Socks grinned. "You might want to fill it up before that, Maggie. The gas gauge doesn't work, but I'm pretty sure you'd be running on fumes before you made it to the FDR. Oh, yeah, do you know how to go? Alex printed out directions from MapQuest, so that should help."

Maggie turned to look at her co-pilot and navigator. "This ought to be good," she said, putting the 1984 Chevrolet in gear and pulling away from the curb as Socks hurriedly slammed the door.

It wasn't easy to find a gas station in Manhattan, so it was another half hour before Maggie had merged onto the FDR Drive North ramp, and straight into heavy traffic.

"Very good, my dear. There's nothing to do now but drive until we reach the exit that takes us onto something called the Deegan Expressway. At which time you'll allow me to take over the wheel?"

"Oh, yeah, that's going to happen. You don't know how to drive."

"You do, my dear. Ergo, I should be able to do it."

"Chauvinist pig," Maggie said, wondering how offended Socks would be if she had Saint Just take the fuzzy dice off the rear view mirror. "Oh, wait. You mean you think you learned how to drive by osmosis or something?"

"Alas, probably not, as Sterling and I never left the apartment during the time we confined ourselves to living in your mind. No, I think I was being a chauvinist pig, actually. I mean, *you* can do it. If a female can do it, I don't see why a reasonably intelligent man couldn't—"

"You're driving me crazy on purpose, aren't you? Why?"

"Perhaps to keep my mind free of the thought that my life is in your hands? Although I will say that you seem much more competent than Tabby, if you'll remember the small trip Sterling and I took to her summer home. Ah, Exit Eighteen. See it, Maggie? We're heading for the Deegan Expressway now. Very neatly accomplished, my dear."

"That's because you didn't look in the mirror on your side," Maggie said, ignoring the middle-finger salute coming from the driver's seat of the car she'd just cut off. "Next time, Alex, don't leave it until the last second. What's next?"

"Hmm, it appears slightly complicated here. FDR Drive N (and he pronounced all of the letters, to Maggie's mingled amusement and chagrin) has been followed by the Willis Avenue BR—I believe that means bridge—as we head right onto the bridge, which becomes Willis Avenue, then a right onto Bruckner Boulevard, then the Bruckner Expressway, the exit for New Haven, *back* onto the Bruckner Expressway somehow, and that becomes I-95, portions toll, for, oh good, 38.71 miles. I've taken fewer turns traveling from London to John O'Groats."

"Just give me that," Maggie said, snatching the print-out from Alex and reading it as she drove. "God, these directions are nuts.

Look, Alex, just play with the radio or something, and let me drive, okay?"

And he did. He played with the radio. Incessantly, looking for the Mets game until he realized it didn't start until two.

Maggie figured she'd ground down at least one millimeter of tooth enamel before they finally entered the small town that sat on the water, one wrong turn and a good thirty minutes after the fifty-five minute drive time decreed by some guy at MapQuest who'd probably never driven in New York traffic.

"Pretty," Maggie said, driving slowly, on the lookout for a restaurant.

"Picturesque," Saint Just agreed. "Bernice informed me that her house overlooks the water, so I would think we're traveling in the correct direction."

"We will be," Maggie said, turning into a gravel parking lot beside a small cafe bearing the sign Rosie's Place. "First, we eat."

"And then we toddle over there and procure the key," Saint Just said, pointing to the realty office directly across the street. "Ah, smell that air, Maggie. Pure ambrosia."

"It is nice," Maggie said, the smell of the water taking her back to her childhood in Ocean City, New Jersey, where her parents still lived . . . which made it not an entirely pleasant recollection. "Let's go. Hamburgers and fries sound good?"

"Not quite as tempting as a good joint and pudding," Saint Just said, at which time Maggie reminded him, yet again, to add the words "of beef" to "joint," before he got himself in trouble.

Maggie was just paying their bill when the door opened and a short, plump woman of indeterminate years with a very bad dye job came into the restaurant, at which time the man behind the cash register said, "Hi, Lureen. The usual?"

"Yeah, Joe, thanks, and to-go, all right? I've got some nimrods coming up from Manhattan to look at the James house. Look, not rent. I'm not going to retire on that kind of commission—*none.*"

"Excuse me," Saint Just said, bowing to the woman as Maggie retrieved change from a twenty. "Allow me, dear woman, to introduce myself. I am Alex Blakely, here to see Ms. Toland-James's house. And you, I trust, are Mrs. Lureen O'Boyle?"

"Oh shi—shoot," Lureen said, offering her hand, which Saint Just bowed over, turning the woman's pale complexion to rosy red. "I'm . . . I'm . . ."

"Eager to turn over the key and direct my good friend here, Maggie Kelly—Maggie, say hello to Mrs. O'Boyle—to the James house?"

Maggie took the key Lureen fished out of her pocket, listened to the woman's garbled directions, and allowed Saint Just to bow her back out onto the pavement. "Sometimes," she told him as they got into the car, "just sometimes, I really love watching you politely rip idiots to shreds."

"Me? Don't be silly, Maggie. I merely rescued Mrs. O'Boyle from her own folly. We're turning here? Ah, is that it? It's nothing like Tabby's summer home."

"That's because my dear agent's place in the Hamptons is all glass and . . . heck, I think it's all glass, and yellow curtains, thanks to Sterling. This is Connecticut, Alex, and small-town Connecticut goes more for gray Shaker shingles and clapboard, whatever that is. It's pretty, but I can't imagine Bernie living here."

"Neither, it would appear, could Bernice, at least not for any great space of time. Shall we go inside?"

Maggie handed Saint Just the key as he helped her out of the car and he opened the door, letting out damp, musty air and the smell of rotting food. "Hit the lights, Alex, it's dark in here with all the drapes closed."

"I am here only to obey," Saint Just said, and the next moment the living room of the rather small house was bathed in artificial light. "How . . . quaint."

"It's pretty ugly, isn't it? While I was getting dressed Bernie told me she took out all her good stuff and had it replaced with renter type stuff," Maggie said, walking into the room, taking in the faded chintz couches, the maple tables, the overhead light that looked as if it was made out of an old wagon wheel.

She proceeded through the dining room, and opened the drapes on the back wall. "Oh, wow. There you go, Alex, that's what you pay for up here. Look at that view. I think you can see all the way across to Long Island."

"And I can see all the way to the kitchen, and evidence that either Mrs. O'Boyle hasn't inspected the premises since the last tenants vacated, or someone has been living here."

Maggie followed Saint Just's voice into the kitchen, and saw about a dozen Brennerman's pizza boxes scattered on the countertops. Alongside the beer cans. "Buddy. He was here. That explains all the closed drapes. He was here, hiding out. For a while, considering this mess. Sonofagun, Alex, does this help Bernie or hurt her?"

"It does nothing, if we don't tell anyone what we've discovered until we know how such knowledge might affect the case," Saint Just said, heading for the staircase.

Maggie followed, and after peeking into two small bedrooms, found more evidence in the third one, the master bedroom probably, as it had its own bathroom.

"Don't touch anything," Saint Just said, using the tip of his cane to flip open a rather battered suitcase lying on the bed. "Coming or going, Mr. James?" he asked the room at large as Maggie peeked around him to see that the suitcase was half-filled with socks, underwear, and a small plastic bag she was pretty sure contained marijuana.

Maggie got a washcloth from the linen closet in the dirty bathroom and used it as a glove as she opened the closet doors. "Did he spend the last seven years in Hawaii? Look at these shirts, Alex. Pretty flashy."

"Bernice was married to a man who would wear those shirts? The mind boggles. However, I think I've discovered something much more interesting."

Maggie followed him across the room, to what must have been Bernie's makeup table. There, spread out on top, were newspaper clippings, about Kirk's murder, about Bernie's days as the prime suspect, about her being exonerated, the real murderer found, and Bernie having inherited Toland Books and Kirk's private estate.

"He knew," Maggie said as Saint Just poked at the clippings with the tip of his cane. "That's why he came back. He knew, and he wanted in, wanted his share. Damn it, Alex, we can't show this to anyone. It gives Bernie a motive to get rid of him."

"On top of another very reasonable motive, that being the three million dollars in insurance money she would have collected in a few weeks. I'm convinced he would have demanded at least half. Bernice really is much better off with Buddy James dead."

Maggie looked up at him mutely, wishing they both hadn't been thinking the same thing.

"However," he said, "I believe Bernice, if she were to contemplate murder, would have found some other way to dispose of the man. After all, everyone already believed him dead. Who would know?"

"You're right! Why didn't I think of that? Alex, you're brilliant."

"That being the case, I may drive us back to the city?"

"You're not *that* brilliant," Maggie said, heading for the stairs, eager to get back to the city while J.P. was still at the apartment.

CHAPTER 8

The drive back to the city was uneventful, with traffic increasing as they went because the president, they learned via the radio, had come to town for a fund-raiser. Although his visits always snarled traffic, today they included a gift—a total absence of media in front of Maggie's building.

"Socks, there you are," Saint Just said as he helped Maggie from the car. "I have a boon to ask of you."

"I don't know, Alex. I don't have any Boones. Got a couple of Crocketts, and they say my Bowie's pretty sharp."

Saint Just looked at him blankly.

"Ah, come on, that was funny."

"Wrong country, Socks," Maggie said, patting him on the back. "But Alex does a great Beau Brummell impersonation."

Now Socks looked blank. "The Beau Brummells? Hey, I know them. I listen to the oldies station. They're ancient, from the sixties. *Laugh, Laugh. Just a Little.* Bitchin', Alex. I didn't know you could sing."

"No, Socks, not the group, the—never mind," Maggie said, giving up. "Have you been here all day? Is J.P. still up there?"

"The Wicked Witch of the West? No, she's gone. And the lieutenant was here and left again. We weren't here, but Ms. Toland-James told me when she called down to ask if I knew when you were getting back, and to tell me not to buzz up any visitors for at least an hour because she was going to take a bubble bath.

That was about ten minutes ago. Oh, and Sterling really scored in Chinatown. A two-for-one sale on lucky bamboo."

"So Sterling is upstairs?" Saint Just was attempting to get all his ducks, as it were, in a row.

"No, he's at Mario's, storing up on Twinkies. Now I have to go move the car."

"Oh, right," Maggie said, handing him the keys. "Nice key chain."

"Sorry about that. It was a gift from my mom. She's got some really weird ideas about gay people, you know? But she tries. Oh, here comes Sterling. Hey, bro, don't forget you've got all those bags in the corner of the lobby."

"Sterling," Saint Just said, inclining his head toward his good friend, who had half a Twinkie sticking out of his mouth.

"Mmmmfff . . . hullo," Sterling said, then licked sugary white filling from his lips. "Home again, home again, jiggity-jig, right?"

"Sugar high," Maggie whispered to Saint Just.

"Shall we head upstairs?" Saint Just asked, swiping his key-card in the slot and then holding the door open for Sterling and Maggie. "I'll get those," he told Sterling, whose arms were already laden with groceries . . . if sugar and fat and artificial flavors could be called groceries.

"We'll deposit all of Sterling's booty in our apartment, Maggie, and then join you and Bernice," Saint Just said as they exited the elevator.

"I'll get the door. See my new key chain?" Sterling said, holding up a key ring that included a small brass elephant, trunk raised.

"Different animal, same upward gesture," Maggie said. "I guess maybe Socks's mother thought it was good luck?"

"Contain yourself, my dear," Saint Just said, waiting for Sterling to open the door.

"Oh, gloomy hour."

"It is? What's wrong, Sterling?" Saint Just asked, pushing past his friend to enter the apartment.

The living room was a mess. An unmitigated wreck. A disaster of epic proportions.

Couch cushions were on the floor, cut open. Pictures were stripped from the walls. Tables were overturned, their drawers pulled out.

"Henry?" Sterling called out, dropping his packages and heading for the sideboard, which had been overturned. "Henry? Where are you?"

"Ohmigod, Alex," Maggie said, squeezing Saint Just's arm. "If they hurt Henry . . ."

Saint Just was listening but, selfish man that he was, just barely. He was rather involved at the moment, looking from the bare space above the mantle to the floor and his completely destroyed plasma television machine, to the bare space, to the desecrated screen, to the bare wall, to the screen . . . and he had yet to even watch a Mets game on the thing.

"Did you find him, Sterling?" Maggie asked, stepping over a couch pillow.

"Be careful where you step, my dear," Saint Just said, coming back to attention, and to what really mattered, and Henry mattered to Sterling. Very much. "He may have broken out of his cage."

"Oh, damn, didn't think about that one," Maggie said, backing up. "I like Henry. I really do. But I like him in his cage."

Sterling was on his hands and knees, trying to lift the heavy sideboard. "Henry? Henry?"

"Here, Sterling, let me help. But, before we lift this, I must remind you that you are an Englishman. Whatever we discover, you will not flinch," Saint Just said, taking hold of one end of the sideboard.

"Oh, God, Alex, do you really think he's under there?"

"Henry!" Sterling shouted as he put all his weight into it, almost single-handedly lifting the sideboard, so that it fell against the wall with a thud. *"Henry!"*

"I can't look. Alex?"

"The cage is rather smashed," Saint Just said as Sterling dropped to his knees and picked up the cage. "But, wait . . . yes, there he is. Sterling, can you get him out? He's fine, Maggie."

"Henry," Sterling said, standing up, holding the misshapen cage in both hands. He turned and headed for the hallway. "Thank God, you're all right."

"Where's he going with Henry?" Maggie asked, picking up a small silver candy dish, an effort that made little difference in the shambles that had once been Mrs. Goldblum's quite lovely living room.

"He has a second cage in his bedroom that he uses for Henry while he's cleaning the larger cage," Saint Just told her. "And, now that Sterling's world is right again, perhaps you could spare a moment's silence for the demise of my plasma television machine?"

"Oh, Alex," Maggie said, carefully making her way across the room to look down at the broken set. "That was just mean."

"Yes, I do believe that was the point of the exercise, once our visitors realized they hadn't found what they were looking for."

"It."

"Correct. It. I imagine it is no longer feasible for me to try to fob you off with any notion that I have ever considered our visitors a small problem. Shall we inspect the remaining rooms? I doubt their appearance will be much improved over this one."

"We should call Steve."

"Oh, most definitely. Good man. I had no idea he divides his time between *left*-tenanting and housekeeping."

"Wiseass," Maggie said, reaching into her purse for her cell phone. "This is a crime, Alex, it has to be reported."

"On the contrary. This is my problem, and I will solve it."

"So will I," Sterling said, coming back into the living room. He stood straighter, walked taller, and the set of his jaw, and both his chins, was almost impressive.

"Sterling? Henry is all right, isn't he?"

"All right? How can you say that, Saint Just? He had to have been terrified. What sort of monster would do such a thing? I vow, Saint Just, I won't rest until the miscreants are incarcerated!"

"The mouse that roared," Maggie said, picking her way through the debris to hug Sterling, kiss his cheek. "I love you, Sterling."

"Yes, I know," Sterling said, and Saint Just smiled as he watched embarrassed color run up his friend's face. "Like a brother, I remember. Thank you very much, and I apologize for being so fierce. But I am very angry. Exceedingly angry."

"Do you wish to turn over the investigation into these blackguards to Steve Wendell, Sterling?" Saint Just asked.

"What? Not avenge Henry myself? No, Saint Just, I won't have anyone else interfering when I find these horrible people. I want them horsewhipped." Then he frowned. "How are we going to find them, Saint Just?"

"Good question, Sterling," Saint Just said, remembering that he had slid the folder beneath one of the couches. "Maggie? Do you see the folder?"

"Uh-oh," Maggie said, always so wonderfully acute when it came to deducing possible trouble. "Do you think they saw it?"

"Saw what?"

"Shhh, Sterling, and help me move these couches, if you please," Saint Just said, already tossing ruined pillows toward a corner of the room.

Ten minutes and some intense searching later, Saint Just dropped his quizzing glass over his head and rubbed the grosgrain ribbon between his fingers. "I think we can safely deduce that the folder is gone."

"That's probably not good," Maggie said, righting a reasonably intact Chippendale chair and sitting down on it. "I mean, now they know we know about them."

"We do? Isn't that above everything wonderful? What do we know?" Sterling asked, opening a Twinkie. "All I know is that someone broke in here and nearly killed Henry."

Saint Just and Maggie exchanged looks.

"Sterling, I've learned a few things about Mrs. Goldblum and her late husband. Rather disturbing things, and I promise to elaborate on all of them later, as we straighten this mess."

"I looked in the kitchen as I went by, Saint Just. All the cabinets were open and empty, and the floor was full of spilled flour and the like. You'll really help me clean up?"

"Of course I will," Saint Just said, ignoring Maggie's snort of disbelief. "Oh, very well, I'll be phoning Killer and Snake, and possibly even Mary Louise, if you must know."

"What, not Socks, too?"

"I'll have another mission for him," Saint Just said, and went off to inspect his bedchamber.

He stood in the doorway, his hands clenching and unclenching.

"Ah, Alex, all your pretty clothes," Maggie said, touching his arm as she went past him, into the room. "Did they have to throw all your clothing on the floor? Look, I know this is a shock to your . . . your sensibilities. Why don't you go call Mary Louise and I'll hang up everything, put everything back into the closet."

"I'm not going to fall into a sad decline, Maggie," Saint Just said, looking at his Weston designed jacket, the one he'd worn to his "debut" into Maggie's world. One sleeve was torn, and someone's very large feet had stomped all over it, leaving waffle-like treads on the fine fabric. "What was that quote you mentioned to me the other day? 'Don't get mad . . . '?"

"Don't get mad, get even," Maggie said, gathering up a half dozen crisply starched neckcloths that were now rumpled, and wet with the contents of a broken bottle of Obsession for Men, Saint Just's newly acquired favorite scent.

"Yes, that's it. It's not quite enough, is it? I fear I wish to get very much more than even. Considerably more. Stay here, I'll fetch a towel to wipe that up."

Picking up slacks and shirts and, surreptitiously, underwear, Saint Just pushed open the door to the bathroom.

He smelled the boot black before he saw the message written with it on the mirror above the sink: *Your dead.*

"They spelled *you're* wrong," Maggie said from beside him.

Saint Just, left eyebrow raised, looked down at her.

"Well, not that the grammar is important," Maggie said quickly. "I mean, it isn't important, right? What's important is that I think you're the *you* in that message. Or Sterling. Both of you. They must know two people are living here, having seen the bedrooms. And the you're dead business has to be about the file they found. I'm going to go call Steve. Don't say no again, Alex, because I'm going to call him. And I've got to check on Bernie."

Saint Just let her go, returning his interest to the message on the mirror. It was an empty threat. After all, no one killed the person from whom they needed information, needed *it.* What good would that do? It simply wasn't logical.

Then again, none of this was logical.

"Your chamber, too, Saint Just?" Sterling said, looking into the room. "Mine is a shambles."

"Yes, I'm sure it is," Saint Just said, escorting Sterling out of the bedchamber and closing the door behind him before his friend could see the bathroom mirror. No need upsetting poor Sterling further, as he had already advanced several yards beyond Incensed. "Maggie is phoning the *left*-tenant, so I suggest we vacate the premises, not touch anything else."

Sterling frowned, punched his glasses back up on the bridge of his nose. "But I thought we weren't going to ask for his assistance, Saint Just."

"I have reconsidered, to soothe Maggie, you understand. You know females, Sterling. They can be overly volatile at times like this."

"I've never had a time like this, Saint Just," Sterling said, then retreated to his room, quickly emerging with Henry. "However are we going to fix Mrs. Goldblum's furniture? She'll be that displeased."

"But not overly surprised, I imagine. However, she'll be considerably more than displeased when I locate her, Sterling, and ask her a few pertinent questions about her deceased husband, and about *it*."

"Oh, yes. You were going to tell me something, weren't you? You didn't want to tell Maggie, right? I can understand that. Some things are simply too terrible for females, and all of that, as you said. Will you tell me now?"

Saint Just debated about correcting Sterling's misconception as to just whom he might be protecting, but decided against it. He slung an arm around his friend's shoulders. "Come along, Sterling. Henry will be safe enough here now, for I doubt the baddies will return any time soon. Let the two of us adjourn to Mario's for something to eat, and a little talk."

"But . . . but where will we sleep tonight, Saint Just? We can't sleep here, not if you won't let me straighten this mess, and if Lieutenant Wendell puts up that yellow tape the way they do on television programs, barring us from our own door."

"A very good question, Sterling, and one for which, sadly, I have no answer at this exact moment," Saint Just said as they stepped into the elevator.

He did, of course, have one possible answer by the time the elevator reached the lobby.

"Socks, just the man I wanted to see."

Socks looked at Saint Just with widened eyes. "Now what? You look a little . . . and Sterling, you do, too. Are you guys mad at me?"

"On the contrary, my good fellow," Saint Just told him. "Quite the contrary. Now, while Sterling and I are at Mario's, filling our bellies, I fear, I would like you to contact Mary Louise, who will then alert Snake and Killer to report here at, oh, seven o'clock this evening?"

"Sure. Is that all?"

"Not quite. Socks, tell me, how does your mother feel about overnight guests?"

"Huh?"

"Yes, I was afraid so. Probably a sad lack of extra bedchambers?

Oh, well, then there's nothing else for it but for you to assist the others as they set the apartment to rights once the police are gone."

"I'm missing something, right?" Socks asked, looking at Sterling, who was still frowning as he stared intently into the middle distance, as if contemplating mayhem at any moment.

"I would say yes, you're missing something. Or, rather, that Paul missed that something while he held his post here, if he took your place this afternoon. A return visit from Sterling's two hatted gentlemen, as a matter of fact, or others of their ilk. They . . . redecorated our new apartment in our absence."

"Redecorated? Oh, jeez. You mean trashed, don't you?"

"They nearly killed Henry," Sterling said, his hands drawn up into fists.

"Henry? Oh, gosh, Sterling, I'm sorry. But he's all right?"

"Much better than my new television machine which, alas, you no longer will be able to use for that small soiree you and Jay were planning. A celebration of Judy Garland movies, I believe?"

"You knew about that?"

"I make it a point to know most things, Socks. Also, I saw Jay the other day when I was out for a stroll, and he not only thanked me for volunteering my new plasma television machine with its DVD player and surround sound, he also wondered if I preferred jalapeño to onion dip, as he is in charge of procuring refreshments."

"Oh, boy. I was going to ask you . . ."

"I'm sure you were. Mary Louise, Socks. Please contact her as soon as possible."

"Absolutely. Right away," Socks said, heading inside to make the call.

"How do you know everything, Saint Just? Did you really just see Jay-Jayne while you were out and about? I mean, it's a very large city."

Saint Just turned to head for Mario's. "You become unusually astute when agitated, Sterling," he said with a smile. "No, it wasn't a coincidence. Actually, Jay stopped by Maggie's the other day while you were out scootering, to ask if we also had a VCR machine, as some of his July Garland movies were in that format. I think he said format. But don't tell Socks. I'd much rather he think I'm omnipresent."

"All right. I don't think I'm hungry, Saint Just."

"In that case, order us each a cup of tea, if you please. Earl Grey, as I've convinced Mario to provide it. Go on ahead of me, Sterling. There's something I forgot to mention to Socks."

Sterling nodded and continued on to Mario's while Saint Just retraced his steps to the canopy over the front of his building. He smiled, just slightly, in the knowledge that, by the time he joined Sterling, the man would have ordered a Reuben, his new favorite sandwich, and a diet root beer, as he liked the flavor of diet soda. Who could hear that last bit of information and not understand that Sterling Balder was actually a very complex creature?

"Socks?" he asked, reentering the lobby just as the young man put down the phone. "Did you reach them?"

"They'll be here. All but Snake. He's visiting his mother."

"Ah, yes, the dear creature who gifted her child with a switchblade knife, even going so far as to engrave his name on the hilt. Vernon. How could I forget? Where does she reside?"

"For the next eighteen months, she's in jail. Snake visits her once a month."

"I must be nicer to that boy," Saint Just said, shaking his head. "I have one more favor, if you don't mind?"

"Sure. And, you know, you guys could crash at my place, if you don't mind sleeping on the couch. I called Mom, and she said it was okay."

"How very kind of your mother," Saint Just said with a slight bow of his head. "I think we will be able to muddle through, however, now that I've considered the thing. Although I do have another favor to ask."

Socks struck a pose (a Saint Just pose). "I am yours to command, of course." Then he grinned. "How was that? For the audition I'm hoping to snag next week. I thought I'd give the guy a British accent. Soap opera fans like that kind of stuff. It's classy."

"So I've heard," Saint Just said, hoping his smile was gracious, appreciative. Encouraging. "And then there's your paperback romance cover model appearance, which will go a long way toward making you more attractive to prospective employers."

"It's one little paperback book cover, Alex," Socks said, jamming his hands into his pockets.

"Yes, and from little acorns, I'm told, mighty oaks grow."

"But don't give up your day job, right, Alex?" Socks said, running to open the door for Mrs. Yates, from Six-B. She handed him the plastic bag containing the deposit her poodle, Mr. Pinky, had made on the city sidewalk, and kept on going.

"She's a good tipper at Christmas," Socks said, shrugging. "What else did you want me to do, Alex?"

"After you dispose of that, you mean? What I'd like is for you to keep an eye on Sterling. And when I say I want you to keep an eye on him, I really mean both eyes, and I mean around the clock. Is it possible for you to ask Paul or someone to take your place here for a few days?"

"I suppose so. Why? What's wrong with Sterling?"

"Nothing that I can think of, other than a propensity to believe he's a chef. I will be fairly well occupied with Bernice's affairs, I'm afraid, and I'd like to assure myself that Sterling will be in good hands."

"In case those guys come back?"

"Precisely. I would like you to go to the park with him, to Mario's with him, to anywhere he decides to take himself. I want you to stay as close as sticking plaster to the man. Keeping to the maxim that there is safety in numbers, you understand. I don't ask that you protect him. Just that you grab hold of his arm and remove him from the scene of any possible trouble."

"At warp speed. I remember that picture of Mr. Goldblum, you know," Socks said, nodding. "And I can get Jay to help. Days. He's got a really sweet gig uptown this week. He's on stage as Judy Garland at a private club. Great costumes. And you should hear him sing. He almost makes you forget Judy wasn't six feet tall."

Saint Just had nothing to add to that, remembering Jay's flamboyant and quite convincing appearance as Jayne at the WAR costume competition, so he returned to the street and headed for Mario's, to give Sterling a highly edited version of the life and definitely messy demise of one Harold Goldblum.

CHAPTER 9

"Are you sure you're all right, Bernie?"

"Only until I explode because you keep looking at me as if you think I will," Bernie said, sliding her knees up beneath the hem of her satin caftan as she lounged on one of the couches.

Her eyes were wide, a little wild, her movements jerky, uncoordinated. "No, really, I'm fine. Strong. Recovered. Confident. Whatever you want, kiddo, I'm it. I'm back up to fighting strength, whatever that means. No more being scared out of my mind. I don't like me scared, you know? Not exactly the image I want to project."

"But you haven't had a drink since I got back here," Maggie said, not happy to be bringing up the subject, except that somebody had to, didn't they? But she'd keep quiet about the wild eyes, the jerky movements, and the way Bernie's words nearly tumbled over themselves as she spoke quickly, too quickly.

Maggie was getting nervous. She didn't think Bernie would explode, pop like a balloon. But she could.

"You're counting my drinks now? Oh, wait. Is that where you're going? You want to talk about my friend Johnny Walker? I'm not on the wagon, if that's what you're hoping. I'm . . . I'm on the cart. Cutting back. Slowly. I get another drink in," she squinted at her watch, "five minutes. No, four and a half. That's it, four and a half. Four now. My watch is fast."

There was so much tension in the room, so many uncomfortable vibes. Like a pot of Angry, simmering, ready to boil. Maggie bit her lips between her teeth, then said what she had to say. "I don't think that's going to work, Bernie. Tapering off. You've got . . . you've got a problem."

"Yeah, and his name is Buddy James," Bernie said, reaching for Maggie's pack of cigarettes, which was on the table between the couches. "God, and I thought he was trouble the first time he was dead." She dropped the pack, slipped her bare feet onto the floor, and stood up. "Okay, hour's over. I mean, close enough. Johnny, baby, here I come."

"No."

Bernie turned her head, pushed back her flamboyant red hair and said, "What? What did you say?"

Maggie felt the ground shifting under her feet. "Um . . . it was no, Bernie. I said no. I don't think you should have another drink. J.P. said—"

"That was the phone call you took in the other room? My attorney? Operative word in that interrogative sentence, Maggie—*my. My* attorney."

Maggie would have very much liked to be able to pick up one of the throw pillows, to hide behind it. Bernie was looking just a little dangerous. And her voice was getting louder, even faster. Maggie hated raised voices, just hated them. Had hated them all her life. She hated confrontations, period.

But she couldn't back away, back down, hide. This was her friend.

"Bernie, please. J.P. said you might be arrested in the next few days. If that happens you'll get bail, she promised, but if the D.A. wants to be a prick—her word, not mine—he won't arrest you until it's too late in the day to get bail set before the next morning. You'll be locked up, Bernie, and Johnny Walker isn't allowed to visit. So . . ."

"So?" Bernie said, looking rather menacing in her green satin caftan, rather like she was ready to swoop on something. Maybe on Maggie. And, although Bernie was tall, she suddenly seemed bigger. Large, loud, domineering, all the things that set Maggie's insecurities into Red Alert Mode. But she pushed on.

"So, you've got to try to stop, now, before—not that it's really going to happen, but it could—before you're arrested. There, I've said it."

"Well, bully for you." Bernie chewed on the insides of her cheeks, her eyelids narrowed, her stance aggressive. "So you're saying I can't have another drink? Bottom line, Maggie. Redundant as that might be. Is that what you're saying?"

Maggie whimpered, but silently. "Yes, honey, that's what I'm saying. No more scotch."

"Fine, glad you clarified that. It's what I always tell my authors: clarify, clarify, clarify," Bernie said, heading for the drink cabinet. "You have any orange juice to go with this vodka? Never mind, I'll drink it straight."

"Stop showing off. You're not the town drunk, for crying out loud." Maggie clambered off the couch and grabbed the bottle from her friend's hand. "No. No more booze. J.P.'s on her way over with a plan to help you, and I promised her—"

"Oh," Bernie said, backing away, her chin sort of hiccuping as she went. "So that's it. J.P. She your new buddy, Maggie? Are the two of you *chums*? Two good *chums,* with a *plan.* Gee, next thing you'll be exchanging fucking friendship rings—while I'm getting fucked by some Fat Sadie in prison. Or, no. Not prison. A detox, right? You think you're going to lock me up in some detox? *Like a common drunk?"*

"Bernie, don't say the *f* word, please," Maggie said, wishing she herself hadn't said anything at all. It would have been so much easier to let Bernie have one more drink. Just one more, until J.P. got here, until Alex got here, until *somebody* got here. "Please, honey, don't do this."

Bernie grabbed up Maggie's cigarette pack and held it over her head. "How about I toss these in the toilet, Mags? Oh, look, little Maggie flinched. Got to you, didn't I? Poor Maggie, just as hooked as Bernie. They planning on locking you up, too?"

"Not yet, but I'll bet that day is coming," Maggie muttered, trying to marshal her thoughts. "Okay, Bernie, listen to me. You know you have a . . . a problem. I used to think it was social drinking, but since Kirk died and you had to take on so much at work and all—well, you drink all the time now. I'm your friend, you know that, but you're in trouble. You have to get sober."

"I *am* sober," Bernie said. Shouted. "I'm as sober as I want to be, damn it! Now leave me the fuck alone!"

Maggie wanted to back off. Oh, God, did she ever want to back off. The memory of her mother screaming at her, bullying her, dripping her special brand of sarcasm all over her, and over her father and the whole family, set off all the old feelings of just not being quite good enough.

But this wasn't her mother; this was Bernie. This wasn't an increasingly vicious contest of whoever yells the loudest wins, as it had become when her brother, Tate, had hit his teens and started screaming back. And she had to help her friend, not hide in her room, or in a book, or in some fantasy world of her own making. Bernie needed her. "I can't," she said with all the bravado she could muster. "I love you, so I can't leave you alone."

Bernie's shoulders slumped. "Damn you, Maggie. You're such a dweeb. 'Please, Bernie, don't say the *f* word.' Dweeb. This is killing you, isn't it? I love you, too."

Maggie collapsed onto the couch, vodka bottle in hand. "Because I'm a dweeb?"

"No, because you're gutsy," Bernie said, her bottom lip quivering. Bernie hated showing fear, had never shown it, not to this intensity, not in Maggie's memory. It was as if Bernie were more afraid of losing her Johnny Walker than she was of being arrested and sent to prison.

So Maggie tried to let her off the hook, tried a small joke, hiding behind humor when the going got too tough, as she always did. "Because I'm gutsy? I always thought you said it was because I'm neurotic, just like you."

Bernie smiled. "Oh, right, that too." Then her face sort of crumpled. "I need a drink, Mags. I'll admit I'm an alcoholic, if that's what it takes. I'll climb the twelve steps, whatever the hell that means. Give me the knee-jerk phrase and I'll repeat it, sing it to you if you want, for crying out loud. But one more, Mags. Just one more? You have to let me say good-bye, right? I'll just die if I can't have one last drink. My swan song. Maggie, please. I'm begging here."

She'd fought the good fight, maybe even gotten somewhere. But Maggie knew that Bernie wasn't going to be cured or broken or whatever the heck the right word was in one small moment, some melodramatic epiphany. Not with J.P. on the way, J.P. and her *plan.* "Okay," she said, getting to her feet. "Just a small one."

"Dweeb," Bernie said, already heading for the drink cabinet. "I scared you there for a minute, didn't I, Mags? But I knew I'd get to you. You're so easy." She grabbed up the bottle. "Come to Mama, Johnny."

Maggie felt something snap inside of her. Sort of go *sprrro–o-ing!* She shot from the couch like a missile out of its silo. "Give me that damn bottle," she said, capturing the Johnny Walker. "That was low, Bernie. How dare you push my buttons that way, get all loud and bullying, then all soppy and sorry and saying what I wanted to hear—do just what you knew would work on me?"

"Because I'm a desperate drunk?" Bernie asked, tossing back her hair. "Because I'd do anything, even to my best friend, to get a drink? That I'd *kill* for a drink? Is that what you want to hear?"

"I don't think so," Maggie said quietly. "It can't be a good idea to let people think you'd *kill* to get what you want."

"Maggie, put a case of scotch on one side and a million dollars on the other, and I'd go for the scotch, every time. I didn't kill Buddy, Maggie. I don't remember, but I *know.* I did *not* kill that slimy little bastard. And I'm not a drunk. I'm just . . . drinking." She grabbed the bottle and retreated to a corner, like a squirrel off to hide a nut.

"Well, that one line would make one heck of a headline, wouldn't it? 'I did not kill that slimy little bastard,' " Maggie said, then closed her eyes in gratitude as Socks buzzed on the intercom. "Got to get that."

A minute later, J.P. Boxer was in the condo, taking it over, making it her own as she paced the carpet in her orange sneakers and black fleece jogging outfit with the white stripes up the sides.

"Drink up, Bernie," she said matter-of-factly as Bernie held the bottle protectively against her chest. "I want you listening to me, not trying to figure out how to get the next drink."

"I am not a drunk," Bernie said, pouring scotch into a tumbler. "You know how insulting you people are? I drink. Okay, I drink. But it's my problem, not yours, and I am *not* a drunk. Drunks talk to themselves and lie in gutters and drink Ripple. I have a life. I have a very important job. I *function."*

"Right, you're a functioning alcoholic. When you're not blacking out. When you're not waking up with a stiff next to you and can't remember how he got there," J.P. said, rolling her huge eyes. "But you're not a drunk. Why not make that a double, Bernie?"

"Oh, shut the—just shut up," Bernie said, filling a tumbler and all but slamming herself down on the couch. "Maggie says you have a plan. Let's hear it."

"Gladly," J.P. said, pulling out Maggie's desk chair and turning it to face the couches. When she sat down she still was tall, and big, and very imposing, but for some reason Maggie knew she'd never understand, she wasn't the least bit nervous around the woman. "Let's start with the bad news, shall we?"

Bernie saluted the lawyer with the tumbler, then said, "Is this where I get so scared straight I'll listen to any bullshit crap you tell me to do?"

Maggie rallied again. "Bernie! Cut that out. J.P.'s only trying to help. We're all only trying to help."

"Sorry, J.P.," Bernie said, pulling her legs up under her. "Maggie could tell you that I broke a nail earlier and I'm in a bad mood. You know how that sort of thing can screw up what was otherwise a perfectly great day, right?"

"Am I missing something here?" J.P. asked, looking at Maggie.

"We were discussing Bernie's drinking before you got here," Maggie told her. "I'm afraid I was pretty hard on her."

Bernie sprayed scotch and began to choke. "Hard . . . *hard* on me? Yeah, like being beaten to death with marshmallows. J.P.? Allow me to introduce you to my best friend, the Terminator. R–i–i–ght . . ."

"Oh, shut up," Maggie said, reaching for her cigarettes, then hesitating.

"Go on, Maggie. To each her crutch, that's what I always say."

"Thanks, Bernie, but maybe not."

Bernie's eyelids narrowed again. "Take one, damn it! I'm not the only addict in this room."

"Don't call me an addict."

"Why not? You do. Maggie Kelly, the happy nicotine addict."

"It's different."

Bernie downed half her drink. "In a pig's eye, it is. You're hooked, I'm hooked, all God's chillun is hooked on something. It's what makes the world go round. Nicotine, sex, caffeine, junk food, Xanax—booze. Pick your drug of choice, because we've all got one. You know," she said, waving the drink about, so that it sloshed over the rim, "what this world needs is less pointing fingers and more damn *mirrors.* Cripes, that was profound. I am so good. Aren't I, Maggie? I'm right, admit it."

Maggie glowered at Bernie, who glowered back.

"My, my, my, aren't we having fun," J.P. said, getting to her feet. "You two do these chummy sleepovers often? I don't know how to break it to you, but some girls paint each other's nails and talk boys. You two? You're beauts, you really are."

Okay, so maybe Maggie didn't like J.P. all that much. Didn't the woman understand *friendship?*

"Never mind us, J.P. Maggie and I never played well with others, but we understand each other, and that's all that counts. Now, what's your bad news?" Bernie asked, sipping her scotch once more, as Maggie lit her cigarette.

"His name is Dettmer. Chad Dettmer."

Maggie sat up, blew out smoke. "The D.A.? That guy with the pompadour hair weave and the rouged cheeks? He's in on this? *Already?*"

"Are you kidding?" J.P. said, shaking her head. "He's in up to his neck, and happy as a pig in slop. The election's in two months, remember, and good old Chad is having wet dreams about charging Bernie, putting his face in front of the cameras 24/7. You're a gift, Bernie. A high profile, too rich, sensational-headline-producing gift."

There was a knock on the door, and Maggie went to answer it. Obviously the person was someone she knew, and Socks had just buzzed him through.

"I think this is where I go back to saying *doomed, I'm doomed,*" Bernie said, then tossed back the remainder of her drink.

"So this Dettmer guy is going to arrest her?" Maggie asked, looking at Bernie as she opened the door.

"I can answer that one," Lieutenant Steve Wendell said, kissing Maggie's cheek as he entered the living room. "And that answer is, yes, as soon as he's got things nailed down a little tighter. Hi, J.P., and before you toss me out as a spy, I'm off the case."

"What do you mean, you're off the case? Bernie's case?" Maggie took his hand and led him toward the couch. "Why?"

J.P. said, "Let me count the reasons for you. Wendell is friends with the prime suspect. Also—nope, that's probably enough."

"Enough for what? Maggie, my dear, I could hear you yelping from the elevator," Saint Just said, closing the door behind him. "Sterling is downstairs with Socks, waiting for our jolly helpers. Hello, *Left*-tenant. J.P., you're looking well. What am I missing here?"

Maggie returned to the couch. "Steve is off Bernie's case, Alex," she told him, caught in what was becoming a familiar dilemma. Who did she go to, trust more, need more—Steve or Saint Just? Right now she—and Bernie—needed them both.

"Really," Saint Just said, looking at Steve. "How unfortunate. However did you manage that?"

"We already covered that one, Alex. The D.A. tossed him for conflict of interest," J.P. said. "How far off, Steve?"

He sat down beside Maggie, ran his fingers through his shaggy hair. "About as far as I can get. Dettmer suggested I use a couple of weeks of vacation I've had hanging for about a year now. He suggested it real strong, you understand."

"Pissed him off, did you?" J.P. asked.

"You could say that. He doesn't understand why I don't already have Bernie cooling her heels in an interrogation room. And he wasn't exactly pleased to hear you're on the case, J.P. I'm not saying you're not on his Christmas card list, but I don't think he likes you much."

J.P. snorted. "I'm a traitor, according to Chad. Left the good guys to defend the scum of the earth, and all for the money."

"That would be me. Scum, paying the money, all of it," Bernie said, hoisting her empty glass to Maggie in a sort of salute.

"Right," J.P. said, nodding. "But mostly it's because I win more than I lose. Steve? Did he threaten you, or did you just take the hint before it got that far?"

"You know how it is, J.P. First the suggestion, then the threat of unpaid leave, a whiff of I.A.B. waved in my direction. Internal Affairs would have had a field day. I will admit, the crime scene was a circus. I didn't come off looking too good, giving out favors, practically having a tea party in the suspect's living room. Doing tours through the crime scene. I'm not proud of any of that."

"You were being a good friend," Maggie said, squeezing his hand. "Besides, you know Bernie didn't do it."

"What I know, Maggie, is that we've already got the results from the crime lab on the fingerprints on the murder weapon."

"Bernie's?" Maggie asked, her stomach doing a small flip.

"Bernie's."

"Ah," Saint Just said. "Exactly as I predicted. Our murderer is so very obvious."

Wendell looked at Saint Just, shook his head. "Dettmer wanted me to bring her in, but I told him she'd already lawyered–up and it went downhill from there, especially when he found out J.P. was on the scene before I got there. But he's holding off because fingerprints aren't enough, not if we don't find more, and if Bernie can keep refusing to talk to him."

"But I don't remember anything. It's true, Steve. Maggie, tell him about the blackouts."

J.P. held out her hands. "Wrong. Don't tell him about the blackouts. Blackouts are not a defense. Steve, you tell me something, because I'm not buying this. Why isn't Dettmer here with a warrant?"

Saint Just, Maggie noticed, was being unusually quiet, just standing on the edge of the carpet, watching.

"Because the techs found blood in the shower drain, for one. Until we get results on that, there are still more questions than answers, and Dettmer may be a jerk, but he isn't a joke. He won't move until he's got more than fingerprints."

"Like motive," Maggie said. "Does he know about the insurance policies on Buddy?"

"It's Sunday, so he's still pretty limited. But he will tomorrow. What will he know, Maggie?"

"Well, you see—"

"Shut it, Little Mary Sunshine," J.P. said, stepping in front of her. "Why are you here, Steve?"

At last Saint Just spoke. "To help, of course. I vouch for the *left*-tenant personally, J.P."

J.P. looked around the room. Bernie nodded. Maggie all but preened. Saint Just returned her look levelly, then winked; Maggie felt a tingle down to her toes at that wink. Only Steve appeared the least surprised, and he, too, was looking at Saint Just.

"Okay," J.P. said at last. "As long as we don't have to hold hands and sing 'Kum Ba Yah,' I guess we've got a team. Just don't make me regret this. Spill it, Sunshine."

Maggie sat forward on the couch cushions. "Buddy has about three million in life insurance that becomes Bernie's when the seven years are up, except that they don't have to be up yet because now Buddy's really dead, and Bernie gets the money right away to help Toland Books become really, really solvent again after that mess with Kirk, unless she goes to jail for killing him, but the D.A. will definitely see a motive because if Buddy came back to either get cut in on some of the money Bernie inherited from Kirk, or to make her split the three million, which he would have to have been planning all along, and which doesn't exactly exonerate Bernie anyway, because the two of them could have been in on the whole thing together for seven years but then Bernie got greedy at the last minute—is anyone else getting this?"

"We've got motive," Steve said, patting her hand. "Got ya, sweetheart."

The room was quiet for some moments before Saint Just spoke again. "Explain the blood in the shower drain, Wendell, if you please. Are you saying that the murderer committed his crime, then bathed?"

Steve nodded. "Which makes no sense, because Bernie was covered in blood when you guys first saw her—sprayed with it—and you don't get covered in blood, arterial blood, once the victim is dead.

"Unless she killed him. A slice to the throat, then quick lying on her side while Buddy . . . *spurted,* so that you could see the outline of her body in the blood. Then she took off her pajamas, showered to get rid of the worst of it because it was really disgusting, got back into the pajamas, smeared some blood on her face and hands, and then called us. But why would she do that?"

"Sunshine, stick to fiction," J.P. said, standing behind the facing couch, her beringed hands on Bernie's shoulders. "Most women don't like blood all over them and I'm pretty sure Bernie here is no exception. But that's pushing it. You don't shower to wash off blood, then cover yourself with it again. Nope, there has to be another reason for the blood. No wonder Dettmer isn't here yet, cameras in tow. When he arrests her, he wants to make sure it's going to stick, and that I won't be able to paper his office with motions to dismiss. Steve—did they find the victim's clothes yet?"

Steve nodded. "We did. In the bathroom, all folded and stacked neatly on a stool. Why?"

"My turn, if you don't mind," Saint Just said, perching himself on the arm of the couch, beside Maggie. It was like being between particularly appealing bookends. "I can think of no one, including myself, who would, in the throes of or anticipation of—forgive me, ladies—*passion,* who would take the time to neatly fold his or her clothing. Therefore—"

Maggie held up a hand. "Unless he was in Bernie's bathroom when she came home, waiting for her after sneaking in somehow, and just about to take a shower when she found him there, naked? Argue, argue, sex, sex, sleep—sneak downstairs and get a knife. And he's dead?"

"I would not have sex with that bastard," Bernie pronounced tightly. "Drunk, sober, blacked out, sane or crazy as a loon. I would *not* have sex with Buddy James. And fold his clothes? Buddy? First he'd have to get lessons."

"Steve?" J.P. asked. "The rape kit?"

"Nothing's back yet, not officially."

"Okay, unofficially."

"I'm off the case, J.P., but I'm still a cop. Sorry, but you're going to have to go through channels."

"Ah, a man of honor. How refreshing. And they also performed a tox screen, correct? Although those results are undoubtedly still pending as well?"

This was from Saint Just, and Maggie looked up at him in surprise. "Did you say *tox screen*? Oh, wait. Cop shows. I keep forgetting."

"Actually, my dear, the Learning Channel, as well as the History Channel. But we won't nitpick. So, this Dettmer fellow, hot as he is to arrest Bernie, is still awaiting results from the crime lab that would cement his position, although his intent seems already to be chiseled in stone. How long do we have, J.P.?"

"To solve the crime, or to stash Bernie?"

"Excuse me?" Bernie, who was in the midst of pouring herself another scotch, turned to look at her attorney. "This is happening? Are you really going to stash me somewhere?"

"That's dicey, J.P.," Steve warned her.

"Not with voluntary commitment papers, it isn't. She hasn't been charged. She hasn't even been interviewed. Nobody's pulled her passport. She's as free as you or me, and I'm going to make sure she stays that way. Sort of," J.P. said, opening her attaché case and pulling out some official looking forms. "Alex, you were right. Good call. The man's a sleaze, but he's well known, and hot to get his name in print. He jumped at the idea."

Maggie narrowed her eyelids and looked up at Saint Just. "Who's well known? Who jumped? Cripes, Alex, when do you find the time to get into so much trouble? What did you do?"

"Come on, Bernie," J.P. said. "You won't need luggage, so just throw on some clothes and we're off to see the good doctor and get these papers signed. There was no press when I came in, but that isn't going to last much longer. I want to get out of here without a tail."

"Maggie?" Bernie asked, her voice quavering.

"In a minute, Bernie. Alex? Who jumped? Are we talking Doctor Bob here? *My* Doctor Bob? We are, aren't we?"

Saint Just only smiled at her, then crossed to the other couch and sat down beside Bernie. "We're going to protect you, Bernice," he said in a tone that, even to Maggie, inspired trust. "And Maggie guessed correctly. You remember Doctor Bob, don't you? Maggie's psychiatrist? You published his book, *Love Well, Live Free*?"

"Ah, Jesus, Alex, you're going to have me *committed*?"

"Legally tucked away, my dear," Saint Just corrected. "Doctor Bob, it would seem, carries considerable influence, and he has already made arrangements for you to be a guest at a very lovely establishment in something called the Catskills."

Maggie was stunned. He'd sent J.P. to Doctor Bob? He ridiculed Doctor Bob every chance he got, tried to get her to stop her every-Monday visits to the man's office. And now he'd contacted him? Was *using* him? She didn't know if she should be surprised, disgusted, or damn proud he'd thought of it.

"Still New York State, Bernie," J.P. interrupted. "You won't be crossing state lines, the D.A.'s office is only told you're a patient, and nobody can touch you. It's legal, Bernie, marginally, and I want you out of here almost as much as I want you sober."

Maggie blinked at tears stinging her eyes as Bernie seemed to collapse in on herself, suddenly the small, frightened child sitting where the supremely confident, wisecracking, sophisticated woman had been.

"But . . . but what about my interview with Holly What's-her-face?"

"Canceled," J.P. told her. "I wasn't going to mention it, but now that you've brought it up I might as well tell you. Fox wouldn't go along with Alex's demands for a straight interview, no opinions, so that's done. Fox is interviewing Dettmer instead. You know, Alex, it was a good idea, until it backfired. Now Spivak will be saying how she tried to interview Bernie, give her a chance to tell her story, but that Bernie insisted on controlling the interview, so that, as a *real* reporter, Spivak had to say no. This is *not* going to play well to the jury pool, let me tell you. Now go on, Bernie. Get dressed."

"I'll help you," Maggie said, following a slump-shouldered Bernie into the guest room, then pulling her into her embrace while her friend shivered.

"I don't know, Mags. I don't know what scares me more—being arrested or going cold turkey. I might not make it through this."

"Sure, you will," Maggie said, sniffling. "You're my hero, remember? The bravest, most ballsy woman I know."

Bernie pulled away from Maggie, wiped her streaming nose with the sleeve of her caftan. "I am, aren't I? Ballsy." She took a deep, shaky breath, let it out slowly. "Okay. Okay, Maggie, let's do this."

CHAPTER 10

Saint Just opened the door to Tabitha Leighton, Maggie's agent, and stood back as the woman swept past him, blonde hair moving through the breeze of her quick step, the scarf around her neck floating. He nearly missed the large, soft-sided suitcase she all but tossed into his arms.

"Where's Maggie? She must be devastated! Do you know there are about a dozen reporters outside? What a mess; I had to fight my way through. I was in the Hamptons all weekend, incommunicado on something very important, but then I finally turned on the television and saw it and I've been calling ever since. Doesn't anyone answer a phone here? Maggie—*yoo-hoo!* It's Tabby!"

"Maggie's not here," Saint Just told her, gesturing that she should have a seat. "Although I am assured she would be grateful to know that you have rushed here to be a supporting prop in this, Bernice's hour of need."

"Maggie's gone? Gone where? Oh, no. She's down at the jail, isn't she? They've arrested poor Bernie. I knew it, I just knew it. And *now,* of all times."

"Actually," Saint Just said, depositing the suitcase on the floor beside the couch, "Maggie and Bernice and J.P. Boxer, she would be Bernie's solicitor, are on their way to an undisclosed location where Bernice will be receiving remedial training, shall we say."

"Remedial . . . huh?"

"She's going to get help with her drinking problem."

Tabby nodded her head a single time. "Oh. Well. Good. About time, don't you think? But . . . but isn't she going to be arrested?"

"Only if I have not discovered the true murderer before she is, as they say, dried out, and released. She was not best pleased with the plan, but we managed to convince her of its efficacy. Actually, Maggie should be well on her way home by now, Bernice safely tucked up and neatly tucked away."

"Oh, wow. I'm glad I wasn't here when you were talking her into it. So I guess we won't need the suitcase just yet."

"I don't understand," Saint Just said, looking down at the thing.

"Clothing. I brought clothing for Bernie. Just threw a few things into a bag. You know her wardrobe, Alex. Flashy, expensive. Juries hate that. So I brought her a small selection of outfits."

Saint Just looked at Maggie's literary agent, who was dressed, as usual, in flowing scarves, an ankle-length soft skirt, and a quite sedate blouse. Tabby tended toward natural cottons, pastels, clothing that, to be charitable, was serviceable, if usually two sizes too large.

Bernice, on the other hand, dressed with a flamboyance that complemented her fiery hair, her vivid makeup, and her general arrogant carriage. "Versace versus Laura Ashley" was how Maggie had explained the thing to him.

"That was exceedingly thoughtful of you, Tabitha," Saint Just said, then walked over to the answering machine. Earlier he had turned off the ringer on the telephone, not that many knew Maggie's unlisted number.

But when he'd checked her America OnLine account (a habit he should break but was loath to do, as he not only deplored the amount of penis enhancement and Viagra-clone spams she received, but did the occasional housekeeping that removed all but the most flattering fan mail), he had discovered three hundred and eighty-two messages received via her Web site.

A cursory check had revealed that the majority of e-mails were from various reporters, inventive little cretins that they were. Now, he supposed, it was time to discover how many of them had found a way to procure her telephone number.

"Excuse me for a moment, my dear," he said, and pushed the PLAY button, as the message indicator was flashing. There were three messages from Tabby, one from the head of the condo committee tersely demanding that she remove a murder suspect from the premises and rid their formerly quiet building of the masses of reporters outside, and two others:

"Maggie? Maggie, it's Virginia. I saw the news on television and I just had to call. This is terrible, just terrible. Poor Bernie! I'm sure she didn't do it. Gosh, and to think we were all just together at the WAR conference, and so happy. Well, happy, but not really happy, what with the murder and all, huh? Oh, I hate talking to machines. Call me, Maggie, okay? I know it's stupid, and selfish, but do you think this means I won't get a contract with her like she said? Oh, scratch that. I shouldn't have said anything so stupid. I don't care, really I don't. Okay, so I do. I'm shallow, I admit it. Call me, okay? Oh, and the baby is just great. I'll e-mail a photograph to you next week. Call me!"

Saint Just hit the STOP button. "Virginia Neuendorf," he said as Tabby nodded. "Quite a mix of concern and selfishness, not that I blame her."

"I've already got the contract on my desk to go over," Tabby said. "She's safe."

"Good," Saint Just said, and pressed the PLAY button again.

"Margaret? Margaret, I know you're there. This is your mother, Margaret. Can't you stop? I pick up the newspaper and what do I see? That Bernice woman, that's what I see. A murderess! Well, that's it, Margaret. This it your third strike, young lady, and you are *out*. Your father and I insist that you sell that horrible New York apartment and come home where you belong. Can't you people go more than two weeks without killing someone? I have a reputation here, young lady. How can I hold my head up when you keep trampling our faces into the mud? Never, never have I seen such tawdry—what? Evan, if I say Margaret comes home, she comes home. And stop pushing those chocolate things into your mouth. I swear, you're going to clog every artery in your heart and—what do you mean you're not interested in living forever? Was that supposed to be a dig at me? It was, it was a dig at me. You know what? She's just like you, Evan. Smart mouth. Weasely. Sly. It's all your fault. Heaven knows I tried. Margaret? Margaret, you listen to me. Tate already called, all upset, and Erin and Maureen are embarrassed to be your sisters, what with those artsy-fartsy people you run around with in the city. Your own siblings, ashamed! Must you be such a black sheep, always hurting me? It's that writing you do, all that perverted sex and smut. I always knew that Bernice person was trouble. That hair? And she's got a smart mouth. Didn't surprise me she killed her husband. I still think she killed the other one, I don't care that you say someone else did it. Class will tell, Margaret, and that wom—"

"Now there's a bit of luck. It would appear the machine ran out of space before Mrs. Kelly ran out of invective. Shall we just erase this?"

"Oh, God, yes," Tabby said, hugging herself as she shivered. "Come home? Maggie would rather have someone shove bamboo slivers under her fingernails. You know, Alex, I deal with crazy publishers and crazy writers, day in, day out, but that woman scares me."

"She is unique," Saint Just said, holding down the DELETE button. "There, all gone. Do stay and visit until Maggie returns, and that won't be long. I was just collecting some additional cleaning supplies for Sterling, however, and have to return to my own apartment."

"Cleaning supplies? You?"

He picked up a blue bucket holding a plastic bottle of something called Spic 'N Span, and several sponges. "As I said, for Sterling. Join us, please. We've located one chair that is still reasonably intact."

He opened the door and bowed a frowning Tabby across the hall, then let her into the shambles that was once his apartment. The bedrooms and his private study were nearly back in order, and most of the kitchen, but the living and dining rooms were so far untouched.

"What . . . what on earth happened here?"

Saint Just ushered Tabby to that one intact living room chair. "A long story, not really worth telling. Suffice it to say we have come to the conclusion that the previous tenant has something someone else seems to very much want, and that someone else decided to look for that something themselves."

"A robbery," Tabby said, nodding her head. "No. Not a robbery? Alex, what's going on? And Steve? You're here? *Cleaning*?"

Steve, his sleeves rolled up, a large, bulging white garbage bag in his hand, nodded to Tabby. "Like Alex said, long story. Alex? This place was tossed by pros. You do know that, right?"

"Pros?" Tabby looked from one man to the other. "I'm confused. Does this have something to do with Bernie?"

Seeing that there was nothing else for it but to explain, Saint Just did just that, while Killer and Mary Louise, having proved themselves to be quite accomplished workers, began picking through the debris in the living room and dining room.

"The mob?" Tabby said at last, looking around her rather frantically, as if deciding whether or not to bolt for the nearest exit. "But they're dangerous. Maybe even crazy."

"And most definitely messy," Saint Just agreed as Mary Louise began picking up bits of a broken lamp. "But we'll soon have it all to rights."

"You're going to *stay* here? Tell me you're not going to stay here. They might be back."

"Yes, they might, as every room in the apartment was searched. Unless the last place searched was the one in which they discovered what they were after, I would say our visitors left with their hands empty." He frowned slightly, remembering the folder Holly Spivak had given him. "Mostly empty."

"But not before writing that note," Steve said, having just returned from dropping the garbage bag down the chute in the hallway. "I got a call on my cell while I was dumping the garbage, Alex. That friend I told you about? He says we're probably dealing with the Totila family. Enrico Totila. Minor league, nowhere near a John Gotti. Goldblum was their mouthpiece, but Enrico, the head guy, was upstate on a weapons charge when Goldblum was offed, and nobody could get anything to stick to him. He's out now, been out for about six months. He's our guy, count on it."

Tabby got to her feet. "I . . . I think I'd like a glass of water. And I could help in the kitchen. Really." She grabbed the bucket, then picked her way through the living room.

George, who persisted in going by the name Killer even as Saint Just tried his utmost to bring the boy up to snuff, enter him into the business world (i.e., The Streetcorner Orators and Players), surfaced from behind one of the couches, large pieces of a broken vase in his hands.

Killer was a thin, almost pathetically weasel-like lad with a good heart, the brains and courage of a particularly dense doorstop, and the bladder control of an infant.

"Did he say Enrico Totila?" he asked, dropping the pieces into a previously empty metal waste can, where they broke into even smaller pieces.

"Yes, I do believe that's exactly what the *left*-tenant said, George. Why do you ask? Do you know the man?"

"Me?" Killer's small eyes grew almost large in his head. "No. Not me. Don't know him. Oh no."

"Calm yourself, George," Saint Just soothed as the boy backed up three paces, colliding with the wall. "Hang on to your bladder, remember?" Then he sighed, as Killer remained one of the regrets of his life, a youth he could reach at some levels, but not really effectively change. "No, not literally, George."

"You're from up around Morningside Heights, aren't you, George?" Steve asked as Killer dropped his arms to his sides, blushing. "The Totila family doesn't operate up there."

"No, sir. But his aunt Isabella, she lived next door to my grandma, and Mr. Totila, he'd visit her. He spit on me once."

"How utterly charming. Thank you for sharing that, George. And now, I think perhaps you should toddle off to Mario's for some of his marvelous sandwiches and salads, to reward everyone for their kind assistance. Oh, and do *not* speak to any of the reporters who may remain outside on the flagway."

"Okay," Killer, ever obedient, said, taking the money Saint Just handed him and all but bolting for the door.

"Now," Saint Just said, turning to Wendell. "Where do I find this Enrico Totila person?"

"You don't," Steve said, shaking his head. "He finds you. Hell, he's already found you. What we have to do is find what he sent those goons to find."

"And you don't mind that I've refused to call in your cohorts?"

"Normally, yeah, I'd mind. I'd mind a lot. But let's just say I'm not too happy with my cohorts, as you call them, right now. Besides, this one would go straight to Dettmer, and he's too happy as it is, with Bernie. Plus, I have a feeling you want a piece of these guys. You know, the TV set?"

"I would be a liar if I disagreed. Even Sterling, as you said, would want a piece of them. You can have them after we're done, if that's all right."

"Just don't leave me out of the loop. I'm giving you some rope, I'm not giving you the whole damn lasso."

"Whatever that is. So, you'll help us find the perps and then make the bust yourself after we're done with them?"

"Maggie's right. You watch too much television. We don't say perps. TV cops say perps."

"Really? What do you call them, then?"

"Bastards, pieces of—well, I guess they can't say that on TV, huh?"

"I don't think so, no."

"Cable. They can do it on cable. And movies." Wendell

righted an end table. "You know, Blakely, we're sort of getting along here."

"Yes, I had noticed that," Saint Just said, picking up what had to be a hand-crocheted doily. "Rather odd, considering we're in competition."

"Maggie, right?" Steve ran a hand over his hair. "She told me you're not close cousins."

"Very distant, yes," Saint Just said. "I'm quite . . . fond of her."

Steve grinned. "I guess then we can rule out flipping a coin for her, huh? Just kidding. So, you're staying? Not going back to England?"

"No, I've no plans to return to . . . my estates any time soon. I've been longing to come here for some years, you understand."

"Okay, it was worth a shot. So we're in competition. I can handle that. Doesn't mean we can't be friends, or work together."

Saint Just struck a pose. "Oh, *Left*-tenant, that had to hurt."

"You got that in one. But, hey, we're doing all right, so far. I mean, working together. If we could only keep Maggie from sticking her nose in, that is."

"That adorable little nose is a problem, and I agree that we should collaborate in keeping that nose out of trouble, even while we acknowledge that our intents are the same and our hopes vastly different," Saint Just said.

"If you just said that we protect Maggie, keep her out of trouble, but we're both free to . . . well, go after her, then you got it."

"How very wonderful, and allow me to express my condolences at what I am convinced will be your undoubtedly futile attempts to *get* her. Now, having cried friends, if we might return to the problem at hand? With Bernice safely out of the picture, Maggie will consider herself free to insert her inquisitive nose, not only in the investigation of Buddy James's demise, but also in the small problem we've encountered with this Totila person."

"Who?"

Saint Just closed his eyes, then slowly turned around, to see

Maggie holding on to the doorknob. "Back so soon? How delightful. And is Bernice settled comfortably?"

"Are you kidding? I have imprints from her fingernails on both forearms. Want to see? But J.P. finally peeled her off, and we left. Nobody can visit her or call her. Not even J.P. So, what have I missed? Who's Totila?"

"Like I said, we work together," Steve said quietly to Saint Just.

Saint Just inclined his head a mere fraction in acknowledgment of Wendell's whisper. "Enrico Totila, my dear Maggie, was the late Harry Goldblum's client, his only client, establishing him as our prime suspect in this wanton destruction of my property. The plasma television machine, remember."

"Oh. The mob boss who ordered this place trashed to find whatever it is Harry had and Irene's got? I got it. So? We confront him?"

"Heaven preserve me from females possessing the world's most undesirable trait."

"Here we go," Maggie said, glaring at him. "And what would that be?"

"Pluck," Saint Just said, lifting his quizzing glass to his eye and looking at her through it, knowing his eye was now enlarged by the glass, knowing that she'd love to, in her words, "bop him one" for using that glass on her. "Yes, pluck. It's vastly unbecoming to the gentler sex, whose role in life is to defer, stand back, admire, and then applaud their gentlemen."

"Okay, consider me off the team, at least for now," Steve said, backing up.

"Would you stop, both of you? I'm not going to be insulted, and I'm not going to be diverted, or whatever it is you two have dreamed up between you."

"She heard us," Steve said to Saint Just.

"Yes, I believe I've already deduced as much, thank you, Wendell. Maggie? The *left*-tenant and I have, as you've already heard, joined forces. In Bernice's behalf, and to ferret out whatever is going on here in my apartment. We have also cried friends in protecting you from . . . well, from you, my dear. Which means, behave yourself and don't get into trouble."

As Maggie stood there, jaw dropped, he turned to Wendell and said, "This is where she says *bite me.*"

Maggie closed her mouth, then opened it again to say, "No, it's not. I understand. You want me thinking, helping, but not acting. Not doing anything on my own, getting myself in trouble."

"Or possibly shot at, yes," Saint Just said, patiently waiting for the other shoe to drop. Because this was his Maggie. He'd lived inside her head. He knew the girl, bless her.

"Yeah? Well, you can both go to hell, okay? Bernie's my friend and she needs help, and if that means I end up sticking my neck out for her, then that's what happens. And the same goes for Sterling. You?" she said, pointing to Saint Just. "You just take care of yourself. You, too, Steve. Now, I'm going to bed."

"The moment she's finished looking up Enrico Totila on Google, although I doubt the mob lists its addresses in their directory pages," Saint Just told Wendell, wiping his quizzing glass on his shirt sleeve as Maggie turned to leave the apartment.

"I could seriously hate you sometimes," she said, turning back to glare at him.

"Maggie? Maggie, is that you?"

Saint Just watched in some amusement as Maggie attempted to hide a wince at the sound of Tabitha Leighton's voice. Maggie liked Tabby, very much, but the agent did have this annoying way of saying all the wrong things at precisely the wrong time.

"Hi, Tabby," Maggie said, waving weakly.

Tabby, wearing Sterling's KISS THE COOK apron and large yellow rubber gloves, picked her way across the cluttered floor and put those gloved hands on Maggie's shoulders, brushed cheek against cheek. "How's Bernie? Have they locked her up tight?

She must feel as if she's already in prison. I saw the news before I came here, and they're calling her the Black Widow. She shouldn't wear black to the arraignment. I brought her some clothes, but all of that can wait. I've got the most *fabulous* news!"

Such as now, Saint Just thought, shaking his head.

CHAPTER 11

Maggie wanted a shower, a long, hot one. She wanted something gooey, preferably chocolate. And she wanted to be alone. Completely alone. She wanted to shed a few tears for Bernie, who had looked like a frightened child as she and J.P. had left her at the clinic with a kindly enough woman who also had the build of a fullback and one hamlike hand wrapped tightly around Bernie's arm.

She wanted to look up Enrico Totila on Google, exactly as Alex had said. She wanted to change the sheets on the guest room bed again, and make sure both Sterling and Alex promised to sleep there tonight.

She wanted a cigarette. She'd kill for a cigarette. No, scratch that. Not a good choice of words. But she wanted one, desperately. An hour up to the clinic, an hour there, an hour back—three hours without a cigarette. The thumbnail on her left hand was already bitten down to the quick—a habit she thought she'd lost at twelve.

But Bernie couldn't have a drink. If Bernie couldn't have a drink, then she couldn't have a cigarette. It wouldn't be fair. Not that anyone got locked up because they smoked. Yet.

Maggie stared at her reflection in the bathroom mirror. "I am an addict," she said quietly, forcing out each word. "I am a . . . damn. Nicaholic? No, that's stupid. Try again, Maggie." She lifted her chin. "I am addicted to nicotine."

Her brother Tate had gone to military school, and for some reason a snippet of something he had to repeat to upperclassmen when he was a plebe—freshman—snuck into her mind now. "I am a worm, sir, a wiggly worm, sir. . . ."

Maggie lowered her head, shook it. "Maybe tomorrow," she said, and headed back to the living room, which was pretty much stuffed to the rafters with people she currently wished would all find somewhere else to go.

"Tuna's fine, thanks," Steve Wendell was saying, accepting a wrapped sandwich from Mary Louise as he straddled one of the chairs at the game table.

Killer was sitting in Maggie's favorite spot, the window seat, dangling string cheese into his gaping mouth with all the dexterity of an octopus in boxing gloves.

She looked behind her, to see that Sterling and Alex were conferring in a corner of the kitchen, and Sterling didn't look very happy.

Tabby, spreading a napkin in her lap, her sandwich waiting for her on the coffee table, didn't see her, so Maggie retreated from the living room and went straight to Alex and Sterling.

"What's up?"

Sterling, bless him, immediately looked at the ceiling, before recovering with a sheepish grin. "That's not really what you meant, is it, Maggie? Sorry, and all of that."

"That's okay, Sterling. Hey, I like your gloves."

Alex did one of those highbrow English *tsk-tsk* things and said, "Please don't encourage him, Maggie. Sterling, take those things off. I'm begging you, which is something I don't ordinarily do, but you must know you look ridiculous."

Sterling held up his hands, still encased in bright yellow rubber gloves. "But I still have to clean the bathrooms and Tabby says it's important to protect one's hands when one is . . . oh, all right."

"Bless you," Alex said, then turned to Maggie. "Bernice is really settled in and fine?"

Maggie felt quick tears sting at her eyes. "No," she said, almost whined. "And I'm such a lousy friend. If she's going to dry out, then I shouldn't light up, right? Support her, you know?"

"It's a laudable idea," Alex told her kindly, then added, "but I do believe you have to stop smoking for *you,* not for anyone else."

"Yeah, that's what Doctor Bob says. I see him tomorrow morning."

"Ah, yes, our every-Monday-morning session with the good doctor. You wouldn't consider giving up those sessions for *you,* would you?"

"I know you don't like that I go there."

"Always the mistress of understatement."

"But I think I'm finally getting somewhere, Alex. I mean, I really don't want to smoke. Besides, I want to thank him for helping out with Bernie when you asked. He didn't have to do that."

"No, he didn't," Alex said, nodding his head. "By the way, you owe him five hundred dollars."

"I . . . he . . . you're *kidding.* He did it for money? He's a *doctor.* How could he have done it for *money*?"

"I believe he termed it a consultation fee," Alex said, inspecting his fingernails.

"Oh," Maggie said consideringly. "I guess that makes sense. Five hundred dollars?"

"A pittance compared to what you've paid the man over the years."

"Would you stop? He's helping me."

"Really? Your mother phoned earlier, left a message. She'd like you to move back to New Jersey, tuck yourself under her protective, maternal wing. Demanded it, actually."

"Sweet Jesus," Maggie said, maybe pleaded, as her stomach hit her toes and her knees buckled slightly.

Alex touched a hand to her cheek. "Yes, Doctor Bob has been such a tremendous help. It's so obvious. Maggie, my dearest girl, you're rapidly approaching three and thirty years of age. Isn't it time you stood up to the woman? Faced her down, informed her that you are an adult now, and in charge of your own life?"

"Sure," Maggie said tersely, but not moving, because Alex was touching her, and his comfort, his hand, felt good. "I'll do just that. Right after I can stand up to the dry cleaner when he tells me it's my fault he lost my blue coat. Can we talk about something else?"

Alex smiled at her. "We could *do* something else, to take your mind off all your varied worries."

"Um . . . excuse me?" Sterling said, gulped. "I think I'll go wash up your bathroom, Saint Just, if that's all right with you? I mean, if you're going to be romantical, and all of that. Snake has come back from visiting his mother and he's still over there. He was going to throw out your television machine, Saint Just. I'm so sorry about that. I'll take him a sandwich and we'll keep on straightening up. I can't abide the shambles, I'm afraid. Maggie? Did you know you made me neat? Isn't that amazing?"

Alex was looking at Maggie as Sterling rambled on. Maggie was looking at Alex. Maggie was forgetting that there was anyone else in the room, in the world. She allowed herself to start leaning forward, her eyes on Alex's mouth.

"No!" she said suddenly, stepping back, grabbing onto Sterling's arm. "Alex, tell him no."

"It's all right, Sterling. You may go, since you're so hot to find reasons to wear those atrocious gloves. Remembering your waistcoat, I'd say it's probably the yellow that holds the attraction. Say hello to Vernon for me, if you will, and give him my thanks for his help."

Maggie watched Sterling leave the room, then turned on Alex. "Are you nuts? He'll see the threat on the mirror."

"Actually, no, he won't. It has already been taken care of, removed. Now, as we've put it off long enough, and Tabitha has doubtless finished her sandwich, I suppose it's time we heard her *fabulous* news."

"I could have choked her for that," Maggie said, sighing. "I mean, she means well, but tonight? How can there be any good news tonight?"

"Slap me down for saying so, but I thought we might have been making some *happy* progress a moment ago," Alex said, extending his arm, so that she took it. "Now, to listen to Tabitha and then usher her out. Usher all of them out."

"Stop that," Maggie told him, leaning against his arm. "You don't really think I think sex is the answer to all my problems."

"No, but I thought you might want to consider it."

"Bite me."

"Ah, an invitation. I'd be delighted, my dear. Nibble, that is."

Maggie's stomach tightened. "Cut that out. You're just trying to get me all flustered and make Steve think something was going on in the kitchen. That is so low, Alex."

"Not if it had worked," he said, dropping his arm as she let go of it and headed for the couch, to plop herself rather inelegantly next to Tabby.

"Okay, let's have it. What's this fabulous news?"

Tabby patted her mouth with her napkin and replaced it on her lap. "Maybe this isn't the time?"

"Good," Maggie said, slapping her knees and getting to her feet. "Because you're right, Tabby, now isn't the time. I've got Bernie on my mind, news hounds at the front door, the mob after Alex and Sterling, my mother on my back, and—"

"We sold to the movies."

Maggie stood, mouth still open, and blinked. Blinked again. "*What* did you say?"

Tabby openly preened. "I've been working on this for months, Maggie, with my agent associate in Los Angeles. I didn't want to tell you, get your hopes up, but this weekend cinched it. We've sold your first three books for television movies. Now, I know it's not the big screen, but it's a start, and a good one. Someone else will write the scripts, but we've got approval—

that took some doing, let me tell you—and they've even invited you out there to watch the whole thing. Cast selection, you name it. I worked hard, Maggie. I really did."

Maggie sat down. It was either that or fall down. "We . . . we sold to the movies? Ohmigod . . ."

"Hey, Maggie, that's great," Steve said, sitting himself on the arm of the couch and leaning over to give her a kiss. She blinked again. Her ears had begun to buzz.

Tabby took Maggie's hand in hers, patted it. "I didn't get everything I wanted. It was a package deal, the first three, but I figure that it's better to get less up front for three than just take our chances with one. We have to build an audience, although they're counting on your readers tuning in. And I got some substantial bonus clauses written in, as well as the possibility that, if the ratings are good enough, the third one goes to the large screen. Or, and this could be even better, they turn it into a series. They've even agreed to put your name on them. You know, like *Cleo Dooley's Viscount Saint Just Mysteries—The Case of the Misplaced Earl.* It's long, but having your name there is big, really big. Maggie? Say something."

So she did. She said the first stupid thing that entered her head: "I can't fly to California."

"Oh, jeez," Mary Louise said, grabbing up her purse and motioning for Killer to follow her. "See? Told you she was weird. Come on, let's get out of here. I've got class in the morning. Hey, Maggie, you don't care if I keep the purse, right? You know, the one you loaned me for the conference? I kind of like it."

"I can't fly to California. I just can't."

"Right. Knew you wouldn't mind. See ya, Vic," she said, waving to Alex. "We see Mr. Pierre tomorrow at one, right? Gotta sign on the dotted line."

Vaguely, Maggie heard Alex agree to meet with Mary Louise. She heard Mary Louise, but she didn't seem able to form either the words "I didn't give you that purse, Alex did, and I want it back, damn it!" or "Don't call him Vic. It's Viscount, *Viscount.*"

Alex. Alexandre Blake, the Viscount Saint Just. Her Alex Blakely. He'd heard what Tabby had said. He had to have heard, even understood. Yet he hadn't said anything. Why hadn't he said anything?

"Alex?" she said, leaning forward to see past Steve, to see him standing there, fingering the grosgrain ribbon on his quizzing glass. "What do you think?"

"I'm considering the possibilities, actually. Very good, Tabitha, procuring script approval. And we'll be able to weigh in on who is to play the characters in the books? I should not wish anyone I did not approve of pretending to be—Saint Just."

Maggie rolled her eyes. Oh, this was going to be good. One fictional character casting another fictional character. Casting himself. "Maybe you want to play the role, Alex?" she asked, then immediately wished she hadn't.

"It's another of the possibilities I've been contemplating, yes."

"But . . . but he can't do that. He's gorgeous, and I know you based your Saint Just on him," Tabby said, tugging on Maggie's arm. "But they want real actors. Maggie? Tell him."

"She's right, Alex," Maggie said, grinning at him. "They want real actors, not real characters. Not that it matters, because we're not going."

"Because you can't fly to California," Alex said, inclining his head slightly. "Yes, we've heard. Might we now inquire as to why?"

Maggie looked from one to the other, to Tabby, to Steve, and at last, to Alex. "Because they have earthquakes out there, that's why, and you damn well know it. I don't like to fly anyway, but the minute my plane's wheels hit the tarmac out there, count on it—*bam,* the big one will hit. Next thing we know, Nevada is beach front property. Not that I'll care, because I'll still be strapped to my seat in a tin can, three miles under the ocean and a couple of million pounds of California."

"Quite the verbal picture," Alex said to Steve. "She's a writer, you know. Chock full of imagination."

"Maybe you can talk to Doctor Bob about this tomorrow," Tabby said. "I know he's helping me with David. I'm doing affirmations now. You know. I am a good person, a worthy person, a good, worthy person deserving of love. Really, Maggie. Affirmations."

"Tabby, David sleeps with anything he can catch. How do affirmations change that?"

"I don't know," Tabby said, sounding hurt. "But I know I don't deserve it, because I'm a good, worthy person."

"No, you don't deserve it. You don't deserve David catting around, Tabby. Bernie doesn't deserve to be blamed for Buddy's murder, Alex and Sterling don't deserve to have that apartment over there trashed and their stuff all ruined, and I don't—well, I guess I'm doing okay, aren't I? I'm sorry, Tabby. You're right, this is great news. Me, selling to the movies."

"Made-for-television movies," Tabby corrected. "Wait until Bernie hears about this. She'll be hot to repackage your earlier books, maybe even with photographs of the cast on the covers. Saint Just, in the flesh. Can you imagine the *god* they're going to have to get to be your perfect hero?"

Maggie shifted her gaze to Alex with an unspoken "don't you say it, don't you say a word" flashing in her eyes.

Steve bent down and kissed Maggie, then got to his feet. "Congratulations, Maggie. I'd better get going, though. Alex?"

"Steve," Alex said, and Maggie shook her head. She didn't know why, but she was pretty sure she'd liked it better when they'd addressed each other as Wendell and Blakely. She did not need the two men in her life liking each other. She definitely didn't like them planning ways to keep her in the dark about Bernie's case, about this Enrico Totila guy.

"Hey, where are you two going? If you're going to talk about Bernie or the mob, you can talk right here, damn it."

"Yes, you do that, just as Maggie says," Tabby said, gathering herself and standing up. "I'll just clear away all this food, all right? I really don't want to be involved, you understand. It's not that I don't care, really it isn't. But it's frightening."

Maggie waited until Tabby had loaded plates and glasses on a tray and escaped to domestic bliss in the kitchen before saying, "So? What's next? Start with Bernie."

Alex gave a wave of his hand. "Oh, go ahead. She'll never let us rest, elsewise."

Steve went back to the straight-back chair, straddled it once more. "Okay, here's what I've got. Maggie? You already know about the blood in the drain."

She nodded.

"Okay, but that wasn't all there was."

"It's a shower drain," Maggie said. "There's got to be a lot of stuff in it, right?"

Steve rubbed at the back of his neck. "Yeah, right. The blood. I'll find out when they get an ID on it, through my source, count on that. And . . . the rest of it. Man, this is why I don't like working with women."

"Gee, thanks," Maggie said, looking at Alex. "No wonder you two like each other."

Steve was still rubbing at the back of his neck, and avoiding her eyes. "They found hairs, too. It was easy to identify Bernie's—red, you know? But four others."

"Four other hairs," Maggie said, nodding.

"Four other, um, *donors,*" Steve clarified, his cheeks reddening. "Maybe more. Four different ones so far."

"Oh," Maggie said, looking down at her hands. "Well, she is single, you know. Is that it? Is that all you know?"

"Pretty much, yeah. Nobody signed in as Bernie's guest, I know that, so either she snuck Buddy in the back way, or he got in on his own."

Maggie sat up. "If he got in on his own, so could somebody else."

"Damn, Maggie, I've already got Bernie and Buddy. Don't add to the mix."

"We have to, Steve, unless you think Buddy committed suicide in Bernie's bed, holding Bernie's hand to the knife while he sliced his own throat, and nobody would believe that. So, somebody else could get in if Buddy got in on his own?"

"Anything's possible."

"Not anything, Steve," Alex said, pocketing his quizzing glass. "It is not possible that Bernice murdered Buddy James."

"Wrong. It is possible. I agree, she would have had to be really strong to damn near cut his head off like that, but she could have done it. Crime of passion. And, once Dettmer gets that stuff about the insurance? He's going to see a slam dunk here. I wish I could trace James's steps, backtrack on his moves. I could maybe get something there."

Maggie felt Alex's gaze on her, but wouldn't look at him. "Oh, why not?"

"If you insist, my dear. Steve, it may be possible that Maggie and I have discovered the recent whereabouts of Buddy James."

"Damn. I should just turn in my shield and pack groceries or something. Where?"

Maggie filled him in quickly about Bernie's Connecticut house and the evidence they had found when they drove up there, Alex adding, "The man was a bit of a slob, with a decided appetite for what you call fast food. Pizza in particular. There were bags and boxes everywhere, along with some of his personal belongings. I would deduce that he had been in residence at least a fortnight and, as the bills I saw scattered about included a delivery charge, remained hidden in the house and had his meals brought to him."

"Dettmer has to be told about this."

Alex stiffened, and Maggie fought an urge to duck. "I beg your pardon?"

"Withholding evidence, Blakely. I can't do that."

"Ah, Wendell, but I can, and you're on holiday. We are friends here, talking, and anything we say is in confidence."

Maggie hid a smile. They were back to Wendell and Blakely. Good. "Guys, guys, think about this. So Buddy was at Bernie's house in Connecticut. So what? I mean, face it, Steve, you have to know that Alex and I went through the guy's clothes and everything. There's nothing there for Dettmer to find. Is there, Alex?"

"Don't answer that, because I think I'd have to start yelling if either one of you is naive enough to think contaminating yet another possible crime scene, or at least a scene connected to a crime, is like your good deed for the day, or something. Oh, and you can do a better job examining evidence than the lab boys. Sure you can." He got to his feet and slammed the chair back under the table. "Cripes almighty, I can't believe this."

Alex perched himself on the arm of the couch. "A trifle perturbed, the good *left*-tenant, wouldn't you say? Tell me, Maggie, do you find him more or less appealing this way?"

"Shut up," Maggie hissed at him, then got to her feet and went to Steve. "We're sorry. But it wouldn't be good if you went to Dettmer with this, would it? I mean, now Alex and I have our fingerprints all over the place. And the real estate agent is sure to remember us, come to think of it."

"Aiding and abetting, concealing evidence, corrupting a crime scene, hiding the prime suspect—anything else you two? Or are you all done now? Never mind, I'm on vacation. I don't want to know. Maggie—tomorrow."

Once the door had closed behind him, slammed behind him, Maggie blew out a breath and sat down again. "That wasn't good."

"I agree. He's of no use to us now."

"What? Is that all you can think about? That he won't be of use to us? What about him? What about Steve? He's really mad, Alex."

"No, he's in a snit. He'll move beyond it. He did say he'd see you tomorrow. Now come along, let's roust Sterling and Snake out of the apartment and get some rest."

Maggie looked at the mantel clock; it was almost midnight. "Good idea. These have got to have been the two longest, most screwed up days in my life."

She didn't resist when Alex slid his arm around her waist as they walked to the door, and then across the hallway to the apartment. The door was ajar, but that didn't mean anything.

The note on the floor just inside the door, however, did.

Alex picked it up, Maggie immediately feeling icy panic sliding down her spine as she saw the cut out letters that made up the message:

TErn It oVEr OR the LiTtEL gUy Dies

Below the cut and pasted letters was another line, hastily scribbled: *And the other one to.*

Maggie ran toward the kitchen calling, "Sterling! Sterling! Snake, where are you?" She knew it wouldn't help, that they were gone, but she had to try. From the kitchen to the hallway, into the bedrooms, calling out their names until Alex caught up with her and pulled her close against his chest.

"Oh, Alex, what are we going to do?" She pushed herself free of his arms. "Steve. He just left. Maybe I can still catch him."

She turned to race to the elevator, but Alex took her arm, held her. "He's already gone, Maggie. Go back across the hall and I'll be right with you, after I lock this door."

"But . . . but . . ."

"Now, now, calm yourself. In a situation like this panic, my dear, aids nothing. And I might suggest that we can divest ourselves of Tabitha's presence."

Maggie took a deep breath, which didn't do much to calm her. "Good point. But I'm waiting for you."

CHAPTER 12

"Well, that's all done," Tabby said, entering the living room just as Maggie and Saint Just closed the door to the hallway. "You know, Maggie, it would be a lot less expensive to buy the meat and bread separately and make up your own—what's wrong? You're really pale, Maggie. Something else is wrong, isn't it? Do I want to know?"

"No, you don't," Maggie said, holding her hands to her head. "You don't want to know. Go home, Tabby. Go home, and I'll talk to you tomorrow, okay?"

"That was certainly well played, my dear, although perhaps not quite as subtle as I might have liked. Still, you did restrain yourself from making *shooing* motions with your hands," Saint Just whispered, busying himself with leaning his sword cane, just rescued from the apartment, against the wall.

"You can do better?" she whispered back.

"Go home? Well, it is late." Tabby looked at Saint Just. "Alex?"

He stepped forward and took her hand, bowed over it. "I cannot begin to express my gratitude at your stunning success in settling Maggie's books so nicely, Tabitha. And thank you so much for all your concern, as well as your splendid housekeeping. However, the hour is late, and Maggie, dear girl, is not quite herself. The commotion over Bernice, you understand. Now, might I escort you downstairs to have Paul hail a hack?"

"Show-off," Maggie muttered on her way to the couch.

Tabby frowned. "Um . . . okay." She picked up her sweater, then looked at Maggie, who was sitting and staring at . . . actually she was simply staring. "Get some sleep, honey. I'll call you tomorrow. Ba–bye."

By the time Saint Just returned to Maggie's condo, she had kicked off her shoes and was sitting cross-legged on one of the couches, smoking like the proverbial chimney. To help her think, he knew. "Paul saw nothing, in case you might have thought to ask. As I had to wake him to make my inquiry, I had already fairly well deduced that he'd be no help to us."

"Damn. Socks would have seen something. Okay, okay, let's forget that. I'm calmer now. Here's what we have to do. We have to call Steve," she said, not even looking up at him. "He'll call in the FBI and they'll set up a task force or something in here, waiting for the call from the kidnappers to arrange the drop, and we'll . . ."

"Sterling isn't real, Maggie," Saint Just reminded her, sitting on the opposite couch, neatly crossing one leg over the other. "Thanks to Mary Louise and her inspired forgeries of all the necessary papers, Sterling and I *appear* real, but a closer inspection would prove that the pair of us arrived from nowhere only a few short months ago. Do you really want that? The FBI, and eventually, the media, probing into Sterling's life? Oh, and Wendell, of course. You'd have to tell him. Dear Steve, sit down, I have something to tell you. Alex and Sterling are real, you can see them, they're really here, but they didn't get here in the usual way. They popped out of my head."

"Shit," Maggie said, which Saint Just took to mean *no,* she didn't want that. "So what do we do? That note was so stupid. We still don't even know what *it* is. And you and Sterling might be fictional, Alex, but Snake isn't. And neither are these goons. They *kill* people."

"I am aware of that," Saint Just said tersely. He was holding on, attempting to project an air of calm. But, inside, he very much longed to throttle somebody.

How dare they! How dare they go after Sterling, a completely lovable, guileless, and, unfortunately, often clueless Sterling Balder? If they injured him, if they frightened him, if they harmed a single hair on the man's balding head . . .

"Alex? Alex, I'm talking to you."

"Pardon me, my dear," Saint Just said, only then realizing that his hands had clenched into fists. This wouldn't do. The Viscount Saint Just was the epitome of calm at all times, in any storm. A veritable brick in a crisis. The Viscount Saint Just held all the answers, all the solutions, and possessed all the derring-do necessary to save any day. With aplomb.

Except that, he was realizing more and more, the Viscount Saint Just had Maggie Kelly making sure all the miscreants failed and her perfect hero triumphed in the end. Damn. Damn and blast. The whole thing was quite lowering at best, and at worst it was dangerous.

"Alex? Don't apologize. And stop looking so far away, okay? Talk to me."

Maggie Kelly as Cleo Dooley, setting up problems for her hero to solve, giving him the leading role, the brilliant mind, the inventive ploys, even the current heroine—and most definitely the happy endings. It came from Maggie. Everything came from Maggie. He was a fraud, a fake, a . . . a paper thin creation. Could he really allow Sterling's fate, Vernon's fate, to rest in the hands of such a sham?

But this was no time to lament truths he'd only just realized, or to attempt to play the hero at Sterling's expense. It was lowering, yes, depressing—and, dear God, totally out of *character*—but there it was. He needed help.

Saint Just blinked. "Perhaps we should contact the good *left*–tenant."

"Really? Wow, what hit you?" She grabbed the phone from

the side table and punched in the numbers. Then waited. "He's not answering. I'll try his cell." More number pushing, more waiting. "He has it turned off. Man, he must really be mad at me. Now what do we do?"

Saint Just took his quizzing glass from his pocket and placed it over his head, began fingering the ribbon as the glass swung at the end of it. Perhaps this mindless activity, one of his trademarks courtesy of Maggie, would help him think.

After all, he was more than a cipher, a figment of her imagination. He had gotten himself here, hadn't he? With no help from Maggie. He had, in his arrogance, solved two murders since his arrival.

So why the apprehension? Why this sudden, inexplicable fear? He'd never felt fear, not in any measurable amount.

"I hope Sterling is behaving himself," Maggie said, putting down the phone.

And there it was. Sterling. His Sterling. His friend. His very good friend. Sterling held all the answers to this sudden bout of insecurity and, yes, self-pity.

Because this wasn't a lark, this wasn't an intellectual exercise. This most certainly wasn't fiction. This was Sterling, alone, possibly injured, and with the threat of death hanging above his head unless he, Saint Just, could save him. Knowing Sterling, he also knew his friend depended on him, expected him to arrive on the scene in full rig-out and complete glory to effect a rescue—preferably a flamboyant rescue. He could not, he *would* not let him down.

"I'm sure Sterling is fine, Maggie," Saint Just said, getting to his feet to pour them each a glass of wine. Taking charge, taking command, because that was what he'd been born to do, even if he had only been "born" six years ago, in Maggie's fertile imagination. "As for us? I fear there's little we can do save to wait for some communication from his captors. That, and locating this ridiculous *it* they seem to crave."

Maggie accepted one of the glasses and took a sip. "Yes,

you're right. That's what we need to do. I'll call Steve back, leave messages on both his phones, and tell him to call me on my cell. Where is it? I want to take it with us while we search the apartment again."

"You do know that it would be reasonable to assume that whatever these thugs want departed the apartment with Mrs. Goldblum?"

"I know. But we've got to come up with something. Even a fake something. Something we can say we have so that they agree to meet us and we can see Sterling."

"I concur," Saint Just said, putting down his wine glass. "Shall we?"

Maggie beat him to the door and across the hallway, into the apartment. "Wow, it looks a lot better. They did a good job."

"Yes, they did. Now we must do a better one."

For two hours they searched, knocking on walls, stamping on floorboards.

"Alex, come here," Maggie called from the living room as he contemplated pulling the refrigerator away from the kitchen wall. "I've found something."

He hurried to the living room to see her sitting on the floor, pulling a multitude of crumpled papers out of the bottom of a very large brass pot. "What is it, Maggie?"

"Old bank statements and canceled checks. She must have used them to stuff this pot before she put the plant container in it. You know how old people can't stand to waste anything."

"Actually, I don't. But do go on."

"Shut up and look at this one," she said, holding up one of the statements.

"I don't . . ." He sighed. This being imperfect rather than perfect was beginning to prove a strain on his sensibilities. "Explain, if you please. I'm convinced you're all agog to do just that."

Maggie got to her feet, took the statement from him. "They're from 1995, all of them. I guess she figured she was safe to toss them after seven or so years. IRS, you know."

"Nine years, Maggie. Nineteen ninety-five would mean nine years. And the same year, I believe, her husband was murdered."

"Hey, right. This is good. Anyway, she shows a deposit, third of every month from March on, for a cool fifteen thousand. Was he murdered in February, do you remember? Oh, well, never mind. Ten thousand of that goes out later in the month. She uses a check payable to cash so I can't tell where it goes, but it goes in like clockwork on the third. I'll bet it still does."

"Blackmail? Ill-gotten rewards from illegal activities?"

"I don't know, but I doubt it. I don't think the mob works on the installment plan, Alex. It could be some sort of income Harry set up before he died, was murdered. Something perfectly legal and legitimate. No matter what, Irene wasn't a poor little old lady living on some meager fixed income. She wasn't loaded, but she was plenty comfortable."

"And this aids us how?"

"Wait, I'm not done. You know what I didn't find, Alex?"

He wanted to get back to the refrigerator. He felt certain he could move it if he just found the proper leverage. "You didn't find anything the mob might want."

"No, I didn't. But I also didn't find any canceled checks for rent on this place. Or a monthly condo fee, like I pay. She owns this place, Alex. She owns it and nobody knows. I'll bet Harry made some private arrangement when they bought it, some under the table deal with the seller. Why would they do that?"

Saint Just shrugged. "I'm afraid I must admit my ignorance. To save herself the monthly condominium fee?"

"Or Harry bought the place with those ill-gotten gains you mentioned. Paid cash. Mob money, you know? Under the table bucks the IRS never got to hear about? With some extra bucks for the seller so he kept his mouth shut."

"I believe I'm getting the headache. All this unbecoming cant."

"Slang is slang, and you watch enough TV to know what I

mean." She threw down the papers, the checks fluttering to the recently cleaned hardwood floors. "Yeah, well, it is interesting, and I'd love to get my hands on Irene Goldblum and ask her a few questions. Just not right now, huh? We keep looking?"

"We continue looking, yes," Saint Just agreed, sparing a moment to look at the bare space over the fireplace, where his marvelous plasma television machine had so recently hung in all its glory. "Maggie?"

"Hmmm?" she said, having replaced the small ficus tree and in the process of shoving sphagnum moss around the top once more.

"The landscape. I put it in one of the closets, but Sterling took it downstairs, to the storage area."

"You're kidding. How big is it?"

"Quite large. Quite homely. Shall we? It may mean nothing, but perhaps the area holds other secrets."

"We'd need the key to Mrs. G's bin."

"I saw some keys in one of the kitchen drawers," Saint Just said, already heading that way. He was progressing, doing something, and it felt good. *Remain calm, Sterling, good friend. I will not let any harm come to you.*

Dear Journal,

I'm not really writing this because my hands are tied behind my back, tied to Snake's hands, actually, and the two of us are sitting in a dark room somewhere, but I am writing this inside my head because Saint Just always says that it is helpful to talk to one's self about problems in order to discover workable solutions.

I feel rather silly talking to myself. So now I'll talk to you, inside my head, and see if a workable solution presents itself.

Let's see. First, dear Journal, I opened the door, which, Saint Just would tell me, was not only my first action but my initial mistake. What could I have been thinking? Oh, I remember. I was thinking that perhaps it was Saint Just come to help us finish straightening the apartment. My, perhaps I wasn't thinking but only imagining hopefully.

Dear Saint Just. He wasn't created to be domestic. It isn't his fault. He was created to give orders, not take them.

I, on the other hand, was created mostly to listen to him when he speaks, and make comments he can then answer. But still he talks to himself inside his head, which is a wonderment. Saint Just is quite complicated, as is Maggie. They are so alike, and yet so different. Saint Just will rail and say something witty at me once we are rescued, and Maggie will kiss my cheek and give me a hug. Then she'll rail at me. I don't suppose I would want Saint Just kissing my cheek, so that's all right.

Snake is being terribly quiet, but then, so am I, which has to do with this rag stuffed into my mouth. Quite an ill-bred, ill-mannered pair of captors, if I must say so myself.

But here we are, my having opened the door and those two large men having pointed wicked looking pistols at us and obliging us to leave the building with them without calling out or otherwise bringing any attention to our dilemma.

Not that Paul, who is manning the doors tonight in lieu of Socks, would have noticed if we'd left the building with our hair on fire. The man, as Saint Just would say, is next door to a yahoo, and with the brains of a flea.

And so here we are, dear Journal, Snake and myself. In the dark. Trussed up like chickens, our mouths stuffed shut, and without the faintest idea what will happen next, except to know that Saint Just will be exceedingly put out when he discovers we're gone.

But not to worry. Saint Just will find us, I know that. Snake, poor boy, does not, so he might well be terrified, while I am only mildly upset.

Moderately upset.

But I do know my place in all of this. That place is to sit still, sit quietly, and await rescue. Because rescue is not my job, it's Saint Just's. He is the hero, after all . . . and, oh dear.

You can't see it, dear Journal, but someone is removing my bonds. Is that a good thing or a bad thing? Shall I ask? If that someone removes this horrible rag I could . . . "Well, thank you. That wasn't entirely hygienic, you know. Could I please have a drink? Something diet? And perhaps a light? It's terribly dark in here."

"Shut your pie hole, jerk. Come on, youse and me are gonna go make a movie."

"A movie? Isn't that a coincidence? Tabitha Leighton—I don't believe you've been introduced—told me earlier as we were cleaning up that mess you made—no offense—that we're going to be a movie. Saint Just and myself, you understand. Well, not really *us*. It's rather complic—oh, a light. Thank you. Snake, we have light. Open your eyes, Snake."

"No way, no how, no fuckin' *way*," Snake said, his eyes squeezed shut. "Can't kill you for what you don't see."

"Oh," Sterling said, looking at his captor. "But I'm afraid I have to point out the error in your reasoning, and all of that, because we have already seen—um, never mind."

"Shut up and come here, fatso."

"No. I think not," Sterling said, backing up, backing into Snake. "Saint Just would not obey orders from a—ah, excuse me. I was very nearly brave there for a moment, wasn't I? That's because of what you almost did to Henry, you know. You should be ashamed of that. Truly asham—"

As Sterling lay on the floor, five-pointed stars circling his head, he thought to himself, *Dear Journal. I am a fool. . . .*

"Anything?"

Saint Just looked over his shoulder, his head nearly colliding with Maggie's. He'd taken a knife with him to the basement storage area, and used it to slice open the back of the ugly landscape. "Just this rather odd key," he said, holding it up.

Maggie took it. "That's a safe deposit key. Damn it, Alex, she put the stuff in a safe deposit box. There isn't even a bank name on the key, just some numbers. They don't want a key they can't use—they want what's in the box. This is no help at all."

"I was afraid you might say something along those lines," he said, getting to his feet and brushing down his slacks. The floor was exceedingly hard, and quite dusty. "I am not by nature a violent man, but I have this recurring thought that has something to do with sliding my hands about Mrs. Goldblum's neck and—"

"You're not the Lone Ranger in that one," Maggie said, pocketing the key. "Now what? Do you want to keep looking?"

"We are here," Saint Just said, looking around the small wire mesh cage at the plastic bins, five of them, that were stacked there. "I'll lift one down for you."

"Thanks." Maggie pried off the lid of a deep purple container. "Oh, photograph albums. They're no help. Although I'd like to see a photo of Harry. One with his head on, I mean."

Saint Just lifted layers of clothing from a second container, scattering small white and rather smelly balls over the floor. "What on earth?"

"Mothballs," Maggie said. "My grandmother always smelled of them. Oh, look, here's one of Irene and Harry at their wedding."

Saint Just ignored her and went on to the next container, and the next, and the next, his frustration growing at each new failure. Sterling and Snake were in danger, and he was on his knees, picking up balls for moths. Frustration did not begin to express how he felt.

"Um . . . Alex?"

"All done here, Maggie," he said, more than ready to quit this depressing area and go upstairs, move that blasted refrigerator and hope there was some sort of safe built into the wall behind it. A wall safe he understood. He did not understand basement bins and little white balls that smelled like grandmothers.

"No, Alex, look. I think we've got something. It might not be the something those guys are after, but we've got something. Look—here's a photograph of Enrico Totila. See? It's labeled. You see who he's standing with? Oh, wow."

"A rather well dressed man, in a flashy sort of way. Is that a wig?"

"I don't think so. But you're right, he's well dressed. That's John Gotti, the Dapper Don." She turned the page. "Oh, wow, here's more. And they're all labeled . . . Totila and Gotti . . . the date . . . the place. You know, Gotti's dead now, but he was the big guy. Not a good thing, having your picture taken with him, though, not if you keep saying you're not in the mob. Harry must have taken these photographs, don't you think? He's not in any of them." She turned another page. "Oh, wow."

"Would it be at all possible for you to stop saying *oh, wow?* What do you see?"

"Totila. See him? Now look behind him."

Saint Just leaned in closer, the better to focus on the photograph. "I see pants legs, shoes."

"Yeah. Pants legs and shoes lying on the ground. And the caption, Alex. It says here, *'Enrico Totila and Biggy Two-Ears Mordini. Outside Trenton, August 14, 1989.'* How much do you want to bet that Mordini is dead, and that Totila was posing over him like a hunter over a six-pointed buck?"

"Now I do need a translation," Saint Just said, taking the album from Maggie and helping her to her feet. "May I suggest we adjourn to my apartment, in the faint hope those two imbeciles who absconded with Sterling and Snake might have thought to copy down Mrs. Goldblum's telephone number?"

"Okay, sure. Oh, wow, Alex, wait until Steve sees this. He's going to go *ape.* I mean it. I'll bet, with these dates and everything, they'll be able to put this Totila guy away for a long, long time."

Any trepidation, any sense of not being quite sure of himself, faded in one brilliant instant as Saint Just turned to look at Maggie. "Steve does not see this."

"Why not?"

"He has a commendable sense of honor and respect for the law, Maggie. In other words, if this is some sort of compelling evidence, and you seem to believe it is, the good *left*-tenant will feel it his duty to take it to his superiors, leaving Sterling and Snake very much in the lurch. I repeat, the *left*-tenant does *not* see these photographs."

"But . . . but the mob guys probably don't even *know* these photographs exist, Alex. They'll be delighted to get them and—oh, damn."

"Exactly. We will have given them something they don't know they need in exchange for Sterling and Snake, still leaving them without the something they think we have that they actually want. In other words, these photographs serve no good purpose. Unless . . ."

"Unless what? What are you thinking?"

"Shh, Maggie, I'm concentrating. There must be a way to employ these damning photographs, dangle a few of them in front of Mr. Totila's henchmen in order to be allowed to see—and therefore rescue—Sterling and Snake, *and* some way to use them to assist Bernice."

"Bernie? What do the photos have to do with Bernie?"

"I don't know. Not yet. But I am under the impression that the good District Attorney Dettmer is the sort of man who would relish a coup. These photographs, these days and names, would you consider them a coup?"

"Oh, yeah," Maggie said, rubbing her hands together as they rode up in the elevator. "Steve can take the photographs—some of them—to Dettmer, and we can wave the rest of them in front of the goons when they contact us, and—no. This isn't going to work."

"Really? Why not?"

"I don't know. But it's too easy, especially when you think about the mob end of it. Those people carry guns, Alex. And Steve would have a lot of explaining to do to the D.A."

"You keep assuming that Wendell will be meeting with this Dettmer person. You could not be more wrong."

"You're not . . . *you're* going to . . . ?"

"It's Sterling, Maggie. I will be in charge of everything, every move, every ploy, every stratagem. Had you a single doubt?"

"Me? Damn right I—wait a minute. *You* told me we needed Steve."

Saint Just lifted his chin. "You must have misunderstood. Ah, here we go, our floor. Get a good night's sleep, my dear, for what remains of it. I will adjourn to the apartment in the off-chance the kidnappers phone early in the morning. You may tell Wendell, when he finally is done with his snit and phones you, that you are terribly sorry for having gone sleuthing without telling him and will never do so again. That should delight him down to his badly shod toes."

"I . . . my head hurts. Alex, what are we doing? We're breaking the law, I think."

"How? By not giving away Mrs. Goldblum's personal belongings? After all, are they ours to give? I think not. Go to bed," he said, lightly touching her cheek as he stepped close to her, lowered his mouth toward hers. "I'm here, Maggie."

"Oh, brother," she said, rolling her eyes. "That was so B-movie, Alex." But as he lifted one brow in question, and made to back off she grabbed his shoulders. "Come here."

This was different. The female as aggressor. A part of him found it quite improper . . . while another part of him firmly told the starchier, Regency Era part of him to, well, to take a hike.

He slanted his mouth against hers, accepting the invitation of her parted lips, sliding his tongue against hers, smiling slightly as she eagerly began a duel that could, should, at least in his stories, end with the two of them in his bed.

"I'm sorry you were scared there for a while, Alex," Maggie said, having pushed herself free of him before he could think to hold her close. "No, don't deny it. You were scared. I was scared. I'm still scared. But you're not, are you? You're over it. You're ready to act. Man, I made you brave. Or very, very arrogant. I'll see you at eight, right before I go to Doctor Bob, unless the goons call. I won't stay for the full hour, but I need to talk to him about Bernie. G'night."

Saint Just stood, the photograph album tucked under his arm, staring at Maggie's closed door, wondering why he'd thought, even for an instant, that he, such an accomplished lover, and with an acknowledged insight into the workings of her mind, understood anything about this particular woman.

CHAPTER 13

Maggie knocked on the door a second time. Pounded on it this time. Counted to ten, then heard the dead bolt turn and, before the door had opened more than a few inches, demanded, "Tell me again why you have a key to my place and I don't have one to yours."

"And a pleasant good morning to you, too, my dear," Alex said, stepping back to wave her inside. "And, so that you might not waste your breath, no, I have had no communication from the mobsters. No, I have not discovered anything else of any consequence in the apartment, although it might please you to learn that, yes, I can be injured without your first writing that injury into one of our books. Meaning, refrigerators are heavy as well as cumbersome, and gentlemen were not meant to move them about willy-nilly without assistance. Oh, and I have not as yet partaken of my morning coffee, as I do not possess any, unless I wish to go down to the basement and scoop some out of the garbage gathered up after our, again, mobsters destroyed the kitchen. And how are you?"

Maggie shrugged, pretending not to notice his wince as he turned to close the door and the way he grabbed involuntarily at his back. She also pretended to ignore how absolutely gorgeous the man looked in a pristine white dress shirt still open at the neck, form-fitting black slacks, and, oh God, bare feet. Nor would she notice his disheveled, shower-damp ebony hair, his bluer than blue eyes slightly bruised from lack of sleep, the somehow yummy smell of Dove soap that clung to his tanned skin.

She didn't have time for any of that. Too bad.

"Gee, now I know why you usually don't crawl out of bed until ten," she said, adjusting the strap of her purse on her shoulder, because she needed something to do with her hands that didn't include helping to boost her up as she climbed the man, grabbed him by the ears, and let him get a taste of the coffee she'd just finished as he plunged his tongue into her mouth and . . . Okay, that was enough of that, too.

"I'm assured the mobsters—must we call them mobsters?—will be contacting us sometime today. Although I discovered, unfortunately only a few minutes ago, that both phones here in the apartment have had their cords ripped out of the wall. Is there some establishment nearby where I can purchase new equipment?"

Maggie reached behind the end table beside the couch pushed against the wall, and came out with a cord that no longer had that little clip thingie at the end. "You don't need new phones, Alex. I can fix this. I'm sure I have some of this stuff somewhere."

"Good. Where?"

"I don't know. In my desk? I'll go look."

"No, I will. You'll be late for Doctor Bob, remember?"

"Oh, right," Maggie said, in no rush to keep her appointment. "I don't know if I should be thanking him or asking if he takes MasterCard or Visa. Although I already know the answer to that one, he takes both. You know, maybe it's wrong of me, but I can't believe he actually charged five hundred bucks to help Bernie. I mean, she's his publisher, for crying out loud. I'm the one who gave his manuscript to Tabby, so without me, and without Bernie, who bought it, where would he be? Not on the talk shows, I'll tell you that much. I had no idea he was so cheap."

"Isn't that strange? Like usually has no problem in recognizing like," Alex said, and she threw a pillow at him as he left the apartment, then looked at her watch. She still had plenty of time. Maybe even time enough to take another look around the apartment, hoping for a miracle.

There was a large walk-in closet located in the hallway that led to the bedrooms, and Mrs. Goldblum had transferred all of her wardrobe there before running away. The clothing had almost all been ripped from the rods, but Mary Louise, or someone, had replaced them. There were shoes on the floor of the closet and purses stacked on shelves above the clothes rods.

Nothing much to look for, nothing much to see, but Maggie had the time, and it still bugged her that they'd found nothing useful in the apartment.

A second glance told her that these were all winter clothes, with no summer clothes, sandals, or straw purses anywhere. Everything summery was gone. Obviously Mrs. Goldblum hadn't headed for Nome, and she didn't pack light.

One by one, she pulled down the huge old-lady purses, looking through them. Scented hankies, crumpled tissues—"Ick!"—wrapped peppermints, a few loose pennies, a bus schedule, a passport, an emery board, a small roll of antacids, a—"A *passport?"*

Maggie flipped the now empty purse on the floor and opened the passport, winced. "Man, nobody looks good in these things, but they don't usually look like they've been dead for three days," she said, then pressed on. It was a current passport, with one stamp in it, for Freeport, in the Bahamas. "She left in a hurry. I wonder if she's missing this right about now."

Ignoring the mess she'd made on the floor, Maggie went looking for Alex, who should have found the cord by now. Holding up the passport like a trophy, she crossed the hall and pushed open the already ajar door to her own condo . . . and stopped dead.

Alex was sitting in her computer chair, reading something. Several typewritten pages held together at the top left corner with a staple. What did she have that was stapled?

And why did he look like that? Sorrowful. Yes, that was it. Sorrowful. His shoulders almost slumped, his entire posture speaking most eloquently of some unhappiness she'd never seen him show, never had thought to allow the character of the Viscount Saint Just to show. Yet he wore even sorrow well, almost elegantly, with just enough reluctance to feel whatever emotions were filling him to be achingly attractive, curiously vulnerable.

"Alex? What's wrong? What do you have?"

He looked up, his eyes clouded for only a moment before he blinked, flipped the pages over and replaced them in the drawer she'd hadn't noticed had been pulled open. "Nothing important. I found the cord. Several of them, actually. They're fairly well tangled but I believe I can manage to fix that."

"Uh-huh," Maggie said, watching as he stood up, tangled cords in hand, and brushed past her, into the hallway. He was gone approximately one-and-one-third seconds before Maggie had tossed the passport on the desk, yanked the drawer open, and was pulling out the pages.

She frowned, flipping them over quickly. "This . . . this is the character description I wrote about him when I first thought him up," she said out loud. "What's in here that would make him . . . ? Hair, black, eyes, killer blue, height, six foot two. Gee, it rhymes. Slender face, can lift his left eyebrow in amusement or as an insult. Bullet scar on his left shoulder. Right. I added that after I had him shot. Lives in Grosvenor Square mansion when in London, right. Quizzing glass, right. Estranged from father, mother died having him. No siblings."

She frowned, scanning the rest, which was nothing more than scribblings she'd added from time to time as she developed his character more fully, like putting in that bit about the young Clint Eastwood slashes in his cheeks.

"There's nothing here that—no," she said, looking at the door to the hall. "He couldn't actually . . . Alex?" She headed back across the hall. He was on his way to the kitchen, a telephone cord in his hand. "Alex? Hold it right there a minute, okay? You were looking at your character description, weren't you? What upset you? This stuff about your parents?"

He looked at her levelly. "Is that so amazing? That I should mourn a dead parent, perhaps even mourn the estrangement from the remaining parent?"

Maggie blinked. "Uh . . . no, I guess—wait a minute. You don't *have* parents. I made them up. I made *you* up."

"True, but you didn't make me heartless," Alex said, running the cord between his fingers.

"No, I didn't make you heartless. But I've never written a single thing about your parents, not in six books. That was just information I needed for me. How can you feel what I haven't created you to feel?"

His jaw set as he looked at her. Maggie nearly backed up a step. "Yes, you created me. I am a figment of your imagination, or at least I was. Until I took charge, took control of my own destiny, which, as it happens, brought me here. You made me, Maggie, and now I am making me . . . more."

Maggie looked at him for long moments, moments during which her heart pounded, her throat went a little tight, and she thought, just for an instant, she might actually faint. "But . . . but you can't do that. You're Saint Just."

"Part of me is, yes. A majority of me. But now there is also Alex. *I* am also Alex. I didn't fully realize that, Maggie, not until a few minutes ago. It is rather staggering, isn't it, and explains how I've been reacting since Sterling's disappearance. I am . . . evolving."

Maggie didn't know what to say. She sure couldn't think.

And then the phone rang.

"Get that!" she said, pointing at the phone.

Alex approached the phone leisurely and lifted the receiver to his ear. "Good morning, Alexander Blakley here," he said, then listened, nodding to Maggie, who wished the extension was working. "Might I remind you that if you had not rendered our telephone machines inoperable in your needlessly overwrought and even wanton destruction of the apartment, I could have answered your earlier calls. Far from me to point out the obvious, my good fellow, but you and your thug cohort might wish to consider that eventuality, when next you are running about destroying personal property."

Maggie clapped her hands to her ears and hissed, "Jeez, Alex. Don't piss him off."

He waved her back into silence. "Yes, I quite understand. Yes, we have *it*. We will, of course, expect verification that the gentlemen are unharmed." Maggie watched as he frowned. "I suppose that shall have to suffice. And precisely when would that—?" He looked at the receiver, then replaced it. "He disconnected. He's not a very polite man, and with a remarkably intense disposition."

"Yeah, I got that."

"I'm ashamed of myself, as Sterling and Vernon must be my primary concerns, but I have to tell you, Maggie, I'm going to enjoy bringing these people down."

"Yeah, I got that, too. What did he say? You should have asked to talk to Sterling."

"There wasn't time. According to our caller, we will be able to see for ourselves how Sterling and Vernon are faring when a package is delivered later today. Until then?" He shook his head. "I imagine you'd better go. It wouldn't do to keep the great doctor waiting. Besides, he'll charge you."

"And Steve? We need him, Alex. These guys are going to want us to turn over what we've got and tell us we'll be able to pick up Sterling and Snake on some street corner in Hoboken or something later tonight. But how do we know they'll keep their end of the bargain? We need an experienced negotiator to talk to these guys, set up cops all around the drop area. All that stuff."

"I'll consider it, yes. But not until after this package arrives and we know exactly what we are forced to deal with, all right? My conversation with that man has given me new hope, as he may have been angry, but he didn't sound in the least intelligent. Why else would they be called *thugs*? Now go, I must finish preparing myself for the day."

Maggie backed toward the door, picking up her purse as she went, her eyes still on Alex. "I . . . I'll be back soon," she said, then turned and ran for the elevator.

Her hands were still shaking as the cab headed up the avenue, and she didn't even bother to yell at the driver when he ran a red light and nearly took out a bicycle messenger. Tossing a five at the guy, she bolted from the cab and into Doctor Bob Chalfont's office a full minute before the good doctor started his meter running.

"Margaret, how are you this morning?" Doctor Bob asked as he opened the door to his office as if he'd been standing behind it, listening for her. "And Ms. Toland-James? She's all settled?"

"Yeah, yeah," Maggie said, collapsing into a chair. "Can a person change on their own?"

Doctor Bob sat himself down at his overlarge desk chair and steepled his fingers beneath his nose. "You think Ms. Toland-James could have stopped her alcohol addiction on her own? I can't discuss another patient, Margaret, you know that. I will say that few people are strong enough to change, to evolve, completely on their own. We all need some help from time to time."

"Strong enough," Maggie repeated, nodding. "Okay, that makes sense. I made him strong."

"Him? I beg your pardon. I thought you were referring to Ms. Toland-James."

"Ah . . . that is . . . did I say *him*? I didn't mean to. I meant . . . so, you think Bernie could have kicked the drinking without this clinic thing?"

"Margaret, I cannot—"

"Right. Let's talk about me. Just for a minute, though, because

I really can't stay. I decided that I'm a nicaholic—a nicotine addict—and even though I say that all the time, I've decided now that I really, really want to stop smoking. That's good, right?"

"Is it?"

Maggie curled her top lip back over her teeth. "Don't do that. Don't answer my question with the same question except it comes out of your mouth. Yes. Yes, it's good that I really, really want to quit. I mean, the smelly clothes, the cost—pretty soon crack cocaine is going to be cheaper, if it isn't already. I can't light up in ninety percent of the places I go. I should quit. I want to quit. I mean, if Bernie can quit, I should be able to quit, too. But can I do it on my own?"

"Margaret, you are not alone. I'm here, remember?"

"No insult intended, Doctor Bob, but you've been here for a while now, and I'm still smoking."

"Because smoking, Margaret, is not really your problem. You know that. Smoking is your crutch. You hide behind it, you use it in lieu of expressing yourself verbally anywhere except inside the pages of the books you write; you pretend you will lose your creativity without it. But, in truth, it's your rebellion, begun in your teens, and now you are physically, psychologically, and most definitely emotionally addicted. You are an interesting case, although not unique. With many, I merely have to help the patient over the chemical addiction. With you? There are other considerations."

Maggie began to reach for the box of tissues on the table beside her, then caught herself in time. She'd come here for two reasons. To ask about Alex and Bernie, and to do just a little bragging. "I did something yesterday. I told Bernie she had to stop drinking. She . . . she went a little nuts on me, yelled at me, but I didn't back down. I'm learning. I'm learning to stand my ground when someone starts yelling. So maybe I'm ready to quit smoking, too? And," she added, thinking about Alex, "maybe I can do it on my own."

Doctor Bob removed his new half-glasses and made a big deal

out of polishing them with a small blue cloth. "Has your mother phoned since the stories about Ms. Toland-James appeared in the news, Margaret?"

Damn the man. He might be a pain, but he was also good. Very good.

"Yes," she said, sticking out her chin.

"Did you talk to her?"

The chin lowered slightly. "I was out. She left a message."

"And did you, knowing that she had to be quite put out at the news she'd read, return her call?"

Maggie stood up. "I'll see you next week. Charge me for the full hour."

"Yes, I thought so. You're making strides, Margaret. *We* are making strides. If you work hard the day will come when you need no crutches, neither the nicotine nor me."

Maggie bolted from the office, stopping once she was back on the sidewalk, where she stood and took deep breaths of the polluted air; rather like smoking, if you were hooked on exhaust fumes.

So she'd made Alex strong, given him all the strength she would like to have, but didn't. She gave Sterling all the heart, because balance was necessary. And yet Sterling had gotten as close to violent as she imagined he ever could when he'd thought Henry had been hurt, and Alex had shown emotions, including sorrow and, yes, fear, she'd never written for him.

She'd made him everything she'd ever wanted to be. Witty, arrogant . . . and yes, brave. And he and Sterling both had taken what she'd given them a step farther. Growing. Evolving.

She could do it. If Alex and Sterling could do it, she could do it.

Deciding to walk home, she reached into her purse and pulled out her pack of cigarettes and her lighter. "But not today. I'm not a total idiot."

By the time she got back to the condo the media had set up camp for another day.

"Hey," one of them yelled at her as she put her head down and tried to reach the door before any of them saw her. "Aren't you Cleo Dooley? Toland-James's friend? She up there? What did she tell you? She did it, right?"

Maggie turned, to see that the reporter who'd yelled wasn't the only one coming at her. Television camera lights went on, flashbulbs popped, and now everyone was yelling at once.

Socks burst from the foyer, arms spread, and placed himself in front of Maggie.

"You, fag boy, out of the way!"

Maggie had been so grateful to see Socks, and hiding behind him until the two of them could sort of shuffle toward the door had seemed like a good idea.

But if not today, when? If not for Bernie, for Socks, then for who? Whom? Oh, hell, she had to do it.

She pushed herself past Socks's outflung arm and stepped in front of him. "Who said that? Which one of you cretins said that?"

"Maggie, it's okay," Socks said, tugging on her arm.

"No, Socks, it's not." She took another step forward, as did one of the reporters. It had to be him. He was smirking like it was him.

She stepped right up to him, poked a finger in his chest. "Look. One, this is my friend, so keep your homophobic mouth off him, okay? Two, Ms. Toland-James is not here. She is, however, totally innocent, a victim. Now go chase a fire truck or something."

Someone else yelled: "What about the D.A., Ms. Dooley?"

"That's Kelly. Maggie Kelly," Maggie said, still glaring at the reporter in front of her. "And what about him?"

"He was on TV this morning saying an arrest was imminent, that Toland-James is a stone cold killer. What about that? Any comment?"

Maggie couldn't see the lights. She was too busy seeing red.

"Sure, I've got a comment. The D.A. needs to lose the makeup and get a new hair stylist. Now go away, because two of my windows overlook this sidewalk and I'm thinking of boiling up some pitch. And in case you're going to say it, yes, that rhymes with bitch, so *back off.*"

It wasn't until she was in the foyer that her knees began to wobble a little and she remembered that the cameras had been rolling the whole time. "Oh, God, what did I do?"

"You were bitchin', Maggie," Socks said, all but dancing in his excitement. "That was Rob Bottoms you were poking. Nobody likes him. You're going to be all over the noon news. Man. Bitchin'."

"Stupid. That was stupid. I should have just mumbled *no comment* and kept going."

"Bottoms got you mad," Socks reminded her.

"Oh, right. You okay, Socks?"

"I'm fine. But my mama might send over an apple pie to thank you," he said, leading her toward the elevator.

She stepped inside, waving at Socks and trying to smile as the doors closed, then leaned against the wall. "Man, I do pick my times. *That's Kelly, Maggie Kelly.* Good one. Mom's gonna blow like Vesuvius."

Alex was gone when she entered her condo, a Post-it note stuck to her computer screen. Two of them actually, as Alex's note, written in his lovely copperplate, was more of a message than a note, though damn cryptic:

No more calls, don't expect any until the delivery. Gather Socks, Killer. Assemble here at three. Mary Louise, self, to Pierre at noon. Other errand in the meantime.

The second Post-it was shorter: *If at all possible, fob off Wendell until after we've seen whatever is going to arrive.*

He'd signed it *Saint Just.*

"What the . . . ?" Maggie crumpled the notes and looked around her living room in frustration. "We're waiting for the kidnappers to contact us and he goes off to sign a damn modeling contract? He needs to be here. We need to talk. I didn't even show him the passport yet, for crying out loud."

Then she smoothed out the first note, read it again. *Other errand in the meantime.* What did that mean?

She went into the kitchen to open a can of soda, then wandered back into the living room, feeling about as useful as a snowplow in Miami—where had that one come from? Was she losing her mind?—and saw the photograph album on the coffee table.

"Might as well look at the rest of them," she said, picking it up and laying it in her lap. She turned one page, two, then frowned. "Where's the dead guy? I'm missing Biggy Two-Ears Mordini."

She paged back to the beginning and looked again, saw the four white photo corner holders minus the photo. Saw the caption with no photograph. Checked the entire album quickly, found more empty spots.

"Alex, what are you doing?" she asked, looking at her watch. He wouldn't be back until at least two, and she could either sit here and stew or she could do something. Something brave.

She lit a cigarette (she wasn't that brave), picked up the cordless phone, hit a speed dial number, waited.

"Hello, Mom? It's me, Margaret. Um . . . do you watch Rob Bottoms on the news?"

CHAPTER 14

Saint just had prepared himself as best he could, discarding the black slacks he had hastily donned that morning when Maggie had all but beaten down the door while he was dressing. He exchanged the dark pants for tan slacks that had remarkably retained their knife-sharp creases and resisted wrinkling, even though they'd been tossed to the floor, along with the remainder of his wardrobe.

He'd kept the white dress shirt, one of his favorites and newly returned from the laundry, topped it with yet another navy blazer, eschewing a formal necktie but strapping a tan belt around his waist. Butter soft tan shoes and matching socks. His hair combed into its usual Windswept style, his quizzing glass around his neck, the glass itself tucked into the breast pocket of the jacket.

It wasn't a jacket by Weston, supple buckskins—putting paid to any faint hope of cutting a dashing leg—nor his favorite Hessians, but the ensemble would do.

All that was missing was his sword cane, and he felt vaguely naked without it. But he was aware that security in official buildings included metal detectors, and explaining away his cane would cause undue attention. Perhaps even confiscation.

Still, his free hands seemed to itch to hold something, so he stopped on his way and purchased a bumbershoot—umbrella—at a small, exclusive shop that seemed to understand that such things should be black, should be large, and should include a solid, curved handle and a long point at the opposite end.

There wasn't a cloud in sight, but he felt better now. More himself.

Once inside the building he examined a large directory, then set out to confront his quarry.

"Good morning, Miss Angela Perkins," he said, quickly reading the nameplate on the desk of the young woman who sat in an anteroom outside the main office of that quarry. "I am, of course, Alexander Blakely, here to see Mr. Dettmer. You will kindly apprise him of my arrival?"

"Who?" Ms. Angela Perkins said, obviously caught between staring at him in expected admiration and paging through the appointment calendar in front of her without looking at it. "I don't think . . ."

"Of course," Saint Just said smoothly, inclining his head in a deferential bow. "How silly of me. I forgot to present my calling card." He reached into the inside pocket of his sport coat and extracted a thin white envelope. "If you would only be so kind as to take this to the esteemed gentleman, I believe he'll recall our appointment."

"Uh . . . um . . ." Miss Angela Perkins slowly stood up, holding out her hand.

Saint Just caught it, as he caught her gaze with his own, as he bowed over that hand, brought it to his lips, kissed her fingers. Then he folded those fingers around the envelope. "What a marvelous mouth you have, my dear. You must become weary of the constant compliments."

"Uh . . . uh-huh," she said, still holding out her hand as she backed from the desk, nearly upsetting her chair. She kept backing away, until she encountered the door behind her, then turned and ran into the next office.

"Who the hell are you?"

Saint Just turned to notice the three gentlemen sitting on

leather chairs, looking at him as if they wanted to eject him from the room via the nearest window.

"Is there some problem, gentlemen?" Saint Just asked, gracefully leaning on the handle of his umbrella.

"Yeah. I have the ten o'clock," one of the gentlemen said.

"You? No way. I have the ten o'clock," said another.

"I've got the nine-thirty, so I'm ahead of both of you. And we're all ahead of *him.*"

"Mr. . . . Mr. Blakely?"

Saint Just raised one eyebrow as he smiled, then bowed to the men before turning around, tucking the umbrella under his arm. "Yes, Miss Perkins?"

"You can go in now," she said, plastering herself against the open door, fingers to her lips as he strolled past her into an office at least three times the size of Maggie's very generous living room.

"You brought these?"

"Indeed," Saint Just said, bowing to the large, red-cheeked man of medium height and expanding build just then coming out from behind a desk that, set with china, could have served twelve comfortably, with room for candelabra, etagere, and the family silver salt cellar.

District Attorney Chadwick Dettmer waved the photographs at him. "What the hell are these?"

"I thought that would be obvious," Saint Just said, strolling across the expanse of carpet to visually examine and then avoid the pair of chairs on the opposite side of Dettmer's desk. They were low chairs. His was a much more substantial chair. Saint Just wasn't worried about the size of his consequence, but Dettmer obviously needed to feel an advantage over his visitors. Saint Just was not about to give it to him.

So he took himself over to the small sitting area to one side of the office, stopping only to admire some photographs on a cherrywood credenza.

Dettmer with the mayor. Dettmer with the president. Dettmer and the obligatory family photo; wife, daughter, son. It was this photograph that Saint Just picked up, gazing at it admiringly.

"Ah, what a lovely family. You must be quite fond of them."

"You threatening me?"

Saint Just blinked. "Why, the thought had never occurred. I was merely making a comment. Is that a beach I see behind you, outside the window?"

"Yeah. A beach."

"Your daughter is quite lovely." Saint Just restrained himself from adding something along the lines of how grateful that child must be, how she must go down on her knees nightly, thankful that she resembled her mother and not her father. "And this is your son?"

"Put that down."

"A . . . sturdily put together lad, much like yourself. And what's that he's got written on his shirt?" Saint Just held the photograph closer as he reached for his quizzing glass and raised it toward his eye. "I think I may be able to make it out if I might just—"

Dettmer grabbed the photograph by its silver frame and set it back in place on the credenza. "Angela said your name, but I didn't catch it."

"Blakely. Alexander Blakely," Saint Just said, giving the photograph one last look, then replaced his quizzing glass and took up a seat in the conversation area—the best seat—negligently propping the umbrella against it.

Dettmer didn't seem to notice, but just stood there, waving the photographs his secretary had given him. "Now, what's this all about? I'm a busy man."

"Oh, dear. No polite conversation? No idle chit-chat? No offer of refreshments? It's this hurly burly world we live in, I suppose. Very well then, straight to the point. You know who all is depicted in those photographs, I'll assume?"

"Totila. It's Totila, standing with a couple of the family foot soldiers. And this one, with just Totila and—what the hell? Whose legs are those? Where are they? When was this taken?"

"What unseemly impatience, sir. That will come, that will come . . . as will several dozen more photographs even more, shall we say, interesting. Once we've discussed terms."

Dettmer finally sat down, his beady eyes narrowed. "Terms? You're an informant? An *Englishman*? In the mob? You want to make a trade? For what?"

Saint Just pondered the word informant (as well as the man's overweening stupidity) for a moment, then decided to dismiss it. "I am here, my good man, in order to negotiate a sort of exchange, yes, although I would prefer to term it an agreement between gentlemen."

Dettmer held up the photographs, waved them. "These are evidence. I can take them right now."

"True, you could. But then, alas, you will not know exactly what you have, will you? Not the dates, not the places, both of which could lead to . . . interesting conclusions. Just those photographs, my good sir, and no others, and they are copies. I did not count each and every photograph, but I do believe I have in my possession approximately fifty, spanning the course of perhaps three decades."

Dettmer glared at him.

"Then, again," Saint Just said, getting to his feet, "I understand that Enrico Totila, with his assorted gang of thugs, is only a minor player. A small but irritating thorn in your side now that some earlier district attorney, not you, laboring with federal authorities, I presume, disposed of John Gotti, Senior—forgive me if my information is fuzzy, as I am, as you say, English. You probably don't want Totila anyway. Not much of a feather in your cap in the ongoing struggle against what is known as organized crime? Although thus far, alas, in this election year, you have none."

"Sit down."

Saint Just looked at the District Attorney, smiled. "Oh, I don't think so. Good day."

Neatly tucking the umbrella under his arm, Saint Just bowed, then headed for the door.

He had taken only two steps when Dettmer said, "Name your terms."

Saint Just took two more steps, then turned around to bow once more to the man who had at last begun to show at least a flicker of common sense. "A gentleman of reason. I applaud you, figuratively, of course. Shall we ring for those refreshments now? No, I suppose not, as by the look of that scowl on your face I doubt we're about to become bosom chums. Very well. I happened to catch your television performance with Miss Holly Spivak earlier this morning."

Dettmer tugged at his suit lapels, did some rather odd moving about of his bull-like neck and chin. Could it be preening? "So?"

"I didn't appreciate it," Saint Just said. "I'm sorry, that was blunt, wasn't it? And yet truthful. I have a friend who tells me you were making political hay on Ms. Toland-James. A quaint term. Is that correct?"

"Toland-James? This is about *her*?"

"Oh, most definitely about her, my good man. This business of being a stone cold killer? Your supposedly open and shut case against her? How *do* you Americans come up with these colorful sayings? Especially as, in this particular case, they are not true."

Dettmer got to his feet. "They damn well are."

"Really? Why, then, is Ms. Toland-James not under arrest? Wait, let me make a supposition. You don't have sufficient evidence to arrest her, do you? Which, I fear, begs the question—how much are you going to flog that innocent woman's reputation in the media in order to shore up what I also have heard is your flagging run for reelection?"

"She's a friend of yours?"

"How minimally incisive of you. A very dear friend, yes, and it pains me to see you, or anyone, attacking her character the way you did this morning, in the manner I am assured you intend to continue flogging her good name in order to— What is the term? Oh, yes. Procure airtime. For shame."

Dettmer waved the photographs again. "So what's the deal?"

"You haven't guessed? Careful, sir. If the remainder of Manhattan realized how very thick you are, those poll numbers might take another tumble. But I am happy to explain, in words of the fewest syllables."

"You're walking a thin line, buddy."

"Again with the colorful phrases. Ah, yes, it's above all things wonderful. If you will but promise to not rush hell-bent to arrest Ms. Toland-James until and unless you have sufficient evidence, not just hopeful dreams of your own prominence, and if you will order your underlings to pursue all avenues of investigation into the identity of the *actual* killer, then I will turn over the originals of those photographs and all previously mentioned particulars, so that you may gain the evidence to arrest a *real* criminal, thus according you the same media interest. Understood? Or shall we review this again?"

"Oh, I understand. You're telling me to back off your girlfriend in exchange for some pictures."

"Merely a suggestion. A bird in the hand, my good sir, has always been preferable to one in the bush, or so I've heard. Ms. Toland-James is not guilty, as the evidence will prove in good time. Mr. Enrico Totila most assuredly is guilty of, ah, so many sordid and terrible things. Which, I would ask, is of more importance to a crime-fighting gentleman like yourself?"

"Get out."

Saint Just, who really believed he had been making progress with this ignorant lout, was surprised again by the man's blatant stupidity, his short-sightedness in the face of all reason. He allowed that surprise to show. "I beg your pardon?"

"Damn right you do. Obstructing justice, hindering an investigation—blackmail threats. I should get you and that bitch adjoining cells. And I would, if these photos meant spit without supporting evidence."

"Supporting evidence which you do not desire?"

"Which I don't think you've got, or you would have shown it to me. And if you think I'm calling your bluff, calling you a liar, then you're right. No deal. That woman's a killer."

"Oh, she is not, and you know it as well as I," Saint Just said, waving his umbrella up and onto his shoulder. "But very well. This was, in many ways, a courtesy call. Since you have refused my offer of assistance, I shall simply have to do everything myself."

"What everything? You can't do that. It's interfering with police business, and if you do that I'll have your nuts in a wringer. Besides, you'd never get anywhere."

"Ah, a challenge. That was a challenge, wasn't it, mixed in with the crudity? How delightful. Very well. I make you this promise, sir. I will exonerate Ms. Toland-James of any involvement with the murder of her husband *and* deliver sufficient evidence to the media to arrest, convict, and return to prison one Enrico Totila, and perhaps most of his gang of thugs, even whilst I ponder why you would so readily give up that bird in the hand."

He raised a hand to his hair. "I should probably think about a visit to my barber, don't you think? I wouldn't wish to look shabby when the media calls. Again, good day. Oh, and you may keep those. They're merely copies, as you know, and I have more."

"I'm not kidding. I see you getting in the way and you're going to jail," Dettmer called after him. "Got some big boys there who'd love to make you their bitch, pretty boy."

Saint Just softly closed the door, smiled at Miss Perkins and the now five gentlemen awaiting audiences with the district attorney, and exited the building. He walked only a few steps before standing himself against a decorative indentation in the marble wall and peering around that wall to watch the busy entrance.

And then he waited. Not five seconds later a young man dressed in a suit much better than Saint Just would have expected (and the standard unlovely, heavy-soled police dress shoes) came running out, to stop at the head of the wide steps, looking left, looking right. Then he spoke into his sleeve. "Sir? You said blue blazer? Umbrella? No sir, I don't see him. He must have beat me to a cab. Yes sir. Sorry, sir."

The young man, looking disappointed, reentered the building.

Saint Just twirled the umbrella in one hand, then tucked it beneath his arm as he strolled off to meet Socks around the corner.

"You look kind of mad, Alex," Socks said as he fell into step beside Saint Just.

"Really? I'm foaming at the mouth? How rude of me."

"Okay, not mad. Angry. What's up? I told you he'd throw you out. If he didn't lock you up."

"He should have locked me up, Socks. I hadn't quite realized that when I entered his office, but he made that quite clear. He could have ordered my arrest."

"But he didn't. So that's good, right?"

"In some ways, yes. But he also refused to exchange some courtesy to Bernice for what you and Maggie have already assured me would have been a tremendous coup for the man. He wants Bernice, Socks. He wants her perhaps even more than he wants this publicity you say he craves. Remarkable, and quite unexpected. Now why, do you suppose, is that?"

Socks shrugged. "Because he figures he can get Bernie, *and* the stuff you've got."

"Really? Would you take that chance? With a person you don't know? I could have given him a false name. I could burn the photographs, Socks, or sell them to the media. I could contact

Enrico Totila and exchange them for a good deal of money. So many, many options. Can the esteemed district attorney be that certain that I wouldn't exercise any one of them?"

"No, I don't suppose so. You're right. He really should have arrested you."

"Yes, and that was dicey for a few moments, I must tell you, as I should be of no help to Bernice or Sterling from the guardhouse. I really have to study your American law more thoroughly. Maggie would not have appreciated having to secure my release."

"She'd have killed you," Socks said, nodding. "So now what? You and Mare still going to meet that Pierre guy for lunch?"

Saint Just pulled his watch from its place in his jacket pocket, opened it, and frowned as he considered the time. "Not lunch, Socks, not any more, although Mary Louise was quite put out when I informed her of our change in plans. Instead, we'll meet at noon at the offices of Fragrances by Pierre, simply to sign the contracts. I am very shortly to be delightfully solvent, Socks. I believe Maggie is caught between consternation at losing monetary control over me and doing handsprings in her delight that I will no longer be a drain on her pocketbook."

"And Mare can stop worrying about money and finish college. It's good, Alex. It's really good."

"Yes, we were fortunate. As were you, in procuring that cover model contract when you performed your impromptu performance the final night of the WAR convention. Fortune often favors the brave, as well as those who happen to do nothing more than happily stumble into the right place at the opportune moment."

Saint Just stopped, ran what he'd just said through his mind once more. And thought about his recent visit to the office of D.A. Chadwick Dettmer.

"Hail us a hack, Socks. As I wasn't with the good district attorney above a quarter hour, I believe we have sufficient time to visit Miss Holly Spivak before my appointment."

"You don't want to go back and see if the kidnappers have sent what they're sending?"

"Maggie is perfectly capable of monitoring that, although I don't believe I mentioned to her that the thug who contacted me said that the package would arrive at two. Do you think I should have told her?"

"Not now, I don't," Socks said as he held open the back door of a cab and Saint Just proceeded him inside before telling the cabbie to head for the headquarters of Fox News.

"An address, buddy. It's a big town. I'm supposed to know everything?"

Saint Just leaned forward and gave the address, as he did know most everything.

Socks struggled to fasten his seat belt as the cab pulled back into the traffic. "Aren't you worried? About Sterling and Snake, I mean."

"No, not really. Concerned, definitely. We are at an impasse at the moment, both with Sterling and Bernice, each side wishing to gain what the other has and fearful of making too many moves, lest one of them be wrong. In addition, Socks, if I cannot outwit some thick-as-planks thugs and one overbearing, overweening, definitely *overconfident* district attorney? Why, that isn't even conceivable. Now hush, if you please. I have to think. Something happened while I was in Dettmer's office. Something important, but I can't quite put my finger on it."

"That you got out in one piece?" Socks suggested.

Saint Just waved him to silence, then mentally retraced his visit, settled on something. Yes, that had to be it. Wasn't life odd? Chock full of coincidences . . . and those that doth protest too much. But he was not the sort to go off half-cocked, and although his word was bond, and highly respected by the characters in Maggie's books, he was now in New York, and had to play by the rules here. Those included a multitude of solid evidence, not merely his famous insights and suppositions.

"We're here," Socks said as the cab pulled to the curb.

Five minutes later they were being ushered into Holly Spivak's cramped, crowded office.

"Alex?" she said, getting to her feet. "I didn't expect to see you for a while. You've got something for me?"

"Other than a firm reprimand for putting your career above the rights of the innocent and a reminder that ethics is more than a word? No, I think not. Although I do have a request. Unless you don't wish to be back in my good graces?"

"You've still got Toland-James stashed somewhere and I still want her. So stow the insults and name the favor. But first, did you see the bulletin we just flashed? No, guess not, not if you were on your way here. Toland-James is as good as locked up. You might want to get her to talk to me, Alex, before they slap the cuffs on. You know, tell her side of the story, cry a little, soften up the jury pool."

Saint Just pressed thumb and forefinger to the bridge of his nose. "I am quite certain you know precisely what you're nattering on about, my dear. Now, if we might be similarly enlightened?"

"The bartender," Holly said, sitting down once more and reaching for a VCR tape. "Watch."

Holly inserted the tape and the small television screen immediately filled with her cheerful, only slightly feline-looking face:

"I'm here in front of Brenda's, the upscale watering hole frequented by Bernice Toland-James. With me is Mr. Ray Givens, who was behind the bar Friday night. In an exclusive to Fox News, Mr. Givens has come forward to tell us what he witnessed that night. Mr. Givens?"

Roy Givens squinted into the camera, grabbing at Holly's microphone to pull it close to his mouth. "That's right, Holly. I called Fox News as a good citizen, to tell what . . . um . . . what I witnessed perpetrated that night."

Holly, still smiling, attempted to retrieve her microphone. "And what was that, Mr. Givens?"

He pulled on the microphone again, turning his head to face

the reporter, while keeping his gaze directed at the camera. "She was in here, Holly."

Holly leaned into the frame, to get closer to the microphone. "She, Mr. Givens? Could you be more specific?"

"Her. Johnny Walker Red. Oh, jeez, I shouldn'ta said that. I mean Mrs. Bernice Toland-James, Holly. It was her. She comes in a lot."

With both of them holding onto the microphone, Holly said, "And when did she leave, Roy?"

"She, um, she departed the premises at one, one-thirty, Holly." Roy smiled at the camera. "And she wasn't alone, neither. She left with this *guy*. Hanging all over him."

"Hanging all over him?"

"Yeah." He turned to grin at the camera. "She was pretty smashed, Holly."

"Really? And did you recognize this gentleman?"

"Naw. Never seen him up to that night." Roy stood up straight, obviously excited now to get out the rest of his story. "But I can tell you what he looked like. I seen that picture of the dead guy you showed when you were talking to the D.A. on the tube this morning, and the guy was this Buddy James guy. Yeah, that picture you're holding up now. Stack of bibles, he was him, Holly. You know, the guy she killed."

Holly hit the remote control and sat back in her chair, grinning at Saint Just. "Game, set, match. Now, what was it you wanted me to do, Alex? I mean, right after you bang your gorgeous head against the wall for trying to tie my hands so I could interview Toland-James the way you wanted me to. Softball? I don't play softball, Alex. I play hardball. What do you have to trade now? It had better be good."

Fortunately, as he hadn't planned to see Holly Spivak today, Saint Just had happened to reserve some of the copied photographs he'd removed from the album. He'd thought they might be his trump cards if Dettmer proved reluctant. But as he wasn't, Holly Spivak's suggestion to one side, the sort who banged his head against walls, he hadn't used them. Taking the copies from his pocket now, he carefully placed them on top of her disorganized desk.

Holly kicked her chair front and frowned at the photographs. "These aren't file photos. Looks like an amateur took these. Copies, too. Where's the originals? There's Totila, still with his hair, so this one is an old picture, and a bunch of his goombahs with him."

She leaned back again, doing a very good impression of a woman completely unimpressed. "They were probably going out for spumoni. So what?"

"I showed a pair of similar copies to the district attorney, along with informing him that I possessed enough evidence to possibly arrest Mr. Totila again, if he were to agree to relax his clutches on Bernice and pursue other possibilities, delay his arrest of Bernice until more information is learned."

"That took guts, or a total lack of brains. And . . . ?"

"And he turned me down," Saint Just told her.

"Didn't arrest him, either," Socks put in, then stepped back, bowed his head. "Sorry."

Holly waved the photograph again. "You say you've got more?"

"Many more, in addition to documentation of names, places, and dates. I would imagine that comparing these snippets of information with crimes committed in the mentioned areas might be of some importance?"

"Damn straight. At the least, it could make a lot of news. But Dettmer didn't bite?"

"Not so much as a nibble. Interesting, yes?"

"No. That's nuts," Holly said. "What's one woman slicing up her husband over getting to take credit for nabbing Totila, maybe turning him, offering him a deal if he rolled on a bunch of others?"

"My question precisely, although I do believe the man had second thoughts, as he sent some underling chasing after me as I departed the building. Poor fellow, I imagine he got quite a dressing-down for having missed me."

"He was trying to put a tail on you?" Socks said. "You didn't tell me that."

"I rarely tell anyone everything, Socks. Now, Holly. As Dettmer doesn't seem to want those photographs, or the many others I have, along with the documentation as to where they were taken and when—perhaps you might?"

"Are you kidding? I'd bang you for them, Alex. Hell, I'd bang you anyway if you weren't gay."

"But he's not—"

"Socks, hadn't you said you were thirsty? Why don't you toddle off to locate a vending machine somewhere and then meet me on the flagway in, say, five minutes?"

"Oh. Okay," Socks said. "Sorry. I'll see you outside."

"Now," Saint Just said, taking the photograph from the desk before Holly could grab it, "how long will it take an excellent, hardballing, ethical reporter like yourself to assemble comprehensive biographies of Chadwick Dettmer and Willard James, and have them delivered to the apartment of my good friend, Maggie Kelly, hmmm? By, say, seven this evening? There's a dear."

CHAPTER 15

"Where the hell were you?" Maggie asked as Alex opened the door and walked into the living room carrying a small brown bag showing a grease stain at the bottom.

"Out and about, on the strut. But I've brought a peace offering," he said, raising the bag. "White cream, not custard filled."

"Gimme that," Maggie said, snatching the bag and opening it, sniffing its contents. "You are *so* lucky. Now, where were you?"

"Signing my contract with Mr. Pierre, of course, as he leaves for Paris tomorrow for an extended stay, and I could not fob him off. A bird in the hand, Maggie. Don't you think that's a sound choice? The bird in the hand? Ah, well. Has the package been delivered as yet? I saw nothing waiting in the foyer with Paul, or sitting outside my door. I arrived half hoping I'd see some hired street urchin approaching the building, package in one hand, a fiver in the other."

"Nothing. I'm going crazy here. Oh, and J.P.'s coming over. And Steve. I couldn't fob—head them off. They'll both be here soon." She dug in the bag for a doughnut. "Do you realize all that's happened since I got up Saturday morning? And you know what I've been thinking? I've been thinking that my life started going crazy right after you showed up. Like you brought trouble with you. I used to have a quiet life, Alex, a calm life, a—"

"A boring life?"

"Shut up, I'm on a roll here. Back to the last couple of days, okay? Saturday morning. All I wanted was to be a slob all weekend, maybe get some writing done. I mean, I don't ask for much. Then Bernie called. Then we saw a body. Then we drove all the hell the way up to Connecticut. Then your apartment got tossed. Then Sterling and Snake got kidnapped. Oh, and we're going to my parents' house for a family Thanksgiving dinner, and don't try to get out of it because this is partly your fault."

"My fault? Really? And how is that?"

Maggie bit into one of the doughnuts, closed her eyes as the sugary white cream hit her tongue. Barely noticing that, when she squeezed the doughnut and then licked more of the cream filling, Alex lowered his head, began inspecting his cuffs. But definitely noticing. After all, she *had* seen *Tom Jones*.

"Parents, Alex. Subconscious motivations. Evolving, growing, changing, whether we want to or not. You name it, it's in there, and you're all over it."

"Fascinating," Alex said, taking a seat on the facing couch. "Do go on. Although you might first remove that bit of cream from your upper lip and . . . ah. Of course, why employ the napkin?"

"Pay attention," Maggie said, running her tongue over her bottom lip, too, just for good measure. She'd been sitting at her computer, playing Snood for the past few hours, and thinking. Letting her mind drift, land where it wanted.

She'd already figured out that she'd subconsciously given the Viscount Saint Just his quizzing glass and sword cane so he'd have things to fiddle with, keep his hands occupied, use as props, even as defenses (hence the sword in the cane). Much as smoking kept her hands occupied, gave her something to do, even had the happy side effect of keeping away people she didn't want close. But that revelation, although stunning to her, could wait. "I created you."

"We're in agreement so far. Do go on," Alex said, pulling out his quizzing glass and polishing it on his sleeve.

She closed her eyes for a moment. Was he on the defensive?

Perhaps even a little nervous? Good. She sort of liked this particular revelation. "But then something happened, after you got here. You began to change. You're still Saint Just, but you're also . . . I don't know."

"Ah, yes. May I quote Jane Welsh Carlyle and say, 'I am not at all the sort of person you and I took me for'?"

"You, too? Right, I guess we're both confused. Because, yes, you've started creating *more* of you."

"Unknowingly, yes."

"Right. It's that unknowingly bit. Now shut up and listen. When I sat down to make you up, a blank piece of paper in front of me, I wanted to make you the perfect hero. I did that." She looked at his gorgeous face, and winced. "Cripes, did I do that. But then I had to give you some flaws, to make you more real."

"I don't care for broccoli, and Sterling is saddened by my penchant for disposing of damp towels on the bathroom floor. Guilty as charged."

"Knock it off, I'm being serious here. I made you arrogant, sarcastic. Women love that, if you do it right—and, before you ask, I'm not really loving it right now. But I also had to make you human."

"And my most sincere congratulations on that head, my dear, as you obviously did just that. Perhaps we should both rise, take bows?"

"Stop it, I want to get this out. I gave you a father you're estranged from, and a dead mother, a woman you never knew. You know, the obligatory dysfunctional family, the lousy childhood."

"And then neither mentioned nor used said parents in any of our books."

"True. When I research, when I do character descriptions, I need all this information for me, to maybe use someday, or maybe not to use, but just so I know it, know the character, what he or she has had to overcome. With you, what I did was give you all the junk that I wish I had. Then added some of the bad stuff."

"Such as?"

Maggie fought a cringe as she remembered her explosion in front of the media. "Well, like being brave. That was a good thing. I try to be brave, but I'm really not, except sometimes I just sort of . . . sort of *blow*. You got all the rest of it. And my parents. You got them, too. That was the bad stuff."

Alex sat forward, looked at her intently. "I beg your pardon."

Maggie held out her hands. "It fits, Alex. You're estranged from your father. Pencil in my mother. Your mother is dead, you never knew her. My father is alive, but he's nothing more than . . . than a cipher. I don't know him at all. It's like he's not really there, you understand?"

She blew out a breath. "Man, and I always swear I don't put anything of myself into characters. I've learned a lot since you got here, Alex, and I'm not exactly sure I couldn't have lived without the information."

Alex looked at her levelly for a few moments, then said, "And Thanksgiving dinner?"

"Your fault. I got brave. Told myself I was getting brave—evolving—and called home. But you've got most of the brave, I only got a little, and it ran out about five minutes into Mom telling me what an ungrateful child I am. So, like I said, your fault."

"And so I'm now sentenced to Thanksgiving dinner. You have such an interesting mind, my dear, at times almost frightening," Alex said, then stood up and skirted the coffee table, to sit down beside her. "But you do know that I am not you, and you are not me."

"Parts of us are."

"True. And we'll include Sterling, if you will. But we are not all the same person." He slid an arm behind her on the couch, settled his hand on her shoulder. Cupped her shoulder. Pulled her closer to him. "It is the opposites in us that attract."

Maggie tried to swallow, but her mouth was suddenly too dry. "You know, Alex, I don't think I'd like anything more right now than to just grab on to you and let you make love to me so that I don't have to think about Bernie or Sterling or Rob Bottoms or my mother or—"

"Shhh, sweetness," he said, lowering his head toward her. "Worries can always wait." He hesitated. "Rob Bottoms? Who or what, pray tell, is Rob Bottoms?"

"Did I say him? You'll find out, but he isn't important now."

"Good."

"Yeah. Good," Maggie said, closing her eyes.

And then he kissed her.

And Maggie melted.

And someone knocked on the door.

Alex sighed. "If you don't mind another quote that has just leapt into my mind, I will tell you that it was Michael Drayton who said, 'These poor half-kisses kill me quite.' "

"Michael whoever has a point," she said, pushing at his shoulders. "That's either J.P. or Steve."

"Both of whom I would happily consign to the devil at any other time," Alex said, kissing her one more time before heading for the door.

"Did you see it?" J.P. asked, brushing past Alex, tossing her briefcase at him. "Got anything to eat? I skipped lunch to get here and this magnificent body of mine needs fuel." She threw her bulk onto the couch. "Damn. Talk about your *presents.* So? Did you see it?"

Maggie and Alex exchanged shrugs. "No," Maggie said. Could J.P. be talking about Rob Bottoms? "What did we miss?"

"The bartender," J.P. said, toeing off her orange sneakers and curling her legs up under her on the couch. "One photo. Spivak showed him one photo. Not an array, not any kind of variety—here's a photo lineup, do you see anyone you recognize? Nope, not Spivak. She shows him just one, Buddy. Blows the bartender as a witness. Completely corrupts his testimony. Plus, dollars to doughnuts, they paid him. His credibility is shot. Totally shot." She raised her head, sniffed the air. "Speaking of doughnuts?"

"Here, go wild." Maggie tossed her the bag. "What bartender?"

J.P. explained while Alex played host, got them all cold drinks.

"So the prosecution won't be able to use him?" Maggie asked when J.P. was done.

"Oh, they'll try to use him, but I'll rip him to shreds on the stand. Were you paid to appear on television, Mr. Bartender? Really. How much? I'm telling you—that's one witness we don't have to worry about."

"Yes, but what he said is still interesting," Alex said, then took a sip of soda. "Bernice was seen with another man, seen leaving the watering hole, visually intoxicated, with that man. And, the next time anyone sees Bernice, she's covered in blood and a man is dead in her bed."

"Yeah, well, Tonto, one victory at a time, okay?"

"J.P.?" Maggie said, almost able to feel the wheels turning inside her head. "Is it possible the man she left with is the killer?"

"What? Oh, wait. You're thinking she got picked up by some serial killer, took him home, and damn, there's Buddy back from the dead, choosing that night of all nights to show up and claim his share of the three million in insurance? That's too pat. Plus, a serial killer would have knifed her, too."

"I guess so," Maggie said, looking to Alex. "Well? You have any ideas?"

"Several, my dear, but none I wish to share at the moment. J.P.? Have you been able to learn how Bernice is faring?"

"That's the other reason I'm here. Gloating about how Dettmer's going to be pissed about the bartender isn't all of it. I got that Doctor Chalfont to call up to the clinic, and he found out Bernie's behaving herself, not asking for a drink, saying nothing's wrong, she's fine, so can she get out of there."

"No horrible withdrawal symptoms?" Maggie asked. "That's wonderful. Or maybe it's too soon for that?"

"Chalfont says they're beginning to think she was on a binge.

Didn't you say her drinking got worse after her husband—first one—was murdered?"

Maggie nodded. "Bernie drinks. She always did. But not like she did when Kirk was killed. Since then? It's been pretty bad. So she isn't an alcoholic?"

J.P. shrugged. "Beats the hell out of me. Could be one doozy of a bender, and that could mean she's also an alcoholic, or maybe she's just depressed and it was easier to get alcohol than Prozac. I just know she's being good, and wants out."

"And can she get out?"

"She signed herself in voluntarily. That's all Chalfont and I could get her to do. Three days, according to the rules at this clinic, and she's free to leave. Maybe sooner. Chalfont was kind of vague on that one."

"So she could be coming back to the city—when? Wednesday or Thursday? I mean, maybe they don't count Sunday, because she checked in so late? But she'll be arrested."

"Possibly. Probably. If she even comes back here, which I'm sure she will. She's not stupid enough to run, and I've got her passport. Anyway, I wanted you all to know, and to watch for her if she shows up, let me know right away. But I've got court starting tomorrow, so I can't baby-sit her."

"Alex?" Maggie looked to him for support. "What do we do if she shows up?"

"Ridding this apartment of spirits would be my first suggestion, although that could prove embarrassing for her. Oh, and pray the few media persons remaining on the flagway will have disappeared by then. Other than that?"

"Other than that," J.P. said, "I'm outta here. Oh, and Mary Sunshine? You did great today. Bottoms deserved every bit of it. Just don't do it again, okay?"

Maggie sat and examined the contents of her glass while Alex escorted J.P. to the door, handed her the attaché case.

"Bottoms? I've heard that name before, haven't I, Maggie? What did you do?"

"Nothing," she said, taking a sip of Pepsi. "Well, not exactly nothing. Rob Bottoms is a reporter for one of the stations, I forget which. He shoved a microphone at me when I was coming in and I told him Bernie was innocent or something like that. J.P. must have seen it on the noon news." She shrugged. "That's about it. Nothing big."

"Big enough for you to have mentioned his name in your litany of complaints," Alex pointed out, because he probably hated her and wanted to watch her suffer.

"Okay, okay, so he said something nasty to Socks when Socks tried to keep me off-camera and I . . . I went a little nuts."

She waited, still not looking at him.

"I see," he said at last. "One of those impossible to hold back moments of bravery. You may not stand up for yourself with enough regularity to please me, but you are a tiger for your friends. My congratulations. Did it feel good, Maggie?"

She looked up at him, grinned. "You mean until I realized what I'd done and started to shake? Yeah. It felt good."

"In that case, my dear, hold up your head and let the world know you not only did it, you're prepared to do it again, in a heartbeat. A good third of brave is actually bravado, I've always found. Now, that must be the good *left*-tenant. Are you ready for him? Chin lifted?"

"Oh, open the damn door," Maggie said, giving straightening her spine her best shot.

"Maggie. Blakely," Wendell said as he entered. "The doorman gave me this to bring upstairs."

"Ohmigod, the ransom stuff!" Maggie said, leaping off the couch, ready to grab the package out of Wendell's hands.

But he reacted quickly, holding the package above his head. "You were expecting this? And you didn't call me? Do I have to remind you that I'm a—"

"Oh, cut line, Wendell, we know who you are," Alex said, neatly divesting the man of his prize. "I merely wanted to inspect the thing myself, before calling you in. Maggie had nothing to do with it. Here you go, my dear," he then said, tossing the box to her.

"So much for fingerprints on the packaging," Wendell said, sitting down beside Maggie. "Okay, sweetheart, this is what we do. You open it, but slowly, touching it as little as possible. Unless you want me to take it downtown?"

"No time for that, Wendell," Alex said. "And might I remind you, speed in recovering Sterling is of the utmost importance right now. You may obtain fingerprints directly from the kidnappers once we've apprehended them."

"Speaking of fingers . . ." Maggie hesitated. "What . . . what if Sterling's little finger is in here? They do that sometimes, Alex. Kidnappers. You want proof, so they send you fingers, and ears, and—here, you open it."

Wendell shook his head. "You two are a real pair."

"Ah, you've noticed. How remarkably observant of you, *left*-tenant," Alex said, retrieving a scissors from Maggie's desk and cutting the string that held the brown paper wrapping over the contents, then pushing back the paper with the tip of the scissors. "We were discussing exactly that before your arrival, as a matter of fact. Well, hello. I believe we have a videotape."

"Handle it by the corners, Maggie."

Maggie, who'd had her hands over her eyes, lowered them slowly, to press them against her cheeks, then looked at the thing in her lap. "They made a tape?"

"I have to take that downtown, Maggie. I mean, I can't believe I'm letting you two talk me into what I've done so far. Why am I letting you do this?"

"Because you don't trust the FBI not to screw it up and get Sterling and Snake killed, and because you hate Dettmer and don't want him to get the glory," Maggie reminded him. "You're as bad as we are, and that's why we like you so much. You just pretend to go by the book."

Alex chuckled, then inserted the tape in the VCR and picked up the remote control. "Here we go. Ah . . . Sterling, there you are, my friend."

Maggie bit her lips between her teeth as Sterling's face appeared on the screen. "Where are his glasses? Freeze that, Alex. Oh, look. He's got a black eye, and his glasses are missing."

Alex had paused the tape and continued to stare at Sterling's frozen image even when Maggie was eager for him to start it again. "Alex?"

As if it took him a moment to understand that she'd said his name, Alex gave a small start, then composed himself, although Maggie could see a muscle working in his cheek. "Yes, of course. Forgive my small lapse."

"Alex, it's okay. It's a black eye. Sterling's okay."

"For now," Wendell said tersely. "Are you sure you two don't want to rethink this?"

"Even less so now than before, thank you, Steve," Alex said quietly, and picked up the remote once more.

"Got you, Alex. Play the rest of the tape."

Maggie grabbed a notepad and pen from the coffee table, ready to take notes.

Sterling seemed to be listening to someone off-camera, squinting at someone off-camera. "Oh. Oh, yes. You did say for me to do that, didn't you? Sorry, I'm feeling a bit befuddled, which is not all that out of the ordinary for me, as Saint Just might tell you. Like this?" he asked, raising a newspaper in front of him, holding onto both edges.

"Today's paper," Wendell said. "So we know they were alive this morning. Sterling, at least."

"Shhh," Maggie said, leaning closer to the set.

Sterling put the newspaper down and looked off-camera once more, nodding several times as he heard what was to Maggie no more than a mumble.

An arm appeared on the screen, shoving a piece of paper at Sterling, who took it. "And now this? Not that I wish to complain, far be it from me to do any such thing, but don't you think this is all rather dramatic?"

There was another rumble of a deep voice and Sterling sighed. "That wasn't very nice. Snake becomes frightened when you say such things, don't you, Snake? And Saint Just won't be best pleased, I should warn you of that. Oh, and if you could step back with that camera? The light is blinding me."

More mumbling.

"I wish we could hear what that bastard's saying," Wendell said, and Alex raised the volume.

The camera panned back, showing more of the room Sterling sat in, his hands free, his feet trussed together at the ankles.

Sterling squinted at the paper. "Do . . . what we dish? No, wish. Wish. Do what we wish—or less . . ." He looked off-camera. "You might have meant *else* here, not less. E-l-s-e. Just a friendly observation. And I'm having a deuce of a time reading this. You broke my spectacles, remember? Perhaps it would be better all round if you read the message yourself?"

The screen went dark, then there was Sterling again, with Snake sitting beside him, his ankles also tied, and now Snake held the paper, which shook in his hands.

" 'Do what we wish—or else.' " Snake looked at the camera, his handsome face pale. "Or else what?" he asked.

"I don't think you want to pursue that train of thought, Snake," Sterling said, speaking out of the corner of his mouth. "Just read that, if you please. These two lovely gentlemen who are not that far away have promised us lavatory privileges once we've performed for them, as it were, remember? Yes, performed for them, that's the word I want. To return to my current dilemma? That door back there, with the light over it? I don't wish to be crude, but I believe that light is calling to me, and all of that, and it's not that far away. And I'm feeling quite peckish, what with smelling the air filled with the aroma of Chinese food. I particularly enjoy wonton soup. Now, finish it, Snake."

Snake visibly swallowed, nodded. "Bring what we want to

the Staten Island ferry at midnight tonight . . . or the . . . *they* are both dead." Snake looked at the camera, blinked. "Oh. That's what else. Fuckin' A."

And that was it, the end of the tape.

"I want to know who delivered that tape," Wendell said, and was out the door before Maggie could tell him that Paul was on duty, which meant he was wasting his time.

Alex rewound the tape, then put down the remote controller. "Bless Sterling. What a brick in a crisis," he said, shaking his head. "I am truly overwhelmed by his genius."

"Clues, you mean?"

"Most definitely. They are being held near, beside, or above a Chinese restaurant."

"Yeah," Maggie said, rolling her eyes as she reached for her cigarettes and lighter. "Only a couple of those in Manhattan. Should be a snap. God only knows why I was worried."

Alex silenced her with a look. "He also talked them into moving the video camera back so that we could see more of the room. What did you think of it?"

"That it was pretty shabby-looking?" Maggie offered, shrugging. "And there were two bathrooms, one marked MEN, the other WOMEN. So they're holding them somewhere normally used by the public, not an apartment or house. The room was big, and pretty empty—there was almost an echo. Did I miss anything?"

"There are still only two kidnappers."

Maggie looked down at her notes. "Oh, right. Boy, Sterling *is* good. Another case of evolving, right? I wrote down everything he said, word for word, so we can go over it again, for more clues."

"Sterling was always highly intelligent. He just has had no opportunity to remove his light from beneath the bushel basket of his more subservient role in our books."

"Okay," Maggie said, pretty much deciding she'd been an unwitting genius when she'd created Sterling and Saint Just, and then looked up as Steve reentered the room. "Anything?"

"Nothing. Jackass says he was emptying a trash can and came back to see the package addressed to Saint Just and Maggie Kelly—Sterling must have given them the names. From the smell on him, I'd say he'd been out back with a reefer, but I'm homicide, not narcotics, so I don't give a crap." He nodded toward the television. "Did you play it again?"

"No, not yet. There's really no need," Alex said. "Tell me about this Staten Island ferry?"

"Forget it," Wendell said, sitting down beside Maggie and taking her hand in his. "From here on out, it's my ball game. Maggie, you do understand that, don't you? I'm a professional. Sterling and Snake are in real trouble, and they need professionals."

"I agree totally," Alex said. "You'll probably want the tape?"

Maggie's head jerked around so she could goggle at Alex. Now what was he up to? It was getting so she couldn't tell the players without a scorecard.

Steve looked at Maggie. "Yeah . . . I need that. What the hell is going on inside that head of yours now, Blakely? I—"

"Here you go then," Alex said, handing over the tape, the wrapping, even the string. "We are counting on you to do your utmost. You or one of your compatriots will, I am assured, be clad as me when you prepare to make the exchange? Do make sure he isn't wearing ugly shoes. I have my reputation as a gentleman of good taste to consider."

"You . . . you don't want in?"

"Passionately. But Maggie has convinced me that this is no time for me to insist upon taking charge. I know you have to be off now, so don't let us detain you. Please keep us apprised."

"God, I'm crazy. All right. You know, we still don't even know what it is that they want. I'll just have to fake it when they show up."

"You?" Alex sighed. "Definitely other shoes. And perhaps a haircut?"

"Every time I start to like you . . ." Wendell said, then kissed Maggie on the cheek and left the apartment.

"And what the *hell* was that all about? Why didn't we tell Steve about the photographs?"

She watched as Alex moved to her desk and sat down, put his hand on the mouse controller of her computer. "Because we may need them. I have every confidence that I will be the one to effect Sterling's rescue, and long before midnight. However, if I have overestimated myself, it would not do for the police to bollix such a delicate exchange and lose what we have. Now, to get to work on Sterling's clues."

Maggie leaned over his shoulder as he searched Google for *restaurants Chinese Manhattan.* "Have you been to Chinatown, Alex?"

"No, I don't believe I've as yet had that pleasure."

"I didn't think so. You'll never find Sterling that way. I'll get that. Cripes, we've got Grand Central Station here today."

Maggie opened the door and Socks, Killer, and Mary Louise straggled in. When Killer asked if they'd found Snake yet Maggie shook her head, and waved them to the couches.

"All we know is the kidnappers want us to bring what they want to the Staten Island Ferry at midnight. Presumably, that's when we'll get Sterling and Snake back," she explained as Socks took her place leaning over Alex's shoulder.

"What you looking for?"

"Chinese restaurants."

"Can't help you. I hate the smell of those places."

"Ah, yes, the smell," Alex said, then turned the chair to face the room. "Thank you all for coming here this afternoon. We've had a communication from the kidnappers that consists of a videotape of both Sterling and Snake that proves they are still in good health."

"Aces," Killer said, raising a fist, sticking up his thumb. "Now what?"

Maggie looked to Alex. *Now what? Good question.*

"Now, George, I am afraid we do nothing. *Left*-tenant Wendell and New York's finest will take things from here. Although I'm certain Sterling would appreciate it if you were to go across the hall and feed Henry?"

"Sure," Killer said. Alex flipped him the key, and he was gone.

"Good move, Vic," Mary Louise said, munching on a pretzel from the bag she'd taken from the kitchen. "He's been driving me nuts. 'Snake's in big trouble.' 'Snake's gonna be killed.' 'Snake's gonna die.' I was thinking about buying the guy some Depends."

Maggie coughed into her hand.

"So you're really looking for Chinese restaurants?"

"Yes, Socks," Alex told him. "Sterling was brilliant enough to try to lead us to him by way of some clues he mentioned in the tape. In addition to those he so outstandingly laid out for us, he has proved to us that the thugs holding him and Vernon are dumb as red bricks—something good to know. But Maggie here tells me that locating one Chinese restaurant in Manhattan is a fruitless exercise."

"Man, I'll say so. What did Sterling say about a Chinese restaurant? Is that where they're holding him?"

"Possibly," Alex said, reaching into his jacket pocket for a cheroot. "But that was only one of several clues Sterling managed to give us with his captors none the wiser. It is quite lowering, really, that two such unintelligent buffoons could have us so thoroughly baffled."

"Now you know how I felt when Paul got promoted to head doorman over me," Socks said, nodding. "What other clues? I mean, we're here, right?"

"Very well. Maggie?"

Maggie picked up the notepad she'd scribbled on earlier. "Two kidnappers. Snake and Sterling in old, straight-back wooden chairs. You know, like the kind institutions use. Schools. Ankles tied. Sterling's with rope, Snake's with something that looked like a really thick drapery cord. You know—deep maroon, shiny, like two pieces of cloth wrapped around each other."

Alex held up a hand. "This was impromptu, not well planned out," he said, looking happier. "They took them in daylight, close to dusk, but still in daylight. They could have put them in a vehicle with tinted windows or the like and taken them anywhere, but I doubt they wanted to move them too far, as they'd still wish to watch us. And I believe that most especially because Sterling said very nearly those very words, twice. *Not that far away.*"

"Somewhere between here and the Staten Island ferry, is that what you're saying?" Maggie asked. "That narrows the search a little, but it's still a lot of Chinese restaurants. If that's what Sterling smelled."

Alex closed his eyes. "Pessimism is not helpful at this point. We're making progress. Please continue. Every word Sterling uttered could be another clue."

Maggie shook her head. Poor Alex. He couldn't help himself, he had to be a hero, not understanding that *she* planted all the clues for him in their books. God, she was even starting to think of them as *their* books. Pitiful.

Or did he know all of that, and still he pressed on? What would that make him? A real hero? Yeah . . . it would.

She brought herself back to attention. "Okay. First the rest of my notes. The room was pretty big, really bare. Echo in there, in fact. Wood floors. Dark. In fact, the only real light beyond that from the video camera came from the light Sterling talked about, over the restrooms. It was red, and kept blinking. You know, not regularly, but like there was something wrong with the bulb. That's it."

Mary Louise, bag of pretzels still in her hand, stood up. "That's nothing. I'm going to go help Killer."

Alex turned back to the computer. "Maggie? Is there a way to narrow this search to the area between here and the ferry port?"

"I don't know," Maggie said, putting down her notes, which Socks immediately picked up. "I guess we can give it a shot."

So Alex and Maggie surfed the net, and Socks read Maggie's notes, her word-for-word transcription of everything Sterling had said.

"Um . . . Alex?"

"Yes, Socks. You want to help us search?"

"No . . . and this is going to sound really screwy, but . . . but I think I know where they are."

It all got a little weird after that. . . .

CHAPTER 16

There is a lot to be said for dumb luck, as Maggie would call it, Saint Just thought as he and his coterie of eager assistants stood at the curb a full block away from Maisie's Chinese, waiting for Wendell to arrive.

"You know," Maggie said now, seemingly having some trouble speaking around the large amount of chewing gum in her mouth, "I'm really not thinking about this as any kind of fun, or some adventure or something. I'm thinking about Sterling. Really. But it is exciting, I have to admit that. And then there's—Mare? That's my purse."

"Yeah. You said I could keep it."

"Bull! That's Coach. I did not. When did I say that?"

"Let it go, Maggie," Saint Just said, taking her elbow and guiding her away from the curb. "Are you sure you want to do this?"

She blew a small bubble, let it pop. "Are you kidding? You're doing it. Killer and Mare are doing it. Socks is doing it. I'm supposed to wait on the curb? I don't think so."

"Wendell is not going to be best pleased."

"Yeah. And don't think I didn't hear the two of you planning to keep me out of trouble from here on out. Do you have any idea how insulting that is? I can do anything you can do."

"You are rather necessary to the plot," Saint Just agreed, adding, "especially if you could . . . is the word hike? Hitch?"

"Hike up my skirt? Again? You're kidding. It's already two inches above my knees. I roll the waistband any more and I won't have a waist."

"It was only in the way of a suggestion."

"I can open another button on my blouse."

Saint Just sighed. "I suppose that will have to do."

"What's the matter with my—with me?"

"Not a thing, my dear. You are perfection."

"But you like my legs best."

"My dear, I am a Regency hero. Bosoms were always on display. Gentleman of my era, however, were regularly enticed and all but rendered stupid by the merest glimpse of an ankle. Why, I'm amazed I haven't as yet swooned at the sight of your legs."

"Oh, shut up." She leaned forward, looking up the one-way street. "Steve should have been here by now. Are my legs really that good?"

"A lady doesn't fish for compliments. But, yes, they are outstanding," Saint Just said, adjusting his cuffs. "Now, I am counting on you to stay with Mary Louise, completely out of the way except to perform as I've asked you both to do."

"We're the diversion. I know. Oh, here comes Steve. Get ready for fireworks."

Saint Just watched as Wendell climbed out of the front seat of what he had learned was called a "black-and-white," followed by the uniformed driver.

Steve spared a look for the others, then headed for Maggie, hooking a thumb over his shoulder. "What are they doing here? And where's the costume party?" Then he looked more closely at Maggie, frowned. "You, too? Oh no. Absolutely not. Whatever you've got cooked up, I don't want to know about it and you're not doing it anyway, so I don't care what it is."

"Tch, tch, *left*-tenant," Saint Just drawled as he lit a cheroot. "Have you forgotten that you are here as an invited guest?"

"On what's probably a wild goose chase. Whose idea was this?"

"Actually, Socks is the one who put all of Sterling's clues together. Socks? Toddle over here a moment, if you please."

Socks crossed to them, rubbing his hands together. "What's up? We ready to move? Curtain up, light the lights?"

"Jeez Louise," Wendell said, looking at Socks. "Are you wearing make-up?"

Socks closed his eyes. "Just a trace of shadow. And some blush. Why?"

"Hey, no reason," Wendell said, rolling his eyes. "But I repeat, you all know this is probably a wild goose chase, right? There have to be a couple of hundred rehearsal halls in the city."

"With a blinking light over the bathrooms, right across from the stage? Do you know how hard it is to concentrate on being a tree in a windstorm with a red light flashing at you? And the Chinese food? I used to have to go home after my lesson and take Pepto-Bismol, and all I did was *smell* the stuff. That was about six months ago, and they've closed the place, I heard. But that's it, I'm one hundred and ten percent positive."

"Yeah, yeah, okay," Wendell said as Saint Just merely stood back, allowed the man to have his moment.

"Jake and I have already gone around the block for a look-see. There's a back door, and Jake will cover that. I couldn't call anyone else in or I'd have the brass all over me for a—hey, why not say it again—a damn wild goose chase. But, because you'll go with or without me, I'm here. Socks, you've been in the place. What's it like through the front door?"

Socks lifted his chin, smiled, obviously now enjoying *his* moment. "Let me see. We enter through the front door. Narrow hallway, flight of stairs. Steep flight, up to the rehearsal hall. Anteroom first, office to the right, coat rack to the left. Door straight ahead, into the hall. Stage on the right, bathrooms on the opposite wall. Two windows, but they're blacked out. Oh, and there's a short hallway at the back, on one side of the windows, I don't remember which side. Anyway, that leads to a door and more steps that go straight to the street."

"Probably leading to that back door you mentioned," Saint Just said when Socks was through, and all but taking a bow.

Wendell scratched at a spot just behind his ear. "Okay. If you're right, and we all know you're not, they probably have Sterling and Snake in the rehearsal hall. Or in the office, and moved them to the rehearsal hall to make the tape. We can't know which. Blakely, you've had more time to think about this. What's your plan? And tell me it includes Maggie and Mary Louise out on the street, waiting for you to do your big rescue."

"I told you not to call him," Maggie muttered under her breath.

"Maggie? Are you chewing bubble gum?"

"Our plan, Wendell," Saint Just said, as the man looked at Maggie, frustration evident in his expression, "is to enter the building as if we are a troupe of hopeful thespians and their teacher."

"Let me take a wild shot at this. You're the teacher?"

"I'm hardly suited for the role of ingenue, *left*-tenant," Saint Just said, fingering his quizzing glass. "If the small foyer is unguarded, we will proceed into the rehearsal hall, quite casually, while you stay back to inspect the office Socks mentioned. If it's occupied by Sterling and Snake, you will release them while we cause a diversion in the rehearsal hall. If Sterling and Vernon are not being kept in the office, we will know that when we enter the rehearsal hall, and you will follow us, to gather up the baddies once the ladies and gentlemen, and myself of course, have confused and diverted them. You are, I presume, armed?"

"I shouldn't be. I should be locked up somewhere. Okay, you said there's only two of them. I'm not even going to ask how you know that one. Now here's how it goes. Jake gets inside, up the back steps, ready for anything. I stay in touch with him by radio—don't ask, Alex, I can do that, okay? We go in the front, *I* go into the rehearsal hall while you grab Sterling and Snake from the office. If they're not in there, I'll have already drawn down on the kidnappers and called Jake in for backup. Everyone else?"

Wendell glared at Maggie. "Everyone else damn well stays here. Either that, or I call for another squad car now, because I'm not putting civilians in harm's way."

"You're letting Alex go with you," Maggie pointed out, blowing another bubble. The girl was obviously, as Socks explained when he himself did it, "getting herself into the role."

Wendell looked at Saint Just. "You still got a sword in that thing?"

"Need you ask?"

"Right. Look, I walked out on the prep for the exchange at the ferry, saying I was following up one last lead, and they're soon going to be looking for me. Let's do this."

Wendell patted the small bulge in the side of his ill-fitting jacket, motioned to the uniformed officer, and started off down the street, Socks, Killer, and Mary Louise just about skipping after them.

"He's only one cop," Maggie said as she and Saint Just hung back, strolled more than skipped or stomped (Wendell did the stomping). "One person. And that Jake guy looks about twelve. I like your idea much better. The more people that come crashing into the rehearsal hall, the more confused those two goons will be, the less they'll be apt to pull out their guns, and the better our chances. Besides, I want to do this."

Saint Just grinned down at her. "Yes, I'd already sensed that. It is fun, isn't it? Danger, derring-do, the flamboyant act, the ingenious rescue, the brilliant capture. Serious business, I grant you, but Sterling would expect no less of me. You've written it, Maggie, many times. Now it's your turn to shine."

"You're doing this for me? Because . . . because I don't think I'm brave?"

"In part. Why, does that upset you?"

"If you think we're maybe putting Sterling and Snake in more danger, yes. But . . . but if you really think I can do it?"

"I know you can do it, my dear. I, after all, am a hero, and you created me. Ergo—"

"We're talking fiction here, bucko," Maggie said as they joined the others outside the door to the rehearsal hall. "This is real life. I can't go back and rewrite it if it all goes belly up."

"Yes, yes, of course," Saint Just said, stepping closer to Wendell. "Shouldn't you go with the officer? Just to make certain the door isn't locked? I mean," he said, lowering his voice, "I believe I still see the dew on that boy's chin. I wouldn't wish to see him come to grief. We'll await your return, once the lad is in place."

Saint Just then looked pointedly at the uniformed cop, to see him gripping a baton with white-knuckled fingers as two red flags of color stained his peach fuzz cheeks.

"So very young," he said, sighing. "And you're quite sure he won't shoot himself in the foot?"

"You're such a pain in my—Jake. Follow me." But first he jabbed a finger in Saint Just's chest. "Wait for me."

Saint Just brushed at his shirt, to be sure there were no wrinkles, and waved Wendell on his way. "Well, that was simple. It is so lamentably easy to mislead an honest man," he said, opening the door to the rehearsal hall and bowing for the ladies to precede him into the small foyer.

Which smelled of Chinese food, almost more so than the air on the street.

"What about the lieutenant?" Socks asked, closing the outer door softly. "Aren't we going to wait for him?"

"He'll catch up. Ready, ladies and gentlemen?"

Killer, his face as white as his shirt, raised a hand. "Uh . . . I gotta go."

"Oh, for crying out loud," Mary Louise said, rolling her eyes. "Didn't you go before we left the apartment? I *told* you to go."

"Sorry, Mare." Killer hung his head. "I forgot?"

"Very well, George. When nature calls, what use are we to deny the summons? You're excused."

"Oh, great. Thanks. I'll bet there's a bathroom next door, at the restaurant. I'll be right back."

The door opened and closed once more.

"Moron. Great big *ma-roon,*" Mary Louise said, one hand on the bannister. "Are we really going to wait for him?"

"Hardly," Saint Just said, tucking his sword cane beneath one arm as he surveyed his troops one last time:

Mary Louise, lamentably but, at the moment, fortunately clothed in her more usual garb. He had dressed her for the cover-model contest, which gained the naturally beautiful young woman her own contract with Fragrances by Pierre, but this afternoon she had chosen to dress herself: what Saint Just had recognized as cowboy boots. A pair of shorts that began two inches below her navel and ended approximately eight inches later. What could only be a large handkerchief tied around her small bosoms. But she had agreed not to color her hair pink, and had left out all the facial adornment save five earrings, all of them most mercifully in her ears.

Mary Louise, Saint Just knew, remained a work in progress.

Socks, bless him, had ingeniously dressed himself as exactly who he was, a doorman and hopeful actor and now cover model who still lived with his beloved mother, could impersonate Barbra Streisand with remarkable accuracy and range, counted a female impersonator as one of his closest chums, and in his off hours had proven himself to be the proud possessor of at least a half dozen pair of extremely slim black imitation leather slacks and twice as many skin-tight black T-shirts. He had a lean and hungry look about him, as well as a most endearing vulnerability.

He looked, in short, exactly like someone who had come to the rehearsal hall to . . . rehearse.

And then there was Maggie. The lovely body most often hidden beneath too-large clothing and depressingly uninspired pajamas, showed very much to advantage in her current too-short skirt, high strappy heels, and knit blouse. She'd tousled her artfully streaked hair, wore at least one too many pieces of jewelry, and even now she was pushing yet another stick of pink chewing gum into her mouth, past her overly red lips.

If the thugs upstairs weren't diverted, they were either eunuchs or blind. Or Socks. Hmmm . . . no, he didn't think so.

Saint Just started up the stairs, careful not to touch the railing, which appeared to be rather sticky, his troupe following behind. A bare bulb hung at the top of the stairs, illuminating a second foyer, and the door to the office.

Motioning for everyone to remain quiet, he drew his sword and then signaled for Socks to open the door.

Socks did, pushing it in even as he kept his back to the wall, and Saint Just stepped through into another room lit by a bare bulb. There were two chairs. There was evidence of lengths of rope, lengths of satin cords on the floor. There was nothing else.

He exited the room, shook his head, and replaced the sword. "They've been moved, but hopefully are still on the premises. Stage in this direction, correct, Socks?"

Socks nodded, his eyes wide. "I was right, they're here? Wow."

"In full throat, people," Saint Just said as he heard the door to the street open and heavy footfalls on the stairs. Clearly Wendell was on his way up, and with all the finesse of a charging bull. *"Now."*

Saint Just flung open the double doors to the rehearsal hall, his arms remaining spread wide as he visually sized up the interior and its occupants before he turned to everyone and said, "Ah, my young thespians, here we are. Home of the muse. Haven of the artist. The cathedral of sweet creation. Step lively, my lovelies, and we will commence. As Abelard said, 'What a King, what a court, how fine a palace!' "

Still with his back to the room, sure he could feel an angry glare boring between his shoulder blades, he continued to move backwards, waving his fingers to encourage everyone else to follow him, even as he kept his eyes on Maggie. Tightly on Maggie. "Come now. Come, come."

Maggie inclined her head to the left, then turned to her right and could not suppress a smile.

Yes, he already knew that. Thugs to the left, Sterling and

Snake to the right. A rather loud, obviously laboring fan running somewhere, most probably inside one of the bathrooms. That could turn out to be a stroke of luck.

Mary Louise took up the dialogue, as she'd volunteered to go first, and had the only real rehearsed lines. The rest would be, as Socks had termed it, improvisation. "Oh, wow, a real stage! I haven't been on a real stage since high school. I was Eliza. Well, her understudy. Hey—who are these guys?"

Curtain up.

Saint Just turned around, but not before seeing Wendell at the door, and waving him back into the shadows. The man was set up well enough to look the actor, but he also all but screamed *copper.* It was imperative he remain out of sight until Sterling and Vernon were safe.

"Youse! Who the hell do youse think youse are? G'outta here."

Saint Just wheeled about. "Enunciation, my good man, e–*nun*-ciation. *You,* not *use. Get out of.* Three distinct words. Clearly, and from the belly, speaking to the balcony." Then he frowned, added: "I say, are you here to join our group?"

As the man blinked and glared, Saint Just got his first clear look at the enemy's face. One of them, at least. Pitiful creature. Overweight. Huge, but soft. And with egg noodles trailing down his shirt.

Maggie and Mary Louise, as earlier directed, now hastened past Saint Just, all the way across the large room, to the wall near the hallway to the rear door.

Wendell might have wished to know that Socks and Saint Just had tended to that door an hour earlier, making sure it was unlocked, so that Maggie and Mary Louise could have an easy escape of it if necessary, if the moment became truly dangerous.

Now Saint Just was in front of the stage, Socks to one side of the room that had to be at least forty feet square, the ladies far to the other side. Too many places for one man, even two, to look at the same time.

A perfect flanking maneuver, if he did say so himself, even with George and his nervous bladder absent.

The thug was at it again, advancing on Saint Just, his arms hanging away from his body, rather like an ape on the move. "I said, youse get out. Youse can't be here. This here's private."

Saint Just frowned at the thug. "I beg your pardon? Are we early? I was certain I was promised use of this hall from five to seven."

"Yeah, well, Twinkletoes, youse *don't* got it," the man said, his hands balled into fists the size of hams. "Now get out."

"Oh, but he can't get out, Bruno." Sterling's voice came from behind Saint Just, from the near dark of the stage. "You see, it's exactly the way I told you. He's—"

"Oh, wonderful. More students. Bruno, you say? Wonderful name," Saint Just said quickly, placing himself in front of center-stage, where Sterling and Snake sat perched on the edge, surrounded by opened white boxes of Chinese food.

Snake, never the brightest star in any galaxy, still had a plastic fork halfway to his mouth, dripping noodles. "Uh . . . hey, hi, Al—"

"Yes, students!" Saint Just said, cutting him off. "Come, come, everybody. Today we begin *Macbeth.* 'Macbeth shall never vanquish'd be until Great Birnam wood to high Dunsinane hill shall come against him.' Tell me, children, what does that mean?"

"Oh, I know that one," Sterling said, raising his hand. "Great Birnam wood was near Macbeth's castle, and the attacking army cut off branches and put them on, then advanced on Dunsinane. Macbeth thought it couldn't happen, but it did. Because the soldiers pretended to be trees and—oh."

Wonderful. Sterling understood. He, Saint Just, and the rest of his small entourage, were Birnam wood, and had come in disguise to conquer Dunsinane.

Saint Just, his back to the stage, pretended to count heads, using the tip of his cane to do so, while actually checking on everyone's positions. Maggie and Mary Louise to the right, a lovely diversion. They were to preen, pose. Stay out of the way, even as their mere presence made them very much in the way.

But Mary Louise seemed to wish to enlarge her role. "Louise?" she said, stroking Maggie's arm. "How 'bout we practice that lesbian kiss again while we're waiting?"

"Okay, we could do that, *Thelma,*" Maggie said, not missing a beat. "But not so much tongue this time. You're not Madonna."

"You're no Britney yourself. Now, open up."

Bruno's attention was instantly diverted, and Saint Just motioned toward the bathrooms. "Logical, yes?" he said quietly, and Socks nodded, then started across the room.

"Saint Just? *Pssst,* Saint Just?" Sterling whispered, leaning front on the stage. "I knew you'd come. I told them you'd come. I told them you're a hero and—"

"Yes, yes. Hush now. Sterling, Vernon, hop down from there and start for the door. Now, while Socks diverts the man. I have your backs."

"Gotta piss," Socks said loudly, rolling his shoulders as he went.

Bruno, who seemed to have his attention and his hopes elsewhere, belatedly sprang to attention. "Hey, you. Where do youse think you're goin'? I told youse all, youse gotta go," the man called Bruno growled.

"God, man. Didn't I just *say* that?" Socks said, giving his head a little slap with the heel of his hand. "Duh. Be right back, dude." Then he hesitated, put a hand to his hip, looked Bruno up and down, winked. "Unless you want to come along, sweetbuns?"

"Go screw yourself."

"How boring," Socks said, and kept going, breaking into the chorus of "It's Raining Men" as he went.

Bruno watched Socks for a moment, then turned back to Maggie and Mary Louise, then back to Socks again. Poor fellow. So easily confused.

But Bruno wasn't *that* stupid.

"I don't think youse jerks are getting this. We've got the room.

Youse get out," Bruno said, advancing toward Saint Just again, hitching up his pants by pressing both forearms against his waist and hefting at his protruding stomach. "Else somebody's gonna get hurt."

"Oh, I know that one. That's from *Guys and Dolls,* right?" Maggie asked brightly. "I'll just bet that's where it's from."

Saint Just turned to see that she was on the move, blister it, ignoring his strictures, advancing on the thug, perilously close to getting very much in the way.

"Mag . . . er, Louise? Return to your place, please."

But the dratted woman had the bit between her teeth now, and wasn't to be turned away.

"Say, you're kinda cute," Maggie said, then pointed at Bruno. "Didn't I see you in that Swiffer commercial last month? Sure, I did. Hi, I'm Louise. What's your name again?" Then she blew a bubble.

"Sterling, Snake," Saint Just hissed. "I'll most certainly throttle her later, but don't waste this. *Move.*"

"In a twinkle, Saint Just," Sterling said. "I knew you'd come. I was just telling Bruno about how you foiled that attempt to assassinate Prinney by—um, Saint Just? The jig is up. Bruno has pulled out his pistol."

"Alex, watch out!" Maggie yelled at much the same time.

Saint Just, who had calculated distances and possibilities earlier, anticipating just such a move on Bruno's part, swung about with one graceful motion, wielding his cane like a club, so that it slammed against Bruno's forearm. The man's weapon skittered across the floor and Mary Louise snatched it up, held it in both hands as she aimed it at Bruno.

"I got him, Vic. Is this cool, or what?"

"Socks!" Saint Just called out. "The door! Close the door!"

The door to the men's room was opening, and Socks kicked it shut again, the second mobster's hand caught between the door and the wall, the gun he had in that hand falling to the floor. Socks picked it up, grinned at Saint Just.

The entire adventure had lasted no longer than two inspired minutes.

"Unbelievable," Wendell said, stepping into the room with his own weapon drawn, even as Jake came through from the back. "Un-freaking-believable. I had the drop on him the entire time you bunch of clowns were fooling around out here, you know," he said, looking down at Bruno, who was rolling from side to side, moaning, "My arm, my arm. Youse broke my freakin' arm."

"There was never a doubt in my mind, *Left*-tenant. Perhaps you'd care to assist Socks now? I believe he's having some difficulty keeping our second thug contained."

Wendell did a head tip thing toward the bathrooms. "Jake. Handle that."

"My arm! My arm!"

Wendell bent down. "Hey, bozo, you have the right to remain silent. Use it." Then he grinned up at Maggie. "I've always wanted to say that, just like a TV cop. Why should you guys have all the fun?"

"Inspired, *Left*–tenant. Wasn't it, Bruno?"

"Screw you," Bruno said, then looked up at Wendell. "You're a cop? Youse is all cops? Cripes, he's gonna kill me. I'm a dead man."

"Who's going to kill you?" Wendell asked, leaning closer.

Saint Just picked up one of the small white containers, sniffed it, then put it down again. "I believe the gentleman may be referring to one Enrico Totila, don't you?"

Bruno moaned.

The second mobster, a near clone of Bruno, his hands cuffed behind him, his trousers pooled around his ankles, was being half shuffled, half dragged toward the group, Jake on one side, a grinning Socks on the other, holding the man by the elbows.

"Shut it, Bruno," the man warned. "We say nuthin'."

"He broke my arm, Nick. He freakin' broke it."

"Call for the wagon, Jake," Wendell said, motioning for Nick to sit down beside his partner. "Makes no never mind to me, boys. We already have Totila nailed. But, first one of you who decides to help, hey, I'm not making any promises. Just think about it."

"A pity they're both incapacitated," Saint Just said, then sighed. "I really would have liked to pummel them. I had been quite looking forward to it, actually."

"And me," Sterling said. "You know, Saint Just—Henry, and all of that."

"Ah, well, we'll have to comfort ourselves that we carried off our plan so wonderfully. Shall we take our bows and depart?" Saint Just took out his handkerchief and lightly rubbed at Maggie's too-red lips, then motioned for everyone to leave the building.

Maggie nearly danced as she walked. "We were all wonderful, weren't we? We were all wonderful! Sterling? How's the eye?"

"Not so bad. Did anyone think to bring my spare spectacles?"

Mary Louise opened her purse and pulled them out. "Here you go, Sterl-man." Then she grinned at Snake. "Come here, you big jerk," she said, and opened her arms to him.

"Maggie, wait," Wendell called out, jogging over to them all just as they neared the stairs. "I'm going to need statements from Sterling and Snake here."

"Later, Wendell, if you please," Saint Just said, and Sterling, who believed Saint Just's word to be law, waved to the lieutenant and headed down the stairs.

"Yeah, all right, later. I've got to go call off the stakeout at the ferry anyway. I'm telling you, that was nuts in there, and if you ever try something like that again I'll—"

"Never complain about success, Wendell," Saint Just interrupted. "But thank you so much for your assistance. Truth to tell, I saw your participation in this exercise as being one of, well, cleaning up after us."

"Why, you—"

"Steve, please. All I want to do now is go home and wash my face. And take off these shoes. Is there anything else, or can it wait?"

"Yeah, there's something else. About Bernie." Wendell waited until Socks took the hint and went down the stairs, then said, "As long as I was at the station anyway, I checked the lab, pulled in a favor, and got something new for us to think about."

"And . . . ?" Maggie prodded when Wendell didn't say anything else.

"J.P. has to find out through channels, okay? My ass—my neck is already in a sling over Bernie's case, and now I've got to explain what happened here. I'll be lucky if I don't end up walking a beat at the Staten Island ferry. You don't mind if I sort of twist what happened here around a little, so I don't look like a complete jerk?"

"Understood. Our lips are sealed," Saint Just said. "But I take it this is good news for us, and unfortunate for Dettmer?"

"I think so, but who knows? Blood work on Bernie came back. Alcohol level? She was up there. But they also found Rohypnol."

Maggie staggered where she stood and Saint Just reached out to steady her. "Was she raped?"

"No. No assault. Just the Rohypnol."

"Excuse me?" Saint Just said. "Loath as I am to admit such a thing, I find myself adrift here."

"Oh, God, I'm sorry, Alex. Rohypnol," Maggie told him. "They call it the date rape drug. Right, Steve?"

"Right. It makes you look really drunk. A guy can pour some in a drink, and next thing you know he's walking the victim out of the bar. She'll do anything he wants, and remember next to nothing the next morning. It's a bitch. And, if we don't get the blood fast enough, we can't even trace it. Bernie's must have been one hell of a dose."

"So she's innocent," Maggie said, and Saint Just squeezed her hand. "I mean, we always knew she was innocent, and it's terrible that somebody slipped that stuff into her drink—but she couldn't have Rohypnol in her system and cut Buddy's throat, too. Could she?"

"I doubt it. Time of death establishes that Bernie was full of the drug at the time. But, that's up to the experts, and I'm sure there will be plenty on both sides. Personally? No way. No way in hell."

CHAPTER 17

Maggie dragged herself into the apartment, aimed her body at one of the couches, and dove in, her nose buried in the pillows. "I've never been so exhausted in my entire life," she mumbled.

"Yes, so you've said. In the hack, in the elevator, and again now," Alex said, placing his cane against the wall beside the door. "Am I to assume that your excursion into playing the heroine is one you don't wish to repeat?"

"Not any time soon, no," Maggie said, turning onto her back, to look up at him. "But we were great, weren't we?"

"I know my performance bordered on the superb, but that was only to be expected," he said, grinning at her as he walked over to her computer, brought up the screen and her America OnLine account.

"I'd have a comeback for that one, but I'm too tired. Catch me tomorrow, after a good night's sleep, and I'll zing you with it. What are you doing?"

"Eliminating your spam, of course."

Maggie closed her eyes, too tired to get up, stagger to the desk, bop him over the head. "You're doing *what*?"

"I see no need for you to read so much as the subject headers of some of the garbage you receive. Ah, another one. And we bid a fond farewell to *Size does matter.*"

Maggie giggled. "Are you deleting those for me or for you? What's the *matter,* Alex? Do those messages embarrass you?"

He ignored her, his hand still on the mouse, obviously still deleting like mad.

"There, done," he said at last. "Only six from journalists begging interviews. In a city this size, it would appear that Bernice is rapidly becoming yesterday's news."

"I'm sure she'd like nothing better, but I doubt you're right," Maggie said, stretching her arms over her head. "Where's Sterling?"

"Safe as houses in our own apartment, now that we've so thoroughly routed the baddies. You do know that Wendell could have put a period to our little adventure at any time? And yet he didn't."

"I know. And then he did that bit about the creeps having the right to remain silent. He had fun, didn't he? I mean, he broke darn near every rule in the cop manual, or whatever it is, and he *enjoyed* it."

"And now we must reward him. This could prove difficult."

Maggie pushed herself up against the cushions, bent to unstrap her shoes. "Why? We give him the photographs, he's a big hero all around, the mayor pins a medal on him, and Enrico Totila is hauled off to jail. Where's the problem?"

Alex poured them each a glass of wine, handed one to her, then sat down on the facing couch. "For one, I do believe I remember promising the photographs to Holly Spivak."

Okay, she wasn't tired anymore. "You *what*?! What in *hell* were you thinking?"

He shrugged. "A moment of madness? And, I'm hopeful, one that will bear fruit very soon. And it's not as if Wendell knows we've discovered anything, remember. As far as he knows, we have been dealing with an unknown, undiscovered *it.* Fortunately, we have managed to discover two *its.* Tell me, do you think Wendell would be satisfied with the key we found behind the landscape?"

Maggie blew out her cheeks, shook her head. "I doubt it, not once those photographs hit the news. Would Spivak? No, wait, never mind. She can't do anything with a safe deposit key. The cops can. Except, you know, none of this stuff is ours to give to anybody. It all belongs to Mrs. Goldblum."

"Who is not here. Who departed rather precipitously and may never return. I'm not too well versed in your American law, but doesn't this mean that the person in possession of the photographs, the key, is the one who is in charge of same?"

"Meaning you?"

"I would be my first choice, yes. At the moment, the coppers know that Sterling and Snake were kidnapped, held for some sort of ransom, and then rescued. Hopefully, Bruno and his friend will be singing—is that the word? singing?—to them about their employer, how they were merely following his orders."

Maggie sipped from her glass. "It could . . . no, wait. The goons know, don't they, and that's what they'll tell the cops when they try to make their deals? Even if they don't know, if Totila didn't tell them what they were supposed to pick up, if they only trashed your apartment as a warning or something, when those photos hit the news Steve is going to know just how they got there. We can't get out of it, Alex. We have to turn them over, first thing tomorrow, or sooner if Steve insists."

"Miss Spivak will not be best pleased."

"She'll be pissed," Maggie agreed. "Boy, Alex, you really screwed up this time. Shame on me, but some small part of me is laughing like hell."

"Anything to amuse you, dear lady," he said, executing a flawless "leg," as a formal Regency bow, complete with arm flourishes, was called. And he'd pulled it off beautifully in twenty-first century clothes. Man, she'd given him panache, in spades.

"Gee, thanks, but this isn't funny. We have to give the album to Steve, no question. Look how Spivak messed up that bartender interview. We don't want her messing up this one. I don't want anyone else coming after Sterling."

"Nor do I," Alex said, and Maggie felt a tingle skip down her spine at his tone. Gone was any hint of his usual good humor, and even sarcasm. His tone had gone flat, and definitely dangerous.

"Alex? You okay?"

"Right as a trivet," he said, smiling. "Then it's settled," Alex added, getting to his feet. "The photograph album goes to the coppers tomorrow. Wednesday at the latest. As they don't know we have it, they also won't know when we first recovered the thing."

"The police, Alex. Stop saying coppers. You sound like an old movie."

He smiled. "I'm so glad you agree. It goes to the *police.* And now, if you'll excuse me, I wish to go check on Sterling now that his undoubtedly emotional reunion with Henry is over. May I suggest you go wash your face?"

"You can suggest it," Maggie said, getting up and padding after him, barefoot. "I want to give him another hug."

When Alex opened the door the sound of a piano reached them as they stepped into the hallway.

"Piano? Sterling doesn't play the piano," Maggie said, putting her ear to the door. "Who's playing the piano in there?"

"Well, my dear, we have two avenues to pursue on that head," Alex said. "We could stand out here and discuss possibilities, or we could open the door and find out."

"You're really starting to get on my nerves," Maggie said, turning the knob and stepping into the apartment. "And this should be locked. Why isn't this locked?"

"Probably so that you won't feel it necessary to knock it down," Alex suggested as they both turned to see who was playing the baby grand. "Felicity?"

"Faith?" Maggie added, blinking.

Sterling either saw or heard them, because he came running

over, smiling. "Isn't she wonderful? She was here when I came home. That's Mozart she's playing now. We should be quiet, not disturb her."

"What's she—" Maggie hesitated, because Sterling frowned at her, then lowered her voice to an angry whisper, began again. "What's she doing here?"

The music stopped abruptly and Felicity stood up, her hands still outstretched, her manicured fingers curved over imaginary keys. "Hello, Maggie. Alex. I told you I played."

"Bully for you," Maggie said, grabbing a spot on one of the couches. "Who let you in here?"

Felicity sat down at the piano once more and idly ran up the scales as she said, "A very nice young man. Paul, I think. When I told him I was expected he escorted me up here, let me into this lovely apartment that I so wanted to see again." She frowned. "It looks different somehow. Wasn't there more furniture? Oh, well, I couldn't wait at your apartment anyway, Maggie. He didn't have a key that fit yours."

"And now you know why," Maggie said as Felicity's fingers cascaded over the keys to the opening of "Autumn Leaves." "Yeah, yeah, we're all impressed. Now cut that out."

"Maggie's had a very long day," Alex said, his hand on the keyboard cover, ready to slip it back into place as soon as Felicity removed her hands—which she did with some alacrity. "Delighted as we all are to see you, Felicity, is there some special reason you're here?"

Felicity shrugged her shoulders, swiveled around on the bench to face the room. "I came to see Bernie, of course. But she isn't here. I have a present for her." She then smiled at Maggie. "And one for you, of course," she added, her nose all crinkled up as she spoke as if to a child who might otherwise pout. "I could never forget *you.*"

Maggie glared at her, because that was all she could do. "You are so lucky I'm beat, Faith."

"Yes, you are, aren't you? This is a new look for you. I wasn't going to say anything, but you do look . . . oh, dear, *hard* is such a nasty word."

"Sterling," Maggie said, still glaring at Faith, "take a note, will you? Kill Faith. Pencil it in for, oh, Thursday?"

Sterling patted at his pockets. "I . . . I don't have, that is . . . I'll remember, Maggie. Oh, wait. You didn't really mean that, did you?"

Felicity laughed, a sound halfway between a bray and a trill. "So? Where is Bernie? You've hidden her somewhere, haven't you? I mean, you said she wasn't here the last time I tried to see her, but I knew you just had her in a bedroom or something because, well, you'd do that sort of thing, wouldn't you, Maggie?"

Maggie stood up, hugged Sterling. "I'm going home. You guys can stay here. Have a sing-along or something."

"No, wait," Felicity said, reaching into her oversize bag. "Don't forget the presents."

"Maggie . . . ?" Alex said quietly, and her shoulders sagged. "There's a good girl."

Maggie turned to Faith, held out her hands. "Okay, okay, give me the presents."

Felicity handed them over; two envelopes, each tied with a large pink bow. "I just think they're the neatest things. I mean I was with Jerold today—he's my broker—and it hit me. The perfect gift. Enjoy!"

"Wednesday," Maggie muttered under her breath. "I don't think I can hold out until Thursday." But knowing Alex would just prompt her anyway, she smiled and thanked Felicity for the gifts. "Bernie will be delighted," she said, figuring that was close enough to a thank you.

"Oh, you're angry, aren't you? You never could be graceful about these things, could you? I remember when you won your single Harriet. Was that at the Detroit conference? I think it was. 'Romancing Detroit.' WAR always comes up with such innovative names for the convention. You just mumbled, then got off the stage. I've had prepared speeches for *all* of my Harriets. Of course, now that I've been installed in the hall of honor in my category, I'm not eligible for the the contest anymore."

Maggie was just standing there, tapping her foot. "Done now?" she asked, smiling brightly. "Good. Faith, Sterling and Alex are gentlemen, so they won't boot you out of here, but we've had a long couple of days, so . . . ?" she ended, turning to look pointedly at the door.

Felicity gathered up her bag and light jacket. "You will tell Bernie I was here? And that she's in my thoughts? I leave tomorrow morning for a whirlwind tour for the new book, but she *is* in my thoughts."

"We'll tell her," Maggie said, opening the door, then closing it almost on Felicity's heels. "In her thoughts. Right. At least Bernie won't be crowded for space." Then she counted to three, turned and looked at Alex. "What?" she said, spreading her arms. "What did I do wrong? I thanked her."

"You won't allow her to be grateful, Maggie. That isn't kind. And, if I might put forth a theory, until you gush and gurgle and ask her to possibly go to the shops with you or share a suite at next year's WAR convention, I would say she will continue knocking on your door—or ours."

Maggie considered this. "You're saying she'll keep coming around, giving me presents, until I start *liking* her again?"

"Exactly," Alex said, rolling his head on his shoulders, obviously feeling weary himself. "Then, and only then, will she be able to snub you once more. It's fairly obvious."

"That's sick. Twisted." Maggie bit her lips between her teeth. "And *so* Faith." She looked down at the pair of envelopes. "I wonder what she got me this time."

"Yes," Sterling said, stepping closer. "Open it, Maggie. I like to see presents."

Maggie looked at the envelopes again. "Tomorrow, okay? If she did something dumb I'll just get angrier, and I need to get some sleep. What time is it, anyway?"

Alex pulled out his pocket watch. "Not quite seven."

"*Seven?* It feels like midnight. How can I be so tired? I can't go to bed yet. Steve is probably coming over to take statements from Sterling and Snake—who isn't here, by the way—and I haven't even had dinner. Only seven?"

"Yes, and with Holly Spivak on her way, if she has gathered everything I want. A decision, Maggie. Do we want the information or not?"

"Well, now, there's a question," Maggie said, stepping out into the hallway, looking both ways, to be sure Felicity wasn't still there, hunkered down behind a potted plant and ready to spring. "What information?"

Alex opened the door to Maggie's condo and ushered her inside. "I'd rather not raise your hopes merely to dash them," he said, picking up his wineglass once more, "but I believe the information will go a long way toward solving the murder of one Buddy James."

Maggie, who had snatched up and begun downing the last of her wine, sputtered and choked. "It . . . it *what?* What is it? Don't do this, Alex, don't keep secrets. We're *partners,* remember?"

"That we are, my dear. But I would rather be more certain of my suppositions before involving you."

"Your theory's full of holes, right?"

"Rather large, gaping ones, yes," Alex said, taking her wineglass and refilling them both. "You will allow a gentlemen some small latitude until he feels more certain?"

"I guess." Then she held up a hand. "But there's a limit. How much latitude?"

"Enough to tell Wendell that we still don't know what *it* is?"

"And here we go round the merry-go-round. Again. I'm getting pretty tired of playing devil's advocate here, but I think I should point out that he'll want to bring people in to search the place."

"Will he? He does, after all, know that Bruno and—Nick, was it?—didn't find anything when they performed their search. Why would he expect to find what they did not?"

Maggie rubbed at her forehead. "I'm too tired, because that sounds logical. But not too tired to know there's a stiff penalty for withholding evidence."

"Which we will not do," he said, and Maggie could tell that he was thinking even as he was speaking. "What we will do when next we see him is tell Wendell nothing, agreed? He goes away frustrated, no unfamiliar feeling for the dear man, and we show the album to Holly Spivak when she arrives, telling her she'll have photocopies of each page as soon as possible."

"Then, after Spivak hands over what you want from her, we give the album to Steve, saying we found it . . . Where did we find it?"

"I would suggest behind the refrigerator," Alex said, touching the small of his back.

"So why don't we go right now, photocopy the damn thing, and give it to him tonight? Get this over with?"

"One, time constraints. I expect Holly Spivak at any moment. And two, I may wish to employ it again before Wendell takes possession."

"Employ it for what?"

"Nothing to worry your head about. Now, perhaps you'd like to shower before the good *left*-tenant arrives? Are you hungry, my dear? I can phone out for a pizza or two. I think Sterling would like that."

"Yeah. Eat Chinese, you're always hungry an hour later," Maggie said, and put down her wineglass. She stood up, felt her head go light and her knees weak. "Wow. One-and-a-half glasses of wine, and I'm feeling it. I do need to eat. Okay, I'll shower, you get the pizza. Give me a half hour."

"Done," Saint Just said, just as the telephone rang. "Would you like me to—"

"I'll get it," Maggie said at the same time, and picked up the portable phone. "Hello?" She covered the mouthpiece. "It's Steve."

Alex picked up the extension:

Steve: I'm not going to make it there tonight, sweetheart. It's all going to hell here.

Maggie: What's wrong? Did they find out about us being there?

Steve: No. Jake's cool on that. But our boys clammed up immediately, and then their mouthpiece showed up.

Alex: Explain, please.

Steve: Cripes, Blakely, you're on here? You're always around.

Alex: And a veritable thorn in your paw, Wendell, yes. Now, what is a mouthpiece?

Maggie: Lawyer, Alex. Bruno and Nick already have a lawyer. Bet it's Totila's lawyer.

Steve: Bingo. And he's already arranged bail. It's not a done deal. They have to be arraigned at night court, but they're getting out before morning, Maggie, and everyone here knows it. Unlawful restraint, they're calling it unlawful restraint, not felony kidnap. So they get bail. Can you believe that? Who says the mob doesn't own judges anymore? Blakely? Stash Sterling and Snake someplace safe, okay? Unless you want me to take them into protective custody?

Alex: I'll do just that, thank you. So we won't be seeing you this evening? Aren't you finished the moment the thugs are locked behind bars?

Steve: Are you kidding? I'll be writing reports until midnight. And here I am, the guy who never took creative writing. Anyway, they'll be back on the street and I'll be here. Like they say, there's no justice.

Maggie: Awww, Steve . . .

Alex: Yes, well, I believe I'm done here and will hang up now. Feel free to bill and coo.

Maggie: Damn it, Alex, don't—

She covered the mouthpiece again. "Don't *do* that. Go home. *Your* home. And call for that pizza. Jeez. . . ." She turned her back to him and headed down the hall to her bedroom, holding on to the phone with both hands.

CHAPTER 18

Saint Just waited until Maggie had closed her bedroom door behind her before picking up the photograph album and his cane and heading across the hall.

"Sterling? Is it all arranged as I requested?"

Sterling nodded. "Mare and Snake will meet you at Mario's as soon as Miss Spivak leaves. Oh, and Mare dropped this off, saying you'd asked for it." He handed over a cell phone. "Saint Just, exactly what are you planning?"

"Nothing you need to worry your head about, my friend. Have you been putting ice on that?" he asked, looking at the purple bruising around Sterling's eye.

"This? Oh, yes, yes. But with my glasses on, I can't put the ice bag where it's needed, and with my glasses off, I can't see past the tip of my nose. It's a conundrum."

"One easily solved," Saint Just said, leading Sterling to one of the couches, the one with the cushions placed there upside down so the slashes in the fabric didn't show. "Lie yourself down and I'll fetch the ice bag."

"You're so good, thank you," Sterling said, toeing off his sneakers and pushing them onto the floor. "Oh. Mrs. Goldblum phoned. Did I tell you? Such a nice lady. I didn't have the heart to tell her what happened to her apartment."

Saint Just had stopped dead; he slowly turned to face his friend. "She phoned? When?"

"Let's see. We've been so busy. Ah, I remember. Just before Miss Simmons played the Mozart. I was going to come find you, but I couldn't be a neglectful host, and you arrived only a few minutes later and—was that all right?"

Saint Just fetched the ice bag and returned to the living room. "It was fine, Sterling. Just fine." He sat down on the facing couch. "So. Is Mrs. Goldblum enjoying her vacation?"

Sterling put the ice bag to his eye, then winced.

He did not see Saint Just's hands close into white-knuckled fists.

"She didn't say, actually. She just wanted to know if everything was fine here and I told her it certainly was, right as rain, because she's dead old, Saint Just, and I wouldn't want to shock her."

"You've a good heart, Sterling."

Sterling eased back against the cushions. "And a very sore head. She'll be here tomorrow evening. Yes, that's it. Tuesday. That's tomorrow."

"I beg your pardon. She's returning to the city?"

"Only to pick up something she forgot. Some passing thing? I really couldn't hear her, as there was a lot of noise in the background. Bells ringing, voices, music. She wants to talk to you when she arrives, Saint Just."

"And I her," he said, feeling his jaw tighten. "I'm going to phone for some pizzas to be delivered to Maggie's in about an hour or so. Why don't you rest until then?"

Sterling sighed, then smiled. "Yes, that sounds wonderful. You'll come get me?"

"Someone will, Sterling, in the event I'm still out and about on my errands," Saint Just said before returning to Maggie's apartment to use her telephone. He listened for a dial tone, which was rather unnecessary, as he could hear her shower running, then used the speed dial to order pizza, and some of Sterling's favorite cheese sticks. Poor man; he was too overset to remember those himself, but Saint Just was certain he'd miss them if they were not there.

Then he was off again, the photograph album tucked under his arm, his cane in his right hand, to wait for Holly Spivak in the foyer of the building.

She was already late, but by seven-thirty she was walking into the building, carrying a large brown manila envelope.

"We meet again," she said, holding up the envelope. "Where do we go to do this?"

Saint Just motioned to the single faux leather couch in the foyer and Holly sat down, patted the seat beside her. "You first this time. Show me."

For a good quarter hour Holly Spivak grinned and gasped and several times descended to a variety of expletives a gentleman pretends not to be hearing pass a lady's lips.

Besides, he was fairly well engrossed reading the material she had brought to him. He uttered a few expletives himself, but only in his mind, and manfully refrained from uttering a "huzza!" when he discovered what he'd been hoping would be there; that nebulous thing that he did not know to look for, but would recognize if he found it.

The gaping holes in his hopeful theory began to draw in on themselves like a noose.

At last Holly closed the album, laid the palms of her hands on the cover. "I'm going to *own* that station, Alex. Where did you get this?"

Saint Just carefully extracted the photo album from her grasp and placed it beneath the envelope. "That, my dear, is information you neither need nor want. Suffice it to say that copies of each and every page of the album will be yours to do with as you please . . . Wednesday. Perhaps sometime tomorrow, but Wednesday at the latest."

She made a grab for the album. "No. No! I want it now. You have to give it to me *now.*"

"My dearest Holly," he said, holding out a hand and helping her to her feet. "What you have just seen is evidence, correct?"

"Damn straight, it is. Totila goes down hard with that stuff, and so do a bunch of other wise guys. Stefano Tiberio, to name one big wise guy. Nasty son of a bitch."

"Wise guys?" Saint Just shook his head. "Never mind, my dear, I'm sure I'll be able to figure that out on my own, eventually. But, back to the album. In its original form, it is evidence, and the police will doubtless confiscate it immediately, as well as ask you some very pointed questions."

"So? I'm a reporter. I don't reveal my sources. They can put me in jail, but I won't talk, won't give them your name."

"How gratifying, I'm sure. However, if the police were to come into possession of the original, and doubtless announce what it contains, but not publish any of those contents for public consumption . . ."

He paused, waiting for her to pick up the thread. Which she did, as she was not a stupid woman.

"Then I can show the copies and say I was sent them anonymously, hint that they came from the cops themselves—and I'm home free."

And here it was. He either stopped now or was committed to going forward. There was no real decision; nobody was safe until and unless Enrico Totila and his group were removed from the board.

"I believe I would be happier if you hint that the photocopies came from Enrico Totila himself."

"Really? Wow, he'd be dead meat if I did that—turning on his own, maybe making a deal to inform on his buddies. But I like it. Totila will sing like a bird to the cops once I show the photocopies, he'd have no choice if he wanted to stay alive. I mean, not that I'm worried he'd try to come after me, but he could. God, Alex, you're a genius. A real fucking *genius.*"

"Modesty to one side, yes, I do believe I am. So? You're pleased?"

"Absolutely. When do I get the photocopies again?"

"No later than Wednesday. We must be certain the original album is already in police hands before you present your copies on the air, hinting that you believe they came to you courtesy of one Enrico Totila. Timing, you will agree, is fairly crucial."

Holly nodded. She pulled a card from her purse. "Here. Here's my home address. Send them there. I don't want anyone else at the station seeing them before I have my hands on them. I owe you, Alex. That stuff I gave you? Bunch of junk, all of it."

"Possibly. Did you reserve a copy of everything for yourself?"

"Do fish swim? You get anything out of that mess, and I'll be able to figure it out, and use it. Man, am I going to be the fair-haired girl at the station. Love you," she said, kissed his cheek, and ran out of the foyer on her high heels.

Saint Just picked up the album and his cane, and was off once more. Next stop, Mario's.

Mary Louise and Snake were sitting in the back, sharing a large cold roast beef sandwich, a soda bottle in front of each of them. "Hiya, Vic," Mary Louise said, waving him over to the table. "Mario put this stuff on your bill, okay?"

"Certainly."

"You get the phone?"

"I did. And it is untraceable?"

"Use it and lose it," Mary Louise said, grinning.

"Splendid."

"Not really. Anybody can get one."

"And modest with it all. Very well. You have the numbers?"

Mary Louise chewed several more times, then swallowed. "Give them to him, Snake."

Snake reached into his pocket and pulled out two crumpled slips of paper. "Killer's aunt Isabella's daughter Annuziata who lives where his Aunt Isabella used to live before she croaked got it from Totila's cousin Concetta who lives where his grandma used to live because Annuziata told her that her nephew Maurizio got stiffed by his boss and he wants to ask a favor of Totila. Like cracking a couple heads."

"These intricacies truly boggle the mind," Saint Just said, pocketing the papers. "How did you procure the second one? I have managed the address through another source, but not the telephone number."

Mary Louise grinned around a mouthful of sandwich. "I did that one. I know this cop, see? Started talking to him about how high and mighty the big guys live, while the cops who do the *real* work are out there holding the thin blue line, taking the bullets. Said I bet our guy lives in some mansion somewhere. And he told me where. The rest I got from this cross-directory I just happen to have. Sometimes it's just too easy, you know?"

"Easy enough to abandon, I pray, now that you've got your contract and a considerable step up in the world?"

"Hey, I told you I'm retired. You're the one asked me to do it. Shame on you, Vic."

"Too true. I am corrupting the easily corruptible. I should be, and am, ashamed. And now, thank you and farewell. Oh, and Mary Louise?"

"Here it comes," she said, rolling her eyes. "What is it this time, Vic?"

He reached into his slacks pocket and pulled out several large bills. "Go shopping, if you please. Our initial photography session is in less than two weeks."

Snake laughed. "Yeah, Mare, go shopping. Maybe then guys won't be walking up to you and asking how much."

"At least I'm not like Killer. I don't spend half my life walking with my legs crossed."

Saint Just left Mario's, a smile on his face. A smile that faded quickly.

Busy. Busy. And so very grateful for all the attention he had paid previously to both the Learning Channel and various police dramas.

Once away from the deli, he extracted the cell phone from his pocket, found the number he wanted, and punched in the numbers:

"Dettmer residence. Who is calling, please?"

"Alex Blakely for District Attorney Dettmer, concerning our meeting earlier today."

"I don't think—"

"How wonderful. Are you paid to do that? Not think? Please give my name to the gentleman. I'll wait."

Saint Just continued to stroll along the flagway, nodding to passersby who for the most part ignored him. How he adored New York.

"Blakely? Dettmer here. I'm in the middle of a dinner party. How the hell did you get this number?"

"And a good evening to you, my good fellow. I won't detain you. I'm only calling to ascertain whether or not there has been a change of heart on your part and you are now interested in the proposition I forwarded this morning."

"Pictures of Totila."

"Indeed. I have them with me now, even as we speak, and would be happy to meet with you, make you a gift of the whole lot. In exchange for a more, shall we say, civilized *treatment of Ms. Toland-James."*

"No deal. She's guilty and we're bringing her in. Like we don't know where she is? The hell we don't, and Boxer better start worrying about her license. I'm giving her name to the review board."

"Boxer, you say? I don't believe I know the name."

"Bull. And don't pull that crap about those pictures again. They're fakes. They've got to be fakes."

"Are they? Is your zeal to arrest Ms. Toland-James so intense that you can take that chance? I must ask myself, Dettmer—Why is the man so hot to have her under lock and key?"

The phone went dead.

"And now I'm certain," Saint Just said, smiling thinly.

He took out the second number, made yet another call.

This one took longer, but when it was done and a meeting arranged, he strolled to the corner, crossed the street, and walked a good three blocks to the south and another three to the west before stopping.

He wiped down the cell phone, smashed it beneath his heel, and then tossed it into a large dumpster before hailing a hack to take him to the nearest Kinko's, where he photocopied the entire photograph album, returning to Maggie's condo just as the pizza delivery van pulled away from the curb.

Timing is all. Timing is everything.

And Saint Just was always in the nick of time.

"Saint Just, there you are," Sterling said as he picked out a slice of pizza and aimed it toward his mouth.

"Sterling. Maggie. Shall I procure napkins from the kitchen, or would you rather simply pretend you're at the trough?"

"Nice try, Alex," Maggie said, expertly using her tongue to whip a string of pizza all the way into her mouth. "I will not be diverted. Where were you?"

"Off to see the wizard?" he suggested, having been forced on the occasion of a previous pizza-devouring gathering to sit through *The Wizard of Oz* while Maggie explained the plot to him and Socks sang along with Judy Garland.

"You mean the witch, don't you, or didn't you meet with Holly Spivak?"

"I met with her, yes."

"And you took that album with you."

"So observant. Have you also noticed that I've brought it back? I thought I might have more need of it this evening, but as it turns out, the party wasn't interested. And, before you ask, I have photocopied the thing for Holly Spivak, so you may feel free to phone the good *left*-tenant and apprise him of the fact that, goodness gracious, we have discovered *it* behind Mrs. Goldblum's refrigerator. He can then turn the album in to his superiors and receive a pat on what they will doubtless consider his fair head."

"Stop trying to score points off Steve, okay? Sit down and eat, and tell us what Spivak said. Did she go for it? I guess she did, right?"

"She saw the wisdom of my plan, yes," Saint Just said, selecting a slice, holding it slightly aloft over the box while oil drained off onto the cardboard. "Did Sterling inform you of his telephone conversation with Mrs. Goldblum?"

Once Maggie was done coughing, Saint Just explained the call, hoping she might know what a "passing thing" might be.

"Oh. Oh! I found it in her closet." Maggie unfolded her crossed legs and headed for her computer desk. "Where is that?" she asked, rummaging through the perennial mess that made up her corner of the writing world. "Okay, here it is. Her passport, Alex. She's coming back for her passport. She can't leave the country without it."

Saint Just took possession of the thing, paging through it, manfully not wincing at the photograph that should, by rights, have had Irene Goldblum challenging the photographer to pistols at dawn.

"She also wants to speak with me," he said as he handed the passport back to Maggie, who wiped her hand on her shorts, then took it, stuck the thing in her pocket.

"Maybe she wants to sell you the apartment. Remember, she does own it. We learned that much. Oh, and you can't afford it. Neither can I, so don't ask."

"Not even as an investment?" Saint Just asked, mostly because he rather enjoyed watching Maggie's green eyes flash in anger.

"Forget it. Although . . ." she added, biting her lip. "You know, it beats the hell out of the alternative."

"Oh! I know that one. Having us move back in here. That's the alternative," Sterling supplied, then dropped his chin. "Sorry, Saint Just. I lost my head there for a moment."

Maggie giggled.

"That's quite all right, Sterling. But to return to Mrs. Goldblum, if we might? According to Sterling, she will be dropping by tomorrow evening."

"You know what I don't get?" Maggie said, waving around a slice of pizza. "If Mrs. G. has been blackmailing Totila, why did she go overseas to do it? If that's what those trips were about. Why the postcards? And why in hell would she come back now, after Totila figured out it was her blackmailing him? Wouldn't she know that she's still in danger?"

"One would assume so, but then again, we all know the danger in assuming things."

"I don't think we have any other choice," Maggie said. "Until she shows up, that is. Man, do I have a bunch of questions for that woman. I think I'll make a list."

"Yes, I agree. Mostly, I'd like to know where she made her mistake, so that Totila discovered her. Indeed, there are still ends to be tied up there, even as we progress to other things."

"Other things being Bernie."

"Exactly."

"You're not going to tell me what you're thinking yet, are you?"

Saint Just got up, removed the manila envelope from the small pile that included the photo album and the photocopies, and tossed it on the couch. "Here you go, my dear, bedtime reading. We'll talk again tomorrow. For now? Well, I think best while walking, so if you'll excuse me I believe I'll take a stroll, breathe in some clear night air before turning in. Sterling, you also should be heading for your bed."

"It's eight-thirty, Saint Just. Isn't that early to be crawling into bed?"

Saint Just looked at Maggie, who was yawning behind her hand, even as she held up the envelope, squinted at it. "Whatever you wish. I have my key, Sterling, so don't wait up, although I won't be long."

And then he picked up his cane, patted his pocket to be sure he had everything he needed. He opened the door, pausing to look at Sterling, at Maggie. They'd be fine, the two of them. Safe. And they would remain so.

He, Alexandre Blake, Viscount Saint Just, was going to see to that.

CHAPTER 19

Maggie opened her eyes and rolled over, looked at the bedside clock. "Seven o'clock? It should be at least ten."

Throwing back the covers, she stumbled to the bathroom, made a face at her reflection in the mirror, stripped, and stood under the shower for five minutes before she had the energy to wash herself.

Teeth, brushed. Hair, too damn bad. Clean underwear, a pair of jeans, T-shirt.

Good to go.

Bacon and eggs. Bacon and eggs sounded good. And Sterling deserved a nice breakfast. Alex? Okay, he could eat, too.

Bacon draining, scrambled eggs on a plate and topped by another one so they'd stay warm, Maggie put two slices of wheat bread in the toaster and padded barefoot through the living room, opened the door to the hall.

"Alex?"

His back was to her as he was inserting his key in the lock. "Ah, good morning, Maggie," he said, slowly turning around to face her, the morning newspaper tucked beneath one arm, the ever-present cane tucked there with it. He raised one eyebrow. "Been in a contretemps with a garden rake?"

Maggie pushed her fingers through her still damp hair. "Bite me." She stepped closer, squinted up at him. "You didn't shave yet. And aren't those yesterday's clothes?"

"Sadly, yes. I fell asleep on the couch last night, and decided to visit Mario's for my morning tea. Shame on me."

She thought he looked pretty good in a morning beard, but she wasn't about to say so. "I made bacon and eggs. I was just coming over to get you and Sterling. Mostly Sterling," she added, because the man looked entirely too good, rumpled. She could imagine waking next to him, his head on the pillow, a slow, sleepy smile on his face. "Do you want some or not?"

"How could I possibly refuse such a gracious offer? Let me see if Sterling has stirred yet."

Maggie followed him into the apartment, pulling the newspaper out from under his arm as she went. "Wasn't he up before you went to Mario's?"

"My, so many questions. And one answer, I don't know. This apartment is so large, you understand, so much larger than yours, that he may have been awake and I simply did not hear him."

"You don't have to get snarky," Maggie said, stung. "Man, and I thought I didn't get enough sleep."

"You didn't," Alex said, grinning. "Now, if you'll excuse me for a few moments, I'd like to splash some cold water on my face and clean my teeth. Sterling."

"Oh, hullo, Saint Just." Sterling entered the living room, the left side of his face and his eye a rainbow of ugly purples, reds, and yellows. "Good morning, Maggie."

"Sterling," Maggie said, tipping her head to one side. "Oh, does it still hurt? It looks like it still hurts. I cooked breakfast for you, sweetheart."

"Thank you, Maggie," Sterling said, and when Alex returned to the room, the trio crossed the hall together.

Sterling and Saint Just sat at the table and Maggie served them, feeling extremely domestic, a feeling that would probably evaporate in a rush when she had to wash the dishes.

"Did you have a chance to read the information Miss Spivak

provided, Maggie?" Alex asked, patting his mouth with the cloth napkin he insisted upon rather than paper napkins, then neatly folding it and placing it on the table.

"Some of it. Bios of Dettmer and Buddy. So what? What's the connection?"

"Are you going to eat that last piece of toast, Saint Just?"

"No, Sterling, you may have it with my blessings. Read all of the information, Maggie. I think you'll understand."

"Go ahead, Maggie. I'll clean up here," Sterling offered, and she didn't wait for him to say it twice.

"I left everything in my bedroom," she told Alex. "You go sit down, and I'll get it."

By the time she entered the living room Alex was sitting at his ease in front of her computer, probably deleting spam again. For some reason this made her feel all soft and fuzzy for him, because he cared enough to shield her from what he had to think was information not suited for the eyes of a gentle lady.

"Cut that out," she said, because he expected her to, then sat down, slipped on her reading glasses, and pulled everything out of the envelope. "Okay, what am I looking for here?"

"You really want a hint? That's not very sporting."

"Yeah? Well I don't *feel* very sporting this morning."

"Very well," Alex said, seating himself on the facing couch. "You know that I paid a call on District Attorney Dettmer yesterday morning? Oh, wait. I don't think you do."

"I do now," Maggie said. "Why would you go to see him?"

"As a supplicant? I had hoped to appeal to his better instincts, so that he would be . . . less aggressive in his condemnation of Bernice."

"Oh, wow. You're lucky he didn't lock you up."

Alex lifted one hand, visually inspected his fingernails. "So I've been told. At any rate, while I was in his office—"

"You actually got in? Wow. Oh, oh, I'm sorry. Keep talking."

"Thank you. While I was in his office—rude man, he didn't

even offer refreshments—I happened to notice a family photograph. He has a wife and two children, one boy, one girl. Teenagers."

Maggie narrowed her eyelids, shook her head. "So?"

"The photograph was taken in a room, the background of which was rather . . . shall we say homely? You know, Maggie. Rather like Bernice's home in Connecticut."

"Early American," Maggie said, nodding.

"Definitely not recent," Alex said, and Maggie bit back a smile. "Also, behind them was a very large window looking out over a beach, the ocean."

"They were on vacation. I don't get it."

"Dettmer was rather unhappy that I was inspecting the photograph, which could have been simply because he is not, I would think, a happy man by nature. But he did agree that a beach was part of the photograph."

"If you're going to drag this out any more I may be reaching for my cigarettes, and it would be your fault."

"A beach, Maggie. We'd just been to the beach, you and I. You know how deeply I believe in coincidence?"

"There are a lot of beaches between here and Connecticut, Alex."

"True, which is why I had Holly Spivak gather information about our friend Dettmer."

"And Buddy."

"And Buddy," Alex agreed. "Now, would you care to read over that information again, or shall I simply tell you?"

"How about I just guess? The beach behind Dettmer and his family is in Connecticut?"

"Very good, Maggie. Yes, it is. Dettmer is separated from his wife of twenty-seven years, but not yet divorced, perhaps for the sake of his political career, perhaps because he is lazy. That's one piece of information. Another is that before Dettmer moved to Manhattan to take up his political career, he practiced the law from his home. In Connecticut. His wife and children still reside there."

Maggie reached for her cigarettes without even thinking about it. "Where in Connecticut? In the same town as Bernie and Buddy? Bernie never mentioned it."

"Bernice never bothered to meet her neighbors," Alex said.

"True." She frowned. "Dettmer made D.A. here in only ten years or so?"

"He left Connecticut fifteen years ago, actually, long before Buddy disappeared. Although I will admit that his political star did rise quite rapidly. If you'll read Holly's report, you'll see that he was very well financed in his bid for election."

"I have to write this down," Maggie said, grabbing a pen off the coffee table and using the envelope to write on. "Okay. Dettmer and Buddy both lived in the same town in Connecticut. Dettmer left fifteen years ago. Buddy disappeared seven years ago." She looked at what she'd written. "Nope. I still don't get it. So they once lived in the same town. So what?"

Alex crossed one long leg over the other. "They did more than live in the same town. They both sailed, both belonged to the same sailing club, as a matter of fact. On the last page, Maggie, you'll see that they often sailed as a team, and won trophies together. They were lifelong chums, friends."

Maggie paged through everything until she came to the last page. "So why didn't he say that when he gave that stupid interview to Holly Spivak? He really could have milked that, you know, and all to his advantage. What's he hiding?"

"Oh, dear, you got there more quickly than I'd thought. That is the problem, Maggie. I don't know what he's hiding. But he is hiding something. I offered him the photographs, if you must know, if he would desist in besmirching Bernice's good name in the media, and he refused."

Maggie sat up straight. "You offered *him* the album? Cripes, Alex, is there anyone you *didn't* offer that thing to? We could have put it up on eBay and made a bundle."

"You'll be contacting Wendell this morning?"

"Right. He's the lucky winner, and let me tell you, I'll be glad to have that thing out of here. Once the police have it, Totila and his goons won't bother us anymore, don't you think? I mean, they might be mad, but they won't be back. You agree?"

Alex got up, walked over to the table and retrieved the pink bow-tied envelopes. "I see you haven't opened your present from Felicity."

"Huh? Oh, right. Do I have to? I want to think about this Dettmer-Buddy connection some more."

"Very well. If you'll excuse me, I'm going to go clean up my dirt and change into fresh clothing."

"Okay, sure," Maggie said, still frowning at the pages and pages of information.

She was still at it an hour later when Socks buzzed her to say that J.P. Boxer was downstairs.

"And so begins another day in Cloud Cuckooland." Maggie sighed, and told him to send her up.

"Have you heard from Bernie?" Maggie asked, waiting in the hallway as the elevator doors opened and she saw not only J.P. but also Steve. "Oh, hi."

"Hi yourself," Steve said, kissing her on the mouth. "Ummm, you taste good."

"Bacon," Maggie said, smiling up at him. He was so good, so kind, so sweet. So *not* Alex. It would be so easy if only she was half as attracted to him as she was to the dangerous, yes, dangerous personality of her no longer quite so imaginary hero.

"To answer your question," J.P. said once they were in the condo and she was sitting on the couch, facing Maggie, "Bernie is fine. As a matter of fact, she's so fine that they're going to allow her a personal phone call. Only one, which is why I'm here—I wrangled a continuance on my case for court. You talk to her, I talk to her, anyone who wants to talks to her, and then she's incommunicado again for another week. Okay?"

Maggie blinked back sudden tears. "That was so nice of you, J.P., to have the call come here. When?"

J.P. looked at the man-size watch on her left wrist. "Any time now. What are those papers? Anything to do with Bernie?"

Maggie looked down at the papers strewn beside her on the couch. "Uh . . . well, maybe. We're not sure."

" 'We' meaning our English friend? Where is he, anyway?"

"He lives across the hall. He'll be here soon."

Steve picked up the papers and started looking through them, and Maggie was torn between being glad he was interested and wondering if she should snatch them away from him. Which was stupid. He was on their side.

It was just that she really wanted to be the one who solved the crime, made the final connection, cleared Bernie. And Alex, of course. He'd already found some connection between Dettmer and Buddy.

Hoping to distract Steve, she said, "Ohmigosh, I forgot. Steve? We found what Totila's men were after."

Well, that worked. He put down the papers at once. "What? Where?"

Maggie fetched the photo album and dropped it into his lap. "Don't worry about fingerprints. I think half of Manhattan's are on there."

"What?"

"Never mind," she said, sitting down again, watching as he paged through the album. "Alex found it behind Mrs. Goldblum's refrigerator." Then she decided to play dumb, because that seemed safest. "What do you think? Is it important?"

"Important? This . . . this is . . . I've got to get this downtown. Maggie, J.P.? I was going to break it to Alex that I had to send a team out here to search, but this is—I have to go." He blew out a breath, squeezed the album between his hands. "Wow. I mean, *wow.* Thank you." He grabbed Maggie, kissed her hard on the mouth. "Gotta go."

"I've always liked him," J.P. said as the door closed on Steve's back. "Doesn't even pretend to be hard-boiled. Costs him when it comes to moving up the ladder, but he's one of the good ones. What was that anyway, Sunshine?"

"Nothing important," Maggie said, picking up the envelope with her name on it. "I guess it's time I open this."

"And I guess it's time I mind my own business," J.P. said, slapping her hands on her knees.

"Oh, I'm sorry," Maggie said, sitting down again. "It's just . . . well, I have this . . . acquaintance. Yes, this acquaintance, and she keeps giving me expensive presents, even when I ask her not to."

"I should have such problems. Open it."

Sighing, Maggie did just that, sliding off the pink ribbon, then ripping open the envelope. She removed a single sheet of scented note paper as well as a second piece, typewriter size and of good quality.

She unfolded the larger paper first, scanned it quickly. "I don't believe this. I think she's giving me *stock.* Why would she give me stock?"

J.P. grabbed the paper out of her hand. Whistled through her teeth. "Five hundred shares of Johnson & Johnson? Interesting friends you have, Sunshine."

"Are they worth a lot?"

"Enough. What does the note say?"

Maggie fought down an insane urge to correct J.P., because the note didn't *say* anything; Faith had written something in the note. But that was just her writer self, and she pushed away the urge.

"God, one more curlicue and nobody could read this," she said, squinting at Felicity's florid script. She retrieved her reading glasses from the coffee table, slid them on. "Hey, at least she doesn't dot her i's with little hearts. I should be grateful for small favors."

"Does this person know you can't stand her?" J.P. asked. "Because if she's looking for a new friend . . . ?"

But Maggie wasn't listening. She was reading. And fuming.

"I don't believe this. I do not freaking *believe* this. Listen to this. 'Dearest Maggie. Just in case the writing falls through, so you won't have to take a second job. Ha-ha. Love, Felicity.' God, how I *detest* that woman. She can't do anything nice without putting a dig in it. Second job, my sweet—"

She shut her mouth. Blinked. Second job? That rang a bell. Why did that ring a bell?

"Something wrong, Sunshine?" J.P. asked, aiming herself toward the bowl of M&Ms perpetually on Maggie's computer desk.

"I don't know," Maggie said, reading the note once more. "Second job. Second job . . . don't eat the blue ones. I save those for last."

"And I thought my orange sneakers were eccentric," J.P. said. "So? What's bothering you about a second job?"

Maggie crushed Felicity's note in one hand and got up to pace. "Second job, second job. Don't make enough money, you take a second job. Moonlighting. No, not moonlighting, just a second job. If you need the money. If you can't get by on the job you have, you take a second job. . . ."

"God, this is scintillating," J.P. said, shoving more M&Ms into her mouth. "You belong to Mensa? The weird ones usually do."

"Shh!" Maggie ordered with a wave of her hand. "Second job, second job. Got it! Oh, wow, I've got it! Be right back."

Alex was in his bedroom, still bare to his waist. Long, lean muscles running across his shoulders, down his arms. Six-pack stomach. Good enough to eat, or at least crawl all over, but she'd already pretty much decided to add that on her To Do list. "I've got it! Alex, I have *got* it!"

"My felicitations," he said, removing a navy silk pullover from his closet and sliding it over his head, then smoothing his hair once more. "Are you going to share it?"

"Buddy. He had a second job," Maggie said, pacing once more. "I remember Bernie saying so, that she wouldn't mingle—that's the word, right? mingle?—she wouldn't mingle their finances. He sold insurance. Buddy sold insurance. But he needed a second job, too. Maybe to afford that boat of his, right? Especially since Bernie could care less about boats, and wouldn't help him there."

Alex put a hand to his forehead. "No, sorry. I don't know where this is going."

"Good. Because I do. I'll bet, I'll just bet, that Buddy worked for Dettmer. Part-time."

"Lawyering?"

"Paperwork? Research? I don't know. Just go with me here. He worked for him, and he found out something on him and—no, I'm still thinking blackmail. Why am I thinking blackmail?"

"Possibly because the former tenant of this very apartment dabbled in that particular pot?"

"Yeah, right," Maggie said, sitting down on the edge of his bed. "It felt so *right*, you know? Bernie—ohmigod, Bernie's going to be calling, any minute now. Let's go."

J.P. was talking on the phone when they entered Maggie's apartment, and waved them to silence. "Absolutely, Red. No, I'd tell you if I knew. You can stay put, so do it. I can wangle you at least another week, ten days, no problem. Okay, here's your friend."

Maggie grabbed the phone. "Bernie? How are you?"

"Thirsty," Bernie said, and Maggie grinned.

"But it's going okay?"

"It's going great. I can't tell you who else is here, but I think Random House is going to be majorly pissed the next time a certain author's contract comes up. J.P. says I can stay."

"I know. And Alex and I, and Steve, we're working to find the real murderer, so you'll be able to stay as long as . . . as long as you need to stay."

"Ah, the Three Mouseketeers. I don't know why I was worried. Look, Mags, this is a public phone, and believe it or not—and I can't, not for what this place is costing me—everyone has to use the same one. There's a line, so I have to go."

"Okay," Maggie said, holding on to the phone with both

hands. "I miss you. Oh—wait, don't hang up. Buddy, Bernie. You said he had to take a second job, remember? What was it?"

"Why?"

"No reason. We're just . . . just gathering information. Do you remember where he had that second job? Like maybe it was for Dettmer?"

"Who? Hey, Blue Eyes, I'm trying to hear here. Thanks. Man, Maggie, I feel like a prisoner sometimes. But I'm handling it."

"I know you can handle it, honey. You're a brick. Now. Dettmer. The D.A. He used to live up in Connecticut, too. You never met him up there?"

"No. I prided myself on not meeting anybody *up there.* The mob is getting restless, Mags, I have to hang up."

"The job, Bernie. What was Buddy's second job?"

"Tax collector. Can you imagine that? Bye."

Maggie hit the OFF button, tossed the phone on the couch.

"And?" Alex prompted.

"He was the tax collector." She looked at Alex. "What the hell can a tax collector do that might make him want to fake his death? That might get him killed?"

J.P. snorted. "Oh, Sunshine, let me count the ways. Slip me some cash and I'll look the other way while you go delinquent for three years. Skim some off the top at tax time, cook the books. And the ever popular blackmail."

Maggie's head jerked up. "Blackmail?"

"Sure. You want to sit down? I'll tell you about one I know about."

Maggie sat, and Alex sat down beside her. She grabbed his hand, and didn't say a word when J.P. extracted a blue M&M from the bowl and popped it into her mouth.

"Okay, you're the tax collector in some small town. For a lot of years that didn't mean all that much. Part-time work, small salary, busy once or twice a year, no big deal. Nobody even hated you for being the tax collector. But then it started. The federal government started cutting taxes."

"The federal government doesn't set local taxes, property taxes, that kind of thing," Maggie said, confused.

"Button it, Sunshine. No, it doesn't. What the federal government does is cut taxes, which is one surefire way of getting reelected. But—big but here—lower federal taxes means not as much federal money going to the states. What does go to the states is a list of unfunded mandates."

Maggie raised her hand. "I know that one. The federal government looks good, yelling about education, cheaper prescriptions, the environment, all that good stuff, but when they pass the laws for all of it they don't give the states any money to help fund any of it. Unfunded mandates. They sound good, noble, but no bucks. Mama, pin a rose on the President and Congress."

"But with plenty of penalties for the states if they don't live up to the mandates. Okay, onward. The states have less money, right? That means less state money to the towns, the cities, the boroughs, you name it."

"So local taxes go up," Maggie said, feeling as if maybe they were getting closer to something important.

"Along with state taxes, right. But the states try to be helpful to their towns, and so they don't have to raise the state taxes too high and get themselves booted out of office come election day. So they send out helpful hints on how the towns can make money on their own to take up the slack. New fees, higher fees, new kinds of taxes. A whole raft of new fees and taxes. And the beauty of it is, by the time the taxpayer figures out he's going broke, there's nobody to point a finger at, no big federal or state government to vote out of office, nothing. Instead of screaming where the screaming, and voting, will do some good, what you've got is a bunch of disorganized taxpayers, all hit by parts of these fees and new taxes, and with no clout, no way to mount any kind of ballot box rebellion. It's like being nibbled to death by ducks, and it's getting worse every year. Tax cut? Watch your wallet. Oh, and watch services decline while you're at it—education, after-school programs, senior citizen benefits, aid to the poor, clean air and water, you name it."

Alex squeezed Maggie's hand, then let it go, stood up. "I may be wrong, and correct me if I am, but I believe we've just witnessed a soapbox oratory."

"Yeah, okay, I get carried away sometimes. It's the bleeding heart in me, I guess."

"Nevertheless, I believe I'd like to borrow your eloquence for a small enterprise I oversee here in the city."

"Oh, good grief," Maggie said, rolling her eyes. "Can we get back to the point of this?"

J.P. held out her hands, fingers spread. "What I'm saying is, there are a lot of new nibbled-by-ducks taxes out there, on the local level. And, with those taxes and fees, a lot of new regulations, including, in a lot of small towns, the right for the tax collector to audit anyone, any business he wants to audit. For no reason at all, with no recourse for the taxpayer or business owner. He can go anywhere, look at anything. Inventory, equipment, all the books."

"Without reason?" Alex sat down again.

"Totally without reason. And with the very real threat of audit. I had this client when I was practicing in—well, we'll leave the state out of it. I was only there for a year before I knew I had to get back to New York, where at least when someone spits on you, you can spit back. Anyway, the town passed one of these new taxes, but nobody really knew about it. My client moved into the town, set up shop, paid all the taxes he thought he had to pay, only to find out ten years later that he'd missed one, the new one. A nibbled-by-ducks one; but get enough ducks together and those nibbles become big bites."

"Ignorance of the law is no excuse," Maggie said. "I've always thought that was stupid. I mean, if you *meant* to do something wrong it's one thing, but if you didn't know? At the least, the law could cut you a break."

"We'll get to that later, all right? One outrage at a time. Anyway, he paid all his other taxes, so the tax collector knew what he did for a living. But he never told the guy, just let it slide for ten long years. Then he pounced."

"Pounced how?"

"Demanded an audit, ten years of audit. A real fishing expedition. I read the ordinance, and my client didn't have a prayer. The ordinance let the tax collector do anything, no statute of limitations, nothing. My client was looking at ten years of back taxes, fines, plus monthly interest, monthly penalties—compounded over those ten years—plus the threat of some pretty substantial jail time. But it was the audit that really spooked him. The town had hired on a private auditor who could, either ordered by the tax collector or on his own—remember that, on his own, and then worry about the state of our government—could demand audits going back to the dawn of time if he wanted to. The IRS is in a straitjacket, compared to what these guys can do."

"Excuse me," Maggie said. "This is still America, right?"

"Ah, the dewy-eyed innocent. It's all legal. That's bad. What's really bad is when the auditor and the tax collector get together and go around threatening audits—unless the target comes up with some bucks under the table. The law lets them in, and greed does the rest."

"Blackmail," Maggie said. "I knew it. I knew it all along. Buddy was blackmailing half of his town, I'll bet you, and one of them scared him enough that he took a hike. Then he came back, was seen, and one of them killed him. God, I'm *good.*"

"Yes, my dear, you are. It is a very workable theory, and I'm sure at least some of it fits the criteria we've considered as motive. And we even know who, don't we? Now all that is left is to ascertain *how.* Shall we put our heads together?"

J.P. winked. "Let me tell you, handsome, that's the best offer I've had all month."

CHAPTER 20

The press conference was called for three o'clock, on the steps of the building housing the District Attorney's office.

Saint Just ushered Maggie ahead of him into the small crowd of reporters and other interested onlookers, heading straight for Holly Spivak, who was checking shooting angles with her cameraman.

"Good afternoon, my dear, how nice of you to meet us here," he said. "Delightful day, isn't it? The sun in the sky, not a cloud to hide it. Your complexion shows well in sunlight."

"Alex," Holly said, turning around and grabbing him, giving him a hug. Holding him close, she whispered, "You sent it over, right?"

An actor friend of Socks's, a very large, very Italian-looking gentleman who worked days filleting flounders in a fish market, had been given the job of delivering the photocopies to Holly's doorman, in case anyone decided to ask that man for a physical description of the messenger.

"Everything is proceeding according to plan, yes. But, alas, I fear I need another favor."

"Name it, handsome. I told you I owed you one. Maybe three or four, but don't push it. I'm about to be a very, very big deal, you know. Today New York, tomorrow the nation, the world." She squeezed him again. "Oh, I love you."

"Pardon me," Maggie said, talking to the cameraman. "You have a barf bag around here anywhere?"

"Maggie, behave," Saint Just said as Wendell joined them on the flagway. "*Left*-tenant. Thank you for apprising us of the time of Dettmer's hour upon the stage. Although I would have thought you'd be on the dais along with our esteemed district attorney, sharing the glory."

Wendell scratched at his cheek. "Yeah, you'd think so, wouldn't you? My captain decided to stand in for me, take the credit. Oh, and not put me up on charges for the sloppy way I handled this whole thing."

"Politics," Holly Spivak said, shaking her head. "It's everywhere. What did you do, anyway? I take it you're a part of this?"

Saint Just took Holly's elbow, walked her a distance away from the crowd. "I do believe the good *left*-tenant desires his anonymity in this entire matter, as do I."

"But—"

"That favor, my dear." He extracted a folded paper from his pocket and slipped it into her hand. "When Dettmer calls for questions, I'd like you to ask him this one. And follow it quickly with the second and most definitely the third one. They're written out for you. It is not my usual denouement in the parlor, with all the suspects gathered 'round, but it will have to do."

"Huh?" Holly tried to open the note, but Saint Just squeezed her hand shut.

"When the time is right."

"If you were anyone else . . ."

"Ah, but I'm not, am I? Thank you, my dear."

The sound of feedback had them both looking toward the top of the wide marble steps, and Holly quickly ran back to her place in the small crowd as Dettmer and four heavily braided and gilded uniformed officers approached the tangle of microphones.

"Good afternoon," Dettmer said, his florid face pressed close to the microphones, setting off another round of screeching, until he stepped back, smiled at his audience.

He pulled a folded page from the breast pocket of his suit and shook it open, began to read. "I am here to announce a major breakthrough in my administration's concentrated war on organized crime in this city. Through months of hard work by the people behind me, coupled with my personal involvement in each and every stage of the investigation, my office is now in possession of irrefutable physical, photographic evidence implicating the heads of two crime families in the crimes of murder, extortion, and other crimes whose details I will not go into at this juncture. Suffice it to say that warrants have been issued for thirty-seven members of organized crime, most notably one Stefano Tiberio and one Enrico Totila, and the roundup of these individuals and their underlings by my personal task force is underway even as I speak to you."

He grinned, turning this way and that for the cameras. "That is the end of my prepared statement, copies of which will be available to the press. As duty calls, I'll only be able to take a few questions."

"You'd better have a damn good reason," Holly whispered, then grabbed her microphone. "District Attorney Dettmer!" she called out loudly, getting her question in first. "Holly Spivak, Fox News. On another matter, sir, if I might. Is it true that you were personally acquainted with one Willard James, recently murdered in this city? And I have a follow-up."

Dettmer frowned down at her. "I scarcely see where that—this press conference was called to report on a major victory in the war against organized crime, and I—"

"Yes, sir," Holly interrupted. "My congratulations, sir, on a job well done. Is it true that not only were you and Willard James acquainted but that you were friends? That you sailed together when you both resided in Connecticut? That your zeal, sir, in proclaiming James's widow a stone cold killer comes from personal motivations?"

Saint Just smiled at Maggie. The crowd had stilled, until a person might be able to hear the proverbial pin drop. Or, when it dropped, and it would, the other shoe.

"Sir?" Holly called out, after referring to Saint Just's note. "One more thing, learned from an anonymous source, if you'll forgive the melodrama."

The district attorney leaned closer to the microphones. "I don't give credence to anonymous sources, Ms. Spivak."

Saint Just stepped closer to Holly, and gifted Dettmer with a jaunty salute, then faded into the crowd once more. After all, a man should know his accuser.

Dettmer went pale behind his rouge.

"Almost done, sir, and again, that anonymous source. Is it also true that additional evidence that will exonerate Bernice Toland-James is expected to be discovered at Willard James's Connecticut home?"

"And now he knows what we know," Maggie whispered. "Or, what we want him to think we know."

Dettmer turned to one of the uniformed officers. "Take over," he said, and then returned to the microphone. Smiled. "Buddy James and I were friends, yes. He was a good man, a good sailor, a good friend. But that has nothing to do with the pursuit of justice, especially in a crime so vicious and hideous, so callous, as that perpetrated on Buddy James. I welcome any and all evidence that might aid in convicting his killer. Captain O'Hara will take over now, as I've got criminals to catch."

One more smile for the cameras, and he was gone.

Holly lowered the microphone as other reporters yelled out questions. "Oh boy. It's a good thing I've got those photocopies, or my ass would be grass back at the station. I looked like a jerk."

"You were magnificent," Saint Just said, and lifted her hand to his lips. "Thank you, my dear."

"Thank her for what?" Wendell asked. "What am I missing here?"

Maggie took his hand. "Come on, Steve. Show us where Dettmer parks his car."

"What? Why do you need to know that?"

Saint Just sighed. "Because the good district attorney is doubtless about to depart shortly for Connecticut. I thought that would be self-explanatory."

"Yeah, well, it's not. What are you two doing?"

"Shut up and move," Holly Spivak said, motioning for her cameraman to follow as well. "Something's obviously going down, and I don't want to miss it."

"He's got a driver," Wendell said as he led the way around the rear of the building, heading for a five-floor, open-sided parking garage.

"I doubt he'll avail himself of the convenience," Saint Just said, standing back so that Maggie could precede him up the cement stairwell, moving fast in her worn sneakers.

"Hey, wait up," Holly Spivak called after him, slowed by her very high heels. "Damn it, these are steep. Don't wait for me, follow them, I'll catch up," she told her cameraman.

By the time they'd reached the third floor Holly had caught up. Minus her shoes. The woman was truly dedicated.

Wendell stopped on the fourth floor, motioned for everyone to wait while he checked the deck, returning a minute later to say, "I see his Lincoln, on the far left, near the outside wall. And now, if nobody minds, what the hell are we doing? I've already been lucky enough to have my ass pulled out of one wringer, I don't want to have to do it again. Sorry, Maggie."

"We're waiting," Saint Just said, leaning on his cane. "Although I would prefer to be closer, with Miss Spivak and her companion tucked neatly out of sight, but positioned so as to be able to record everything."

"Everything *what?*" Steve asked, and this time it was obvious he wasn't going to be fobbed off.

"Very well, as we seem to have time." Saint Just paused behind one of the large cement pillars, and smiled at Maggie. "Would you care to begin?"

She made a face. "You know I want to. Steve, it's like this. We're not one hundred percent sure, not even fifty percent sure, as a matter of fact. . . ."

"I probably should not have suggested you begin," Saint Just said, sighing.

"Shut up, I'm trying to be honest here, and to be honest here, we don't know a heck of a lot. But—*but*—we do know that Buddy James was the tax collector before he faked his death seven years ago, and we're betting that he faked his death because he'd been playing fast and loose with his perks as tax collector, either skimming off money or blackmailing people. Probably both. One of his victims threatened him, and he took off."

"Dettmer," Steve said. "He knew James, lived there, was friends with him. You think James had something on Dettmer? Wait a minute. James disappeared seven years ago. Dettmer was an assistant D.A. by then, probably getting ready for his run for D.A. If he had some kind of monkey business in his past he sure wouldn't have wanted it brought up."

"Or he was tired of paying so it wasn't brought up," Maggie suggested. "Except that he had a very well financed campaign, so I'll bet he was part of the blackmail scheme, not a victim. So we decided to go with the second one."

"Could you guys talk a little louder? Joe's barely getting this."

"Holly," Saint Just said, shaking his head. "Did I say you could film our discussion?"

Maggie leaned against the post. "Sometimes I feel like I'm in an old *Seinfeld* episode. Maybe the one where they get lost in a parking garage. All I need is a plastic bag with a goldfish swimming in it."

Steve smiled. "Only if I'm Jerry. Alex can be Kramer. He does live across the hall, right?"

Saint Just ignored them, as he didn't understand them, and

was fairly certainly he wouldn't appreciate their humor if he did. And then the large metal door opened and Dettmer was striding across the garage, on his way to his car, and there was no time for anything but the Plan.

"Heigh-ho? Dettmer?" he called out brightly, stepping out in front of the D.A., blocking his path. "Delightful running into you here. I have a question. Does your son enjoy his employment at Brennerman's?"

It was a gamble, because he'd not been able to read the imprint on the boy's shirt, not clearly, but a gamble he had to take.

Dettmer had backed up three paces. "I don't know what—get out of my way."

"No, no, please," Saint Just said, extending his cane, even more effectively blocking Dettmer from his vehicle, unless the man wished to dance about and make a complete ass of himself, trying to dodge Saint Just and his cane. "You'll remember that I admired that photograph of your lovely family yesterday, in your office? I was most taken with the fact that the photograph had been framed in front of a beach—I so love the beach, don't you? It wasn't until my mind was jogged by . . . shall we say *other* things, that I realized what else I had seen. Your son's shirt, Dettmer. The wording on that shirt. Brennerman's Pizza."

"So?"

Saint Just smiled. He really was very good at this detecting business.

"So," Maggie said, stepping out from behind the pillar, "when we drove up to Bernie's house in Connecticut we found Buddy James's suitcases and a bunch of bags and boxes from Brennerman's Pizza."

"Yes, I can imagine it now," Saint Just said, sensing Holly Spivak and her cameraman edging in closer. "A visit to Connecticut, perhaps to drop in on your children, perhaps to take a sail. You love to sail, don't you, Dettmer? You speak with your son, ask him how he's coming along, and he tells you that he's fine, and did you know that someone's living in the James house again? Perhaps he tipped well, or perhaps your son mentioned the man because he did not tip well? Or the man looked familiar. Or he was simply making conversation. But he told you, didn't he?"

"I'm not going to stand here and listen to this."

"Please, feel free to leave. Miss Spivak? Could you possibly ask your assistant to record the flight?"

"He's not going anywhere." Maggie pointed a finger at Dettmer. "You knew he'd come back. Didn't you? You knew Buddy was back."

Wendell, who had been keeping silent, added his mite to the conversation. "Buddy's back. That has a nice ring to it."

This called Dettmer's attention to his own lieutenant. "Arrest these people. Her, too," he said, pointing to Holly Spivak.

"On what charge, sir?" Wendell asked.

"On . . . on . . . just arrest them, damn it."

"But this is public property of a sort, sir. They're allowed to be here. And I heard this gentleman say you were free to leave at any time."

Dettmer set his jaw, glared at Wendell. "You were always a troublemaker. That's why you're not going anywhere. You're too damn *cute.*"

"Handsome, in a faintly bucolic way," Saint Just interrupted. "But I wouldn't say cute."

"He doesn't mean it that way, Alex," Maggie said, grabbing at his arm, shaking it. "We're losing steam here. Do something."

"Dettmer?" Saint Just said, and the man turned to look at him. "If we could return to the matter at hand? We have a theory, if you don't mind. A theory that includes your friendship with one Willard James, and a plan the two of you implemented several years ago. A plan to line your own pockets through the threat of James's office of tax collector."

Dettmer shifted his gaze to the cameraman, then back to Saint Just. Said nothing.

"At first, I thought perhaps Buddy—you don't mind if I call him Buddy, this good friend of yours? At first I thought he had found a way to blackmail you for something you'd done in your position as lawyer. But then I remembered that you two were bosom chums, sailing together. It made much more sense that the two of you, perhaps after chatting while sailing, decided that, together, you could relieve quite a considerable number of your town's residents of a portion of their income."

Maggie stepped forward. "He'd threaten to audit them, they'd come to you, the lawyer, to get out of it, and you'd arrange the deal. It was perfect. Perfect! What happened? When you decided you wanted public office Buddy threatened *you*? Threatened to expose you? Even if he didn't, could you afford to have Buddy as the skeleton in your closet?"

Saint Just watched Dettmer's face, attempting to gauge how much of their theory had struck the target.

He pushed on, for what was the mind of a sleuth for, a fiction writer for, if not to formulate theories?

"Buddy feigned his own death because he knew you were out to eliminate him before you could feel safe in declaring yourself for office, or you sabotaged his boat and he escaped, then realized the benefits to being assumed dead. Does it matter which is correct? Not really. What matters is that Buddy came back. You must have been horrified, poor man. All your hopes, all your dreams, so nearly within your reach, just to have them all snatched away by the dastardly, damned inconvenient Buddy James."

"Isn't that almost a line from one of my books?" Maggie asked, then shook her head. "Never mind. Keep going."

"So how did he get Buddy to Bernie's penthouse? That's where this is going, right?"

"Correct, *Left*-tenant. That is precisely where we are going. Having discussed all of this today with Miss Kelly here, and attorney J.P. Boxer, we have come up with a possible scenario. Would you care to hear?"

Dettmer took two steps to his left, moving away from Saint Just, who extended his cane once more, blocking him.

"His son told him about the man living in Bernie's house, and he went to check, found Buddy, and pretended he was happy to see him," Maggie said, her words nearly tumbling over themselves in her excitement. "Buddy told him he'd come back to get the three million in life insurance from Bernie now that the seven years were just about up and he was declared legally dead—plus more money from Toland Books, because he knew Bernie had inherited the company. He had newspaper clippings all over the house. He *knew*. Alex?"

"Happily. You, Dettmer, convinced Buddy that you were his friend, delighted to see him again, and would assist him in his quest. You brought him to the city, in secret, to help him confront Bernice."

"Wait a minute," Wendell said, holding up a hand. "Dettmer got him into the penthouse? That works. We have bypass keys for elevators. It would explain how they got in, probably through the freight elevator. And the Rohypnol? The evidence locker. He could get it from there. It fits. Damn, it all fits."

"Yes, it does, doesn't it?" Saint Just said, feeling rather proud of himself, even if he knew most of the more technical explanations, the business of the pass keys, the evidence locker, had come from J.P. Boxer, and Maggie. "Once Dettmer had Buddy's confidence, he sent him off to Brenda's, to slip the dastardly Rohypnol in her drink and fetch her back to the penthouse. Either he slipped it into her drink without her taking notice of him, then sat back and waited for the drug to work, or he wore a disguise. We'll have to ask the bartender, won't we?"

"This is crazy," Dettmer said.

"Not really, if I might continue. Thanks to your department's investigation into Kirk Toland's death, you already knew much about Bernice's habits, including her proclivity to social drinking. To continue? You had Buddy James drug her, then help her home, upstairs via that same freight elevator. At that point, you subdued Buddy James. How, I'm not sure as of yet, but it will come to me."

"I can help with that," Wendell said. "I didn't tell you, but the medical examiner found a hell of an egg on the back of Buddy's head. Blunt force trauma, he said. Dettmer knocked him out."

Maggie raised her hand, and when she wasn't "called on," spoke up anyway. "Cold-cocks him, strips him, tapes his wrists, mouth, and ankles. Undresses Bernie, re-dresses her in her pj's, plops her unconscious body on one side of her bed, Buddy on the other. Except Buddy's awake now. That's why his eyes were open, Alex. The man saw everything. *Euuuwww.*"

"You're all insane," Dettmer said. But he was sweating. Sweating, and shivering.

Holly Spivak ordered her cameraman to do a close-up.

Maggie kept going; she was on a roll now. "You killed Buddy, pressed Bernie's hand around the knife, for fingerprints. Then you cleaned up, took a shower to get the blood off you, and left. Oh, and on your way out you put the tape in the trash that was picked up early Saturday morning, which is why no one found it."

She turned to grin at Wendell. "Hey, it's a possibility. I called Bernie's building to find out when the garbage was picked up. We've been very thorough. And Dettmer's been very bad."

"Yes," Saint Just said. "What did you call it a few minutes ago, Dettmer? Oh, yes. 'A crime so vicious and hideous, so callous.' "

Steve added his mite: "Even folded James's clothing, so it looked like he was some sort of invited guest, taking a shower before crawling into the sack. I kept trying to figure out why the clothes were folded."

"Hey, good one, Steve," Maggie said. "We hadn't thought about that one. So Bernie wakes up the next morning, covered in blood, Buddy's on the bed beside her, dead, and she can't remember anything." She pointed a finger at Dettmer. "Oh, and we're betting you cut yourself at some point, because murder's messy, isn't it, even if you wear rubber gloves, and it's your so far unidentified blood that was found in Bernie's shower drain.

But that can be proved very easily. DNA, Dettmer, DNA from the DA. It wasn't the perfect crime, bucko, and they would have gotten your sooner or later. We just made it sooner."

She raised both hands, grinned. "Ta-da! Hey—where's he going?"

Saint Just, who had been enjoying Maggie's enjoyment, turned just a moment too late to stop Dettmer, who had taken off across the garage, Maggie in hot pursuit.

"No!" she yelled. "Don't you jump! You have to tell the truth! Don't—"

Saint Just winced as Maggie positively *launched* herself at the running man, bringing him down by the simple expedient of wrapping her arms tightly around one of his legs.

Dettmer fell forward onto the low cement wall that caught him across the thighs, grabbed at the wall with his hands and attempted to boost himself over . . . Maggie still holding onto his leg . . . Saint Just and Steve running to help . . . Holly Spivak and the cameraman right behind them.

While Steve grabbed Dettmer at the shoulders, Saint Just pried Maggie loose and took hold of the man's legs, and the DA was pulled to safety and then almost immediately cuffed.

Saint Just helped Maggie to her feet as she winced in pain.

"Oh, boy, my knees. Look at my knees. They're bleeding. Why did I wear a skirt? I had to stop him, Alex. If he jumped, Bernie might still be in trouble."

"You must insist on playing the heroine, mustn't you?" Saint Just said, lifting her hand to his lips, turning it over and placing a kiss in her palm. "Don't do that again."

"Okay," she said, her voice small and her eyes wide as she saw the camera pointed in her direction. "Oh, God. My mother's going to *kill* me."

"Not until you spend at least a few hours giving statements," Steve said. "All of you."

CHAPTER 21

A few hours turned into four hours, and it was only when Maggie begged Wendell to be allowed to go home and take a shower that they were freed to leave.

Sterling greeted them at the elevator, doubtless alerted by Socks. "I saw it. I saw it all, on the television machine. You were magnificent, Saint Just. You, too, Maggie. I was so proud. And Bernie will be that thrilled," he continued as Saint Just pointed his cane toward their own door.

"Thank you, Sterling. Now please tell me we haven't missed Mrs. Goldblum's arrival."

Sterling shook his head. "I've kept the door open to the hall so I would see her, but she hasn't appeared."

"Good," Maggie said, dragging herself into her apartment. "I'm heading for the shower. If she shows up, hang on to her. Tackle her if you have to."

Sterling watched her go. "Poor thing. Being a heroine is difficult work."

"Yes, I do believe that realization came to Maggie, probably as she propelled herself across the parking garage like a shot from a cannon. Shall we adjourn to our domicile? Oh, and if there might be anything to eat?"

"I had Mario make up some sandwiches, yes," Sterling said. "Oh, and I set up a small drinks table. Would you care for a glass of wine?"

"Yes, thank you, I—I'll get a glass for both of us. It's time we nip this notion of yours that I am in charge and you are somehow somewhat less than me. We are friends, Sterling. Equals."

"I know that," Sterling said, raising his chin. "But I do what I do and you do what you do. I prefer it that way, Saint Just, I truly do."

"I don't value you nearly well enough, my friend," Saint Just said, knowing that he was feeling maudlin, for all his success earlier today. "But I will say that I am honored to be your friend."

Sterling blushed to the roots of his hair, held out a plate. "Liverwurst?"

There was a knock on the door, more of a pounding, and Saint Just said, "We really must give her a key."

Sterling let Maggie in and she sat down beside Saint Just, picked up half of his sandwich. "No potato chips? I like to crush potato chips on top of the liverwurst and then squeeze it all between the bread slices. Stop making faces. Never mind, I'm starving, I'll eat it like this."

"Have you brought your list?" Saint Just asked a few minutes later, when Socks buzzed to alert them that Irene Goldblum was on her way up.

"Right here, next to the passport that she doesn't get until she answers all of our questions," Maggie said, patting her jeans pocket. "Bring her on."

Sterling stood sentry at the door, opening it even before Mrs. Goldblum could knock, then escorted her to a chair as Saint Just, ever the gentleman, stood and bowed his welcome.

"Oh, so glad you're all right—I mean, so glad you're home," Mrs. Goldblum said, smiling at Saint Just. "I'm only here for a few moments. I forgot something, you understand. Honestly, I'd forget my head if it wasn't attached. Oh! I shouldn't say that, should I?"

Saint Just and Maggie exchanged glances.

"How's your sister, Mrs. Goldblum?" Maggie asked, dragging her notes out of her pocket.

"My sister?"

"Yes, you know. The broken hip?"

"Oh! Oh, the broken hip. Of course. I—" She stopped, sighed. "You know, don't you?"

"That you've been blackmailing Enrico Totila for the past ten years and you left town when he got onto you and left Alex and Sterling here to take the fall for you? Is that what you mean?"

Mrs. Goldblum frowned. "What? Enrico Totila? That horrible man? You think I was *blackmailing* him? I should be so stupid."

Maggie said it all again, adding, "Sterling nearly got killed because of you."

Mrs. Goldblum pressed her heavily ringed fingers to her ample breast. "Me? Truly, I didn't think anything would happen if I was gone." She looked at Saint Just. "I didn't know what he wanted."

Maggie snorted. "Yeah, right."

Saint Just put his hand on her thigh. "I believe her, Maggie. She truly doesn't know what we're saying." He smiled at Mrs. Goldblum. "Perhaps, as you've realized now that we have earned the right to be curious, you will tell us about these past ten years? The postcards? The trips that were *not* to visit your sister? Your abrupt departure Saturday morning?"

Mrs. Goldblum put a hand to her mouth. "First Mildred, and now you. Well, I suppose there's no reason to keep secrets any more, is there?"

"You're right, Alex," Maggie whispered. "She's either really good, or she's got a whole other something else going on here."

Sterling offered Mrs. Goldblum a cup of tea, an offer she gratefully accepted, and Sterling escaped into the kitchen, obviously unnerved by the woman's upsetment and off to do what he believed might help.

"Where do I start?" she asked, looking around the room. "Oh. You got rid of the landscape. Thank you. You know, Harry bought it for me, telling me that some day it would be worth a lot of money, but I've always hated it."

"That's it," Maggie said, shaking her head. "She really doesn't know. Mrs. Goldblum? Where have you been since Saturday?"

"Hmmm?" Mrs. Goldblum, who had continued her visual inventory of the room, undoubtedly counting up all the lamps and vases that were no longer there, said, "Oh. Atlantic City. We always go to Atlantic City. To the Taj Mahal. Isaac prefers poker, you understand, and there's a lovely poker room there. I like the slots, myself. Those new nickel slots? They're such fun! Stripping chickens, dancing hats—even Lucy, from *I Love Lucy.* I always liked her—have you been?"

Maggie rubbed her forehead. "I wonder if it's okay for me to take more aspirin yet."

"Headache, dear? I'm so sorry. But I should tell you everything, since I seem to have caused so much trouble. I mean, now that Mildred knows, I imagine there's no reason to keep secrets."

"Certainly not," Saint Just said encouragingly. "Please, start at the beginning, and tell us everything."

Mrs. Goldblum opened her large purse and extracted a packet of tissues, one of which she used to dab at the corners of her mouth, where her very red lipstick had begun to leak into the creases. "At the beginning? Well, I suppose that would be two years or more before Harry . . . died. I'd always been very partial to his brother—Isaac, you understand—but as Harry became more secretive, more *standoffish,* I found myself confiding more and more in dear Isaac."

She blew her nose. "Mildred is Isaac's wife. Horrible woman. But Isaac said it was easier to keep our . . . our love a secret."

Saint Just nodded his head. "So he'd go overseas every now and then, send you a postcard, and you'd join him?"

"Heavens, no. Why would we do that? The postcards were our signal. Whenever one arrives, I take the bus to Atlantic City. He always sends such lovely postcards. You know about the postcards? I suppose Socks told you. Didn't he mention that they are all postmarked Chicago? Isaac drops one in the mail as our signal, even though I always know the date of our next rendezvous anyway. Isaac likes to be silly and romantic. Such a dear. We were to meet in two weeks, this time for a full six weeks, as Mildred had planned to visit her daughter. From her first marriage, you understand. That's why I thought you could stay here, to keep an eye on the place. I was going to return the bulk of your rental fee. But then I had to leave early."

"You always met Isaac in Atlantic City?"

"Yes, Alex, always. I don't like to go far away from my doctors, you understand. My cardiologist, my internist, my rheumatologist. Oh, and my podiatrist, of course. I have these most awful corns, and—"

"So you were never blackmailing Enrico Totila?"

Mrs. Goldblum pulled herself up straight. "No, Miss Kelly, I most certainly never was doing anything of the sort. An adulteress, yes, even a hussy, shamed as I am to say it, but a blackmailer? Never. Besides, he's not a nice man."

"So you've met him."

"Only once, Miss Kelly, just last week. He was not, after all, welcome at Harry's funeral. I saw him on the street and said hello, because politeness demands such things. He stopped, asked who I was and if I wanted anything from him, and I told him no, thank you, you gave me quite enough through Harry. Then he asked me if I'd recognized him from his photographs in the newspapers and I said no, not in the newspapers, but that Harry kept this rather extensive photograph album that I only discovered after his unfortunate death—I was very daring, wasn't I, speaking of Harry's death?—and said that I recognized him from many of the photographs."

"You said that?" Maggie asked, wincing.

Mrs. Goldblum frowned. "Yes, I'm sure I did. I was very, very nervous, knowing I shouldn't have said hello in the first place, so I was sort of jabbering, running on and on. I told him that Harry had written all the names and even dates and places beneath every photograph, so that was how—oh. Oh, dear, is that what they wanted? Well, why didn't they just say so instead of saying all those horrible things to me on the phone? I would have given it to them. What do I want with all those old photographs? I put them in the basement."

Maggie made a rather rude sound in her throat. "They didn't have to do it. They didn't have to threaten Mrs. Goldblum and send her running. They didn't have to trash this place, or kidnap Sterling. If they'd asked, she would have handed it over. If they'd done nothing, no one would ever have known. If they'd just left well enough alone. Amazing. Freaking amazing."

"Mind-boggling, I agree."

"But you're all fine, yes?" Mrs. Goldblum asked, taking the cup and saucer from Sterling. "Thank you. You're such a dear. Oh, and that's the other thing. Alex?"

He was still sorting through everything in his mind. "Yes?"

"Mildred found out. Isaac and I were going to meet in Atlantic City in two weeks, as I said, but when that horrible man called on the telephone and said he was coming to get something from me in the morning and I'd better have it ready for him, or else . . . well, I called Isaac in a panic and Mildred listened in on the extension. She's like that, horribly suspicious. So, Mildred knows."

"We all have our problems," Maggie said, fingering her nicotine inhaler. "I can't believe this comedy of errors, because that's what it is. It is. Really. Except it's not funny. But, hey, I'm sorry, Mrs. Goldblum. What happened with Mildred? Oh, and here's your passport," she ended, fishing the passport out of her pocket and handing it over to the woman.

"Thank you, dear. Isaac wants to celebrate, fly to Freeport for a few days, and I may need this. Lovely casino in Freeport. But I left in such a hurry. I mean, between that awful man, and Isaac being so upset that Mildred had found us out . . ."

"You've had a trying few days, Mrs. Goldblum," Saint Just said, wishing the woman's story over, wishing her gone. Because Wendell would be showing up sooner or later, probably sooner, and he needed to have all of his wits about him.

"I have, Alex, I most definitely have," Mrs. Goldblum said, then smiled. "But it's all settled now, if you'd be so kind as to agree to purchase this apartment. You see, Mildred has moved out, gone to Palm Springs to live with her daughter permanently, and Isaac has invited me to come live with him. Living in sin. I'm seventy-three, and about to live in sin. Isn't that delicious?"

Maggie sat forward. "That was the other thing. Thanks for reminding me. Mrs. Goldblum, why did you keep it a secret that you own this place? That rent control business?"

Mrs. Goldblum fingered the pendant on her necklace. "That was Harry, dear. He purchased this place in a . . . a rather unorthodox way, and told me never to say anything. After all, dear, if people believe you to be poor, they're less apt to rob you. Alex? Would you like to buy the apartment? You can have everything, even all this lovely furniture, as I won't need it."

Saint Just gave a moment's thought to "all this lovely furniture," knowing much of it had to be replaced. "Maggie?"

"You'll have to pay me back."

"Fragrances by Pierre," Saint Just said quietly.

"That, and not wanting to go back to having the top left off my toothpaste. Okay, okay. Mrs. Goldblum? How do you want to do this?"

"Oh, I'll just call down to have Socks send Isaac up here. He's very good at that sort of thing. He's a lawyer, you know."

Maggie coughed into her hand. "Corporate?"

"Criminal," Mrs. Goldblum said, smiling. "Just like his brother. It's very lucrative. Tell you what, dear. It's late. I'll wait for Isaac at the elevator and we'll go to a hotel, come back tomorrow."

Saint Just quickly agreed, before Maggie could say anything else, and Mrs. Goldblum and her passport were reunited with Isaac (the spitting image of his late brother), and sent on their way while Sterling lingered behind to feed Henry and Saint Just and Maggie retired to her apartment.

"We had it wrong. We had it all wrong," Maggie said, sinking into the couch cushions. "And we still ended up smelling like roses. Alex, you're the luckiest man in the world."

"I consider myself fortunate, yes," he said, crossing to answer the knock on the door, admit Wendell. "*Left*-tenant. How is District Attorney Dettmer this evening?"

"No longer running for reelection, for one thing." Steve took three steps into the living room, and stopped. "I'm on a quick dinner break. I can't stay, but I wanted you all to know that you guys don't have anything else to worry about. It's over."

Saint Just closed the door, kept his back to the room.

"Over? What are we talking about here, Steve?" Maggie asked. "Dettmer, or the other?"

"The other, Maggie. Dettmer's pleading not guilty through reason of diminished capacity—says he's nuts—but that'll get tossed. I'm talking about Totila."

"You found him?"

"Yeah, you could say that. We picked up Bruno, too, not Nick, but we'll find him, or he'll turn himself in. He'd be nuts not to. The task force rounded up an even dozen of Totila's men, along with about the same for Stefano Tiberio's guys. We just didn't get them in time. I'm trying to feel sorry about that, but I can't do it."

And here it was, Saint Just knew. He seated himself on one of the couches. Took out his quizzing glass, held on to it halfway up the ribbon, began swinging it lazily. "In time for what, Wendell?"

"In time to keep Tiberio from putting out a hit on Totila. Word travels fast, and we figure Tiberio found out about the photograph album and blamed Totila. Who knows, maybe Nick went to him, looking to cut a deal when he figured his boss's boat was sinking. Anyway, a uniform found Totila about an hour ago in an alley, behind a dumpster. He'd been dead for a while, we think, maybe since late last night. Somebody put a knife clean through his heart."

"Totila's dead?" Maggie looked at Saint Just. "Wow."

"Yeah," Wendell said. "Tiberio's screaming he didn't order

the hit, didn't do it, that he didn't know anything about any photographs until we showed them to him. But that's a crock, we know he did it. He's been getting away with murder for years, but not this time. Anyway, I've got to get back. We're going to be interviewing and booking all night, but I wanted to let you know. Nothing else to worry about. It's over."

"Over," Saint Just repeated. "Yes, it is."

Steve kissed Maggie, who stood up, walked him to the door.

"Oh, one more thing. Totila must have been planning something when he was killed. We found a safe deposit box key in his pocket, and we're betting it's loaded with cash because he was about to leave town, or maybe even evidence he'd been gathering to protect himself in case he ever had to make a deal with us. Either way, it's going to be just more proof that Totila was dirty. We'll know in the morning. G'night."

"Thank you, Wendell," Saint Just said, replacing the quizzing glass in his pocket. He'd had to leave the key with the body. Totila had to be found with incriminating evidence in his possession. If it couldn't be the photograph album, it had to be the key.

"Good night, Steve," Maggie said, slowly closing the door, even more slowly turning to look at Saint Just. "Alex?" Her voice was low, tremulous.

"Some things must be done," he said as he got to his feet. He looked straight into her eyes. "To protect those we care about."

Maggie swallowed down hard, stumbled to her desk chair and collapsed into it. "You . . . you *killed* him? Last night . . . you went out. You . . . you were just coming home when I saw you. That's why you hadn't shaved. You'd been out killing somebody. And then you sat down and ate bacon and eggs? Just like that?"

"Not *somebody,* Maggie. Enrico Totila, a man who very much deserved to be dead. I could not trust your welfare, or Sterling's, to anyone or anything less than myself," he said quietly, firmly. "And it was a fair fight, even if I admit to having instigated the thing. The man was armed. But I am who I am, Maggie, and I do what I must do. Surely you understand that."

She didn't say anything. She just kept looking at him.

"Maggie. He's not the first man I've been forced to kill."

Her eyes went wide. "I . . . get out, okay?" She raised her hands in front of her, her fingers spread. Her hands shaking. "Just . . . I need time to . . . I mean, *I'm* responsible. I taught you how to kill, Alex. I *made* you."

"And I have made me more, so rid yourself of guilt," Saint Just said quietly, but in a firm voice filled with the conviction he felt, which he hoped she'd come to understand. "At the heart of it, my dearest love, at the bottom of it, I am Alexandre Blake, the Viscount Saint Just. And the Viscount Saint Just takes care of his own."

"Oh, my God," Maggie said, closing her eyes. "I have to think. Alex? Go home now, okay? I have to think. . . ."

He retrieved his cane, ignoring her wince as he picked it up, and let himself out into the hallway. Sterling would want to talk to him and he wasn't ready for that, not just yet.

He turned toward the elevator, pressed the button, and stepped inside when the car came, his back to the wall. As the doors closed he wondered . . . wondered if he really had made himself more, now that he was also Alex Blakely. More . . . or less?

EPILOGUE

Dear Journal, I've been neglecting my duty to you these past days, although I did speak to you in my mind. Which probably doesn't count for much, but I will say that I am glad you were there during a difficult time.

Has it only been a few short days since last I took up my pen and prepared to record the events of my life? It seems so much longer. Years longer.

So much has happened. Dear Bernie was in a very bad way for some moments, accused of murdering her dead husband, but that has all worked out, thanks to Saint Just. Oh, and Maggie. Not me, certainly, as I was rather occupied with other things.

Saint Just has told me I am a hero and I suppose I am, of sorts. Being a hero is not everything one might suppose it to be, by the way, and I am going to strive very hard not to be a hero ever again.

Oh, Bernie has gone away, to "dry out," Socks says, and I think Maggie must miss her very much, because she looks quite sad, and is barely even speaking to Saint Just, which he says is nothing to worry my head about, even though I do. They had been rubbing along together so well that, I will admit it, I had begun to harbor High Hopes in that direction.

But I must get busy. Saint Just is purchasing Mrs. Goldblum's lovely apartment that is not so lovely now but will be once we have bought new furnishings. I have taken over that chore for the most part, having convinced Saint Just that we must incorporate proper feng shui to promote harmony, serenity, good health, and all of that.

He is for the most part fine with that, as he is a kind and generous man, but he tells me that he draws the line at wind chimes hung just outside his bedroom window. I read in one of my feng shui books that wind chimes only bring good luck when they are not annoying to others, so I have returned the wind chimes to the shop, exchanging them for a lovely brass elephant for the coffee table. Trunk pointing up, of course.

That's for good luck, Dear Journal, and I must say we seem to be in frequent need of that particular commodity. Let me tell you about these past few days. . . .